Nicole

of

Prie Mer

Nicole

of

Prie Mer

Book One of the Latter Annals of Lystra

Robin Hardy

Westford Press

Nicole of Prie Mer: Book One of the Latter Annals of Lystra
2nd edition
Christian fantasy/romance

ISBN: 978-1497339859
Copyright © 2003, 2014 Robin Hardy.

Westford Press
mail@westfordpress.com

Cover photo copyright kuznetcov_konstantin

Scripture quotations are from the RSV: Revised Standard Version of the Bible, © 1946, 1952, © 1971, 1973 by the Division of Christian Education of the National Council of the Churches of Christ in the United States of America.

To Janice Hardy

these three remain: faith, hope, and love

Three things are too wonderful for me;
four I do not understand:
the way of an eagle in the sky,
the way of a serpent on a rock,
the way of a ship on the high seas,
and the way of a man with a maiden.

Proverbs 30:18-19

The Continent

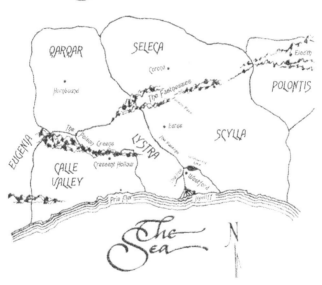

The Sea

N

I

The Lady Nicole of Prie Mer, sitting in the open carriage, gazed ahead at the gargantuan, iron-banded palace gates of Westford, marveling at their standing open—to admit her! She could hardly contain the thrill. All agog, heart pounding, she clasped the padded rail of the carriage as the driver clucked to the horse and the carriage lurched over the bridge spanning the Passage.

The driver, an affable soul named Niles, now turned his neverending soliloquy onto the history of Westford. But since Nicole had discovered hours ago that he talked much of matters he knew nothing about, it was not necessary for her to actually listen to him in order to respond with, "Really, you say?" and "My word," whenever he paused.

It had been a hard day's drive from Prie Mer in Calle Valley, as they had left before dawn and it was now late afternoon. But since her father could scrape together barely enough silver to rent the driver and the rig, much less mounted guards, the early morning hours were the only remotely safe time to travel along the coastal highway of Calle Valley. Once they had crossed the border into Lystra, they could relax, as the Lystran Commander kept the roads mercilessly purged of robbers. So now, only a little tired, with a trunkload of elegant dresses, Nicole had arrived.

As they passed through the gates into the courtyard, Nicole's gaze traveled up to the scores of soldiers along the parapet, many of whom were gazing back down at her. Unheeding, she looked around the palace courtyard. It was huge, and every bit cobbled, crammed with the chaotic traffic of merchants, servants, and upper-caste townspeople. And above it all, like warrior angels, the soldiers on the parapets looked down in silent watchfulness.

After negotiating his way through the crowd with agile steering and swearing, Niles pulled the rig up to the steps of the palace itself. A handsome young sentry in an ornamental breastplate of gleaming brass shot down the steps to grab the nag's bridle impatiently. "Get this beast—" his tirade was cut short by a glance at Nicole. He fell dumb, looking at her.

In righteous vindication, Niles said haughtily, "The Lady Nicole of Prie Mer is here at the invitation of her cousin, the Chataine Renée."

Nicole had only to smile at the young sentry for him to open the door of the carriage, lower the step, and extend his hand. "Welcome to Westford, Lady Nicole. I will have your belongings brought in and the Chataine apprised of your arrival."

"Thank you, sir," she replied with a pretty inclination of her head. But once having assisted her to alight, he stood paralyzed. So with a toss of her head, Nicole hiked the skirts of her travel dress and trotted up the steps, where two other sentries opened the great doors into the foyer.

Glancing up at one sentry long enough to see his slack, lovestruck expression, Nicole sighed faintly in relief. Her primary concern prior to this visit was whether the men in Westford would react to her the same as they did in Prie Mer. They did, and it bode well for her designs.

Nicole had never considered herself beautiful. After her

mother had died when Nicole was barely toddling, her father Robert was left with no relatives to watch her while he worked painstakingly at his trade as a tailor.

Hour upon hour he would sit and stitch, and the quality of his work earned him fame throughout the whole southern region of Calle Valley. Since he himself could not both watch her and earn a living, he hired out her care to a neighbor woman with six children of her own.

The woman ignored her completely, and Nicole turned into a wild child of the coastline. She spent her days ranging over craggy bluffs and rocky inlets, white-sand beaches and inland meadows. Then at eventide she would go home to her father, who blithely assumed she had been under the neighbor's watchful eye all day.

As the shoemaker's children go barefoot, so Nicole wore dresses handed down by the woman's four daughters. By the time the dresses came to her, they were very nearly rags. So whenever Nicole happened into a middle-caste house not her own, she was roundly scorned and shooed out the back door.

She never even looked into a real mirror until, at thirteen, she had encountered one at the fair. (Robert conducted business without one; years later, she was to wonder how.) To her eyes, the reflection was less than spectacular, dominated by the coarse, patched dress, too small and too tight. That was but four years ago.

The seventeen-year-old stood waiting in the grand foyer, lifting her eyes to the staircase that was broad enough to accommodate a team of plow horses. Today, the ragged child was dressed in an elegant travel suit of brown linen. It was simply cut, neither fashionable nor revealing (as the fashion of the time was to be revealing), but tailored so impeccably that the charms of the lady were apparent at a distance of fifty yards to alert eyes. For this, and the entire wardrobe the Lady Nicole carried, were constructed by a master tailor.

Robert had never lost sight of his daughter's ultimate

good. No matter how many hours he might put in on his customers' needs, not a day went by that he did not spend at least an hour on Nicole's trousseau.

When a particularly fine piece of silk fell into his hands, he would stash it away in the trunk that sat behind her now. Whenever he measured a lady who seemed about the size of his darling wife (God rest her soul), he cut the silk according to those measurements. Whenever a short string of beads was left over from a gown laden with them, he would add it to a headpiece that went into the trunk. For although the title was entirely fictitious, Robert was determined that his daughter would one day be presented as a lady.

A bell tolled somewhere in the palace complex. Waiting for Renée, Nicole watched the staring, whispering courtiers. People would always talk; it didn't bother her. They just wanted to know who she was.

But as no one approached her directly to ask, she spoke to no one. Thirty feet to her left was a massive fireplace with a comfortable fire. In late April, it was still cool enough to require generous feeding of the flames. But even in midsummer, this fire would be never be allowed to burn out. The foyer fire was always kept burning, year-round. It was the fire from which every other flame in the palace was lit.

By the time her visit came to a close at the end of September, other fires around the palace would be burning during the day, as well. She must complete her objective by then. She had five months to find a husband, if not a nobleman, then at least rich. Her father had ordained it. That she had no dowry to offer made the proposition that much more challenging.

Thirty feet to her right was the doorway to the chapel, open to anyone in the city whenever the palace doors were open. Nicole looked in at the rows of benches and the rough-hewn wooden cross standing at the far end. On the foyer wall beside the doorway, stretching to the very staircase, were the huge banners commemorating the reigns of the houses of Westford: Karel, Galapos, Roman, Ariel, Bobadil, Talus, and Cedric, the present Surchatain. Cedric's was by far the largest and most ornate of the banners; the earlier ones, especially, were rat-gnawed and dirty. Was Cedric married now? As Renée's father, he once had been, but even on the coast of Calle Valley they had heard reports years ago of his wife's infidelity and deposal.

In the excitement of the moment, Nicole wondered what her chances might be with Cedric, were he single. Then she blushed in shame at the thought, remembering her estate. It would be a daunting enough task to snag a nobleman; a royal husband was out of the question. She put it firmly out of her mind so as not to embarrass herself with overweening aspirations, ever.

Nicole began walking the length of the wall to distract herself with a closer look at the banners. She knew much of Westfordian history without the tutelage of Niles; the Valley was most interested in keeping up with the affairs of its neighbors.

She had even been afforded the rare opportunity of reading the entire *Annals of Lystra*, written during the reign of the great Roman of Westford. Becker, a monk who lived in a hovel on the shore, had taught her to read and unlocked for her the storehouse of books hidden in his charge. The summer of her twelfth year she had spent mostly sitting on the floor of his hut, reading. Not only did it open her mind to the joy of learning, but it changed her speech—she no longer sounded quite so much like an ignorant pauper. But Becker got to bothering her with his hands that wanted to roam over her developing body. She endured it long enough to finish the last book of the *Annals*; then she left and never returned.

She paused in front of Roman's banner. As she regarded the faded lion and cross, something stirred inside her—almost a pain of recognition. But that was quite impossible, as he had reigned a hundred years ago. Under him, Lystra had gained the greatest stature in her history, covering almost three times the territory she had now. Roman's son Ariel enjoyed a long reign of peace and prosperity, but Ariel's son Bobadil, raised without the advantages of hardship and struggle, almost brought the country to ruin. Lystra was only now scrabbling to recover under the watchful eye of her covetous neighbors, including Calle Valley.

Nicole stepped away from the wall to get a clearer view of the banner and blindly collided with a man striding toward the front doors. The collision would have knocked her breathless to the stone floor had he not caught her shoulders, whereupon her feet got under his, and he was forced to dance a two-step to keep from falling down and taking her with him. Gales of laughter billowed from onlookers all over the great hall, and Nicole looked in the man's face. She gasped as soon as her breath returned.

He was tall, broad-shouldered, and solid as a stone wall. He wore black pants and a black waistcoat embroidered also in black, with just the frill of his white shirt showing under the standing collar. He had dark brown hair cut short, out of his eyes.

But all she saw—and what made her gasp—was the hideous scar running the length of his face. It separated his right eyebrow, resumed deep and purple on his cheek, and terminated only at his jawline. When she could tear her eyes away from the scar to look at his eyes, she saw them regarding her with no expression at all.

He was looking into impish, upturned eyes, effusively fringed. She had luminous skin and full lips. Curiously, her bottom lip had an indention that matched the top, only fuller. It was a small feature that irritated her greatly upon discovery, but that men seemed to find fascinating. They were always trying to put their mouths on it.

But her pride was her glossy mane of chestnut hair which

(when clean) had the feel of silk. It flowed halfway down her back, and the sunlight glinting off it could blind a man.

There was little sunlight in the great foyer. As the man set her back on her feet and began to move away, she obeyed the sudden impulse to curtsy and murmur, "Forgive me, my lord." There was nothing in his mode of dress or adornment that elicited her use of the title—only in his bearing.

His eyes darted back to her face in what might have been surprise. Then he lowered his face, or nodded in response—she couldn't really tell which—before carefully stepping around her to resume his brisk walk, his long sword strapped at his hip. A subordinate who was following him regarded her with a moment's intense curiosity before catching up to the man ahead.

Feeling slightly disoriented, Nicole returned to stand beside her trunk. She reached down to pat it reassuringly. Everything she had of value—everything that might bolster her status as a lady—was in this trunk. Regardless, she did not really feel nervous about her ability to blend in here, with what she knew of Renée.

They had met at the spring fair in Crescent Hollow just a few weeks ago—Nicole always accompanied her father when he took his creations to the spring and autumn fairs. One look at Renée's gown told Nicole that she was someone special, but Renée hardly glanced at Nicole's gown—one made by Robert, which Nicole wore in advertisement of her father's trade.

Instead, drawn to something in Nicole's face like a long-lost sister, Renée kept her at her side the whole day, and then insisted that Nicole come stay the spring and summer at Westford. Upon hearing, Robert was jubilant. The only other event that would approach a visit at Westford for sheer number of prospects was the annual betrothal fest at Calle Valley, and it had become so decadent that Robert would not permit his treasure to attend. Besides, she wasn't invited.

The Chataine Renée returned home after that one day at

the fair, leaving instructions for Nicole to come as soon as possible. In the twelve days before Nicole's departure, Robert almost wrecked his health staying up till all hours finishing her trousseau, while she received intensive training from a local nobleman in palace etiquette (in exchange for free tailoring).

"Nicole!" The scream resounded in the great hall, and everyone turned to look at Renée poised on the enormous staircase. Her objective accomplished (in getting everyone to look), Renée then lifted her brocade skirts (revealing a naughty, bare ankle) and skipped down the stairs to greet her guest.

Nicole embraced her. "Oh, Renée, you are so beautiful!"

She was, actually. Renée, two years older than Nicole, had blond hair and fair, pampered skin. Her eyes, very large and very blue, could beseech anything out of anybody, which she did, frequently. And she was always dressed in the most sumptuous clothes.

"Take her baggage up to my apartments," Renée ordered a nearby soldier. Interrupted, he looked at her, looked at the trunk, then shrugged and gestured at a fellow to help. Watching them hoist her treasure, Nicole observed the smiling whisper that passed between them. "Come, let's get you out of that drab dress," Renée chirped, hugging her arm, and Nicole felt her heart sink.

Upstairs, Nicole tried hard not to stare at the opulence of the Chataine's quarters. It was an astounding act of generosity for the Chataine to invite a commoner to share her personal quarters during her visit. Nicole gazed at the cloudlike feather bed in wonder—but no, that was presumptuous. She would sleep on a pallet.

Meanwhile, Renée was bending over her trunk in delight. "Hurry and open it. I can't wait to see what you have! Oh, we're going to have fun today!" Nicole removed the trunk key from a ribbon hidden in her bodice, and unlocked the trunk.

Renée threw open the lid and began to dig through the contents. Nicole bit her lip, watching the precious fabrics being pawed like so much hay.

Renée lifted out the first dress, holding it up by the shoulders. "My, how . . . lovely. How quaint," she murmured, then draped it carelessly over her arm to rifle through the others. "No matter," she decided, standing. "Change into this quickly. I've so much to show you."

Renée's personal attendant brought water for Nicole to wash and a light meal, since she had not eaten since early that morning and dinner was still hours away. In front of Renée's full-length mirror (a thing Nicole had never seen before), she slipped into a dress of yellow silk and fur-lined surcoat. A beaded silk cap held her hair back over her shoulders, and little yellow slippers went on her feet.

Nicole stood before the mirror, touching her father's handiwork with fondness and pride. She turned to the Chataine, beaming, and Renée took her hand. "Come," she said with a devilish grin.

Hand in hand, they raced down the corridor toward the stairs. Most of the servants and courtiers had the good sense to get out of the way, but one man in elegant robes, wearing a gold chain of authority, planted himself in front of them and bowed formally. Nicole slid to a stop within inches of his pert nose. "My dear Chataine, please introduce me to your captivating friend," he said in a prim tone.

Renée drew up impatiently. "Counselor Carmine, this is my cousin [another fabrication] Lady Nicole of Prie Mer. She will be summering with us."

Nicole curtsied low to him, knowing that the counselor was second in status only to the royal family. He held out a hand heavy with gold rings. "How charming," he said.

"I am honored, my Lord Counselor," she replied, touching his hand in the appropriate manner. One must not grab or clasp the proffered hand of a superior, but touch it with

17

the respect due a religious relic. Kissing the hand was also appropriate, but Nicole was not forward enough to carry that out.

"You will give the Commander a rest today, darling?" he addressed Renée.

She laughed wickedly. "Where is he?"

"In the pugiling pen, I believe," he said, cocking his head as he studied Nicole. He had nice features, and beautiful light brown hair that curled to his shoulders, but there was something dissipated and weary in his manner.

"Perfect!" Renée laughed, seizing Nicole's wrist to drag her in another direction. She turned to attempt to bid a proper goodbye to the Counselor, but Renée said, "Don't bother. He won't be marrying anybody." Without Nicole's objective ever having been stated, Renée knew what it was. Her own father had similar designs for herself.

They raced to an interior row of windows that looked out over a huge grassy quadrangle. At the far end of the complex were the soldiers' barracks and servants' quarters, stables and pens. In between, in neatly demarcated plots, were training fields—the archers in a corner plot, swordsmen in another, hand-to-hand combatants in another—all receiving tutoring in their disciplines. Sheep grazed placidly in unoccupied plots, until that ground was needed for an exercise and they were shooed to the next.

Renée leaned far out of the window to look. "Good! He's there." Nicole looked down. Six feet from the wall, thirty feet beneath them, a shirtless man stood in a roped-off ring holding a pugil stick—one of those long poles with pads of wool and leather on each end. Scores of soldiers circled the ring, attending as he lectured on its use. He twirled the pole expertly as he talked. When several of the soldiers grinned knowingly at the girls in the upper window, Renée pulled Nicole away. "Come quickly."

They darted back into the corridor, where Renée seemed

to be searching for something. Nicole was startled by the sudden tolling of a bell, very loud and clear. "What is that?"

"The bell, darling. The bell tower is just around the corner here." Renée stopped to count. "Six. Dinner is at eight. When the bell tolls eight, we must be at table." She spotted a chambermaid lugging a bucket.

"Aha!" Renée pounced on the startled maid and seized the bucket, which slopped wash water over their feet. Nicole gasped as the soapy water drenched the hem of her silk dress. "Help me with this!" Renée ordered. Nicole obediently assisted her in carrying the bucket to the quadrangle window and hoisting it onto the sill.

Renée looked out cautiously, and Nicole saw the man in the ring below demonstrating maneuvers with the stick. Just when a few of the onlookers stepped away from the ring, seeing a prank in progress, Renée tipped the bucket with well-practiced accuracy. The wash water cascaded down to drench the man. "A perfect hit!" she exulted.

As the victim turned to look up at the window, the two culprits retreated. Renée tossed the empty bucket at the feet of the chambermaid, who was giggling. "It makes my whole day worthwhile to get him once really good," Renée gloated.

"Darling, surely—surely that wasn't the commander of your army?" Nicole asked in subdued alarm.

"Yes," Renée admitted.

"Whatever will he do to you? Won't he be furious?" Nicole asked. She had heard whisperings that the Lystran Commander killed his own soldiers when it suited him.

Renée laughed. "Silly dear, he's madly in love with me. He would sit on his haunches and bark like a dog if I asked him to. Men are either beasts or patsies, and he is my patsy."

"Shall you marry him?" Nicole asked hesitantly.

"Don't be absurd!" Renée screeched, laughing. "Chatains from around the Continent are standing in line to meet me. Do you know that the eldest Chatain of Polontis traveled for weeks over mountains and plains to come beg for my hand? I sent him away just two days ago."

"Why?" Nicole asked in wonder.

"A Polonti? Never, darling," the Chataine sniffed.

"But—your own Roman was half-Polonti," Nicole said. Renée laughed in disbelief, and Nicole insisted, "He was the son of a Polonti prostitute."

"Oh, you will go on so," Renée laughed again. "Then you should have been here. You could have had the Chatain. There will be more coming."

"Oh, no," Nicole ducked her head self-consciously, remembering the middle-caste houses that were too good for her. "I wouldn't dream of it. I would be content only to aim a water bucket as well as you." She looked up slyly.

"Then you shall practice tomorrow," Renée avowed. "Come." Hand in hand, they trotted down a back stairway and through a passageway floored with rough-hewn planks. Nicole hobbled, picking splinters from her soles, then they continued on to the back entrance of the kitchen pantry.

Nicole gazed in awe at the long shelves stocked with jars of compotes, sacks of grain, spices, salted meats, dried fruits, and many other foodstuffs illuminated by the narrow shafts of waning sunlight descending from holes in the roof. Grain dust rose in the light like offerings of incense. A servant was up on the roof now, patching it on the outside with tufts of hay and pitch.

Renée knelt beside the wine rack to remove a bottle by its neck. "Hurry now." She seemed a little more anxious in this escapade, as if it were riskier than the last.

With the purloined bottle, they headed down the rough-hewn passageway until it intersected a stone portico; this they traversed, emerging into the open-air laundry pit. Renée plopped down on the edge of the great stone pit where the washing was done. A dozen laundresses were stirring the clothes in the soapy, water-filled pit, beating them, rinsing them, then hanging them to dry. Nicole sat gingerly as Renée popped out the cork from the bottle and took a swig. A sudden splash jolted Nicole to her feet again, and she turned to look at the new stains on her skirts.

"Here." Renée offered her the bottle, and Nicole took a drink. It was much stronger than the heavily diluted varieties she was used to, and she swayed a little in sitting again. "Hey ho, Merle," Renée called, and a wimpled woman came over, to whom Renée offered the bottle. "Tell us what you know," Renée invited.

After the laundress had quenched her considerable thirst, she began a recitation of palace gossip: who was sleeping with whom, who lusted after whom, who had rejected the attentions of whom, and who had fallen out of favor with whom. Not knowing any of the persons involved, Nicole found all of this less than intriguing. But she came to attention when Renée asked with dripping irony, "And what of the Commander's love affair with Lady Rhea?"

Merle snorted, spewing little drops of wine. "He's upped his offer to her father to fifty royals—he's desperate to be married. Her father wants it so, naturally, but the lady drags her feet. Lucinda herself heard her tell Portia that she'll never marry him, just wants to see how high he'll go."

The nearby Lucinda nodded confirmation of this information. "He's too proud to go to the whores or chambermaids—says he'll produce no bastards for the abbey's care. But *I* think that beggars shan't be choosers, and he'd best take what's offered," Merle squinted judgmentally.

"Oh!" her small eyes widened in remembrance of something crucial. Setting the bottle on the stone ledge, she drew Renée aside. Nicole picked up the bottle (lest it fall into the pit) to follow. "Tanny said that messengers are to be dispatched to Eurus very soon. One or both of Ossian's sons are to be invited to come meet you."

Renée cast a knowing glance at Nicole. This particular

match made excellent sense. Surchatain Ossian, ruler of neighboring Scylla, had carved out a kingdom for himself from the fragments of vanquished territories, including part of Lystra itself. A marriage alliance might very well satisfy all parties with the least loss of blood. Renée knew this because there had been an unpleasant scene at dinner one evening when the Commander had emphatically advised her father that Lystra was ill prepared to fight any war with Scylla, defensive or otherwise.

"Well," Renée smirked. Taking the bottle from Nicole, she offered it up in a toast: "Here's to love, gentle ladies." Then she upended the bottle and chugged for six seconds. "Nicole! Try this!" Thrusting the bottle at Merle (who finished it off), Renée took a running start, then slid standing up for ten feet on the slick slate floor encompassing the pit. She caught herself on a wooden pillar to stop. "Now your turn!"

Both dizzy and emboldened from the wine, Nicole lowered her head and ran the same stretch. She began sliding immediately, and would have tumbled down had she not caught herself on another wooden pillar. Hugging it, she heard the sound of fabric tearing, and looked down at a fresh rip on the inside of her right sleeve.

"Again!" Renée called happily, trotting back to the starting point.

"I will watch you," Nicole said, leaning on the pillar.

Renée did it thrice more, never stumbling, falling, or even soiling her dress. Nicole shook her head, looking down at the ruins of her silk ensemble. "Darling, I must change before dinner," she said dismally. She had brought six dresses, not including her linen travel suit. At this rate, she would have nothing left to wear in a week.

The bell tolled the hour: bong, bong, bong, bong, bong, bong, bong, bong. Nicole listened, counting. Then straightened off the pole. "Was that—?"

The Chataine was momentarily frozen, then she seized

Nicole by the hand, crying, "Come!" They tore through the portico, sliding about in wet slippers. They ran through the pantry and kitchen, down a short hallway to an antechamber that was occupied by a solitary gentleman with a list in hand. "Georges?" Renée breathlessly inquired.

He looked profoundly relieved. "You are on time, ladies." He peered through the curtained doorway into the great banquet hall, lit by hundreds of candles in the chandeliers suspended from the ceiling, as well as tapers on the table. "Please go in now."

"Thank you," the Chataine breathed, but Nicole was sick to be presented to the royal table in such a state. Dinner in any palace was the most important and inflexible of institutions. Courtiers could be banished from the royal table forever by a single lapse.

Two attendants met Renée and Nicole at the door of the great hall and offered their arms. Nicole laid her left hand atop the right hand of the attendant and kept her right arm close by her side, to hide the tear. The girls were then escorted to their seats toward the head of the table.

Seating was rigorously determined by social status and favor with the Surchatain. Those at the foot of the table, the least favored still able to dine in the presence of royalty, were seated first. The table was then filled by courtiers, merchants, or officials, depending on rank.

By the time the Chataine and her guest were shown to their chairs, about thirty people were already present. Everyone was to stand behind his chair until the Surchatain arrived and was seated. The lesser bowed to the greater as they entered, and the whole table bobbed in unison as Renée took her place on one side of the table and Nicole on the other, directly across from her. One never spoke to a person of higher rank first, but it was courteous to acknowledge the presence of those below. So Nicole turned and curtsied prettily to the table, which pleased them immensely.

"Lady Nicole, may I present Lady Rhea and her father, Lord Notham?" Renée offered meaningfully, nodding down the table, and Nicole looked at a man and young woman bowing. The man was obviously a well-to-do merchant—certainly better off than Nicole's father—but the woman had a thin, pinched face, unpleasant even when she tried to smile, and Nicole suddenly pitied the Commander. She nodded benignly to them.

She then looked at the man standing to her right, and vaguely recognized him from—where? He stood tall and straight, with clean-shaven, boyish features. (She began to realize that few of the men here wore beards.) He was dressed in a smart uniform of leather with some military insignia around the collar.

But it was only when she looked in his eyes, and saw his expression, that she remembered where she had seen him. There was that curiosity again—less intense, but still discernible—tinged with a definite glint of humor. He had been at the side of the man who had almost fallen over her in the foyer. The recognition of that, and what it probably meant now, caused something like consternation to rise in her throat. He realized that at once, and responded with a subtle smile of reassurance. He was trying to reassure her.

As she gazed at him, male voices drifted in, along with the sound of purposeful footsteps. Nicole was about to turn when Counselor Carmine took his place to Renée's right, next to the head of the table. "Ah, Lady Nicole," he said in his cultured voice. "It is so very pleasant to see you again. May I present Commander Ares?"

In near terror, Nicole turned weakly to the figure in black at her left. And the man with the scarred face looked down at her as he nodded slightly.

2

Nicole was in such a state that she missed bowing when the rest of the table bowed, and had to make a solo curtsy to the Commander and Counselor. Across the table, Renée smirked at the Commander, "Your hair looks damp, sir. Did it rain today?"

He smiled mildly. "I enjoyed the shower, Chataine. And was relieved to find it water."

Told you so, Renée's finely arched brows communicated to Nicole. She, in turn, wondered what had been dumped on him before. She nervously rested her hands on the high back of the chair, whereupon the tear on her sleeve puckered open. She dropped her right arm hastily to her side again, and the Commander pretended not to notice.

A childish roar startled her, and she turned just as a small form landed on the Commander's back. He calmly peeled the sticky thing off his back to hold in his arms. "Chatain Henry, we have a guest at table tonight," the Commander said. "May I present the Lady Nicole of Prie Mer."

Resting in Ares' substantial arms, the young boy evaluated her while Nicole curtsied to him (in concert with the rest of the table, this time). He was a delicate child of seven, with pale skin and gray eyes. "She's pretty, Ares," he whispered.

Nicole did not know whether to thank him or not, as the comment had not been directed to her, but the Commander said, "Yes, she is."

"Do you like her?" Henry pressed.

"The Lady Nicole is here as a guest of your sister. Not to see me," the Commander told him.

That seemed to exhaust the young Chatain's interest in her. At the Commander's urging, he stood indifferently beside a small chair engraved with a royal insigne at the head of the table. Two larger chairs with identical insignia also sat at the head of the table, awaiting the Surchatain and, evidently, his wife. Contrary to expectation, the small chair sat on the corner next to the Commander. And Henry wore a miniature version of the military uniform that the Commander's subordinate wore.

Georges, the dinner master, announced, "Surchatain Cedric and Surchataine Elise." Everyone at table then turned to face the entering royalty, and kept their faces to them until they took their seats. Then the table bowed before sitting themselves. Nicole noticed that the Commander went down on one knee; she did not realize that the man behind her did likewise. She stepped to the right to enter her chair as she was supposed to—a great, heavy, wooden piece with brocaded seat —and was startled when the Commander pulled it out from the table for her. As she sat and he pushed back in, she whispered, "Thank you." The Counselor did the same for the Chataine, who did not comment.

The guests sat before plates and utensils of pewter (gold for the royal family) and Cedric motioned to the wine steward to begin pouring. He started with the head of the table, of course, and Nicole watched. Cedric himself was in the prime of manhood, rather ruddy, with curling, dark blond hair. He wore an understated, finely made suit of wool, eschewing any crown. And Elise was clearly the most beautiful woman in the province, probably on the Continent, with mounds of pale blond hair held by a circlet of gold. Her perfect skin and large gray eyes had been finely reproduced in her son Henry.

The wine steward worked his way down the table from one side to the other: after Cedric and Elise, Henry was served a little that was then diluted; then the Counselor, the Commander, the Chataine, the Lady Nicole, and so on. Nicole wondered briefly about the propriety of seating the Counselor and the Commander above the Chataine—but considered that, realistically, Renée's worth would be determined by whom she married. Henry was heir, but Renée was a bargaining chip. Such was life.

"High Lord and Lady, the Chataine's guest arrived this afternoon from Prie Mer. This is the Lady Nicole," Counselor Carmine said suddenly.

The Surchatain glanced at her and Nicole almost panicked, being unable to rise from the chair to curtsy. So she bowed her head, and a chestnut curl dropped into the Commander's wine cup. "Welcome to Westford," Cedric said as Nicole stared helplessly at the offending lock.

"Thank you, High Lord," she murmured. Commander Ares, smiling, lifted the dripping lock from his cup and draped it over her shoulder, barely stroking her hair with the back of his hand. Then he picked up his cup and drained it in one eager draft. The rest of the table (those who could see) watched this interlude with interest.

Nicole stared at him as he lifted his cup behind her chair in a signal to the wine steward for a refill. (She was to learn much later that the Commander was the only one who could presume to make such a demand.) As she studied him, the scar that defined his face and his marital status seemed to fade somewhat. He turned his eyes to her, and she saw they were smoky brown.

"Well, Lady Nicole, did you and your retinue have any

difficulties on the trip?" Cedric asked conversationally.

Retinue! Any number of people here would know she came without a retinue. And lying to the Surchatain could cost one one's head. "No, Surchatain. Once we crossed the border into Lystra, I knew I had no more need of escorts. The safety of your roads is legendary," she replied with a glance at the Commander.

"Indeed," Cedric agreed. "Tell me about your family's holdings, lady."

Nicole looked at Renée. It was the Chataine's idea to pass her off as a lady, as that was the only way she would be allowed to stay in the palace. An artisan's daughter was just not of sufficient rank —not unless, or until, he made enough to acquire land holdings. Renée narrowed her eyes, thinking fast.

"They should benefit from the waterway, High Lord. Has the Counselor shown you the plans?" Commander Ares asked.

"You've drawn up plans already?" Cedric asked, looking to Carmine in interest.

"Quite so, High Lord." Carmine flicked his wrist toward an attendant, who scurried off. "While we're waiting for them, let me explain our rationale. Years ago, Hycliff was an adequate port, but the cliffs have eroded to the point that the harbors are virtually unusable. When was the last time we received ships from beyond the Sea? Trade has dried up both ways, and that has hurt our revenue.

"So the Commander and I were studying the lay of the Village Branch, and noted how strong it has been flowing in recent years, pushing farther toward the coast. So we reasoned, why not help it along a bit? A canal only three miles long would be sufficient to connect it to the Sea and reopen trade. We have even selected a natural harbor site."

The attendant ran back in with a large rolled parchment which he delivered into the Counselor's hands. He, in turn, spread it open before the Surchatain. As the first course of shellfish was presented and Cedric leaned over the map, Nicole looked at the Commander. The care with which he took not to look at her confirmed that he had deliberately changed the subject. Was it to spare her? He leaned toward the map to point out some pertinent feature.

Cedric waved at the table to begin eating, and Nicole picked up a clam only after others had done so. She knew how to eat clams, having eaten them all her life, but the nobleman had not shown her how it was done at Westford. She doubted they used the same technique as Prie Mer paupers.

Nicole watched Renée open one and insert a small fork, then dip the flesh in a sauce before eating it. There was one bowl of sauce between every two people: Renée and Carmine shared a bowl, as did Ares and Nicole. She opened the shell and forked out the meat adequately enough, only to see it slip off the fork and sink in the sauce.

As she was opening a second clam, Cedric pronounced himself satisfied with the plans for the waterway, rolled them up, and turned his attention to dinner. Nicole sat very quietly so that he might forget his previous line of thought. Happily, he did. And the Commander, dipping his fork in the sauce, was surprised to bring it out with two lumps, both of which he ate.

The following courses of eggs, plover, and venison followed quickly, with large loaves of bread making their way around the table as diners pulled off handfuls. When the man to her right handed her a loaf, he leaned forward to speak around her. "The smith brought the new-style hauberks for you to inspect, Commander. They're in the armory."

"Fine," he nodded, then glanced up. "Have you been introduced? Lady, this is my Second in Command, Thom."

"Lady Nicole," he nodded, and she could have sworn there was fondness in his voice. "Please meet my wife, Deirdre."

Nicole looked past him to the pretty young woman

smiling warmly at her. Nicole nodded, and Deirdre began, "Oh, you are lovely. I've heard so much about you. I—" Thom leaned forward in a sudden spasm of coughing and his wife patted his back, fretting.

Nicole watched in some alarm, not over his coughing fit, but over what Thom's wife might have heard. Was there already suspicion that she wasn't nobility? She looked at the Commander, who studiously looked away. But Renée's alert eyes took on a gleam of interest, and the Counselor murmured, "Dear me," in an amused way.

"So, Lady Nicole, you were telling us about your family," Surchataine Elise said kindly. She looked down the table at the quaking girl in the soiled yellow silk.

There was a moment of profound silence. Cedric looked at her. Nicole raised her face, looking between the great rulers, and opened her mouth to confess her duplicity.

Then three other people began talking loudly all at once, and none would yield the floor to the others. The Commander, the Counselor, and the Chataine were spewing various and wildly conflicting details of Nicole's illustrious family history to their royal persons. Cedric divided his attention between them, imagining that he could understand them all, but Elise shouted, "Enough! Really."

They fell silent, but Carmine required the last word: "So you see, Surchataine, that the lady's family is a virtual institution in the southern region of the Valley."

"That is likely to be useful," Cedric noted, and Nicole stared at the Counselor in wordless gratitude. He winked at her, and Renée smiled at Ares as she chewed on the lip of her gold cup.

Chatain Henry, who had been up and down and all around the table during dinner, finally was allowed to crawl into the Commander's lap as dessert plates were placed on the table. The guests helped themselves to glazed peach slices with their fingers. Seeing that Ares let the serving platter go by rather than reach around Henry, Nicole offered him a slice. She almost put it to his lips, but hesitated, so he reached a hand up to take it. But Henry opened his mouth wide: "Ahhh!" Taking the hint, Nicole fed him a candied slice, and he grinned.

"Georges! What is our entertainment this evening?" Renée asked, leaning forward in anticipation.

"Dancing, my lady! Shall I send in the musicians?" he asked.

"Yes, and we shall pick leaves!" Renée exclaimed. She pushed her chair back forcefully and skipped from the table.

"Hmm. And I wonder who shall dance with the Lady Nicole," Counselor Carmine murmured over his candy.

"What are the leaves?" Nicole leaned forward to whisper.

"Mulberry leaves, my dear. Each man's name is scratched on a leaf which the ladies draw from a basket. The name the lady draws is her partner for that dance," Carmine explained.

"She's up to something," Nicole observed, which drew confirming snickers from several quarters.

The musicians came in with their harp, lyre, viele, and bells to begin playing practice tunes. Soon Renée swept in with a basket, which she offered first to the ladies at the foot of the table. Taking care to hide their eyes, they each picked a leaf, then laughingly displayed their selection all around. The lucky partners were tapped on the shoulder and presented the leaf.

"Now, how shall she work this?" Carmine muttered over the table to Nicole and Ares. "She and the Surchataine must draw last. How shall she make the choice falls as she wishes?"

"What is it she wishes?" Nicole whispered back.

"Watch," Carmine winked.

Deirdre drew, then the steward's wife reached up her hand into the basket that Renée held high. "I can't feel a one," the woman complained.

"Oh, just pick!" Renée said in exasperation, leading her hand to a leaf.

"Ah. Lord Notham," she cooed, looking down the table. The gentleman squirmed in his seat. He had evidently been hoping for someone else.

Meanwhile, Renée had turned her back momentarily to the table. When she turned back around, she held the basket under Nicole's nose, ordering, "Pick."

Nicole looked down, where three names lay exposed on the tender undersides of the mulberry leaves: Cedric, Carmine, and Ares. Nicole felt sure she knew whom Renée wanted her to choose, but she did not know why. Rather than play that way, Nicole squeezed her eyes shut and turned her head away. She sifted through the three leaves and brought one out truly blind: Ares.

Turning in her seat, she presented it to him: "I have picked your name, Lord Commander."

"So you have," he said quietly. Standing, he drew back her chair and offered his hand. Nicole responded, and his warm hand closed over hers, swallowing it. He led her to the line of dancers which had already formed, and, with her hand atop his, they faced the same direction as all the others. Renée, paired with Carmine, and Cedric, paired with his wife, joined them.

The music began, and the dancers moved in concert. The nobleman had taught Nicole a form of this dance, but it contained idiosyncrasies known to Westford alone, so Nicole intently watched the steps of the woman closest to her line of sight. It would have been easy to learn but for the billowing skirts hiding the feet.

Suddenly she felt a tug from the Commander, and the dancers broke off into pairs. Taking her right hand in his left, he slipped his right loosely around her waist. She had no idea what was coming next.

Her panic must have been evident, for he whispered, "Follow my lead." She looked down at his feet: forward (backwards for her), to the side, back (forwards for her), to the other side. The same square was then repeated over and over. After only a few measures of this, she felt confident enough to look up. Other dancers were elaborating on this basic pattern; Renée and Carmine, in particular, were twirling about the great room with breathtaking finesse. But Ares kept it simple for Nicole.

She looked up at his smoky brown eyes and mild expression, and gratitude welled up in her for his unfathomable kindness. "Oh, Commander, I am so sorry for the trick we played on you today."

His knees bent as he laughed—a wonderful, rich, deep laugh. "Why are you sorry? It was delightful."

"You can't be serious. It was mean-spirited," she countered, offended. It was disturbing to watch the scar move and gape as he talked.

"Not at all," he insisted. "I enjoyed it."

For some inexplicable reason, she was growing angry. "You couldn't enjoy it. It was a mean trick to make people laugh at your expense. You deserve respect, not to be played with like a toy."

He looked down at her, something profound happening behind his eyes, and he whispered, "Play with me. I am delighted to be your plaything. Do to me whatever your heart desires. I will not complain."

Such frank humility caused tears to well up in her eyes, and he looked thoroughly alarmed. Turning his face to obscure the scar, he whispered, "Forgive me, lady. I meant no offense."

"You have in no way erred," she replied. Of its own accord, without her knowledge, her hand slipped from resting on his shoulder to his neck. He dropped his face so that his unmarred cheek was a hairbreadth from hers. Nicole watched his broad chest expand and contract in tightly controlled aspiration. She began to enjoy the dance so much that he chanced a turn. She followed effortlessly—he made it so easy!

—and smiled up at him. His arm slipped a little closer around her waist.

Chatain Henry bounded up to them. Ares turned to him shrouded in forbidding thunderclouds just as Renée snatched her young half-brother by the arm and began dragging him away. He howled and twisted, and the Commander turned serenely back to his dance partner. "How he loves you!" she marveled.

"I am the Chatain's guardian. I have to know his whereabouts every moment, for if anything befalls him, I am put to death," the Commander said.

"How cruel!" she said, shocked.

"Really? It insures that the army stays loyal to Cedric's house," he said.

"And anyone wishing you both out of the way has only to do away with the child," she observed.

He smiled tightly. "If anything happens to me, Thom is under orders to kill the Counselor."

"Why do you encourage such barbarism?" she protested.

His look mellowed. "Checks and balances. We hang together or we hang separately. Since we all understand this, we can dispense with treachery and work for the common good."

"I see." And reflecting on it, she did. She lifted her chin, smelling the lingering scent of soap on his hair, and her fingers unconsciously caressed his collar. Again he lowered his head, and brought her right hand a little closer to his shoulder. When she sighed, he lost control of himself and brazenly brushed his cheek to hers. She did not recognize it as an offense.

The next moment she realized something was rather amiss. Looking around, she discovered that most of the other couples had ceased dancing, although the musicians were doggedly continuing the same tune over and over again, so that the dance would not end. When Renée saw her ploy exposed, she motioned to them and they quit in midmeasure.

Henry ran up to Ares again, who released Nicole to lift him. "It's past my bedtime and you must come say my prayers with me," he scolded his guardian.

"Bid the lady goodnight, then," the Commander sighed, all soft and unmilitary. He set Henry on the floor so he could take Nicole's hand and kiss it in a very proper farewell. She offered her hand to the Commander, who bent to kiss it. But somehow between her extending her hand and the touch of his lips on it, it contrived to turn itself palm up.

Nicole, raised on the beaches and meadows, did not understand the implication of intimacy in offering one's palm to a man's lips. But her palm was indeed turned up when his lips met it, so that he kissed it in sudden passion. The heat of it startled her.

The Commander straightened. "Good evening, Lady Nicole. God watch you while you sleep." He bid good evening to the others in the room, going down on his knee again before Cedric and Elise. Then he slung Henry over his shoulder like a sack of flour and carried him out.

Renée rushed at Nicole in sheer exuberance. "Perfect! This is working out better than I ever imagined! Come, we've much to plan!" And she began dragging her out of the room.

"Wait! Oh, Renée, please!" Nicole cried. It was a terrible offense to leave any event before one's betters, and utterly unforgivable to leave without acknowledging the beneficence of the hosts. Grudgingly, Renée allowed her to curtsy to the Counselor and throw herself on her knees before the High Lord and Lady.

"You may go, dear," Elise said with distinct amusement. Cedric nodded thoughtfully. That was well and good, but when Nicole attempted to bid everyone else goodnight, Renée lost all vestiges of patience. Nicole did manage to wave at Thom and Deirdre as she was dragged out.

The two "cousins" ran up the stairs hand in hand and

burst into the Chataine's apartments. Renée took a flying leap onto the massive feather mattress. Nicole came to a dead stop at the foot. "Get up here!" Renée ordered.

In tentative wonder, Nicole climbed onto the soft, shifting mattress. Renée bounced in glee and they laughed riotously, tossing pillows and straining the ropes holding the bed frame together. "Oh," Renée sat up and wiped her eyes. "This is priceless. Now, we must plan." She stuck out her feet for the chambermaid to begin undressing her.

Nicole climbed down from the bed to remove her own clothes. The low fire in the hearth gave a soft, wavering light by which Nicole assessed the sorry state of her attire. What was left of the silks hung on her like mourning rags. The slippers were utterly ruined. How could she have convinced anyone of her nobility tonight?

Stripping, she watched the chambermaids laboriously finish filling two large wooden tubs with water warmed over the fire. One maid inclined her head and gestured to a tub, indicating its readiness. Nicole used the chamber pot with great relief, then climbed into the tub by means of a step stool, sinking down with a sigh on the padded interior. The maid poured warm water over her head and began washing her hair.

From the other tub, Renée was plotting aloud: "Tomorrow you shall send a bodice ribbon to the Commander, and—"

Nicole sat up. She had exactly one bodice ribbon to keep her underwear together. "Why?"

"To let him know of your undying love for him," Renée snickered.

Nicole's heart sank. "Oh, no, darling. Please, no. That's so cruel. What has he done that I should lead him on so cruelly?"

"What is cruel? He loves it! Didn't he tell you so?" Renée insisted. "Ow!" She jerked her head free of the hands of the chambermaid, who murmured apologies.

Rather than ask how Renée knew what he might have told

her, Nicole said, "Well, I'm not sending a bodice ribbon. That is unseemly." She closed her eyes as the chambermaid poured rinse water over her head. "This is divine," she sighed.

"Very well. A hair ribbon, then?" Renée asked.

Nicole thought about it. "I will send a hair ribbon," she agreed. Taking the sponge the maid offered, she began washing herself, and she thought about his hands. Very nice hands, large and well-formed. "I will send it in appreciation for his kindness tonight."

"I will set up a meeting in the garden for you," Renée said lazily. "I will have to discover his schedule, then give you a time tomorrow."

Nicole stepped out of the tub into the great, soft towel the maid held out and sat on the stool for the maid to comb out her hair. "What beautiful hair, my lady," the maid whispered.

"Thank you," Nicole said automatically, and the two maids exchanged glances. "Darling . . . why does the Commander's love life interest you so?"

"I don't know!" Renée laughed. "Since he was in love with me for so long, I suppose I'm just anxious to see him happy!"

Nicole looked at her. "But dearest, you have no desire to see me marry him. Only to make him think I will."

At this, Renée burst into laughter. "Oh, the sweetness of your heart! My dear, he KNOWS you will never marry him! Why do you think he's so happy to let us torment him? He knows that is the closest he will ever come to having you or me!"

That is exactly what he had told her, in so many words. But remembering the passion of his kiss on her hand troubled Nicole. One's heart did not always regard the instruction of the mind, and its disappointments were brutal. She had no desire to cause a worthy man that kind of grief.

Nicole donned fresh linen undergarments as Renée slipped into silks that looked disturbingly similar to what

Nicole had worn earlier. The maids wrapped their damp hair around bits of cloth to make it curl while they gossiped about everyone at table tonight. Then they climbed into the massive bed, and the maids closed the curtains around them. Half the candles were extinguished, and Nicole listened to the maids quietly emptying the tubs and chamber pots.

What a loathsome job they have, she thought, turning onto her side. *If I don't find a husband before my wardrobe expires, I may be doing that.* And the thought struck her, ridiculous in its belatedness, *Why not marry the Commander?* He was not rich, nor noble, but he would obviously be a doting husband.

The more she thought about it, the more sense it made. So what if his face was scarred? The royal family respected him nonetheless. On these musings, she sank into the down pillow and closed her eyes.

ℬ

Nicole awoke before Renée, and climbed quietly out of bed. The room was quite dark. Feeling her way to the window, she opened the curtains and shutters, breathing in new morning air. The sun had lately risen, and the view from this window of the colored sky made her heart rise in gratitude. The birds sang their morning songs, and the spring breeze replied.

Exhaling, Nicole stepped over the sleeping maid to use the chamber pot and wash her face and hands in the basin. The chambermaid awoke with a start. "Oh! My lady—" she began to apologize.

"Shh. No trouble," Nicole whispered.

"Would my lady like a bite of breakfast?" the maid asked.

"Yes, I would; I'm famished. What is your name?" Nicole asked in a whisper.

"Eleanor, my lady." The maid curtsied.

"Eleanor. Thank you."

The maid washed herself hastily and dressed with apologies, obviously used to sleeping later in the morning. After she left with the pot, Nicole unwrapped her own hair and brushed it out. She opened her trunk and took out the best dress she had brought: it was deep blue with a high collar in back and décolleté neckline—so to speak. Compared to the palace style, it was virginal. The long sleeves gathered nicely over her wrists, and the cap held her hair up, instead of smashing it. By the time the maid brought a tray of bread and wine, Nicole was dressed.

"My lady looks lovely," Eleanor said, setting the tray on a table.

"Thank you," Nicole replied a little despondently. Sitting at the table, she said, "I don't look anything like the other ladies, do I?"

"Oh, better, my lady," Eleanor said, which confirmed Nicole's worst suspicions. Her father might be an excellent tailor, but he had no sense of the palace style at Westford. Eleanor excused herself and Nicole ate a solitary breakfast, leisurely examining the stunning tapestries and elegant furnishings that surrounded her.

After eating, Nicole gathered up the remains of her yellow silks and headed downstairs. Pausing at the foot of the stairs leading into the great foyer, she mused, "First things first." She entered the chapel, which was deserted at this hour of the morning except for the priest in his rough goat-hair robe and shaved head. He greeted her, "Good morning, Lady Nicole. Whatever you may need, I am here for you. Do you bring an offering this morning?"

"An offering?" She looked down at her silks. "Oh, no, Father!" she laughed. He looked slightly offended as he withdrew, and only later did she contemplate the fact that he knew her name.

Nonetheless, she knelt before the cross and silently said her morning prayers. It seemed only right to thank the God of heaven for preserving her on the trip here, and through dinner last night. She asked His mercy on the royal family, on the Counselor, and on the Commander. Here, her thoughts wandered a little, but then she reined them back in to ask His assistance in arranging a marriage that would be acceptable to her father.

That accomplished, she gathered up her silks and headed for her original destination. Careful of rough planks and puddles, she made her way to the laundry pit, already bustling. Nicole paused to count the chimes as the bell tolled seven. Spotting the laundry mistress, she called, "Merle! Good morning."

The woman turned, and her face fell to see that Nicole carried nothing to imbibe. "Eh. Yes, morning, lady."

"Merle, I was hoping you might work your magic on my poor dress," Nicole said, holding out the pitiful silks.

Squinting judgmentally, the woman declared, "Lady, if I were you, I'd burn the things and get you something proper. They're making you a laughingstock at table."

"Probably," Nicole whispered, retracting the bundle.

"Not that the Commander cares, but really, Lady, feeding him candies and letting him kiss your palm! Why don't you just sit in his saddle?" Merle chided. Nicole's mouth dropped open in shock. "It did some good, though. After that brazen display, Lord Notham accepted the Commander's offer for the Lady Rhea. And I do have to say she's acted more the part of a lady in this than you have. Who is your father, anyway?"

Staring at this fount of vitriol, Nicole comprehended that every word she herself spoke and every move she made were recorded, catalogued, and repeated for the entertainment of everyone in the palace. Not only was it widely known that she was a commoner, but one not even respectable enough for the Commander.

While absorbing this shock, she was further shaken by the most awful cries and shouts nearby. Soldiers were dragging a group of men in shackles toward the slaughterhouse. There was crying, and pleading—even some of the maids were weeping. But the soldiers shoved away the bystanders and wrestled the prisoners inside.

Then Commander Ares, in linen shirt and breeches, strode to the officer in charge and uttered something final. The lesser saluted as the Commander turned away. While he went about other business, sharp cries resounded from the slaughterhouse.

"What in God's name is happening?" Nicole cried.

Merle looked at her sharply. "The little lamb that eats out of my lady's palm lives up to his name."

Nicole looked at her so pathetically that she softened a bit. "Eh, a few of the soldiers got drunk in town last night and took liberties with a tavern maid, whom some say was not willing. Just some. When the Commander heard of it this morning, he ordered them castrated and expelled from the army. Say, what d'you suppose Georges will be serving at table tonight, eh?"

"Oh!" Dropping her burden of silks, Nicole covered her ears from another anguished howl and ran from the laundry pit, slip-sliding on the slate. She bounded up the great stairs, almost tripping over her own skirts, while courtiers stared after her. She raced down the corridor until she reached the door of the Chataine's apartments, and fell on the wall beside it to cry.

It was a foolish, foolish venture to come here, where there were eyes in the walls and razor-sharp tongues. She had no place here, nor could she ever fit in. What nobleman would accept her for a wife? At this moment, she rued her spineless obedience to her father's pipe dreams and the Chataine's selfish entertainments.

A sentry passed, so Nicole forced herself to stop crying. She leaned her back against the cool stone to think. Where was she to go? Home? Without a husband? Her father might well turn her out. Then what? "Lord of heaven, I am in your hands," she whispered hopelessly.

She looked down as a cat came trotting, tail aloft, around the corner. Any family that housed cats had no fear of losing their stored grain to rats. "You earn your keep well enough, don't you, kitty?" she said, kneeling to seek comfort in the purring furball.

Henry appeared suddenly around the corner in evident pursuit of the cat, with a flustered scribe behind him. "Chatain, please come finish your reading. Chatain, I beg you."

Henry ignored him, scooping up the cat. "My Lord Henry, will it please the Commander that you forsake your lessons to play with the cat?" Nicole asked, smiling. He looked at her sideways, puckering guiltily. She stood, extending her hand. "May I come hear you read?"

The Chatain weighed the offer, then dropped the cat to take her hand. They began following the tutor back to the library. "Do you like Ares?" Henry asked. So he, too, had heard the gossip.

Weighing an answer, Nicole thought about what she had witnessed that morning. In hindsight, it began to look like a reasonable course of action. A few unruly soldiers could make life unbearable for a great many people. Besides, he had been most kind and gentle with her. "Very much," she admitted to Henry and herself.

Henry began to bob in excitement. "He likes you," he confided. "I heard him ask Audry whether he should send you a gift or not, and then they were all arguing about whether it would scare you off or make you like him."

"Really?" she asked. He nodded, and they swung hands as they entered the library.

Nicole caught her breath at the sight. There had to be thousands of volumes here, worth staggering sums. Cedric must value learning. She scanned the rows in awe, reaching up without daring to touch the spines of so many priceless books. The tutor watched her reaction with gratification as Henry patted a large cushioned chair. "You sit here."

She did, and he climbed into her lap. Then the tutor handed him a tall, slender book, opened to a page decorated with glowing colors around the black block text. Henry nestled into a comfortable position and began to read haltingly.

Nicole rested her cheek on the top of his head as she listened. It was a charming story about a race between a tortoise and a hare. Henry giggled as he read, but quieted down as he reached the end of the story. Then he pronounced it totally unsatisfactory: "The hare was faster. He should have won."

"Why didn't he?" she asked.

He looked up at her from his resting place in the crook of her arm. "Because he was bad."

"Maybe he was just—" she broke off upon seeing Commander Ares standing in the doorway, watching them. Henry looked over, then scrambled off her lap to leap for him.

The Commander stopped him with an outstretched hand. "Chatain, to your reading," he said in a low voice. Henry sulkily obeyed, seeing that Ares was not in the mood to play. "May I borrow you for a word, Lady?" Ares asked. He self-consciously turned his unpresentable side away from her, and she was somehow hurt that he felt he needed to.

She rose and joined him in the doorway. Up close, she noticed his misbuttoned coat and sweating brow. Glancing down the corridor, he extended his hand to a small alcove with a window. Nicole entered it ahead of him and turned.

He wiped his face with his sleeve. "Lady—" his voice cracked, and she marveled at the realization that the fierce Commander who castrated soldiers was nervous in her presence. He cleared his throat. "Lady Nicole, I thought to explain to you the circumstances which the—the punishments you heard this morning necessary. These men, of my troops, had—had gone—"

She was shaking her head. "My lord, I would not presume to question your judgment in such matters. For what it is worth—and I fear that is very little—my opinion is that you were justified."

44

They looked at each other while the bell tolled eight. Nicole deduced that he had been told not only of her presence at the laundry pit, but of her tears in this upper corridor, and had fit the two circumstances together incorrectly. For some reason, he felt it imperative to stop what he was doing, dress, and request an audience with her to clear the matter up.

When the echoes of the bell died away, he stirred and said, "May I ask a favor of you?"

"Anything that I am free to give, my lord," she said cautiously.

"I—have duties that wait, and cannot take the time I would like to—talk with you. Will you meet me in the rose garden at seven of the bells tonight?"

She looked downcast. "I am sorry, my lord, that would be highly inappropriate, when you are betrothed."

He laughed aloud. "Really? Well, congratulate me! Who is the fortunate lady?"

She stammered, "I, um, heard that Lord Notham—that Lady Rhea had accepted my lord's proposal—" He cast a canny, bitter glance out the window, which was Nicole's first indication that palace gossip, though pervasive, was not always accurate.

"Your informant was mistaken, Lady," he said. "Will you meet me before dinner?"

"I have no idea where the rose garden is," she said.

"Any soldier will bring you. Will you meet me?"

"Yes," she nodded, smiling down at her shoes. "Yes."

"Thank you." That seemed to conclude their business, but he did not leave and she did not leave. She watched him look at the floor and scratch the stubble on his face, and it occurred to her that he was having a conference inside his head.

She shifted infinitesimally toward him, which caused him to look in her face again. He ventured, "I've . . . been carrying around a small token for some time, with no one to give it to, and would take much delight in seeing it on you, but . . . I

45

don't wish to alarm you, or make you feel indebted in receiving such a trifle from me. . . ."

"What is it?" she asked with a curious smile.

He unknotted the coarse scarf at his neck, and a small, exquisite gold cross on a delicate gold chain fell into his palm. He held it up for her appraisal, repeating, "Just a token of friendship. Nothing more."

Her face lit up, which caused his breathing to quicken. "It's lovely," she said, and bowed her head for him to place it around her neck, which he did, awkwardly. He was too unnerved to lift the masses of chestnut hair over the chain, so she did, shaking out the hair. The cross fell just above her cleavage, and he gazed at it.

"I thank you for your token, especially generous to someone who almost drowned you yesterday," she said, curtsying, and he laughed. She laughed, then that bit of business was concluded. But he did not leave and she did not leave, still.

He leaned toward her the slightest bit and she lifted her face. He looked at her lips and she parted them invitingly. He bent his face, pausing in persistent disbelief at her lack of objection, then just as she felt his light breath on her lips they heard Henry demanding, "What are you doing?"

Ares jumped, then swept him off the floor. "I am taking you back to your lessons, O royal nuisance," he said, carrying him out of the alcove and down the corridor as Nicole watched.

"But what were you doing?" Henry laughed loudly.

She followed them back to the library, where Ares deposited the Chatain. As the Commander strode off, he glanced back at her, and she fingered the necklace. He was so intently watching her that he nearly stumbled into the wall, so Nicole resumed her place in the great chair with Henry, who promptly asked, "What was Ares doing?"

"Talking to me. Now read," she said, opening the book.

46

"What did he tell you?"

"I am not free to repeat it," she said airily. "The next story."

"No one tells me anything," he grumbled.

"Oh, you seem to know plenty," she said. That satisfied his pride enough for him to turn the gilt-edged page.

He read for a long time, and it was good practice for Nicole to help him. About the time the tutor was nodding off in his chair, an attendant passed the door and caught himself. "Lady Nicole, the Chataine summons."

"Ah. Excuse me, Chatain," she said, sliding him off her lap. That set him to pouting again, so she smiled and winked. He watched her, then looked away in a manner distinctly reminiscent of the Commander.

She followed the attendant to the Chataine's apartments, where Renée had just gotten up. She was at the table eating pastries with jam while Eleanor arranged her hair. "How long have you been up? Where have you been?" Renée asked irritably.

"Helping Henry with his lessons," Nicole answered. "May I?" As she leaned over the pastries, the necklace dangled in the air.

"Certainly." Renée gestured carelessly, never seeing it, and Nicole sat beside her to eat. "Now," Renée adjusted the shoulder of her robe, "first thing, we must send a ribbon to the Commander, with a note. Bring paper and quill," she waved at Eleanor, who let her hair drop and left. "We'll say, 'Seeing how kind and gentle you are with everyone has shown me what a large heart—'"

"Renée—darling—" Nicole looked at the sunshine streaming in through the window. "Let's find someone else to torment today."

"Why? Oh, darling, you're not becoming entangled in this question of conscience again, are you? I thought we had that all worked out. He really does enjoy the attention."

"I understand that," Nicole said with her mouth full. She leaned over the table to prevent pastry crumbs from nesting in her dress. "It's just that—there are so many people here, it would be a shame to expend all our effort on one person. So many others are just as deserving of the attention. Like Merle, for example."

"Oh, no. Not Merle. She'd eat you alive, and you'd never get your laundry done," Renée objected. "It has to be someone with at least a shred of humor."

"What about the Counselor?" Nicole asked, then felt immediate guilt. He had been kind to her for no discernible reason.

"No. Not him," Renée said quickly.

"Why do we have to torment anyone? Show me around the palace. There is so much I want to see," Nicole said.

"Really, don't be tiresome, darling," Renée said, then looked up as Eleanor entered with a stack of parchment, quill, and inkstand. "Put those here and finish my hair."

"Let's ride out and look at the river where they're proposing the waterway," Nicole suggested.

"Darling, you are trying my patience," the Chataine said as to an unruly child. Taking a parchment sheet, she dipped the quill in the inkstand. "Now, what shall we say?"

"I haven't a clue." Nicole reached for another pastry.

"Our beginning was good. 'Dear sir: Seeing how kind and gentle you are with everyone has shown me what a large heart beats in that noble breast.'" She read slowly, as the writing was slow. "'May I say that I am counting the minutes'—how do you spell *minutes*?"

"M-I-N-I-T-S," Nicole guessed.

"'May I say that I am counting the minits until I see you at table tonight. Please accept this small token of my love—'"

Nicole looked at her sharply, and Renée amended, "'this small token of my affection for you.' We shan't sign it, of course. Now, I need one of your hair ribbons."

"Oh, dear," Nicole pouted. "My ribbons are so—cheap and plain. He won't be impressed at all. Can't we please use one of yours? They're so much prettier."

"Very well." Renée stood to open a massive wardrobe while Eleanor hung on to her hair. "It can't be too ornate, or he'll know it's not yours," Renée said.

"True," Nicole murmured, gazing at the scores of fabulous dresses that hung crammed together.

"This one?" Renée pulled out a blue ribbon and Nicole shrugged. Then the Chataine carefully blotted the note, rolled it up, and tied the ribbon around it. "Fetch Tanny," she told Eleanor, who finally finished her hair.

The maid bowed and left, returning moments later with one of the male attendants Nicole had seen often yesterday. While he stood outside the door, Renée put the scroll in his hands. "Deliver this to the Commander. Wait to see if he has a reply." He bowed and started off, then she remembered: "Tanny! Tell him it's from Lady Nicole. Do not mention me."

"Chataine," he bowed obediently.

"Well, I should say we'll have a reply within the hour," Renée said in satisfaction. Nicole looked off.

As a matter of fact, the Chataine had barely finished dressing when Tanny knocked on the door of her chambers. "Enter! Already!" she marveled to Nicole.

"Chataine," he bowed at the door, knowing better than to enter the room. He was empty-handed.

"Did you give it to him? What did he say?" Renée asked.

"Yes, Chataine, I gave it into his hands personally while he was at the stables. I watched him open it and read it, then he threw it into the smith's fire," Tanny said.

"What? Did you tell him it was from the Lady Nicole?" Renée asked, pained.

"Yes, Chataine," he said gravely.

"What did he say?"

"Nothing, Chataine. He just tossed it into the fire."

"And the ribbon?" Renée asked.

"Into the fire, Chataine," he said regretfully.

"Oh, dear. I'm sorry, darling," she said to Nicole. "It seems that his affection for you may be less than we had hoped." Nicole looked resigned.

"While I am here, Chataine, I thought to tell you that your father sent messengers this morning to Ossian inviting both of his sons to come visit," Tanny said.

"Both of them! My, however shall I entertain two?" Renée said, as if it would be not difficult at all. "Well. You may go." She waved at Tanny, who bowed and withdrew.

Renée began to pace. "It troubles me that the Commander is not playing along with us anymore. That's very uncivil of him." Nicole said nothing. "Well. Let's go down to the laundry pit and see what Merle has to say."

"Oh, darling," Nicole sniffed delicately, "something down there gave me a terrible headache. I would really rather see . . . your gardens."

"Then go look!" Renée said, exasperated. She swept out, obviously expecting Nicole to follow with a torrent of apologies. But as soon as the Chataine had disappeared down the back staircase, Nicole took off in the opposite direction. She traipsed down the main staircase to tour the palace grounds on her own.

It was a profitable tour in which she learned much. She learned that the great banquet room of last night was actually the audience hall during the day where Cedric held court. He was holding an open audience now, in fact, and Nicole stood in the back of the room behind a throng of people to hear him deliver judgment on a certain matter brought before him. (What it was all about, she couldn't quite hear.) While the Surchatain sat on an ornate (but wooden) throne, the Counselor stood beside him, serious in his role as advisor. No, it was hardly appropriate to dump buckets of water on *him*.

From there, going toward the interior of the palace, she

passed by the kitchen and herb garden. Past that was an entrance to a larger garden, but these were not exclusively roses, so she still did not know where the rose garden might be.

Another corridor brought her to the portico opposite that of the laundry pit, this one looking out to the stables and training pens. A restless stallion ran the circumference of one pen over and over, dodging attempts to rope him, snorting at calming hands. Nicole watched as one trainer finally cast a hood over his head to cover his eyes. Then he could approach the quivering animal to stroke it quietly.

"Lady Nicole," said a deep voice, and she jumped. The soldier at her side diffidently pointed to the stables nearby. "The Commander thought there's something you'd like to see."

"Very well," she said cautiously, lifting her skirts to follow him to the dark enclosure. Pausing at the doorway to let her eyes adjust to the darkness, she heard hoarse, heavy breathing, and she suddenly thought about the soldiers' brutalizing the tavern maid.

"Over here, Lady." It was Ares' voice. Holding her skirts high out of the hay, she tiptoed toward him. In the close, dim stall, he grinned at her and nodded to something massive on the floor. When she could see, she saw a mare, heavy with foal, lying on her side in a bed of hay and panting hard.

"Oh, my!" she whispered in wonder.

"Should be any time now," he whispered. He leaned down to brush aside the mare's tail and reveal the crowning foal. Nicole caught her breath.

An experienced stablehand attended the mare, but no one else was allowed in. Nicole stood very still to watch. As the mare strained to give birth, Nicole leaned into Ares' side. He put a casual arm around her.

The foal, covered by sac, protruded bit by bit until the mare gave a mighty grunt and the whole slid out onto the hay.

Nicole gripped Ares' arms as the dam staggered up to start cleaning her newborn. The little thing's head bobbled, then it stuck up one spindly leg after another and shoved itself up on wobbly supports. Within a matter of minutes it was nursing.

"We've got us a pretty little filly, Commander—" the stablehand whispered as he turned. Seeing Nicole, he amended, "Another pretty filly, sir."

"Oh, Commander!" Nicole turned to hug his neck in joy, and he put his arms around her. But, of course, the stablehand was watching intently.

"Come." Ares walked her out into the bright sunshine with a hand at her back.

"Oh, life is beautiful. Thank you, Commander," she said. He nodded, regarding her necklace, and she added, "I had nothing to do with that silly note, you know."

"I know," he said. Nicole looked at him in work pants and soiled linen shirt. His fine musculature was far more apparent in this humble attire than in formal dress—why was it just the opposite with women's clothing? Observing how the scar disrupted even the line of his beard stubble, she opened her mouth, then shut it self-consciously. "Ask me," he said.

"Commander?"

"Ask your question." He did not presume to tell her what that was, even though he knew.

So she asked, "Do you love the Chataine?"

He looked surprised, then smiled. "Of course I do. Just like I love Henry."

Nicole lowered her head, embarrassed at her own for-wardness. What a question!

"What you're asking, however, is, do I *love* her," he continued in a soft voice. "And, at one time, I'm sure I did. Our dear Chataine likes to make sure every man does. But I never harbored any illusions of having her. That a soldier should marry a Chataine—well, that came about once in Lystra's history. It's never liable to be so again, and if it were, it wouldn't be me." He said that as if it should have been obvious.

"And how did *that* happen, Commander?" she asked, glancing at his scar.

That was the question he had been expecting. "When I was a child, younger than Henry, I stumbled into a group of drunken soldiers fighting over—who knows what. Their honor, I suppose. It was an accidental slashing. I'm sure the man who did it—whoever that was—had no idea what he had done. But it shaped my life. I determined that day no one would ever hurt me again without a fight. I became a soldier."

"So . . . it was ordained," she said.

"Yes, I feel it was," he said.

"Are our lives ordained, Commander?" she asked.

"What comes to us is ordained. What leaves is what we have made of it," he said, standing as close to her as he dared. He would not attempt to kiss her in view of the whole world here. She looked down at the brown fingers that she grasped without realizing it.

A soldier approached his back. "Commander, there's a gentleman—" When Ares turned and the man saw Nicole, he sputtered, "A thousand pardons, Commander!"

"I had best go. The Chataine will be having fits looking for me," Nicole said, hiking her skirts. As she did, she inspected them, and found them clean. The stables, apparently, were kept cleaner than the laundry pit.

Ares gestured. "Dirk, accompany the lady to her destination."

The soldier saluted and offered Nicole his arm. She turned to curtsy to Ares. "Thank you, my Lord Commander."

He mouthed in reply, *Seven*, and she inclined her head. *It's not likely that I will forget, Commander.*

4

At the foot of the stairs in the great foyer, Nicole told the soldier, "You may leave me here." He bowed formally to her, and she turned up the stairway. Ascending, she passed stationed on the stairs soldier after soldier whose eyes seemed to follow her. But when she looked directly at them, they were always focused on a far-off point just over her head.

In the upper corridor, she passed a sentry who stood at the door of a locked storage room, then paused and returned to him. "Do you know who I am?"

He straightened as before the Commander himself. "Yes, Lady Nicole."

"And . . . have you been given any orders concerning me?" she asked.

"Yes, Lady," he confirmed.

"And what would they be?" she asked tensely.

"To safeguard your person and execute any request you might make in our hearing," he replied, all the while looking at the wall. It was insufferable for a soldier or servant to look a superior in the eye unless instructed to do so.

Nicole contemplated his use of the plural. "Well. Please tell the Commander I thank him," she murmured, and was startled when he bolted off the wall down the stairs. She hadn't meant for him to leave his post to deliver a trivial message. But a moment later another soldier came to take his place. He acknowledged her with a formal bow, then stood at the door as the first had done.

Nicole left him and continued down the corridor to enter the Chataine's apartments. They were empty, so she opened the window and sat on the cushioned window seat to look out. This window faced east, toward Willowring Lake, and she could see in the distance, past orchards and grain fields, the ancient weaving willows and hazy glints from the water. She leaned against the casing and thought about the Commander. Then she lifted the cross to study its wonderful filigree.

How could men lay out their hearts before a stranger like that? She never understood it. She had certainly never done it. Were it in her power, she would take many months to test out a man before deciding whether he was someone she wanted to love.

But she had no such luxury of choice here. The Commander was the obvious (and only) candidate to fulfill her father's requirements. And she felt sure that he would be good to her—as long as she pleased him. What might happen when he tired of her was another matter altogether, one that was useless to speculate upon.

The door to the chambers opened and Eleanor came in, carrying a bundle of fresh laundry. Seeing Nicole at the window, she said, "Oh! The Chataine has been looking everywhere for you, and here you are! Please go to her in the anteroom, my lady."

"I will do that," Nicole decided. Eleanor glanced at her, curtsying, and Nicole knew it sounded strange for her to deliberate whether to obey or not. But now Nicole felt like she had a choice—in regards to that, at least.

Downstairs, she found the anteroom outside the great hall, where Renée was in the process of instructing a servant to bring a basket of delicacies to the front courtyard. Seeing Nicole, she exclaimed, "There you are! Darling, I was beginning to worry! Where were you?"

Nicole looked surprised. "I was touring the grounds, as you told me to. I watched a foal being born," she said.

"Oh. Well, come." Renée took her hand to lead her out the front doors, where a litter manned by four servants waited at the steps. "You wanted a trip, so we're going into town. I promise we will be back by dinner tonight."

"Are we both riding in that?" Nicole asked.

"Yes, of course, what did you think, dear? The men are strong. They won't drop us."

The kitchen servant placed a basket of refreshments in the litter and Renée got in, assisted by one of the carriers. Nicole resisted, knowing there was no way Renée would have her back in time for her tryst with the Commander without being let in on every detail. "I want soldiers to accompany us," Nicole said suddenly. "At least two. And I want to go on horseback."

Renée stared at her through the embroidered curtains of the litter, then she got out again and faced Nicole on the steps. "Why all these demands, dear heart?" she asked in a cold voice.

"Don't you see, darling? It would be terribly demeaning for you to have a commoner—for that is what I am—ride with you through the streets of the city in your personal litter. What if some fool sees us who does not know which one of us is the Chataine, and repeats what he has seen? It will surely reach your father's ears. Then what will become of our summer together?" Nicole argued. Renée's bright blue eyes took on a worried cast.

"Moreover, what if some ruffian sees the litter, and decides to gather more of his kind to get what they can from it? How can your servants carry the litter and defend us at the same time?" Now Renée looked frightened. "Let me ride a horse beside you, with mounted soldiers. Then I am clearly a friendly subordinate, and the soldiers will scare off anyone looking to make mischief," Nicole urged.

"Oh, you are so right, darling. I am so glad you have such good sense." Renée turned to a servant. "We need two soldiers on horseback and a pretty mare. Quickly!" The servant scurried off, and Renée said, "Well, it's likely to take them forever, lazy beasts, so let's see what the kitchen has for us." Nicole agreed, and they sat in the grounded litter to pilfer the basket.

In a very short while, a procession came around the corner into the courtyard. Much of the normal bustle was suspended while the people watched. Nicole climbed out of the litter as four of the biggest men she had ever seen, wearing breastplates emblazoned with the royal insigne, rode up on massive war horses. Between them, they led a small white horse, primped like a dream creature, adorned with hoof guards, bells and a delicate sidesaddle. Nicole had never seen anything so beautiful.

The soldiers dismounted and went down on one knee before the litter. When the Chataine bid them rise, the lead soldier said, "The Commander wishes my ladies a most pleasant outing."

"Oh, thank you," Nicole breathed, stroking the mare's neck and mane. "Oh, she is precious." She glanced up at Renée's pensive face, and feared for a moment that she would take the horse for herself, but, not practiced in horsemanship, Renée returned to the litter.

Nicole hiked her skirts to mount, whereupon one of the soldiers got down on his hands and knees as a step stool for her. The lead soldier gave her his arm, and she paused. In an audacious test of his loyalty, she whispered, "I must be back at the palace by seven, and the Chataine must not know why."

His chest seemed to swell as he whispered back, "It shall be so, Lady."

So, she thought, *he knows*. Whereupon he assisted her into the saddle, the soldiers mounted, the carriers lifted the litter, and they proceeded out of the cobbled courtyard into the city streets. The bell tolled five.

There was some momentary confusion as to formation: the ranking soldier wished to lead the mare by a strap, as the reins were nonfunctional silken cords. But the Chataine wished Nicole to ride alongside the litter so they could talk, and most of the streets were not wide enough for the three of them abreast.

Nicole convinced the soldier that she was capable of riding unaided, so he acquiesced to allow two of the men to precede the litter, Nicole to ride at its side, and two of them, including himself, to form the rearguard. He looped the strap across the mare's neck as reins, and again they set off.

The townspeople, of course, were agog at this show, and craned their necks to see into the litter. The carriers were somewhat harried in keeping their feet clear of the mare's hooves, so Nicole tried to ride her not so close to the litter's side. The only horse she had ever ridden before was the plowman's great, broadbacked workhorse, but this was easy.

They stayed to the better streets, of course, in which the best shops were located. They stopped first at the dressmaker's where the Chataine had several gowns on order. Walking into this shop, seeing the sheer volume of fabrics and trims and workers, put into perspective for Nicole her father's one-man operation. By comparison, it was rather shabby.

While the Chataine tried on a dress in progress with the assistance of the shop owner, the man's wife curtsied to Nicole. "What may I assist my lady with today?"

"I am not here to buy," Nicole said.

"Oh!" Regarding her dress, the woman looked offended, and left her alone.

Nicole had to stay in the shop to contribute appropriate comments and encouragement when the sleeves of one voluptuous gown were found to be wanting. While Renée fretted over this disaster, Nicole glanced outside where their retinue waited. Were the bells audible from here?

Finally, all possible business in this shop was exhausted, and they exited. Renée climbed into the litter, and the soldier went down on his hands and knees in the street beside the mare. Standing on his back, Nicole stopped as she heard the faint tolling of the bells. How many? She glanced at the lead soldier to see him nod and hold up six fingers.

As they resumed their foray deeper into town, Nicole grew uneasy. Her responses to Renée's happy chatter were vague and distracted. She wanted to get back early to wash up before meeting him—but that was unlikely. It would be difficult enough to get back on time, and she could not imagine how the soldiers would manage it.

Their next stop, which at twilight must be their last, was the jewelry shop, kept open tonight solely for them. Dismounting the mare, Nicole almost moaned at the thought of standing around in another shop, watching Renée fret over selections of gold and jewels. This shop employed their own armed guard, who appraised the royal soldiers enviously.

As feared, Renée lingered maddeningly over the display cases, and Nicole began to pace. The minutes slipped by; it was growing dark outside. Candles were lit in the shop.

Finally, when she thought she would grab Renée and drag her out, the lead soldier leaned into the shop and said, "A thousand pardons. Will my ladies kindly allow us to deliver them to the palace before dark, so as not to alarm the Surchatain?"

"We're coming," Renée said, and continued to look.

A few minutes later, the soldier assayed again, "Forgive me, Chataine, but—"

"We'll be out when I'm done!" Renée said angrily.

Nicole's heart sank. It appeared that Renée was intent on staying out as long as possible, just to prove that she could.

Glancing at the soldier, she saw him furtively gesture for her to come. Nicole took a step back. "My, these necklaces are lovely," she said, wandering to another case closer to the door where the soldier stood.

As she began to inch her way out, the sharp-eyed shop guard said, "Where are you going?"

The royal soldier then stepped full into the shop with his hand on the hilt of his sword and fire on his brow. Nicole glanced at Renée, who was oblivious to this scene. Then Nicole slipped out the door under the arm of the soldier.

Outside, he dispensed with formalities and lifted her straight into the saddle. "Come," he said, mounting his own horse and digging in his heels. As the charger took off, the little mare followed with bells tinkling wildly, and Nicole grasped her mane to stay on.

They loped up dark streets, scattering small creatures. When Nicole felt herself slipping from the saddle, she heaved herself up under the heavy skirts and willed herself to stay on. As they clambered over the bridge, Nicole gasped to see the palace gates closing. The soldier saw it, too, and gave a piercing whistle, which he repeated twice more. The ponderous gates stopped moving.

They clattered into the courtyard as the bell tolled seven. Nicole fell off the mare into the arms of a sentry. "Take me to the rose garden," she gasped. He started to lead her, but she changed her mind: "Wait." She returned to the lead soldier, who was dismounting. "You. What is your name?"

"Oswald, my lady," he bowed.

"Oswald, you shall take me to the rose garden," she said.

"You honor me, lady," he said, extending his arm. She placed her hand atop it and he escorted her into the palace.

They entered the garden she had seen earlier that day. In the darkness, it was lit by scores of globed candles on wrought-iron stands along the pebbled paths. Following one such path, they came upon a matching wrought-iron gate leading into a separate, smaller garden. Here, the spring roses were just beginning to bloom, and the air was heady with their fragrance.

Commander Ares, standing beside a stone bench, turned at their approach. Oswald stopped and saluted, and Nicole curtsied. Ares returned the salute and Oswald melted into the darkness of the receding path.

Nicole paused to catch her breath while the Commander studied her. "He had quite a time getting me out of the jewelry shop where the Chataine had taken up lodging," she smiled, then added, "She does not know that I am here." He nodded.

"Oh! Thank you for sending the lovely mare. I so enjoyed riding her," Nicole said. He nodded again. Then she waited for him to speak his mind, growing worried over his formality. He was acting differently toward her, and she did not know why.

He cleared his throat. "Lady, tell me about your family. The truth."

She lowered her head. "My father is the tailor of Prie Mer. He is not nobility. We have no land. But I met the Chataine at the spring fair, and she wanted me to come visit her here, so I agreed to the deception. I am sorry."

"So your father made your clothes," he said. She nodded. "They are very fine work," he added.

With as much dignity as she could muster, she said, "I thank you."

There was a moment of silence. "So . . . the only reason you are here is to provide entertainment for the Chataine."

"As far as she is concerned, yes. But the whole reason my father made these clothes—spent years on them—was to make me presentable at court. He sent me here to get a rich or noble husband," she said. He might as well know.

He looked off. "Well," he said, assuming a studiously casual air, "I am neither rich nor a nobleman, but I am available. Will you have me?"

"Yes," she said. Was it wrong that all she felt was relief?

He looked hard at her, not attempting to obscure the scar. "Prove it."

"My lord?"

He took a step toward her, something building in him. "Give me a token as proof of what you say. I'll play no more games with you, not about this. Give me something from your person to prove you agreed to marry me."

She opened her hands. What could she give besides a cap or a shoe? And appear at dinner with head uncovered or one shoe missing? But he was certainly justified in demanding a token. And she could not give back the necklace, for who would believe she had accepted it from him in the first place?

"Oh, turn around," she groaned. He looked uncertain, as if fearing she would run off as soon as his back was turned. "If you want a token, turn around, my Lord Commander," she insisted.

He turned his back to her, and she reached into her bodice to begin unlacing the bodice ribbon. He shifted slightly, and she ordered, "No peeking." He raised his head to wait patiently, hands clasped behind his back.

She drew out the ribbon, then rearranged herself, hoping to stay together just through dinner. "You may turn around." He did, and she offered into his outstretched hand the plain, slightly sweaty ribbon. "There is your token, sir."

He kissed it and tied it around his neck, stuffing it under his shirt collar to hide it from the rest of the world. Then he took her hands and kissed them, brushing one hand against the scar. Eyeing her, he turned the palms up and kissed them. He placed a warm hand on the back of her neck, beneath her hair, and brought her mouth to his.

He had the good sense to kiss her softly and not be overbearing about it, but the longing seeped out through his hands as he caressed her shoulders and back, then drew her tightly into his chest, pressing harder on her mouth.

When a tiny complaint rose in her throat, he released her.

"I must go ask leave of the Surchatain to marry you," he whispered, and she could feel his pulse racing in his wrists. "But I will see you at dinner. Oh, I will crow shamelessly at dinner!" he promised. He kissed her again for good measure, then started down the path at a run, scattering pebbles.

"My, that went well." The question of a dowry had not even come up. She collected herself for a moment, then headed out of the garden toward the anteroom.

Oswald met her on the way, bowing. "Congratulate me, Oswald. I am betrothed to the Commander."

He raised his fists in triumph. "God be praised, Lady!" She grinned at his joy. But he had another matter to address: "Lady, we thought to inform you that the Chataine has just now returned, and she appears to be in ill humor at your disappearance. The sentries have informed her that you preceded her home—beyond that, they know no more. You may wish to consider what you should tell her."

"Yes, Oswald, thank you," she said pensively. She nodded to herself, then entered the anteroom.

As she was early, the anteroom was crowded with courtiers awaiting Georges' permission to take their places for dinner. They, in turn, were stirred with interest at her arrival. Most of those toward the upper end of the table took great care not to wait in the anteroom with the masses.

Seeing Thom and his wife, Nicole made her way to them immediately. Drawing them close, she whispered, "I am betrothed to the Commander."

Deirdre covered her mouth in delight. Thom asked quietly, "Has the Surchatain given his leave?"

"The Commander is now asking," Nicole replied. "Is there a reason he should not?"

"Not that I know of, Lady. God bless you," Thom said.

Deirdre began chattering to her, and Nicole tried to listen, but was distracted by her own troubled thoughts. She glimpsed Lady Rhea watching her with a rather unpleasant smirk.

Georges announced the table ready, and the guests began entering by pairs or singly, as Georges so directed, until Nicole was left in the anteroom all alone. Just as he began to get distressed over the Chataine's absence, Renée swept in, refreshed from a visit to her chambers. At first she said nothing, not even deigning to look at Nicole, then turned coolly and said, "Do you have an explanation?"

"No, Chataine, I am very sorry," Nicole said. "Only that you can afford to be late to dinner, and your father would do nothing. Were I to walk in late, even with you, he would put me out of the palace. I am sorry, Chataine. I will not risk your father's displeasure even for you."

Georges looked at the Chataine in something like triumph, and she looked chagrined. Hugging Nicole, she said, "Oh, darling, you're right. I am the one at fault. I love you so much, I just forget we are not sisters, with sisterly privilege."

Nicole hugged her in return, and Georges said, "Excellent. You may enter now, ladies." So Nicole and Renée entered on the arms of their attendants and received the greetings of the table. Nicole curtsied in response and Renée rolled her eyes.

They waited; it seemed like a long time. Then the Counselor came in with Henry bounding on his heels. He came to a dead stop at the absence of his guardian. Nicole curtsied to them, glancing anxiously at the Commander's vacant place to her left. Ares was always supposed to enter with the Counselor, before the Chatain.

Carmine looked concerned, but Henry was livid. "Where is Ares?" he demanded of her.

"I do not know, my lord Henry," she said.

Exhaling, he put his hands on his little hips and began pacing around the table in a show of displeasure that would have been comical had the circumstances not been so foreboding.

"Where IS he?" he shouted, but no one could answer. The

Counselor, studying his manicure, saw something in the cuticles that depressed him a great deal.

Rapid footfalls sounded, and everyone turned to look. The Commander came striding in with fury brimming in every move. Nicole shrank back as he took his place beside her and nodded curtly to the Counselor. But Ares ignored Henry, which enraged him. "Where have you been, Ares?"

"With your father, Chatain," Ares replied through gritted teeth. That the interview went unfavorably was apparent to all. Nicole bowed to him, as the rest of the table did, save Renée, who was owed obeisance from *him*.

He glanced at Nicole beside him, then took her hand and kissed it. Then he took her in his arms and kissed her full on the lips, to the astonished gasps of the other guests. Nicole received him without hesitation, feeling his anguished disappointment as her own. Henry was speechless.

"Surchatain Cedric and Surchataine Elise," Georges announced, and all those at table turned to face them except the Commander. Nicole tugged pleadingly on his sleeve until he also turned.

Cedric greeted the table and all were seated, then he motioned for the wine. No one dared attempt to break the tension while the Commander stared ahead vacantly. Henry tried to climb on his lap, but Ares put him firmly in his own chair. With tears brimming in his eyes, Henry cried, "What's wrong with you?"

Ares exhaled, dropping his shoulders, and opened his hands to the boy. Henry clambered up into the proffered arms, but repeated, "Why are you so sad?" Ares said nothing.

Cedric suddenly demanded, "Is your family noble, Lady Nicole? Yes or no! And no one answer for her!"

"No, High Lord," she said calmly.

"Well, *really*!" the Counselor huffed in an exaggerated show of indignation. Brightening, he offered, "Then that makes her worthless for either of Ossian's sons, Surchatain, so there's really no reason the Commander can't have her, is there?"

Renée gasped, "Oh, darling! Are you going to marry our precious patsy?"

"If the Surchatain will allow it," Nicole answered quietly.

The Chataine turned on her father, crying, "Let them marry, you beast! How could you deny him that? Have you any idea what he puts up with?"

Henry clambered down from Ares' lap to run over to his father and begin kicking him violently in the shins. "Give him Nicole! He wants her! You give her to him right now!" Ares jumped up from his seat and lifted Henry under the arms, then reseated himself with the Chatain confined on his lap.

Elise turned pleadingly to her husband. "High Lord, please let them know some of the happiness we have known."

With the weight of the table so firmly against him, Cedric began to waver. He glanced around uncertainly. But the royal pride was at stake. He needed a gracious way to change his mind.

Leaning forward, the Counselor murmured seductively, "High Lord, let us consider the most politically expedient course. Shall we offer a beautiful but common girl to a son of the man who has beautiful noblewomen from across the Continent at his court, or shall we give her to the Commander of your army, in appreciation for the many years of selfless, loyal service he and his thousands of soldiers have given you, uncomplaining, undemanding . . . ?"

"You may have her, Ares," Cedric said grumpily.

The table erupted in cheers. Ares put Henry off his lap, stood, and then fell on his knees at Cedric's feet. "Thank you, High Lord," he said, choked.

"Enough," Cedric muttered, pleased. Henry fell on Ares' back, laughing, and the Commander stood to peel the tick off and place him in his chair yet again. Returning to his seat, he kissed Nicole's hand, and his eyes were full.

"When shall you wed?" Renée cried, clapping her hands.

"Tonight. As soon as we are dismissed," Ares said promptly.

Renée objected, "No! We must have decorations, and a dress, and—"

"With all respect, Chataine," Ares said loudly, then, having secured her full attention, finished in a normal voice: "Tonight."

5

With that small matter disposed of, Cedric became a benign and convivial host. He even attempted small teasings directed at the happy couple: "Well, Nicole, are you sure you want to dine next to that monstrosity day after day?"

"He is not offensive to me, High Lord," she replied, successfully defanging a personal affront. After having paraded the roast pig around the table for all to admire, the servers were now in the process of cutting it up and serving it. Ares serenely cracked a hazelnut in his bare hand and offered it to her. "Um. That's delicious," she said, so he scooped up a score of them to crack for her.

"Oh, but he's so *old*," Cedric groaned, leaning back like a weary old man. The Commander smiled and nodded at the private joke. "You see, Nicole, the Commander and I were born within three months of each other thirty-four years ago. Thirty-four long years . . . but our families go back even farther, eh, Ares?" The Commander nodded.

In truth, Cedric was thirty-seven, three years older than Ares, but the Commander did not know that, and Cedric relished the little deception, believing he looked so much younger than the other man.

Contemplatively, Cedric continued, "But you are sitting there, and I, here. . . ." Ares cracked a handful of nuts in his fist and picked out the shell fragments before depositing the meat in Nicole's palm.

"That is so sweet," Renée cooed. "Then the note must have had some effect after all." Henry hovered between them, wanting a lap, but he knew he had to stay off until the Commander finished his dinner. That much, Ares insisted on.

Cedric picked up his golden goblet and the rest of the table answered with theirs. "To Commander Ares and his lady," Cedric said, and there was the slightest irony in his voice. "May she stay by your side the rest of your life."

The table drank the toast, and Ares turned to her. "I will love you forever," he whispered. She lowered her eyes.

As dinner progressed, he grew increasingly restless, anxious to get it done. He wolfed down his portion with little of the social self-consciousness he had evidenced last night, and eschewed dessert altogether, until at last he was sitting with his hands on his knees, waiting for the word. Most of the other diners cooperated by eating hastily, but Cedric refused to allow the few stragglers (such as Lord Notham and his daughter) to be rushed.

Finally, with a tolerant smile, Cedric deemed it time to remove the tables and chairs and call in the priest. Thom was ready: a signal to the sentries lining the wall brought soldiers out in force to clear out the furnishings, which they did within seconds. Ares gripped Nicole by the hand, but she said firmly, "My lord, you must allow me to retire momentarily to wash." He looked distressed, but let her go upstairs with Renée.

Once again, they ran hand in hand to her apartments. While Nicole used the chamber pot and washed in the basin, Renée rifled through her own wardrobe. "This one," she decided, pulling out a gown of milky damask and taffeta. "You shall be married in this."

Nicole touched the dress. "Darling, I . . . I can't. I cannot wear your dress. It's too . . . extravagant. I'm only—"

"Don't be absurd," Renée said briskly. "I insist. I am giving you this dress because it goes so nicely with your hair."

Nicole embraced her. "You are a true friend."

"Hush, now, let's get you dressed. At least you are marrying someone you really care for," Renée said, and Nicole turned her gaze to the flickering candle on the bedstand.

Dressed, with flowers twined in her hair and beaded slippers on her feet, Nicole stared at her reflection in the mirror. Renée said, "There. You look worthy of Ossian himself." Eleanor murmured agreement, fussily arranging the taffeta to expose enough of her shoulders to cause fainting spells among the men. The cross glittered red-gold in the firelight.

"Thank you," Nicole whispered. She turned to the door, but her feet would not move.

Unheeding, the Chataine took her hand to lead her downstairs. The bell chimed ten. "Poor Ares," she snickered. "We've kept him waiting for the better part of an hour. Well, I got him good one last time."

Nicole did not hear, nor was she fully aware of descending the staircase. She did not really see the doors to the great hall standing open, and the hundreds of soldiers crammed inside. Craning their necks to catch a glimpse of her, they opened a path for her down the middle of the room. At the far end of the hall, Ares sprang up and woke the priest.

The Chataine gave her a little push. "Go!" But it was impossible that Nicole should be walking down the hall in marriage—she had arrived here only yesterday! *Wait! It's too soon!* Her heart rebelled in panic, but her feet did as they were told.

By hesitant steps, Nicole made her way alone down the great expanse toward her future life. The freedom of life in the marshes flashed before her, of skipping home to stir the pot of stew for her father bent over needlework, of running herds with the goatherd and digging for crabs in the surf—

She looked aside wildly at the faces—all the faces blending together, hemming her in, compelling her to go on. Her throat constricted, her mouth went dry, and the faces began to move in strange circles.

There was a hand clasping hers, and she looked up at Ares' scar. *Who are you behind that scar? I do not know you.* With so little knowledge of the man, and so little time to know him, her heart shrank back. He had taken her hand, and with his other arm around her waist, he escorted her the rest of the distance—half the way—to the priest at the end of the room. Blinking, she squeezed his hand, and he directed her to kneel as he did.

The priest said some words over them that she did not understand, and sprinkled them with water from a basin. Then he said, "Commander Ares, do you swear before God to take this woman Nicole as your only wife, to love her, to be faithful to her, until death parts you?"

"Yes," Ares said firmly.

"Nicole, do you swear before God to take this man Ares as your husband, to love him, to be faithful to him, till death parts you?"

To love him? She had to swear to love him? How could she do that when she did not know her own heart?—did not know him? Part of it urged her to flee; part of it said, *But he loves you.* Nicole was silent, grappling with this, and Ares slowly turned to her.

She had already given her word to marry him; that's what the bodice ribbon was about. She gave it to him freely. So it had to be an act of love to go through with the marriage when she did not know how she felt. To fill the awful silence, the priest was repeating, "Nicole, do you swear—"

"Yes," she whispered, and Ares dropped his head in relief.

The priest continued, "God and Father of our Lord Jesus Christ, I pray your blessing on Ares and his wife Nicole. 'What God has joined together, let man not separate.' Amen."

Ares lifted Nicole, by now quite limp, to her feet to kiss her, and the crowd of soldiers roared. Nicole covered her ears and Ares chuckled, covering her with his arms, pressing his face into her hair. Dazed to the point of stupidity, she just stood there.

He was saying something to her in the din, pointing, and she looked down at Henry, sleepy-eyed, pulling on her skirts. She came to herself enough to kneel. Henry said, "I stayed awake to see you married."

"Thank you, my lord," she whispered. And somehow, that brought her out of the mists. In his childish way, Henry knew when a good thing was happening. He knew what was worth staying up to watch. The marriage was a fact now; get on with it.

She stood, feeling a little stronger. Ares took her hand to lead her out of the hall, and she smiled shyly at the soldiers who applauded and shouted and reached out to slap him on the back. Leaving the mob behind, he hurried her down one corridor and up another, lit by globed candles. Then he stopped at one door and swung it open, wordlessly inviting her inside.

Her first impression was of the stables, only with a stone floor. But she could see little beyond the low fire and the circle of light cast by the solitary candle burning in its holder. Nicole stepped in and he shut and bolted the door behind them.

"I had them bring in a bed for you," he said, lifting the candle to show her. It was straw—a straw-filled bed with straw-stuffed pillows. "I've never slept in a bed before, but I knew a pallet would never do for you."

"Thank you, my lord," she said.

He reached out to touch the taffeta, which thoroughly

intimidated him. "I don't want to damage the dress," he whispered.

Nicole turned abruptly and looked at the bolt on the door. Then she closed her eyes and said, "The buttons are along the back. I cannot unfasten them myself." Under her guidance, he patiently undid the long row of pearl buttons. Then he divested himself of his clothes posthaste as she laid the gown across an empty chair. Her linen undergarments he could handle by himself. Then he brought her, shaking, to bed.

He was very gentle, but determined to avail himself of his conjugal rights. And he was careful not to hurt her. Once he felt her relax somewhat, he went full force after his desire, and soon his sweat drenched her from neck to knee. He gripped her head, pressing his smooth check to her face, breathing hard in her ear. At last he was done; at last he withdrew, and the new bride dropped immediately to sleep.

For a while. From the blackness, she heard him whisper, "My love, are you awake? . . . Nicole, will you wake?" When she stirred, he embraced her again, and she did not protest.

It was not unpleasant, for he was too tender, too affectionate. But she was clearly not feeling what he was feeling. She had not the benefit of the pain, or the rejection, or the frustration he had endured in finding an acceptable and accepting partner. She had not been privileged with years of suffering at the hands of women who relished the power they had to torment a man.

Wanting to please him, Nicole let him do as he wished, only—he was insatiable. He would have her and sink down beside her only to wake her again an hour later. This went on for most of the night, with her cooperating in a state of semi-consciousness. At last, she had a few uninterrupted hours of dead sleep, and then it was morning.

The early sunlight woke her—sunlight peeping in through a crack of his shuttered windows. She saw it haloing his head, bowed, facing her. She blinked sleepily. He was kneeling beside the bed, gripping her hands as he whispered intently.

She heard only fragments of what he said: ". . . this treasure, this jewel you have given me. How you made her to accept me, I will never know, only, my gratitude will—will never end—" He kissed the cross lying across her breast, and she felt wetness. Then she fell back asleep.

Later in the morning, when the sunlight pervaded the room, she awoke again. She still lay on her left side facing the window, and Ares lay at her back, his arms around her. When she moved, he stroked her softly. Although his hands were rough, it was not unpleasant. She thought of the monk's hands, and how she had abhorred his doing the same thing. She knew even then he had no right to touch her so.

But Ares had the right to pet her body; it belonged to him now. And she thought that she might enjoy being his pet. She stretched luxuriously, reaching back to embrace his head, which caused his arms to close over her like steel bands. He moaned something unintelligible into her hair.

"I'm hungry," she murmured.

He promptly raised up. "Breakfast is waiting, my love."

She climbed out of the straw bed and donned her linen undergarments, seeing as Ares had on loose breeches. He was actually a comely man, but for the terrible scar.

She smiled a little self-consciously as he sat her at a table and poured her a cup of sweet wine. Taking a sip, Nicole brushed her hair back and glanced around. The room was ample in size, but as she had surmised last night, devoid of anything ornamental or comfortable. There was a large fireplace chiseled out of the rock wall in which a low fire burned. Next to it were louvered wooden doors. In the corner were a tub and a chest. Her trunk sat at the foot of the bed, and a wooden honeycomb against the far wall of patchworked stone held an assortment of parchments. She was aware of a muffled sound like a babbling brook, but could not tell whence it came.

Ares, meanwhile, had uncovered a platter of meat-filled pastries, fresh from the kitchen. "My lord, I can't eat these. They are for the royal family alone," she protested.

He laughed, "No one is going to tell me you can't have them!"

Picking one up, she sighed, "You treat me like a lady, even though I'm not."

He regarded her as he took a bite of pastry himself. "Of course you are," he said thickly.

"We got that all cleared up last night, remember, my lord?" she said. "Um, these are wonderful."

He washed down the mouthful with a swig of wine. "There are some advantages to marriage with me. My rank elevates you. We are Commander Ares and Lady Nicole."

"Really?" she cried, and he nodded firmly. "Oh, that will so please Father!"

"Yes, it should," he said, then glanced at the bed. Getting up, he said, "I've sent a horse after him; he should be here by evening." He looked at the rumpled straw bed, littered with limp blossoms from her hair, and stripped the bottom sheet from it. This he held up to examine the spots of blood on it before folding it up and putting it aside. "He will want to see this."

Yes, her father would be interested in the evidence attesting to her virginity as of her wedding night. "You sent for him to come here?"

"I did," he confirmed.

"For how long?" she asked.

"As long as he wishes to stay," he smiled.

"Oh! But—how did you know where to find him?"

He sat back down, gingerly, it seemed. "Ah, dear Nicole. Do you really think I would take the Chataine's word for who you were? After you almost brought me to my knees in the foyer day before yesterday, I told Thom to find out everything there was to know about you, and he sent out two of our best trackers. They located your father by evening, and spoke with several of his regular customers in Prie Mer before returning yesterday. Lady Brigid wants her new surcoat trimmed in silver fox instead of red, by the way."

"Then, last night, when you asked about my family—"

"I already knew. What I did not know was whether you would tell me the truth," he said levelly. He finished off the pastry and wiped his hands.

"Oh." She looked around again, uneasily this time. "My lord, where is your, um, chamber pot?"

He shuddered. "I don't use one. They're nasty."

She looked toward the shuttered window, dismayed at the thought of using the common latrine outside. "Oh, dear."

He got up and opened the louvered doors. They exposed a garderobe, or water closet, cut out of the rock. A stream poured out of a high opening in one side of the closet, then cascaded down the graded wall to disappear underground just beyond the opposite wall.

"An underground stream," he said. "My engineers found it when we were trying to locate all the branches of the Passage. That's why I took these quarters rather than those upstairs. No one else has running water."

"That's amazing!" she exclaimed. Ares demonstrated how to crouch inside and hold on to the ledges to relieve herself. He had to hold her when she first tried, but it didn't take her long to learn. She leaned back on the rocks where the water flowed. "Oh, it's warm," she said. "If only you could bathe in here! Why is the water warm?"

"The fire heats the surrounding rock," he said, lifting her out. "No, you don't want to bathe over the latrine. Here." He wheeled the tub (which rested on casters) to sit in front of the closet, then reached up for an angled wooden trough suspended on ropes from the garderobe ceiling. The end of the trough fit into a groove in the rock under the fountain, thus diverting a generous flow of warm water into the tub.

Nicole cried in delight, "Who built you this?" as she threw off her undergarments to climb into the tub.

"I did," he said. "Actually, I designed it. I had men build it. Does my lady care to wash?" He held out a sponge and cake of soap.

Sinking down in the rapidly filling tub, she sighed, "Oh, yes!" He stood by eager to offer further assistance, but she demurred.

When she was finished, he took his turn in the tub. At this point, he showed her an additional feature of his invention: once the tub was filled, a little slot could be opened in the bottom of the tub to drain it into the closet, thus allowing for a continuous stream of clean, warm water. "You've had the comfort of running water, but not a proper bed," she observed.

He smiled grimly. "I cannot sit at the Surchatain's table smelling like a street beggar. My position is tenuous enough as it is."

While she dried her hair in front of the fire with a great towel, she watched the erstwhile bachelor Commander make his toilet. First, she was amazed to see him run a rough cloth over his teeth and the entire insides of his mouth.

"Sister Agnes taught me to do that," he muttered, embarrassed at her staring. Now she realized why it was pleasant to kiss him—he had all of his teeth, and they were clean. Sitting up, she took the cloth after him and cleaned her mouth, too.

Next, he shaved his face with the edge of a sharp knife entirely by feel, without a mirror. Then he picked up the bottle of wine, and, to her astonishment, poured it down his scar. Toweling up the excess, he explained, "Wigzell, the doctor, makes me do that. Everyone thinks he is mad because he pours wine in open wounds and washes his hands constantly. But he seems to keep people on their feet, so I do as he says." She nodded.

While he dressed in deerskin breeches and a cotton shirt,

Nicole opened her trunk and pulled out a red linsey-woolsey dress. Being the last gown Robert had time to complete, it had few flourishes, but it was comfortable, and Nicole knew that Ares would not care what she wore. It was wonderfully liberating to not have to worry about her clothes anymore.

Ares drained the tub, put it away, and shut the water closet. As he turned to her, she was brushing her hair over her head, upside down. She twisted the hair into a long, high ponytail which she drew through the top of her red wool cap. Then she tied it under her chin and smiled at him. He shook his head in mild disbelief. "You are so beautiful."

"Come." She held out her hand. "Are you still my plaything?"

He said plaintively, "Lady, that should be obvious. All you need is a leash to lead me with—" and he showed her the bodice ribbon he still wore under his shirt.

She laughed, placing a hand on the cross that would never leave her neck. Skipping out of the room into the nearby portico, she said, "First, I want to see the foal born yesterday. And then we must—my lord?" He had disappeared. She looked all around.

He came around the corner, walking in a slow, stilted manner, with a rather strained expression. "My lord? What is it?"

He leaned a hand against the wall to bend over in pain. Then he started laughing. "I, um, overused some very rusty equipment last night, and almost broke it. This is my just punishment for not allowing you to sleep."

Staring, she offered by means of comparison: "I don't hurt."

"Then what they say about women being the weaker sex is quite a load of crock," he vented, so she laughed, "I will go slow for you."

With her arm in his, they went to the stables looking for the newest foal. The stablehand pointed them to a grassy pen, and there was the dam and its foal, which looked nothing the same. It was sturdy and frisky, eyeing them curiously even as it pressed close to its mother. Nicole desired to pet it, but the dam flattened its ears, so Ares pulled her away.

They headed back into the bustle of the palace. In the foyer, Nicole paused. "I forgot something important," she said. When he queried her, she led him into the chapel. "I must acknowledge that my prayers have been heard."

"Yours? Yours have? Lady, I am in paradise," he countered. As they were agreed that thanks were in order, they knelt together at the cross for private morning prayers.

Leaving there, he said, "Ah. I remember now what I wanted to show you. Here, it's only a short ways from the palace." He spoke to a sentry, who darted off and returned momentarily with a blanket, which Ares stuffed under his arm.

As they started out of the courtyard on foot, Nicole said, "Oh, let's ride!"—thinking of the lovely white horse. Ares turned slightly green, and she said, "Would that be painful?"

"Exquisitely," he said.

"It's hard enough to walk, isn't it?"

"Quite," he said placidly.

"Then you must really love me to take me out today, suffering as you are," she suggested, snuggling his arm.

"You will never know." He shook his head.

"How much you are suffering?" she grinned.

"How much I love you," he growled. "And am suffering."

They took the main road north out of Westford, then turned off on a sheep path. As they walked, she absorbed the wet greenness of spring, the cool, earthy breeze, the fervent calls of mating birds, and wondered how many generations of lovers had enjoyed this tableau. Thinking along those lines —"Did you really offer Lord Notham fifty royals for Lady Rhea's hand in marriage?" she asked.

"Yes," he said.

"And she led you on, to up the price?"

"Yes," he said.

"And accepted you after all, after we had made such a spectacle of ourselves?"

"Yes," he said.

"But—you told me I was mistaken!" she exclaimed.

"Actually," he said, "you knew more than I did. Word of her acceptance got around to you before it did me. By the time I heard it—quite by accident, by the way—you were upstairs changing for our wedding. Upon investigating, I found that the soldier who received the word from Lord Notham's messenger threatened him with a thrashing and turned him out, then went and told the chambermaid he sleeps with—not me. I am still trying to decide how to punish Lucus for that," he ended pensively.

She felt a vague concern as she watched storks lift off from an unseen arm of the lake ahead. "My Lord Commander, if you had a standing offer to Lady Rhea, which she then accepted, are you not required to make good on it?"

"No, actually, technically," he said anxiously, "because of the tardiness of her reply. Gracious lady, I negotiated with her father for almost four months! How long am I obligated to wait in case she changes her mind? The last word I had from her was 'no' before I proposed to you. So no, I am not bound." Then he muttered, "On second thought, perhaps I should reward Lucus instead."

"Did you ever kiss her?" she asked wickedly.

"She wouldn't allow it," he said tautly. Nicole felt terrible for having asked, but he continued, "And she had stipulated that, were she to accept me in marriage, I would have to wear a hood whenever we were—intimate, so that she did not see or feel the scar."

"She is unworthy of you, my lord," Nicole said angrily, and he dropped his head.

While they walked, she laced her fingers in his, admiring their size, and he lifted her hand to help her up a small incline.

Raising her eyes from the path, she cried, "Oh! Oh! Oh!" while he watched her, smiling. "Oh, Commander! Why could I not see this from the upper window?" Filling the hollow that lay between this small ridge and the lake were hundreds, perhaps thousands, of bright yellow jonquils. The hollow was dense with them. They nodded and bowed to her, elbowing each other jealously.

"The depression, you see," he said, indicating the low-lying area. "The tradition is that Surchatain Roman scattered a handful of bulbs on the grave of their stillborn child for his wife Deirdre, and this resulted. I always thought it fitting, that consolation cannot be seen but by those who come to the valley of despair. . . ."

Nicole was skipping on down the barely discernible path, holding up her skirts lest they crush the upturned yellow heads. Ares circumvented the field of flowers to spread the blanket beneath a great, old willow tree near the water's edge, where he sat to watch her.

She reached the middle of the field and twirled in exultation, surrounded by a priceless horde of living gold. Then she bent to pick a few to make a chain.

Oh, the glory of the day! How sweet it was! She ranged over the field, harvesting volunteers, then looked up at Ares sitting on the blanket a ways off. She stilled with her arms full of flowers.

Why had she been seized with such fear to marry him? What exactly had she lost by keeping her word? Clearly, her fear had been illusory—more than that, cowardly. How pathetic it would have been for her had she succumbed to such fear and left him standing alone! He stood now, trying to see what had made her stop so suddenly.

Nicole made her way to him, careful not to trample the flowers not destined for her chain. As she approached, he sat back down, and she plopped onto the blanket beside him. "You gave me a necklace, so I shall make the most magnificent necklace ever for you," she declared, proceeding to twine stems.

"So that I shall look like the most magnificent carthorse ever," he said, and she laughed. Many merchants decorated their horses with garlands.

"You are so very clever," she said admiringly.

"I must be," he murmured, studying her. He lay on his back to look up at her while she worked. "I will tell you something entertaining that happened a fortnight ago. Henry was running down a corridor, as he will do, and someone opened a door right in his path. He hit it face first and fell down, crying to high heaven. But then they brought him to a mirror so he could see this red mark running the length of his face, and that made him very happy. He went 'round the rest of the day swaggering and barking commands."

"What, because he got hurt?" she said, eyes on her chain.

"No, because he looked like me," he explained.

"How did he look like you?" she asked.

"Nicole," he said plaintively.

She glanced down at him. "What?"

He raised up and stared at her, his face clouding. "My scar."

She looked at him again. "Oh, yes. I forgot."

It was manifest that she truly had forgotten about his scar. It was as if she didn't even see it anymore. Ares lay back down on the blanket, exhaling in wonder.

6

icole placed the finished ring of jonquils around Ares' neck and then burst out laughing. "It's true, it's true. You look like the potter's great horse Orion." He eyed her, and she added, "But it's a very handsome animal, my lord."

He leaned forward to kiss her mouth, and she placed her hands on his head. Holding her, he sank back on the blanket, making her lie across him to keep her lips on his. Nicole kissed him, then lifted her lips. He tried to follow, raising up, but she bypassed his mouth and placed her lips reverently on his scar, starting at his jaw and working her way up inch by inch to his forehead. A little mew escaped him, and he clenched her so tightly that she could hardly breathe.

He suddenly turned his head and shifted her protectively to his side. Looking back over her shoulder, she saw a laden figure laboriously trotting down the path toward them. Ares sat up, noting, "We have been discovered. It's Tanny." Nicole watched.

The messenger approached, bowed, and handed a basket to Ares, sitting on the blanket. "From the Chataine, my Lord Commander," he panted.

Nicole looked in it, finding wine, cheese, bread, and

candied flower petals. "What a darling she is! Do thank her, Tanny."

"The Chataine had a message for the Commander," he said, twisting his hands.

"What is it?" Ares squinted up at him in the sunshine.

Tanny hesitated in dismay. "I plead with my Lord Commander to remember that I am but a messenger, obligated to repeat the words my lady has commanded me."

Ares smiled. "Go ahead."

"The Chataine says that my Lord Commander is—forgive me—a wretched beast to not provide properly for a lady on an outing, and that if my Lord Commander, ah, abuses the Lady Nicole, the Chataine shall, ah,"—Tanny gulped—"have him gelded."

Ares burst into laughter, but Nicole straightened indignantly. "Please remind the Chataine that she has no such jurisdiction over *my* property."

Tanny bowed and Ares fell backwards onto the blanket. "I will die of happiness here and now. Plant me with the jonquils."

Tanny returned to the palace to deliver another difficult message while Ares and Nicole ate their fill from the basket. Then he folded up the blanket and they began a leisurely stroll back in the late afternoon sun. Nicole swung the basket as Ares picked crushed jonquils out of his clothes, but their hands were clasped the whole way.

On the steps of the palace, they gave up the basket and blanket to a servant before another presented Ares with a parchment: "From the Counselor, my Lord Commander, who offers his congratulations." Nicole looked at the sheet over Ares' arm—it was a beautifully decorated marriage certificate, set with the Surchatain's seal. It required only the signatures of the couple.

"Ah. Bring a fresh quill and ink bottle to my chambers," Ares said, taking Nicole's hand. Once in his room, he spread the parchment flat on the table and accepted the writing instruments the servant brought. Ares signed first, making his signature bold and readable. Nicole then took the quill, endeavoring to make pretty letters, like Renée's. When the signatures were properly blotted and dried, Ares rolled the parchment up and tied it with the bodice ribbon he took from his neck.

Then he went to the wall behind his parchments and bent to pry at a stone in the wall with his fingertips. Nicole watched in great interest. "What is this?"

"My safe place. I keep my money here, and the signet," he grunted, working the heavy stone from the loose mortar around it. The stone came out, and she knelt to peer into a large hole in the wall.

Ares kissed the scroll, tossed it into the hole, and lifted the stone to painstakingly replace it. "Obviously, you must never mention this. No one else has seen it. But if anything ever happens to me, you know it is here," he said, and she nodded.

While he was replacing the stone, she used the garderobe. Ares glanced over his shoulder at her and smiled in gratification. With the stone in place, he stood, brushing his hands, then looked around and uttered an oath. Stepping outside, he instructed one of the ubiquitous sentries: "Summon Gretchen."

Nicole was washing her hands when Gretchen, wearing a large white wimple, entered the chambers and bowed. She was a tiny woman whom Nicole recognized from the laundry pit. "Gretchen, did you remove the sheet I had folded up here?" Ares asked anxiously.

"Yes, my lord, to wash it with your other dirty things, sir," she said.

"Oh, Gretchen," he winced, "I was saving that to show Nicole's father! Has it been laundered yet?"

"Yes, but my lord's not to worry. Why, a hundred people

saw it, and any of 'em can attest to my lady's purity, sir," Gretchen said, winking and nodding.

Nicole looked at Ares open-mouthed, and he glanced at her. "Uh, yes, well, all right, Gretchen. You may go."

Closing the door behind her, Ares contemplated appropriate words for the moment. Nicole removed her wool cap and shook out her hair, so that he forgot what he was thinking. She stood beside the bed, unfastening the buttons that ran down the front of her dress. "Are you still in very grievous pain, my lord?" she asked.

"No. None. Not at all," he said, trying to bolt the door while watching her unbutton her dress.

"Then, is the equipment serviceable, my lord?" she asked, dropping the dress to the floor.

"Yes, yes!" he cried, fumbling with the reluctant bolt. Nicole crawled into the fresh bed and watched him whimpering over the bolt. At last it slid into place, and he dove for the bed, falling over his clothes. While the daylight waned, they came together again, unhurriedly relishing every sensation.

The bell tolled, and they paused in their embrace, neither having any idea of the time. The bell ceased, and they relaxed. "It's only seven. We've plenty of time," he whispered into her neck, lipping the gold chain. She sighed, arching her back, and he lowered his face.

Then she rolled on top of him, pinning his arms above his head. "You are my prisoner, and you will do as I say," she instructed.

"Command me," he moaned. She lowered herself to him to make her wishes known. In a little while she made him rekindle the fire, as it was getting dark, then he returned to her arms.

The bell tolled again, and on the first strike they both leaped out of bed. Ares could don his dress blacks in seconds, which he did, but Nicole was in harder straits. Unwilling to appear at the table in linsey-woolsey, and with no time to dig in her trunk, she seized Renée's dress still lying across the chair and threw it over her head while burrowing her feet into the beaded slippers left underneath it. "Help me! My buttons!" she cried as the bell tolled ominously.

Ares fastened those that he could, but as the eighth strike echoed away, he seized her hand with half of them undone. "Come now!"

"Oh, Commander! My hair!" she cried. It fell luscious and disheveled about her shoulders and down her back. Ares shook his head helplessly as he threw open the bolt and the door, and they ran down the corridor to the anteroom.

Nicole was almost weeping. Appearing at dinner with unbound hair was offensive to the point of lewdness, inexcusable at the Surchatain's court. She was not so much concerned about the dress falling off her shoulders as the hair flying behind her.

They tore through the anteroom attended by Georges' cry of distress and rushed to the table. Gasps of horror rose around the room; the Counselor murmured, "Oh, dear," covering his eyes, and Thom looked nearly panic-stricken.

He stepped behind Ares to help shield Nicole from view from the anteroom (where the ruling couple would imminently appear) while Ares desperately fastened buttons and Nicole tried to twist her hair together. Henry watched all this, rapt.

Renée smirked at them. "Admit it, Ares: you are a beast," she challenged.

"I am a beast," he said pathetically, fumbling with the tiny buttons.

At that, Renée removed the jeweled clip from her own hair and handed it across the table to Nicole, who grasped it with a little cry and fastened it in her hair just as Georges announced, "Surchatain Cedric and Surchataine Elise."

Those on Ares' side of the table turned and all bowed. The Counselor got a rather extended view of Nicole's back while Renée shook out her hair. After being seated, the royal parents noticed the transgression right away. Elise raised an offended eyebrow; Cedric looked at his daughter once, then again. She looked back defiantly, and he muttered, "I shall never get used to these new fashions."

"You look radiant tonight, Nicole, dear," Elise said, as if to emphasize her propriety by contrast.

"Thank you, Surchataine." Nicole blushed deeply.

As the wine was poured, Ares met Renée's eyes across the table. "I am in your debt, Chataine," he said under his breath, and she smiled.

The dinner progressed decorously from soup to main course, then Cedric asked, "Well, Ares, how goes the trenching?"

The Commander betrayed his own thoughts by nearly spewing his wine. "What—the what, Surchatain?"

"You're going good and deep, aren't you?" Cedric pressed. Ares stared at him helplessly, and Renée laughed into her napkin.

The Counselor dabbed at his pursed lips, then replied with his strictly correct enunciation, "I don't believe the Commander has had the opportunity to observe the waterway trenching that was begun today, High Lord. But from the looks of things, I would say that all is going quite satisfactorily."

Thom snickered loudly, then tried to cover it with a cough. The guests hid their mouths or turned their faces, but were unable to stem the laughter building around the table. It broke in a torrent. Cedric looked at them in amazement, but Elise smiled, and Nicole hid her face.

"I will—be sure to go out—to check it tomorrow, Surchatain," Ares said slowly, as if unsure of the language.

"Beast," Renée laughed at her plate.

"Did you say something, daughter?" Cedric asked testily. He had the general impression that a lot was going on over his head tonight, and she seemed to know something about it.

"It's elk, isn't it, Father?" she said, tossing her head. (At this point, she was having great fun flinging her loose hair around. The more she did it, the more her father determined to ignore it.) A servant had placed the plate with a small mound of pink-brown meat before her, and was now serving the steward to her left.

"Yes, I believe so; isn't it, Giles? Imported from northern Scylla, is that right?" Cedric addressed the steward. Flattered, Giles began an animated recitation of how the large and dangerous animal was purchased in Eurus and transported to Westford on the hoof.

As Giles talked on, transforming a possibly one-word reply into an epic, Ares risked looking at Nicole for the first time since they were seated. She barely turned toward him, eyes downcast. His hand crept to hold hers under the table, and she lifted her lids. The rest of the table pretended to listen to Giles while they watched the newlyweds gaze at each other.

Henry could stand it no longer. He climbed down from his seat and came to stand at Nicole's right, between her and Thom. She smiled at him, and he nudged her right shoulder. Hesitantly, she turned to face the head of the table, as he desired.

With her blocking his parents' view of him, Henry finished buttoning the back of her dress. Then he climbed into Ares' lap with perfect confidence that he would not be expelled, even though the Commander had not finished dinner. Sure enough, Ares held him on his left knee while he ate, which meant he had to let go of Nicole's hand.

A servant entered and spoke in Cedric's ear. "Really? Send them in," the Surchatain gestured. As the servant hastened out, Cedric said, "The messengers I sent to Ossian have just arrived."

The Counselor attended with interest and the Commander

put down his fork, turning to watch two tired, dusty soldiers enter. They saluted the Surchatain, who nodded. "What say you?"

"Surchatain, upon arrival at the palace in Eurus, we were escorted into the presence of Surchatain Ossian, who greeted us cordially. We extended your invitation to him, which he accepted straightway. His sons Magnus the elder and Tancred the younger shall set out tomorrow morning, and should be arriving by nightfall," the ranking scout reported.

"So soon?" Cedric exclaimed.

"He indicated that he was anxious to avail himself of the invitation without delay," the scout explained.

"Excellent. That's excellent," Cedric declared, while a glance passed between the Counselor and the Commander. Cedric dismissed the messengers and they bowed, then saluted the Commander before departing the hall. They knew he would require a much fuller report momentarily. "Tomorrow night! There is much to do to prepare for such esteemed guests, eh, Giles?" the Surchatain asked in distinct good humor.

"Yes, High Lord!" he said, thrilled.

"Then let us begin at once. You are dismissed," the Surchatain waved to the table. They did not look thrilled, being deprived of dessert and entertainment.

After everyone had bowed to the departing royalty, Ares turned to Nicole. "I must—" A servant approached, bowing. "What?" Ares asked testily.

"A thousand pardons, Commander. The lady's father has arrived from Prie Mer."

Nicole gave a little cry of joy and Ares exhaled, smiling. "Send him in. And have set a place for him to eat at this table." She turned to squeeze him as hard as she could, and he kissed the top of her head, above the clip.

The trackers entered with Robert between them, looking thin and nervous. He wore the same clothes he always wore, but with an old, almost shabby surcoat. Nicole rushed forward to embrace him and the soldiers saluted their Commander. He returned their salute and gave them leave to depart.

He then turned to his new father-in-law. "I am Commander Ares, Nicole's husband. I wish you to know that your daughter pleases me exceedingly."

Robert stared at him, then stared at his daughter. Ares waited for several long minutes while Robert looked at Nicole with mounting aversion in his face. "Father? He is Commander of the whole Lystran army," Nicole whispered anxiously. But he was looking specifically at her dress, and Nicole suddenly remembered what she was wearing. It was not anything he had made.

"Oh! The gown," she laughed nervously. "Father, I can explain that. It was a gift from the Chataine for me to be married in! Although—the dresses you made were lovely. Everyone said how lovely they were." She looked at Ares for support.

"Very finely made," he said, evaluating Robert.

Robert looked at him then. "You are a soldier?" he said in dismay.

"I am Commander," Ares corrected him. "I carry the signet of the Surchatain."

"So?" Robert asked blankly.

Ares came close to sputtering. "Sir, only the most trusted officials of the court carry the Surchatain's signet ring to set his seal of authority on decrees and correspondence. Counselor Carmine is the only other person in Lystra to carry a signet besides the Surchatain himself. Even the Surchataine does not."

"Does that make you a nobleman?" Robert asked.

Ares laughed good-naturedly. "I should say not—that would be a step down. Lord Robert, I outrank everyone at Westford but the royal family and the Counselor. Your daughter is a lady by virtue of marriage to me."

Ares' loose use of the title put the tailor somewhat at ease. He glanced at the sumptuous food being set on the table beside them. But—he still had questions. "You have land?"

"What do I want with land?" Ares glanced off impatiently. "I am not a farmer." At Nicole's beseeching eyes, he sighed, "Perhaps I should explain that I am entitled to live with royal privileges until the day I die. Those privileges extend to my wife. If you wish, I can extend them to you."

"What do you mean?" Robert asked.

Ares gestured to the waiting meal. "Food from the Surchatain's table. Living quarters in the palace. Clothes for your back, and servants to carry out your wishes, plus whatever luxuries a lifelong stipend will buy. Come taste what you could have for the rest of your life."

Robert eyed the dinner suspiciously, then sat to sample it. Soon he was gulping mouthfuls. Nicole poured him a cup of wine and sat beside him. "Oh, Father, he's everything you wanted for me. He is so wonderful." She stroked the bony hand that clenched a piece of bread. "This is what you have been working for all your life. Stay with us."

Ares glanced aside at an approaching servant, who bowed. "Forgive me, Lord Commander. My lord Counselor is ready to interview the messengers."

Ares nodded at him, then placed a friendly hand on Robert's back. "Please excuse me. Take your time." He started to move off, but Nicole stood, reaching up to him. He paused long enough to kiss her palms before departing.

Nicole sat back down beside her father as he cleaned his plate, glancing all around. "So do all the noblewomen dress like that here? You look like a whore."

She wilted in dismay. "Father, I—know it's not what you would choose I wear, but—it doesn't matter. I've been wearing your dresses, and—"

He pushed his plate away. "I don't want to hear any more from you. I'm going home now."

"Now? Father, you can't travel to Prie Mer tonight! Oh, just stay the night, and let me show you around in the morning! Come, let me see if they have a room for you. Come, please."

She made inquiries as to where he might sleep, and a servant took them to a spare room in the lower corridor with a pallet and washbasin. Robert, taciturn and skittish, locked himself in the room without another word to her. "Good night, Father," she said outside the door, and turned away in distress.

She went to Ares' chambers to begin undressing, but as soon as she felt the clip in her hair, she left the room. Borrowing a candle from the anteroom, she passed through the foyer toward the great staircase. It was much different at night: deserted but for the few sentries, dark and shadowy, echoing, and cold. It made her want Ares by her side.

By the feeble light of the candle, she ascended the unmanned staircase and turned into the corridor toward the Chataine's apartments. At her door, Nicole knocked and entered to see Renée lounging in the tub as Eleanor washed her hair. "Hello, darling. Tired of him already?" Renée asked with a wicked smile.

Nicole removed the jeweled clip from her hair and set it on a shelf of the great wardrobe. "I came to return your property. You are a dear friend and I thank you from the depth of my heart."

Renée motioned Nicole closer as she leaned forward with her elbows on the side of the tub. When Nicole knelt beside her, Renée whispered, "So what is he like?"

"Oh!" Nicole closed her eyes. "He's wonderful, darling. He is so—tender and funny and—and—masculine, you know," she said shyly.

"Tell me everything!" Renée insisted, as Eleanor tried to pretend not to listen.

Nicole glanced up at her and Renée turned. "You may leave. I'll finish myself." Eleanor bowed and withdrew.

"There now. You have no excuse for not telling me every detail."

"Well," Nicole bit her lip. "At first, it—"

Renée waved impatiently. "I know all that! I mean, what does he do differently from other men when he's making love to you?"

Nicole was profoundly shocked. "Darling, I . . . I don't know. I've never been with another man."

"You haven't?" Now Renée's eyes widened in shock. "What, have you been living in a nunnery all your life?"

"No!" Nicole laughed in disbelief. "I just never. . . . Darling, you haven't . . . have you?"

Renée eased back in the tub, a sensuous smile lingering on her lips. "Perhaps. Would it bother you if I had?"

"Yes!" Nicole cried. "Ossian will expect a virgin to wed his son, and they'll know if you're not. Oh, please tell me you're playing with me, even as cruel a game as this," she said anxiously.

"Dear, sweet Nicole, the pure in heart," Renée murmured, leaning her head back on the padded rim. "It will make no difference at all to them whether I am a virgin or not. What matters is the revenue we can produce, the laborers we can provide, and the loyalty of our soldiers. Let us not mix politics with love, dear heart. I can assure you my father will not be demanding proof of Magnus' virginity," she noted ironically.

"But what if Ossian demands proof of yours?" Nicole asked.

"Then let Magnus choose another," Renée said coldly. "I'm not ashamed that I have been in love."

"Oh." Nicole closed her eyes. "I am afraid for you, Chataine. You do not know what they will do."

Renée laughed. "Save your trembling for *them*, darling. You don't know what *I* can do. You've never seen me angry."

"I hope you're right. I love you." Nicole leaned over to kiss her cheek, then stood.

"Darling." Renée caught her hand. "Do you think less of me?"

"After what you have done for me? Never," Nicole said firmly. "Good night, darling."

On her way out, Nicole heard her say, "I'm glad you're with the one you love, dear heart." Nicole leaned her head on the door, then picked up the candle to light her way downstairs.

Ares was not in his chambers, so Nicole got a chambermaid to help her out of the dress. She folded it up to put it in the trunk, then discovered her yellow silks had been cleaned and repaired and stashed away, as had her linen undergarments. She dismissed the maid, who was yawning, and climbed into bed.

She found herself too restless to sleep, so she opened the shutters to look at the moonlit night. But as the moonlight illumined nothing fairer than the stables and the laundry pit (with their attendant smells wafting in through the open window), Nicole shut the window again and lay down, listening for his step at the door. But he did not come and he did not come, and she could not keep herself awake until he should.

She thought she dreamed he was in bed beside her, but if he was, he did not wake her. In the morning she awoke alone still, and clambered out of bed with a pounding heart. Then she saw his dress blacks lying on the floor, and weapons sitting on the table. Trembling, she dressed in the first thing handy, the yellow silks, while the bell tolled seven.

As she was fitting the cap on her head, there was a knock at the door. "My lady, your father desires you," a maid called.

Nicole opened the door. "Where is the Commander?"

"He is coming to meet you in the foyer, where your father waits, Lady," the maid curtsied.

Nicole rushed to the foyer, already crowded in the early morning. Her father stood pressing his back against the wall by the fireplace, looking rather wild-eyed. "Father! Good morning." She greeted him with a kiss, and felt him all tense and rigid. "Don't I look lovely today?" she asked, spreading her silk skirts.

He didn't even see them. "I'm going home today. They're bringing me a cart."

"Oh, Father, can't you stay but a few days?" she asked.

"I don't belong here. There's no place for me here," he said, eyes darting at the courtiers who looked down their noses at him.

Nicole laughed, "That is exactly what I said a few days ago. But you will see—"

Her heart leaped up at the sight of Ares striding through the massive front doors toward them. She ran to him and threw her arms around his neck. He lifted her off the ground to kiss her good morning.

"Dear, sweet Commander." She sank into his chest. "Oh, Lord Commander," she said, turning her face up anxiously, "my father wants to leave this morning! Will you talk to him?"

He nodded, his face hard. "He is leaving for Prie Mer right away, and you're going with him."

7

The shock of his words was like a knife in her chest. "My lord?" she whispered brokenly.

He clasped her head and pressed his bristly, unscarred cheek to hers, whispering, "I am sending you back home with him, just for a while, just while Ossian's sons are here. Oh, my beautiful bride—it will not matter to them that you were born common, or that you are married to me—if they see you, they will take you. I must put you out of their reach."

"Oh, no, my lord, please, let me stay with you. The Surchatain won't allow them to take me. I will keep myself hidden. Just let me stay with you," she pleaded.

"I can't risk it, Nicole. I will send for you as soon as it's safe. I swear it," he uttered.

She reached up to kiss him, and when he saw the tears in her eyes, his own eyes grew wet. "God grant you a bodyguard of angels, my love." He turned to Robert, still hunkered against the wall. "Come quickly. Your cart is ready."

Robert sprang to follow them out to the courtyard where two mounted soldiers, one of them Oswald, waited beside a one-horse market cart. They were dressed not in uniform, but as mercenaries. "I am sorry it won't be as comfortable as a carriage," Ares said, lifting her onto the seat. No, without the suspension of a carriage, it certainly wouldn't be, but at least the seat was padded with thick blankets. "But we don't want to call attention to you on the road. Oswald and Rhode will be your bodyguard. They are trustworthy." They nodded to her.

As Robert clambered onto the seat beside her, Ares asked him, "Can you drive, man?" He nodded eagerly and took the reins from Ares' hands. "Good. Go! Hiya!" Ares slapped the dappled mare on the hindquarters, and she lurched off at a canter, the soldiers beside her.

Nicole twisted in the seat, watching Ares disappear beyond the palace gates. The cart rattled over the ancient wooden bridge, and then they were on the southbound road. She bent over her knees, heartsick.

They made good time, despite the traffic, and Nicole endured the teeth-jarring ride for several hours, until they got to the coastal highway. There was less traffic here, besides flat, safe areas to pull off the road for a rest. "Stop," she said. "Stop!" Robert, who had not spoken a word on the trip yet, looked at her in irritation, but guided the cart off the road.

Oswald dismounted to help her down, and for the first time she noticed the large, square basket on the floor of the cart behind the seat. Opening it, she discovered that it contained a generous provision of dried meat, bread, wine and smaller packages of delicacies.

She closed her eyes. "He is a good man." Then she handed a bottle to Oswald and a loaf to Rhode. "We eat here," she said, and they inclined their heads to her. Robert, restless, only nibbled as he paced beside the cart. And Nicole knew to eat just enough to assuage her fierce hunger, as they had a good five hours of bone-rattling travel ahead of them.

They relieved themselves in the underbrush, and Nicole walked around to ease the soreness of her buttocks. She was tempted to ask to ride behind Oswald, as the horses had built-in springs, at least, but lacking the courage, she finally assented to his assisting her into the cart once more.

With that wrenching jerk, they were off again. She bundled up the blankets to provide as much padding as possible, meanwhile pitying the kitchen servants who rode carts like this back and forth to market everyday.

Riding along the coastal highway provided a little distraction, for she loved the merciless beauty of the Sea. At certain seasons its storms washed furiously over little Prie Mer, sending the terrified residents scurrying upland for shelter. Nicole did not hate the Sea for that; she respected it. Those who got their living from it, and built their frail little houses near it, learned not to get too attached to anything they made, because the Sea would claim it again.

She was gazing at the waves crashing upon the rocks when Rhode, behind them, began shouting. Nicole and Oswald turned to see clouds of dust raised from the hooves of horses in furious pursuit.

"We cannot outrun them! Off the road!" Oswald gestured, unsheathing his long sword and pointing it at Robert, who so hastily jerked the reins that the mare reared up at the pain of the bit, almost upsetting the cart.

With swords drawn, the two mounted escorts placed themselves between the cart and the five pursuers. They gained them quickly, and Nicole saw their royal insignia. They were Lystran soldiers. As they pulled to a stop beside the cart, the ranking soldier said, "The Surchatain demands the return of the Lady Nicole."

"Show me orders sealed by the Surchatain," Oswald said.

"Written orders are not required from your superior, man," the other sneered, who evidently outranked Oswald. "By the Surchatain's command, turn this cart around."

Oswald and Rhode looked at each other, and there was complete agreement between them. Oswald said, "The Commander himself, who is your superior, made clear to us our duty. She shall not be returned without sealed orders."

"Here are your orders!" the other replied, drawing his sword, and the pursuers attacked.

Nicole apprehended with horror that her defenders intended to die on the road before giving her up. "Stop!" She clambered down from the cart to throw herself between the horses, immediately ceasing the hostilities. "Stop! I will go back with you. I will go back. Let—just let my father take the cart home, and I will ride behind Oswald."

"You will ride behind me, lady," the lead soldier said.

"I will ride behind you," she acquiesced.

"Lady Nicole, you walk into treachery," Oswald protested.

"Shall I let them kill you and then take me?" she asked quietly. To the ranking officer, she said, "What is your name?"

"Lieutenant Antony, Lady," he smirked.

"Let my father go, Lieutenant Antony," she insisted. He waved impatiently at Robert, who slapped the reins frantically on the mare's back.

After watching him disappear down the highway toward Calle Valley, she turned again to the lieutenant: "All of us shall return to Westford. And if Oswald or Rhode is punished in any way upon our return, I shall testify against you to the Surchatain's face." The officer stiffened at this threat.

"Oswald." She gestured for his help to mount. He removed his surcoat and placed it behind the saddle as padding, then helped her straddle the horse's haunches. She heard a tiny rip, and sighed at the abuse inflicted on her poor yellow silks. As they started down the road at a lope, she was obliged to hold tightly on to Antony's waist, which pleased him very much.

Riding behind the saddle was not much better than riding in the cart, but Nicole kept her teeth clenched against complaint and gripped the horse with her knees until her muscles trembled with fatigue.

A few hours into the return trip, Oswald called, "Stop to

let her rest! She's slipping off." Antony heeded the warning, and she practically fell off the animal into Oswald's arms. He assisted her to limp around a bit, then she remounted behind the lieutenant with a groan.

At last, at last they pounded over the wooden bridge and clattered into the cobbled court. She slid down by herself and turned up the palace steps to search out Ares. But the lieutenant caught her by the arm. "You will accompany me, Lady Nicole."

Nicole wheeled and struck him in the face as hard as she could, and he staggered back. With the whole courtyard attending, she asked loudly, "Am I a prisoner?"

He glanced around in alarm. "No, of course not, Lady."

"Then you shall keep your hands to yourself, and I shall gladly go where I am directed, *after* I have seen my husband."

Grimly, he extended his hand toward the open doors. Nicole limped into the foyer, but as soon as she turned to the corridor off the anteroom, Antony and another soldier took her by the arms and escorted her swiftly up the staircase. She was hustled down the corridor past the Chataine's apartments to another door, which was opened for her to be dragged inside.

In the room, the Counselor looked up and gasped, "Animals! Is this how you handle precious things?"

The lieutenant, whose face still bore a red handprint, muttered, "She fights, my lord."

"As well she should! Now get out," Carmine gestured angrily, and they withdrew. "My dear, I deeply apologize for this treatment," he said, bending penitently over her hands. She pulled away suspiciously.

He sighed. "I've much to explain, and not enough time to regain your trust. Let me begin by saying this: the Commander and I were both alarmed over Ossian's response to the Surchatain's invitation. It makes no sense, politically, for him to offer even a nephew in marriage alliance with Lystra, not when there are royal daughters available around the Continent.

Calle Valley has the agriculture; Qarqar the mines; Seleca the forests; and Polontis the men—all the resources that we lack. An alliance with any one of these countries would allow Ossian to waltz through Lystra, as if he could not already. That he is sending both of his sons here, posthaste, signals an ulterior motive not to our liking."

"What do you want of me?" she asked.

"Your help," he said. "Frankly, the Commander violently objected to soliciting your assistance in this matter, as anyone could understand. But I desired to present it to you personally. Will you listen to our plan?"

"I will listen," she said, "as long as you understand that I will not do anything against my husband's wishes."

"Judge for yourself. Have a seat, please, Lady Nicole." He extended his hand to a silk-upholstered chair, and she sat.

Two hours later she left the Counselor's chambers accompanied by a soldier who escorted her to the Chataine's apartments. Here, Eleanor drew Nicole's bath while Renée was dressing for dinner. The Chataine kept glancing at her, wanting to speak, but mindful of the servant's ears. So she said, "Are you all right, darling?"

"Yes," Nicole said. She stepped into the tub to let Eleanor wash her hair.

As Nicole was bathing herself, Renée opened the wardrobe and selected a stunning green gown. Handing it off to Eleanor, she said, "Ask Father if this is acceptable for Nicole tonight." The maid curtsied and left with the dress.

Renée turned to Nicole, whispering, "I heard they brought you back by force."

"Yes," Nicole said.

"Oh, darling! I am so sorry! What will you do?" Renée whispered.

"I don't know yet." Nicole climbed out of the tub and began to dry off.

"Ossian's sons are already here," Renée said.

"Yes," Nicole nodded. "I know."

Eleanor reentered with royal approval of the gown. While Nicole hung her head upside down to dry her hair before the fireplace, Renée sat to apply makeup—sheep's fat and chalk to whiten the skin, rouge for the cheeks and lips, tiny lines of charcoal around the eyes.

Eleanor assisted Nicole into the gown, then sat her down to arrange her hair around the pearl cap. Renée offered her the makeup, but Nicole shook her head. "The last thing I want to do is make myself appealing to them." She touched the cross still adorning her neck.

As the bell tolled eight, the Chataine Renée and the Lady Nicole entered the anteroom. "Marvelous! Oh, heavens, such beauty!" Georges gushed, and Nicole looked away. The attendants offered their arms, and they entered.

Nicole noticed immediately that Thom and Deirdre were not at table. Almost as soon as the two young women took their places, the Counselor appeared, and stood behind a chair at the head of the table to the left of the Surchataine's seat. Nicole looked at the two empty places between her and Renée and the head of the table.

Georges announced, "Surchatain Cedric and Surchataine Elise and their guests the Chatain Magnus and the Chatain Tancred."

Nicole turned to curtsy, and when she raised up, she was looking directly into the eyes of a pretty young man. He stared intently at her as he took the chair to her left—the Commander's place. But Ares was not at table tonight. Significantly, neither was Henry.

"Chatain Magnus, may I present my daughter the Chataine Renée," Cedric said. Nicole looked across the table where Renée curtsied to the young man to her right. He, with harder features than his brother, nodded shortly to her. "Chatain Tancred, may I present the Lady Nicole," Cedric said. Nicole curtsied to him, but he took her hand to kiss it.

Both brothers had heads of short-cropped curls, but Magnus was blonder than Tancred. Little brother also had a remnant of baby fat in his cheeks, for which he was nonetheless appealing. The visiting royalty took their places next to the Surchatain and Surchataine, respectively; the rest of the table sat, and Cedric motioned for the wine.

Tancred could not take his eyes off Nicole as she stared down at her plate. Magnus, looking on with interest, said, "So, are you related to the Chataine, Lady?"

Her eyes flicked up. "No, Chatain. I am a commoner by birth who attained my title by virtue of my marriage to Lord Commander Ares. We are still married."

Cedric seemed to wince, but Magnus laughed, "Lucky man! Where is he?" as he glanced down the table.

Nicole also looked down the table, then said, "I do not know, my lord. He is usually here." She turned to Tancred. "In that chair." The boy blinked.

Magnus uttered, "Then he can't be that important."

Cedric said, "Chatain Magnus, you may be interested in my newest building project. I'm trenching the Passage to the Sea, to reopen the waterway for shipping. When it is completed, it will greatly cut the overland route by which goods come to Eurus from across the Sea."

"Show me," Magnus said, leaning back for the first course to be placed before him. "What is *this*?" he said, screwing up his face in disgust at the entree.

"Scallops, Chatain," Cedric said, distracted in sending a servant after the map. "A delicacy from the Sea—"

"Send it away!" he commanded, and the offending dish was briskly removed.

"I wish to try it," Tancred announced. He turned to Nicole. "Please show me how to eat this."

She opened a shell from her own plate and forked out the meat, which she dipped in the sauce to her left. Tancred followed suit, smiling shyly. He chewed appraisingly, then grinned and mumbled, "I approve." Nicole smiled slightly and inclined her head.

"We are delighted you are pleased, Chatain Tancred," Cedric said thoughtfully.

"He is easily impressed," Magnus sneered at his brother.

The map of the proposed waterway was brought, and the Counselor spread it before Magnus to show him the plans. The Chatain studied it with interest, then asked, "Will it be deep enough for warships?"

"No, Chatain," the Counselor said, rolling up the map.

With the personalities so established, dinner continued. Magnus all but ignored Renée to talk endlessly about himself —his education, his exploits, his courage and cunning. This left nothing for her to contribute except murmurings of admiration, which were so toneless and whispered that several people began to wonder just how flattering their content was. Tancred essayed conversation with Nicole once or twice; she responded politely to his openings and fell silent.

Finally Magnus leaned toward her to say, "It doesn't matter one whit that you're married, you know. You can be easily unmarried."

Nicole replied, "I am sure my Lord Chatain Magnus is an honorable man, as is his father, and respects the oaths that his servants take before the Ruler of heaven and earth."

Magnus' mouth dropped open slightly, and the Counselor murmured, "Well said, dear lady." Tancred looked crestfallen at first, then pensive.

After dinner, dancing was announced. But there would be no picking of the leaves tonight, the partners having been preordained. As the musicians set up, Magnus led the Chataine onto the floor with a flourish. Since she was as poised and confident as he, they made a splendid couple.

Nicole turned to Tancred before he could say a word. "You should know that I am a terrible dancer. It would be most humiliating for you to dance with me," she warned him.

He grinned self-consciously. "I am honestly glad to hear you say that. I never could get the steps down right." He nodded toward the entrance to the garden off the great hall. "May we talk?"

"As you wish, my lord." She inclined her head. Many eyes watched them leave the floor.

At the garden entrance, in full view of the banquet hall, Nicole sat on a stone bench. Seeing that she was disinclined to go farther down the path to more private seating, Tancred sat as well. He took her hand, and she did not pull it away.

"You are so beautiful," he murmured. "More beautiful than the Chataine." Nicole laughed in disbelief and he insisted, "I mean it. With all that stuff on her face, you know—" he gestured over his face with a look of distaste, and Nicole dropped her head.

He contemplated her hand for a moment, then said, "I didn't even want to come, seeing as how Magnus was to get the Chataine, and I the—the seconds, as it were. But the moment I saw you, I realized that for the first time in my life, I have bested Magnus."

Nicole shifted uneasily in the heavy damask gown. Its weight continually pulled it down from her shoulders, baring far more than she was comfortable with. She agreed with her father's assessment of the impression such a dress created. "I will never be your mistress, and you are in no way foolish enough to settle for marriage with a commoner."

"To settle for a commoner, true. But you are far from common, Lady Nicole," he said.

"Explain that to your father," she said dryly.

"I've no need to," he said, resting his elbows on his knees. "He has given his word that I may marry whomever I choose."

Nicole sighed impatiently. His boyishness may have been appealing to her at one time, but after having been intimate with a man seasoned by experience, she felt mismatched with Tancred.

He turned her chin toward him, and she bristled. "I will win you, Lady," he said in the naive confidence of privileged youth.

"How old are you?" she asked suddenly.

"Eighteen, Lady."

"And Magnus?"

"He is twenty-two," Tancred replied.

"Children," Nicole muttered under her breath.

"What?" he said, leaning his ear toward her so that his face hovered over her chest.

Nicole delicately pushed him away. "I said, you remind me of Chatain Henry."

"Thank you," he said, not having met the boy.

"You're welcome," she muttered, looking away.

Nicole did everything she could think of to disengage him so that she could sneak off to Ares' quarters, but everyone in the palace conspired to prevent it, and Tancred himself dogged her side until she honestly pleaded fatigue. He bid her a warm goodnight, even though she refused to kiss him, and two armed soldiers escorted her upstairs toward the Chataine's apartments. The man at her right had an honest face, so she whispered to him, "Where is the Commander?" He glanced at her, then lowered his eyes in dismay.

They deposited her in Renée's rooms with Eleanor and another maid to attend her. Nicole sighed, gesturing to the dress: "Get this burdensome thing off me, dear Eleanor."

She climbed into bed with the curtains pulled long before Renée came up, and did not stir when the Chataine joined her.

Nicole woke in the early morning, and lay still for a moment. At first she did not know where she was—she had been dreaming of the marshes. She felt the down pillow under her head, then counted on her fingers: five. Today was the fifth day since she had arrived here to find a husband. So much had happened in those few days! What would have happened, she wondered, if she had delayed her visit, arriving today instead of five days ago?

She climbed out of the shifting mattress, being careful not to wake Renée, and stepped over Eleanor on her pallet on the floor. She tiptoed to the door and opened it a crack to look out. One of the soldiers stationed there turned to look, and she shut the door again, breathing out. So she woke Eleanor to ask what she should wear. Eleanor left to find out.

By the time Nicole had taken the cloth strips out of her hair and brushed it out, Eleanor had returned with instructions: the ladies were to wear day dresses, suitable for travel. As soon as they were dressed, they were to be escorted to join the men.

In trepidation, Nicole dressed in the deep blue outfit Eleanor selected. This was similar to the linen suit she had arrived in, only much finer, of course. The skirt was very wide, almost circular, allowing her to straddle a horse if necessary, without the bulk of many petticoats. The matching hat was held in place by a ribbon around the back of her head, under her hair, which allowed the curls to cascade over her shoulders. Eleanor wanted to primp her some more, but Nicole rose from the dressing table, kissing her cheek in gratitude. Then she stepped out into the corridor where the soldier waited.

He led her to a balcony at the end of the corridor where Magnus and Tancred were seated at breakfast. Tancred jumped up to greet her; Magnus kept his seat. She curtsied to them. "Good morning, Chatains."

"Lady Nicole, you are even more beautiful in the sunlight," Tancred effused, and Magnus stifled a laugh.

"Excuse him, Lady; originality is not his strong suit," Magnus sneered.

"There is a great deal to be said for sincerity, however," Nicole couldn't help replying. Tancred seated her at their table and the servant offered her a selection of pastries. Taking one, she looked out over the orchard, resplendent in spring finery. Rows upon rows of white-blossomed apple trees and pink-blossomed peach trees stood as if awaiting inspection. Pear and persimmon trees were sporting the delicate green attire of newly sprouted leaves. And the morning sun gave its benediction over all.

"How is this for sincerity, then?" Magnus began, lifting his goblet. "I am not convinced that your quaint little province has much to offer us. I think you would gain a great deal more from an alliance than we would. I need to see more."

"Such as?" Nicole asked.

"First, the waterway project," Magnus said, then looked annoyed. "Where is that lazy Chataine of yours? It must be nigh upon seven of the bells."

"She must have exhausted herself trying to please you last night," Nicole said curtly.

Tancred grinned and Magnus looked at her sharply. Then he eased back with a half-smile, glancing at his brother. "Do you ride, Lady Nicole?"

"Somewhat," she allowed.

"Then you shall accompany us," Magnus decreed, draining his goblet. To a servant, he said, "You may tell Cedric we are ready to depart, and Nicole shall be going."

They allowed her to stop by the Chataine's apartments (where Renée was still sleeping) to freshen up, then the three, with their attendants, went down to the front steps of the palace where horses were waiting for them. The Surchatain and the Counselor joined them, and Nicole was given a plain brown gelding with a regular saddle to ride.

The five of them, plus their retinue, headed out on horseback southwest along the Village Branch of the Passage. Years ago, the poor of the land built their hovels along the Branch (hence its name) but Cedric's father Talus had cleaned them all out, burning their huts to the ground. Now, it was just pasture on either bank.

They rode at a steady lope along the banks, Tancred staying close to Nicole. After the first jittery minutes, she got the feel of moving with the horse, and began to rather enjoy the ride. She did not attempt to rein the horse at all, but let it follow the others. She knew the bit could hurt him if she mishandled it.

The river tapered off as they followed it downstream. Then they saw the workmen from a distance going back and forth like a column of ants. The royal party turned aside to climb a small embankment and look down on the trenching in progress.

There were hundreds of men at work, neatly divided according to tasks which the Counselor explained: twenty feet south of the point where the Branch disappeared underground, one line of men drove plow horses to break up the ground while the plowed earth behind them was shoveled into wheelbarrows which another group of men wheeled away. They, in turn, deposited their loads on the east and west banks of the Branch.

When the trenching was completed to the Sea, the remaining dam of earth would be broken away, and the banks leveled for eventual paving. Staked ropes had already been stretched along either side of the planned trench to mark its boundaries. The work was backbreaking, but for just having started, there was progress to be seen.

As the Counselor made these points, Nicole watched the men labor. Suddenly she sat up. In the midst of them, directing the work, was Ares, shirtless and filthy. She watched him hungrily, drinking in his form, following his every movement. Then he looked up and saw them, and her with them.

8

hile they watched, Ares began making his way up the side of the embankment toward them. He scaled a rather steep incline, then gained the crest to stand before them and bow. He was practically covered in dirt—it had even gotten caked in his scar. The sight was so offensive that Nicole ached to get down from her horse and clean it for him.

"So how goes it?" Cedric asked.

"Very well, High Lord," Ares responded. He kept his eyes off her, as the Chatains would have considered it criminal for such a man to even look at a lady of the court. "Much easier than we expected, in fact. We knew there was a layer of rock beneath the topsoil," he said, pointing, "but didn't discover until we hit it that it's soft limestone. I presume that accounts for the numerous underground streams. We may even hit a cavern along the way." As casually as he replied, Nicole could not guess what was going through his mind.

"When will it be completed?" Magnus asked.

Ares hesitated. "I cannot say for certain, Chatain, as we had to make it wider than we originally planned. If we don't encounter major setbacks, we are hoping to launch the first vessels by next spring—"

"Stop saying 'we,' as if this were your plan," Magnus said irritably.

"A thousand pardons," Ares said dryly. "As foreman, I was allowed to sit in on the planning."

Magnus looked over the workers, then asked, "Where did your labor come from?"

"From our barracks, for the most part, Chatain. There are also peasants and townspeople who wanted to earn a royal a day," Ares said, obscuring a grim smile at the lie.

"You pay them a royal a day? Each?" Magnus exclaimed, turning to Cedric. The Surchatain looked just as shocked, and the Counselor would have to explain to him privately later that the peasants were actually paid five silver pieces a day, a tenth of a royal.

Ares looked surprised at Magnus' objection. "It's hard work, and they keep at it better if they're well paid."

"I'd use whips to keep them at it," Magnus growled.

"I am certain my lord is aware that slave labor uprisings are more costly, in the end," Ares said, folding well-muscled arms over his chest. The reply was neither aggressive nor disrespectful, but it somehow confused the issue of which one of them was subordinate to the other.

As if sensing that, Magnus lifted his chin to appraise the digging. "It looks ample for warships to me."

"Not Surchatain Ossian's cogs, my lord," Ares said succinctly, and Magnus glared at him.

"I've seen enough," he growled, reining his horse around. As they made their way back down the embankment, Nicole twisted in her saddle to look at Ares, still on the crest. "I'd hang a man for having such an ugly face," Magnus said.

"Oh, but he's good for trenching," the Counselor said, casting a surreptitious glance at Nicole. She grinned, fingering the gold cross.

They rode through the streets of Westford for the Chatains to see the bustling commerce, and the merchants eagerly pressed free samples on them which Magnus disdained and Tancred accepted. They visited the jeweler's, the furrier's, the tailor's, the wainwright's, and the silversmith's, until Magnus said, "These weary me. I wish to return to the palace now."

While riding toward the palace gates, Magnus lifted his eyes to a fortress sitting on a hill south of the city. "What is that?" he nodded.

"Just an abbey, my lord," Carmine said lightly, as if trying to deflect suspicion from it. As far as Nicole knew, it was really just an abbey. The nuns there cared for orphaned children.

In the courtyard, Nicole gave up the horse to a servant and turned to the palace steps. Tancred caught her hand. "Dear Lady, I would lunch with you."

"Excuse me to chambers first, my lord," Nicole smiled sweetly.

"For a little while," he allowed as if already her master.

Knowing she was being watched, Nicole headed up the great staircase without hesitation. She entered the Chataine's apartments to find Renée still asleep. Smiling, Nicole undressed and lay down beside her. She was safe here for the time being, because no man, not even the Surchatain, was allowed in the Chataine's quarters. They would have to wait until she chose to come out. Nicole stretched out and went to sleep.

Upon awaking, she lay there a long time, thinking. Renée was gone. Nicole looked out the bed curtains to see the late afternoon sky through the open shutters. She sighed, caressing the feather bed, and wondered how Ares would like it. Then she rolled over on her back, giggling, "Trenching."

There was a movement in the room, and Eleanor stuck her head through the curtains. "Oh, Lady Nicole, I'm so glad you've finally awoke! Chatain Tancred had such a tantrum, but I stood up to him and said that the lady needed her rest, but he's not being patient about it." She bustled to the wardrobe.

Nicole sat up. "Thank you, Eleanor. Is the Chataine downstairs?"

"If that Magnus is, then she is. Oh! What have you done to your hair?" Eleanor fretted. Nicole scratched her head and smiled.

Since Tancred was not likely to let her up here again to change, Nicole dressed in formal dinner attire. She stared at herself in the mirror as Eleanor braided sections of hair. Then Nicole stood to dig through the wardrobe. She pulled out a silk scarf, compatible in color with the rose of her dress, and stuffed it down the front, providing several inches' additional covering of her cleavage. "That's better," she said, and Eleanor shrugged.

The sentry stationed outside took her down the corridor in the opposite direction, to a wing guarded by sentries at all times: the Surchatain's wing. As she approached the far door in the corridor, another sentry leaned over to open it for her, and she found herself in the Surchatain's receiving chambers.

It was larger than Ares' whole quarters, appointed in the richest purple and gold. Cedric, Magnus, and Tancred sat around a table amid wine goblets and parchments. Surchataine Elise lay on a reclining couch nearby, watching but not participating in the proceedings.

Tancred stood to kiss Nicole's hand. "You will make me mad with your dallying."

"It was not intentional, Chatain. I fell asleep," she said innocently, curtsying. Magnus snorted and shook his head.

Cedric leaned back. "Nicole, Tancred wishes to negotiate for your hand."

"I'm sorry; that is not possible, Surchatain," she said.

He pushed a parchment toward her, and she picked it up. It began, "I, Nicole of Prie Mer, present this petition of divorce to my husband Commander Ares, wishing to gain my freedom as of this day—" which was today. There was more legal language, then a space for her to sign and a space for Ares to sign, which neither had. But it already carried the Surchatain's seal of authority.

Nicole laid it back on the table. "I will not sign."

"We can make you," Magnus observed.

"Break my hand if it please my lord, but a coerced signature is not legal under *this* Surchatain," she said.

Tancred burst out, "Lady, do you not understand what I can give you?"

She regarded him. "No, my lord, I do not. I am very sorry."

He turned on his older brother. "We must talk, Magnus."

"I already told you—"

"Now, Magnus!" Tancred shouted. "We talk now!"

Cedric hastily stood. "Come with me, please, Chatains." They preceded him out of the door, and the Surchataine waved the sentry out with them.

Elise then turned her lovely gray eyes on Nicole. "Well done, Lady," she murmured. Nicole exhaled, and Elise raised her voice slightly. "There is someone here who wishes to see you."

Nicole opened her mouth, then saw the wall tapestry behind Elise's chaise wiggle. A small hand appeared at the edge, and Henry's light-brown head peeked out from behind it. "Henry!" Nicole cried, kneeling with outstretched arms. He flung himself at her and she covered him in kisses. "I've missed you, dear Chatain. You are much better company than those other boys."

He grinned up at her, "We miss you, too."

She moaned, "Oh, Henry, do you get to see him? Is he well?"

"He's worried," Henry said, playing with her sleeve.

"Did you hear, darling? Do you understand what happened here just now?" Nicole asked.

"You wouldn't sign something," he said.

117

"A divorce decree. They wanted me to divorce the Commander and I would not. Can you run tell him that for me, Chatain?"

"Yes," he grinned.

Nicole looked up at his mother, who nodded her consent. "You are very brave, like the Commander," Nicole told him. He jumped up and saluted, then wrestled the heavy wooden door open and ran out. Nicole slumped to a sit.

At dinner that evening, Tancred had regained a great deal of poise—more than he had displayed yet, actually. He spoke courteously to Surchatain and servant alike while feigning aloofness toward Nicole. Magnus watched his brother's experiment with an amused eye. Meanwhile, Nicole was relieved not to be the center of attention as Magnus decided to acknowledge Renée's existence. Their slightly barbed flirtations took center stage.

After dessert of honey cakes and figs, Surchatain Cedric and Surchataine Elise stood, signaling an important development. "Honored guests, the Surchataine and I wish to make an announcement that will be proclaimed throughout the province of Lystra tomorrow morning. Chatain Magnus of Scylla has asked for the hand of Chataine Renée in marriage. She will accompany him to Eurus for the royal wedding. Join me in wishing them bliss." He picked up his goblet, as did Elise, and the table stood with their goblets raised.

The toast was made, then Magnus gestured to his servant, who brought him a gold box. "Dear Chataine Renée, please accept this small token of my pledge to wed," he said. It seemed that he could say nothing without a twinge of irony. But Renée accepted the box, and gasped when she opened it. Nicole leaned forward to look, knowing it took a lot to shock the Chataine. She lifted out of the box an ornate gold cross, heavy with gems, and bowed her head for Magnus to place it around her neck. The other guests at table broke out in applause.

Tancred now turned to Nicole with his tail feathers fully spread. "Lady Nicole, I also have a token of my deep affection for you." He gestured to the servant, who came quickly around the table with a smaller gold box. Holding her breath, Nicole stared at Tancred, trying to warn him away from his folly. He presented the box to her, saying, "Lady Nicole, will you"—she was glaring at him with clenched teeth—"accompany me to Eurus to see your dear friend and Chataine wed to my brother?"

Nicole paused without touching the box, so he opened it under her nose. Her sharp intake of breath made Renée blink. Since Nicole would not take it, Tancred lifted a jeweled gold bracelet, cousin of the necklace, and fastened it around her wrist. It was now painfully obvious, especially to Renée, that Tancred had taken one of the gifts meant for her to present to Nicole.

Her heart beat loudly in the ensuing silence. The gift was highly inappropriate, and it would be fraud for her to accept it, as she had no intention of giving him what he wanted. But to refuse it in front of the assembled royalty and guests would be stunningly rude—wars had started over less.

Cedric said, "Nicole, my daughter affixed a title to your name to bring you here just for the pleasure of your company, and stood by you throughout your little charade so that you would suffer no consequences for an offense that has meant banishment for others less favored. As you have made your high principles and your contempt for our guest plain, will you go to Eurus solely as companion for my daughter as she embarks on her new life?"

Nicole hung her head in shame. "Yes, High Lord," she whispered.

"Thank you," he said stiffly, and Tancred beamed.

That night passed in lonely dreariness and despair. Renée hardly spoke before bed, being angry over the bracelet, and Nicole lay wide awake long after the Chataine was breathing deeply. Finally, Nicole got up and tiptoed to the shutters to open them. She leaned on the sill, gazing up at the stars while the night wind played with her hair. As she was unable to visit the chapel, she clasped her hands, pressed them to her forehead, and prayed in the light of the heavens.

Hard upon sunrise, Eleanor had two other maids helping her pack trunks for the Chataine and her companion. They tried to work quietly, but as Nicole was sleeping fitly, she woke and climbed out of bed. "A thousand pardons, Lady. Here, let me see how this looks with your hair," Eleanor said, holding yet another fabulous gown to Nicole's shoulders. "Ah, you grace everything," the maid said, folding it to place in a trunk. "There. That's the last of the gowns."

Nicole looked at the still-full wardrobe. "What is the Chataine taking?"

"Same as you, five dresses, Lady," Eleanor replied, pulling out a brown traveling dress. "This is yours today. The Chataine hates the color. Oh, and the leather shoes. Maddie, pack the makeup but leave out the hair ornaments until we see which the Chataine prefers."

"Why is she taking only five dresses?" Nicole asked.

"Magnus says they're 'provincial'—wants her dressed in northern attire," Eleanor sniffed. "And if you stay, it'll be the same for you."

Something about Eleanor's detachment alarmed Nicole. "But you—you're coming with us, aren't you?"

Tears of anger appeared in Eleanor's eyes. "The Chatain says he has maids aplenty for the ladies. No, you may not bring your own," she said bitterly.

Nicole breakfasted and dressed under a cloud of foreboding. A servant entered with the Surchatain's instructions to wake the Chataine. The guests were anxious to depart.

Shortly thereafter, the packed trunks were sent down and the ladies followed. Renée was lethargic but no longer angry, muttering to Nicole, "Wish I'd gotten the bracelet instead of the necklace. It's like wearing a millstone." Nicole glanced at the fabulous cross hanging about her neck, then touched the bracelet on her own wrist. She had hidden the small cross in the folds of her bodice, for she was afraid Tancred would make her remove it.

The normal activity of the courtyard was suspended while the Scyllan soldiers in the Chatains' retinue made preparations for the return trip, which would take the better part of the day. They loaded the trunks, provisions, and gifts from Cedric onto carts before bringing up an elegant carriage with the most modern suspension and upholstered seats for the ladies.

As the door was opened and the driver offered his hand to Renée, Nicole looked for Tancred. Having got what he wanted thus far, he was now making a point of ignoring her.

She approached him while he was standing with his brother and curtsied low. "Yes, Lady?" he said lightly, extending his hand.

She placed in it the hand adorned with the bracelet. "Chatain Tancred, I do owe you an apology. I misjudged you. You are generous and good, and it is indeed an honor to be invited to visit your royal court."

He looked pleased, but Magnus was watchful. Nicole wished she could separate them, but that would make Magnus all the more suspicious. "Since you are a kind man of royal blood, I have a request of you before we depart."

"Here it comes," uttered Magnus.

"See to your own affairs," Tancred spat at him. "What will you ask of me, Lady Nicole?"

She chose her words carefully. "I wish to say good-bye to my husband. It may be a long time before I see him again, and I wish him to know I bear him no ill will." She said no more, to let the implications sink in of their own weight.

Tancred absorbed that, then raised a hand. "Summon the Lady Nicole's husband," he said grandly.

She curtsied again. "Thank you, Chatain Tancred."

A Lystran soldier shot into the palace as from a bowstring, and the courtyard bustle stilled when Ares, in work clothes, appeared from within. Having not yet been to the waterway today, he was still clean. "Him!" muttered Magnus.

Nicole lifted her skirts to meet him at the foot of the steps, out of Tancred's hearing. She repressed her inclination to bow, but looked up at his smoky eyes, expressionless as that first day she had encountered him in the foyer.

She whispered, "I will come back. I swear it." He blinked slowly, all the response he dared make.

Beside the carriage, Renée called, "Come here, dear patsy."

With restrained stride, Ares approached her and went down on one knee. She held out her hand and he kissed her fingers respectfully. "What shall we do when I am no longer here to soak you from an upper window?" she asked severely.

"I shall assign the task to another, Chataine," he said in a gravelly voice.

She laughed deep in her throat, then ordered, "Stand up." When he did, she threw her arms around his neck to hug him tightly, maybe even whispering something. He held her as if she were still ten and said, "God go with you, Chataine. Remember us."

He released her and looked at Nicole standing by her side. She lifted her arms and he reached for her, but Tancred intervened, "Enough!" Ares turned away, his face a mask, albeit torn.

After the ladies were assisted into the carriage, Magnus leaned his head in to hiss at Renée, "My, that was a disgusting show of familiarity, dear heart."

"As was your pawing the maids, my lord," she muttered in return. He withdrew abruptly and Renée turned to Nicole. "I told Ares it was from you," she said, taking her hand. Nicole leaned on her shoulder to cry as the carriage started out.

Two Lystran diplomats, clearly garbed in Lystran blue, traveled on horseback with them to report back to Surchatain Cedric after the royal wedding. Curiously to some, Cedric and Elise had not been invited to attend.

Travel was fast, as the weather was fair and the road broad, straight and paved. This ancient highway had been the main overland north-south route for centuries, but was not paved with stone until Roman's time, when the Surchatain wished to facilitate travel to Outpost One, then along the border between Lystra and Seleca. When Roman's grandson Bobadil lost the territory to Ossian's great-uncle, the new ruler demolished the outpost but kept the highway, building his capital city of Eurus around it.

Crossing the Passage north of Willowring Lake brought the party into Ossian's province. Except for the servants who manned the carts and the driver of the carriage bearing Nicole and Renée, everyone else was on horseback, proceeding at a fast lope.

The carriage bounced mightily on its springs, throwing the occupants around a bit, but it was nothing like the jarring of a cart. The carriage windows were opened just a crack to admit air without a lot of dust. Nicole looked out of the rear window, pitying those pressed to keep up this pace in carts.

The bumping made it hard to converse, but she and Renée managed. At one point, Renée took her arm to look at the bracelet. Nicole said, "There is much more for you where this came from."

"I know," Renée said. "You deserve it, having to leave Ares." Nicole looked miserable, and Renée added, "You forget, after a while. You'll forget you ever loved him."

"How can you say that?" Nicole cried softly.

"Because it happens. The man I loved. . . . He was a soldier, too. Oh, he had the most beautiful eyes, and when he looked at me, I felt I should never even look at another man. We would meet in the gardens, or the orchard—once even in my chambers," Renée said, and Nicole covered her mouth in shock.

"But gossip got around to my father's ears, and I heard him order my lover brought before him. I got word to him first, and—he disappeared. He left that very night, and I've neither seen nor heard from him since. My father never spoke of it, and . . . so it died." Renée held Nicole's hand as she talked, and a jolt of the carriage suspended them momentarily in midair.

"Love dies," Renée repeated, tossing her head, but Nicole looked at her in sorrow. "I must say that I was disappointed Ares let you go. I thought he would have fought for you."

"He had no choice," Nicole whispered.

"No, he had the same choice we all do: whether to live another day," Renée said.

Nicole studied her. "You don't want to marry Magnus, do you?"

"Would you?" snorted Renée. "He's perfectly horrid."

"I am so sorry," Nicole said, opening her arms, and they held each other while bouncing off the seat.

A few hours later the Chataine pounded on the roof of the carriage. "Stop! Stop this thing and let me out or I shall wet myself!"

The carriage slowed and Nicole, with the same need, opened the door. Immediately she put her hand over her nose. "Ew! What's that?" The strong smell of dead fish permeated the air. She gazed over the field of winter wheat bordering the highway, first thinking it had been burnt. Almost the whole field was black. Then she saw a few heads of blackened, shriveled wheat nearby, and realized the odor was emanating from them.

The carriage door was slammed in her face. "Not here!" Magnus shouted. "We'll stop further up the road!" The carriage jolted forward again while Nicole pressed her face to the crack in the window to look. Field after field they passed was black like the first, acres and acres of it. It was another quarter hour before Magnus would allow them to stop.

Because delays like this were few and far between, the party made such good time that they came within sight of Eurus by midafternoon. They made a brief stop, then a half-hour later they were passing through the city gates.

Nicole shoved the carriage window full open to look. The whole city was enclosed by a wall, as Westford used to be. But over the years, Lystra's rulers had allowed the city wall to crumble, choosing to reinforce the palace complex instead.

As they passed through the gates of Eurus, Nicole studied the towers and sentries, the construction of the gates and the means of their operation. She leaned far out of the carriage to look up at the chamber from which the portcullis was raised and lowered by chains and pulleys. "Sit down; you're embarrassing me," Renée said.

"I want to see," Nicole replied. She evaluated the tall houses along the street with their ground floors made of stone and their second floors of timber set with meurtrières—narrow window slits through which archers could pick off invaders in the street below. She craned to see down side streets and studied the people who stared at the returning royalty.

As they approached the palace complex, one of the mounted soldiers pulled up beside her window, forcing her back inside and blocking her view. So she leaned across Renée to look at the drawbridge they were crossing. From the smell, it was apparent that the palace residents used the moat as a sewer—an effective safeguard against trespassers. She looked back at the twenty-foot-tall stone and earthen walls. "You don't get out much, do you?" Renée asked blandly. Nicole smiled at her.

The party followed a slightly narrower brick road that curved around gardens and ponds before arriving at the palace entry. The carriage door was opened and the step lowered for first Renée and then Nicole to emerge. Alighting on the arm of a sentry, Nicole studied his hauberk and axe. Misinterpreting her interest, he looked down the front of her dress, and she shoved him away. Then she saw that the Lystran diplomats had been blindfolded—probably before they reached the city.

The women were taken into the palace entry hall, where they were instructed to wait. Glancing at the milling courtiers told them volumes: the fashion laws here dictated modest necklines and plunging backs, with half or three-quarter sleeves. Turning her back to the stares and whispers, Renée muttered, "This must be what it feels like to be embarrassed." Nicole, observing the movements of the palace guard, did not reply, so Renée asked painfully, "Have I ever embarrassed you, dearest?"

Nicole looked at her in surprise. "What? Of course not."

Renée lowered her eyes. "I am so glad you came with me. I know it was hard."

"I am glad to be here for you, Chataine. Ares can take care of himself."

Renée nodded, and a tear tracked down her face. Nicole squeezed her hand.

When the trunks were unloaded, the two were escorted up a winding staircase (one of a pair) to guest apartments. Here they were left alone. Renée sat on one trunk with a dismal sigh, but Nicole opened the window to survey the grounds.

A moment later two chambermaids entered and curtsied. "Chatain Magnus instructs my ladies to be promptly dressed in their finest," one said in a clipped accent, something like the Counselor.

"Open the trunks and take your pick," Renée said carelessly. The two maids glanced at each other and giggled in surprise. "What?" the Chataine said ominously. They promptly quieted and turned to the trunks. Nicole suspected they were laughing at Renée's southern accent.

In minutes the Lystran women were freshened and changed. As the pair of sentries who had been stationed outside their quarters led them downstairs, Nicole's eyes swept every detail of their route. She and Renée were deposited in an antechamber by themselves and instructed to wait.

Nicole peeked through the curtain separating them from the great hall, but it was unnecessary for her to tell the Chataine that many people were assembling on the other side. Finally, the heavy curtain was drawn back and two attendants presented their arms to the ladies. Renée was escorted out first with Nicole immediately following.

They walked down the center, carpeted aisle of the great room in the midst of the Scyllans, who craned to see them. On raised thrones at the end of the aisle sat the ruling couple, presumably Ossian and his wife. Standing at the Surchatain's side was Magnus; beside the Surchataine was Tancred, watching with overweening pride.

The ladies and their escorts reached the proper place to stop and curtsy, Nicole still behind Renée. Then Magnus descended to wave away the attendant and take Renée's hand. "Father and Mother, this is the Chataine Renée of Lystra, wearing the token of betrothal I gave her."

She curtsied again, and they motioned her forward to examine her like dry goods. Ossian nodded, but his wife said to her, "That dress will never do. You must find something more suitable to wear for dinner tonight." A tiny ripple of amusement passed through the hall and Magnus glanced around. His mother dismissed him with a wave, then beckoned to her second son beside her.

Magnus pulled Renée to the side as Tancred came down to claim Nicole's hand. Smirking, he led her before his parents and bowed while she curtsied low. Then he said, "Father and Mother, may I present the Lady Nicole of Westford, wearing the token of betrothal I gave her."

9

ancred had her, and he knew it. He knew Nicole dare not murmur a word as he extended her hand with the bracelet before his parents. The Surchataine peered at it and her, then turned to her husband in exasperation. "What are these southern women thinking with these dresses?"

"I think the boys have done well," Ossian said, leaning on his hand. "One can always remove the dress if it is displeasing." A stronger ripple of laughter passed around the room. "Well, Tancred, let us get your brother married off tomorrow, then see what shall be done for you and the Lady Nicole." Ossian waved; he and his wife rose, and the whole room bowed like wheat in the wind.

Without another word from the Chatains, Nicole and Renée were taken back to their apartments upstairs. Along the way, Nicole glanced constantly to the left and the right, seeing how many guards were posted where. When they were placed in their room, Nicole asked the guard, "When is dinner?"

"About an hour, Lady," he said, not unkindly.

"We need a maid," she said.

"You shall have one," he nodded, and she closed the door.

She turned to see Renée leaning on the windowsill, head

down. "I've never been treated so ill in my life," she whispered. Nicole exhaled, then opened their trunks to see what she could do.

When the promised maid entered, Nicole told her, "We need a needle and thread, quickly." The maid bowed and withdrew.

Renée turned listlessly. "What are you doing?"

"We have to make do with what we have, but we can't wear them as they are. Undress, Chataine," Nicole instructed. The maid returned with a sewing basket, which Nicole took, then said, "Get out." The maid bowed, peering around the door as she slowly closed it.

Although Nicole had grown up with a tailor, he had never allowed childish hands to touch his work and thereby learn his craft. Still, she had watched him enough to know something. She had Renée change into another of her dresses, which she then scrutinized.

Taking a breath, Nicole cut a swatch of silk from an inner petticoat the same hue as the outer skirt, and sewed the piece into the bodice to elevate the neckline. Then she unbuttoned the back of the dress a ways and turned the corners to the inside, where she stitched them in place. The sleeves she merely pushed up to three-quarters length, tying ribbons in the creases to make it look less improvisational.

Renée twisted and turned in front of the mirror to evaluate the result. "Darling, you have saved my life."

"Both of ours, I hope," Nicole said, taking out a dress from her trunk. While Renée arranged her own hair, Nicole altered her dress in the same manner.

As Nicole was slipping the dress on over her head, there was a loud knock on the door. "You are summoned to dinner with the Surchatain."

"We need just a moment," Nicole called, as Renée buttoned her dress and she grabbed up her hairpiece.

The sentry then pounded. "You shall come *now*!"

Nicole rushed to the door and flung it open. She looked hard at the sentry, and he at her. She said, "I just wanted to be able to point you out, when the Surchatain asks how we could presume to appear at table in an unpresentable state."

He actually blanched. Seeing as how they were very nearly ready, he stood quietly in the doorway while Renée helped Nicole secure her headpiece. Then they allowed him to escort them downstairs.

They had to wait in the entry hall along with all the other dinner guests, who stared at them frankly without any friendly overtures. Renée gazed off into the distance as if bored, but Nicole assessed the dress, accessories, and relative girth of the guests to ascertain their level of prosperity. She mentally counted the guests as well as the number of soldiers lining the hall, and where they were positioned.

The unseen dinner master gave a signal, and the tide of guests flowed into the hall. Nicole and Renée looked at each other without moving. They should be escorted in. As they waited, even the Chataine began to show some nerves. A servant's head poked into the anteroom through the curtain. "What are you doing here? Come take your seats."

Renée and Nicole stared at each other in astonishment, then entered the hall escorted by the lone servant, who pointed them to one long table where everyone else was already seated on benches. At one end of the table, the two Lystran diplomats jumped up to bow as their Chataine and Lady entered, who sat at the last two places on the far end from their countrymen (having not seen each other in the crowded entry hall). A second table with four chairs sitting off by itself on a dais was as yet unoccupied.

Serving platters of food were already on the table, untouched. No one moved, and only the barest whisper passed from one person to another. A fly buzzed in to land on one uncovered platter of leeks; Nicole brushed it off and a man nearby hissed at her. She glared back at him. Thus they waited, staring at food that could not be eaten. Besides the leeks, Nicole saw cabbage, barley bread, and pieces of capon. Filled wine glasses stood beside the plates, which no one touched, of course.

Long minutes later the dinner master announced: "Surchatain Ossian and Surchataine Danae, Chatain Magnus and Chatain Tancred." Everyone at the long table stood to bow; doing so between a table and bench while wearing a full gown was a feat. Without a glance at the long table, the royal family sat at their separate table while servants hovered around them with the wine pitcher and serving platters.

At some invisible signal, guests at the long table began grabbing food. The capon pieces disappeared instantly, as did the leeks. People served themselves slaw by the handfuls. By the time Nicole and Renée realized they were on their own, there was only a little cabbage and bread left. And no servant appeared to offer refills.

The other guests talked among themselves, and while they stared plenty at the Lystran women, no one addressed them. No one from the royal table so much as looked toward their guests throughout the meal. Servants did pass a large basket of wafers for dessert, and Nicole knew to grab a handful. She shared them with Renée, who was too proud to scrounge for food—yet.

And that was it. The royal family rose from their table and departed, not acknowledging the awkward bowing of their guests. Nicole and Renée were escorted back up to their chambers, where Renée threw herself onto the bed in a weeping fit. Nicole comforted her as best she could.

In the morning, Nicole woke immediately when the chambermaid entered to rekindle the fire. Nicole lay on the feather bed and distrustfully watched without stirring until the maid left. Then she climbed down from the bed holding her stomach, which cramped with hunger. "I shall surely faint away at the wedding," she muttered, then mused, "Why wait?"

As the maid would be back soon, Nicole arranged herself in a sprawl face down on the bare wood floor and closed her eyes. When the maid reentered, she gasped and rushed to revive the lady with handfuls of cold water. "Enough. Enough!" Nicole said, turning her face.

"What happened, Lady?" the maid cried, sure that it would somehow be construed as her fault.

"Oh, I must have fainted from hunger. We've had practically nothing to eat since we arrived—I doubt the Chataine will be able to stand throughout the wedding," Nicole said weakly.

"I will alert the kitchen," the maid promised, hurrying out, and Nicole sat up to dry her face on her underwear.

"What's going on?" Renée asked sleepily from behind the bed curtain.

"I am trying to secure us some breakfast," Nicole said. Renée promptly got up.

The maid returned very soon with barley bread, wine, and dried figs. Nicole sent her away before sitting down to eat. It was poor fare, as the bread was course and the wine thick, but the two of them ate it all. Shortly thereafter, another servant appeared with their actual breakfast. Renée took one look at it and exploded, "I'm sick of this brown bread!"

"A thousand pardons, Chataine," the servant said, bowing nervously. "But the wheat harvest failed, as Calle Valley sold us bad grain."

"Enough excuses. You may go," Renée waved. They were still hungry enough to eat part of this breakfast, hiding the rest for later.

Then they waited, not knowing what was to be required of them next. Nicole altered a second dress for herself and put it on, but Renée contented herself to lounge around in her underwear. Nicole opened the small window to look down on the paved courtyard below. A sentry looked up, and she withdrew from the window.

Not long afterwards another maid entered carrying a heavy, ornate gown. Its train was so long that a second maid was needed to carry it alone. "Your wedding dress, Chataine," she bowed. "It's time to get you ready." Renée acquiesced, sighing.

Nicole watched while the maid dressed the Chataine and primped her in the appropriate tradition. She used no makeup on her face but a little rouge on the lips and cheeks, and the hair was gathered up in tight braids atop the head. When she was all ready, with headpiece and cross, she turned to Nicole. "What do you think, sister dear?"

"You are radiant," Nicole breathed, and they embraced.

Renée was escorted downstairs, the maid and Nicole following with the train. In the anteroom of the great hall they were separated, and a soldier pointed Nicole to a balcony seat. This she found it actually satisfactory: she could sit instead of stand as most of the audience would, and she could see the entire proceedings.

It was a long wait, however, while the aisle carpet was laid and the candles lit around the thrones on the dais. Following that, the guests entered to fill the hall. While surveying the layout of the floor and the movements of the soldiers, Nicole spotted the two Lystran diplomats near the front. (She did not see them after the ceremony, and assumed they were sent directly away.)

Finally, the priest entered, followed by the royal family: Ossian and his wife sat on the thrones; Tancred stood to Ossian's side; and Magnus stood before the priest in front of the dais.

Then the door was opened, and Renée entered on the arm of an official, possibly the Counselor. The guests bowed as she passed, and Nicole was filled with admiration of Renée's poise and grace under the weight of the dress and the occasion.

The Counselor delivered her to Magnus' arm, and they

kneeled for long minutes while the priest spoke unintelligible words over them. At some point along here, they repeated their vows, though Nicole could not hear them. They were sprinkled, and the sign of the cross made over them, then they stood to be kissed and embraced by Surchatain Ossian and Surchataine Danae.

With the ceremony completed, the royal family (including Renée, now) was escorted to sit at a lavish table across the room. Here they ate the wedding dinner while guests helped themselves (with their hands) from smaller tables set up around the room.

Nicole made her way down from the balcony, but found it impossible to get close to the royal table, or even force her way into the great hall, because of the number of people inside. So she looked toward the front of the palace, and discreetly began to explore the avenues of entry.

Her adventuring was cut short by a soldier who took her back up to her quarters. "I haven't had anything to eat," she complained.

He nodded. "Wait here."

An hour later there was a knock on the door, and when she called, "Enter!" Chatain Tancred himself walked in with a platter and a parchment roll. Nicole drew back in slight alarm.

But he set down the platter, saying, "I saved you a portion from our table, Lady Nicole." She immediately moved in to consume the eggs, cheese, and brown beer (which was bitter). Watching her eat, he said, "When we are married, you will join our table, of course. You will have fine dresses, jewelry, and a generous allowance to spend on whatever your heart desires. You and the Chataine shall spend your days in carefree entertainments."

She hung her head, then saw to her dismay that the filigree cross was plainly visible on her chest, and she looked up quickly at Tancred. He had not noticed it. It was so small that no one paid any attention to it.

Tancred continued in a low voice, "However, my father wishes everything to be done correctly, according to law." He handed her the parchment, which she unrolled. It was her petition of divorce. "You must sign it before we can be married. Our new life cannot begin until you end the old one. So summon me when it is done—I shall answer your summons at any time, day or night."

With that he bowed, kissed her fingers, and left. A maid brought in a quill and inkstand which she placed on the table. Nicole put the parchment beside them and did not touch it the rest of the day, but sat at the window to look out and think. When evening came, a maid brought her a modest dinner and took the chamber pot out to empty, but otherwise, Nicole was alone.

She had not signed it in the morning when the maid came again to bring her breakfast and draw her bath. When Nicole was dressed, she asked the sentry at her door, "May I take some exercise in the courtyard?"

"No, Lady," he replied.

"Am I a prisoner, then?" she asked.

"Call yourself whatever you will, Lady. I am instructed you shall do nothing without permission of the Chatain Tancred."

"Then perhaps you will ask the Chatain if he will walk with me," she said. He nodded and moved off, and another soldier came to stand at the door.

In a while, the first soldier returned with a pair of maids who carried a fabulous gown only a little less ornate than the one Renée had been married in. "The Chatain sends your wedding dress, Lady, but he regrets that he cannot come up himself until you have the document signed." The maids hung the gown on the outside of the wardrobe for her to study at her leisure. Then they left, closing the door behind them.

Nicole opened it again. "I wish to see my dear Chataine."

"She is busy, Lady," the sentry said, a corner of his mouth

turning up. So the maids brought her dreary meals and she watched the day turn to evening through the window.

The next two days passed in exactly the same manner, except that Tancred sent up gifts from time to time. There was a jeweled headpiece, and an emerald ring, and a gold necklace, all which Nicole placed in the wardrobe. She put the bracelet there as well, that Tancred had given her in Westford.

She asked repeatedly to see Renée, but was denied. When she signed, they said, she would have company with the Chataine. Not before. The maids did report to Tancred that late into the night, the lady would pace the room, muttering to herself.

Then Tancred sent up one last gift. It was a book, bound in leather-covered wood, of little sayings written in beautiful script, and illustrated in colors. The sayings had to do with love, and were mostly silly or sighing. But there was one quotation that spoke to her soul: "Love is patient and kind; love is not jealous or boastful; it is not arrogant or rude. Love does not insist on its own way; it is not irritable or resentful; it does not rejoice at wrong, but rejoices in the right. Love bears all things, believes all things, hopes all things, endures all things." And from that moment on, for the first time, she knew her own heart.

Early the next morning, after she had dressed and eaten, she opened the door to the sentry outside. "Please summon the Chatain Tancred." He darted away.

While waiting, Nicole put the book in the wardrobe with some visible regret. Then she smoothed out the divorce petition to look it over.

With a knock, Tancred entered, his face eager with expectation. "Did you summon me, Lady?" he bowed.

"Yes. Thank you for coming. I am considering signing the petition, but there is a serious constraint. If I marry you, I shall have a life similar to the Chataine's. But as I have not been allowed to see her since the wedding, I do not know how she is faring. I do not even know that she is alive. If I cannot see for myself how she is, I can never sign this," she said, weighting the edges of the parchment so that it was all smooth and ready for the quill.

"Is that all? That shall be answered immediately, Lady!" he promised, departing in a wink. While Nicole waited, she thought about jonquils, and foals, and Henry—especially Henry.

Some time later the door opened and Renée swept in: "Darling!" Nicole jumped up to embrace her. They hugged each other tightly, then Nicole looked at the sentry standing in the room. It irritated her how the men here felt so much at ease in a lady's apartments. "Get out," Nicole said.

"Darling, allow me." Renée turned to him. "You may wait outside." He bowed to her, making his point that he was not beholden to obey Nicole.

When he was outside with the door shut, Nicole turned seriously to Renée. "How are you, Chataine?" she asked, evaluating her. She looked well enough. She was certainly dressed well.

"Perfectly fine," Renée answered lightly.

"They would not allow me to see you," Nicole said.

"Well, dear, I've hardly been out of chambers," Renée laughed. "You know how it goes."

Nicole lowered her voice. "Darling, you must be perfectly honest with me—a great deal is hanging on it. Are you all right? Are you happy here?"

"Why, sister, such gravity! Yes, I'm very well. Now that I am Magnus' wife, everyone treats me with much more respect. The food isn't as good as at home, and I've missed you terribly, but, all in all—yes, I am happy," Renée said.

Nicole studied her. "I hope you mean that."

Renée returned her gaze. "Of course."

Nicole inhaled deeply, then opened the door. "Please summon Chatain Tancred."

"What are you doing?" Renée asked.

Nicole sat at the table and reached for the quill, which she dipped into the inkwell. "I am going to sign for the divorce from Ares."

Renée looked torn for a moment. "Oh, darling. . . . I'm sorry. I hate to be selfish, but—oh, it will be so lovely to have you with me here. Then our summer visit need never end!" As Renée hugged her shoulders, Nicole debated the importance of Renée's enthusiasm. Then she wiped the quill tip on the lip of the inkwell and carefully signed her name.

When Tancred arrived a few minutes later, Nicole was blotting the signature. "As you wished, my lord Tancred," she said, handing him the document.

"Yes!" he laughed, clenching his fist. "I will show it to Father at once, and then—"

"Excuse me, my lord, but there is another problem," Nicole said levelly.

"What?" He and Renée both looked at her.

"It is in the way the petition is worded," she said, pointing to the first line: "'I, Nicole of Prie Mer, *present* this petition of divorce to my husband Commander Ares'—I must present it to him personally for it to be valid. Were you to merely send it by the hand of a messenger, he would assume I was forced to sign it. Then, knowing the Commander, he would bring an army against you to retrieve me."

Tancred glanced at Renée, who concurred, "He certainly would. Actually, I'm surprised he's not already at your gates."

Tancred's eyes darted around as if searching almost frantically for a solution. "But—if I take you to him—"

"Then I will present it to him, and we will be free to leave," Nicole said.

Tancred looked unconvinced. "You will present it to him? You swear it?"

"Yes," Nicole said. "I swear I will present it to him."

"But—once there, he will keep you," Tancred said.

Nicole shook her head. "He is not like that. He would not keep me against my will." As Tancred looked uneasy still, she nodded to Renée, "Tell him."

The Chataine looked off to a distant view. "Commander Ares is a man of honor. If she wishes to go, he will let her go."

Glancing between them, Tancred made his decision. "We will leave immediately." He strode out clutching the parchment, and Renée paused in the doorway. She looked back at Nicole with heavy eyes, then departed as well.

Nicole summoned a maid to help her change into the brown traveling suit for the most mobility. Fingering the gold filigree cross on her chest, she cast a longing glance at the beautiful book before shutting it up inside the wardrobe.

Tancred summoned her within the half hour, and she was led down to the courtyard where the carriage waited, along with a dozen mounted soldiers. Tancred himself was striding among them, shouting orders, tense with excitement. "No carts!" he bellowed, kicking a wheel. "You there! You carry the provisions! What's the matter with you? Can't carry enough for a day trip?" Soldiers and servants scurried to carry out his fragmented commands as Nicole watched.

When he spotted her, he came forward to take her hand. Seeing it bare, he asked, "Where is the bracelet?"

"My lord, I left it here," she said, amazed that he would even ask. "Why would I take it?"

"Oh, yes. Of course. Since you're coming back," he laughed nervously. He glanced around to ascertain that she had no luggage at all.

Smiling benignly, she allowed him to assist her into the carriage and close the door. The driver climbed up in his seat; Tancred mounted his fast steed, and with his shouted command, they were off.

Exiting the palace grounds, Nicole lowered the window enough to observe the workings of the drawbridge from the inside. She took a second look at the portcullis on their way out of the city, then closed the window and tried to relax for a bumpy ride.

If she thought the ride here was fast—and she did—it was a jaunt compared to the pace they were going now. Nicole gripped the sides of the carriage as it careened down the road, occasionally on two wheels. In his determination to get the thing over with, Tancred was leading the party at a full-out run. She wished he could see that if the horses collapsed, or the carriage broke an axle, or it rolled over and killed her, then the great speed would have been all for nothing. Nicole closed her eyes, committing herself to the Lord of heaven once again, who had so admirably handled her case up till now.

After a while she almost got used to the fits and pitches of the carriage, though it was very tiring to be thrown about like a rag doll. It had a disagreeable effect on her bodily functions as well, for sooner (and more often) than Tancred would have liked, she was pounding on the roof of the carriage to make them stop.

It aggravated him also that she would linger outside the carriage with an eye on the horses' heaving chests. She saw no reason that the beasts should suffer for his impatience. So when she did climb back in, he drove like a madman renewed, forcing other travelers off the road when necessary, cursing them for being there.

Then, sooner than she could have imagined, she felt the carriage crossing the ancient bridge just north of Westford. She flung the window full open to look out—there was Willowring Lake on her left! Her heart lifted as she went airborne once again, and then the carriage rolled into the cobbled courtyard of the palace at Westford.

The driver opened the door and put down the step for her as Tancred demanded that a sentry summon Commander Ares. After being bounced around for hours on end, Nicole felt like a newborn foal herself.

She stumbled from the carriage to hear Tanny, the

experienced messenger, come out to say: "Chatain Tancred, Commander Ares sends a thousand apologies. My Lord Commander was summoned from the waterway when the scouts spotted your party just up the road. He is now endeavoring to make himself presentable to receive you. While you wait, he requested that you and your party take refreshment from our meager store." Tanny gestured to the maids—pretty ones—who were making the rounds among the Scyllan soldiers with large goblets of wine and meat pies.

"We don't want it!" Tancred said, but his men seized the offerings, as there had been no eating on the road, and other servants brought buckets of water to the lathering horses.

Leaning against the carriage, Nicole looked up at the watchful soldiers on the wall, and one waved at her. She smiled, but did not wave. There were at least twenty on the parapet now, with more arriving by the moment—expert archers, all of them. More soldiers began quietly filling the courtyard, nudging the townspeople out.

Nicole turned to Tancred. "The petition, my lord?" Just this one formality, and it was done.

He looked at her blankly, then laughed, "The petition! That's why we're here." He removed the damp, wrinkled roll from his belt and handed it to her.

At that moment, Commander Ares appeared on the palace steps. His hair was wet and clothes damp, though clean. When he saw her, he stopped where he was, with one foot on the step lower than the other.

With her heart in her throat, Nicole approached him. She curtsied, though no words would come out, and extended the parchment to him.

10

A res held the petition for a moment as he came down off the steps, then unrolled it and read it. He raised his eyes to her, and she saw the scar throb once with the force of the blood flowing so closely underneath. Then he calmly and methodically tore the parchment into tiny shreds which he let the breeze take from his hand.

Nicole could endure it no longer. With a cry, she leaped into his arms. He caught her and crushed her to him while she kissed his scar, his beard, his lips. She was only dimly aware of Tancred shouting and soldiers cheering as she whispered into his lips, "I love you, Ares. Henry taught me to love you." For what her heart finally made her mind understand was that a child knows who is worthy of love. Ares started making a funny little choking sound, and when she saw the tears course down his scar like a waterway, she realized he was crying.

"Lady Nicole! You gave your word! You will explain this, Lady!" Tancred was shouting.

She turned in Ares' tight arms. "A thousand pardons, my lord. I gave you my word that I would present the petition to him. That I did. I cannot help that he refused it."

Tancred stood open-mouthed as it dawned on him that the

143

pair of them had acted in concert according to a preordained course, and Nicole turned back to lace her arms around her husband's neck and kiss him deeply.

"But—the gifts! You have taken—" Tancred's outrage was cut short by the remembrance that she had left everything at Eurus, even her own belongings.

Satisfied with the consolation from Nicole's lips, Ares lifted his head. "Chatain Tancred, I thank you for returning my wife. My men will see that you get safely to the border." He turned with Nicole to reenter the palace, but Tancred scrambled after them. "No! Stop, you—trench digger!"

Ares quickly turned and raised a cautionary hand. "Chatain! Look!" he urged, pointing to the top of the wall.

Despite himself, Tancred looked. His soldiers looked, and they saw at least fifty archers with bowstrings drawn tight, arrows aimed at the Chatain's heart. "Go in peace, Chatain," Ares advised. With so little choice, he did.

Weak with happiness, Nicole entered the palace foyer as the Counselor descended from the upper window where he had been watching. She let go of Ares to fling herself on Carmine now, who received her smilingly. "Oh, Counselor, you are a genius!" she exulted. ["He doesn't have a garderobe with running water," Ares objected.] "Every detail of your plan was perfect! I did just what you said, and it all worked perfectly!"

He nodded, but asked, "How is the Chataine, my dear?"

"Except that," she sighed, leaning against him. Ares jealously drew her back into his arms. "I don't know. She was married to Magnus the day after we arrived, and I saw her this morning. She looked well, and said she was happy, but . . . I don't know that I believe her. Tancred may have forced her to try to convince me to stay, but by the time we parted, she knew I would not."

"This is my fault," Carmine said, shaking his head. "I never supposed Magnus would actually marry her."

"Why do you think they came, then?" she asked.

"To spy us out—see how much resistance we would put up to an invasion. That's the reason for all his ridiculous machinations," the Counselor said, with a humorous glance at the Commander.

"They worked well enough," Ares said defensively.

Nicole glanced between them. "What—?"

"Oh, having the troops march out for the Chatains' inspection, for instance. When the leading ranks went out of view, they ran around the palace compound and joined the ranks marching into view," the Counselor said wryly. "It went on and on."

"We tripled our numbers doing that," Ares pointed out.

"And paying the laborers a royal a day?" the Counselor scoffed. "Magnus did not believe that for a moment."

"Oh, no? You didn't see the look on his face," Ares snorted. "And what was your point in making him think that the abbey is an outpost? He's liable to attack it, now," he said angrily.

"My lord," Nicole said mildly, placing a calming hand on her husband's chest.

"There, Lady. He's still annoyed that I persuaded you to our cause," the Counselor said in amusement.

"You overrode my order and brought her back against her will!" Ares said hotly.

"No, darling, I came back willingly. I did not want to leave," she protested gently. "My lord?" she murmured, reaching her lips to his, and he melted.

"Thank you, Lady. I despaired of my life frequently during your absence," the Counselor said dryly.

"I threatened you only once a day," Ares muttered. "And it had better be worthwhile."

"Well, Lady? What information do you have for us?" Carmine asked, folding his jeweled hands.

"Oh, a great deal!" she exclaimed. She then remembered,

"What about the diplomats you sent? Did they return safely?"

"Yes, Lady, but they saw practically nothing, as they were blindfolded upon entering the city. Once they had witnessed the wedding, they were practically driven out again," the Counselor replied. "Apparently, Ossian's fear of spies is what prevented you from bringing so much as a maid. So we are most anxious to receive your observations."

"Well," Nicole began importantly, "When you first enter the city by the main road—"

"Wait," the Counselor said. "To my chambers, please, Lady. Commander, would you care to join us?" Ares just looked at him darkly, with his arm firmly around his wife.

In the Counselor's chambers, they sat with an amanuensis to take notes on Nicole's intelligence. But as she had memorized everything while pacing, she paced now to retrieve the information: "The city gate is secured by an iron bar three handwidths, and a portcullis comes down on the inside. There is a second wall around the palace, gained by a drawbridge over a moat—"

"We know this," Ares observed, as the amanuensis scribbled furiously to keep up.

"Let her continue, Commander," Carmine chided.

Nicole resumed pacing. "The main street to the palace is faced by tall houses with arrow loops in the upper levels, and ditches along the sides of the street—"

"We know all this," Ares said, standing. Entranced by the swinging of her skirts back and forth in front of him, he put his arms around her from behind and brushed the hair from her neck with his lips. The amanuensis watched intently.

"To your notes," the Counselor instructed, and he ducked his head to continue writing. "Commander, can you possibly allow her to continue?"

With Ares kissing her neck, Nicole closed her eyes. "The soldiers wear hauberks of steel, though some looked rusty. They carry axes as sidearms—"

"—Paired with spears. We know, we know," he breathed into her neck. Caressing his arms, Nicole stopped talking.

Carmine sighed. "Perhaps we should continue this later."

"That is an excellent plan," Ares said, taking Nicole's hand with a proprietary look in his eyes. They made haste downstairs to his quarters, where Ares bolted the door before lying across her on the straw bed. He was hampered in getting beneath her skirts, as he did not want to get up to let her undress.

"Oh! I forgot! And the wheat fields were all blackened, and smelly—"

"The wheat smut. We know," he groaned. "That's why we import wheat only from Calle Valley."

"But they got the bad wheat from Calle Valley," she said.

At that, he lifted up. "What?"

"We complained about the brown bread, and the maid said that Calle Valley had sold them bad wheat," she said.

He froze for an instant, then jumped up and threw back the door bolt. Towing her by her hand, he told the sentry outside, "Summon the Counselor to the foyer." The sentry departed at a run, and Ares collared another man. "Have Dirk and—um, Alphonso saddled up with three days' provision out front." That servant scurried off in another direction.

They entered the foyer, where Ares looked pensively toward the front doors. By this time the Counselor was coming down the stairs with the sentry. "Well, did you pry something useful out of her, Commander?" he asked lightly, then paused at Ares' face.

"Tell him," Ares nodded at her.

Nicole faltered, "We—the Chataine and I complained about the brown bread they served us, and the maid said that their wheat harvest failed because Calle Valley had sold them bad grain."

The Counselor's eyes widened. "We must scout the Valley at once."

"Dirk and Alphonso have been summoned," Ares said tensely.

"We must ban all imports of wheat, and inspect grain before spring plantings. What fortuitous timing! The fields are being broken up for planting this very week!" the Counselor said.

"Meaning that we cannot afford to wait for the scouts' report to halt planting. Can we subsidize the farmers who have infected grain?" Ares asked.

"We may have to, if we want bread," the Counselor replied. "Otherwise, it could presage a widespread famine."

Within an hour inspectors were dispatched to all areas of Lystra to check the wheat prior to planting. Dirk and Alphonso were sent off to Calle Valley to see the condition of their winter crops. And the Counselor had a royal proclamation drawn up stating that any infected wheat was to be turned over to the palace for burning. Compensation would be made on a first-come, first-served basis, as stores allowed.

Nicole watched the Counselor take the signet ring he wore on a heavy chain around his neck, under his surcoat, and press it in the hot wax to leave the Surchatain's mark of authority on the proclamation. "Why can you not ever use yours?" he murmured.

"Too much trouble to get it out," Ares replied. After a moment she realized they must be referring to the signet Ares kept hidden away. "You know what else this means," Ares said. "If the Scyllan winter wheat has failed, and Calle Valley's has failed, then Ossian will have nothing stored up to feed his soldiers during a spring campaign. He would have to wait until summer—"

"And by then, they could have famine in Eurus. They will certainly be in no condition to wage a campaign against anyone," the Counselor finished.

"It may already be bad. Renée said the food was poor. What they fed me was certainly miserable. If the royalty are eating poorly, what are the commoners eating?" Nicole wondered. One good thing about living in the shadow of the capricious Sea, she realized, was its generous provenance.

Ares glanced with some self-reproach at his wife. "You did well, my precious spy."

Carmine seconded, "Well done, Lady Nicole. Now, did you give the Commander all of the information you gathered?"

"No," Nicole said, drawing up. Ares slumped only slightly, and they returned to his quarters where he sat and listened patiently as she recited everything she knew about Eurus. It was rather torturous in more ways than one, for she still had to pace, and would not be confined to his arms while she talked.

When she had finished her recitation, he nodded thought-fully, allowing a minute of silence before he stood to take her in his arms. But now she wanted to know, "How is Henry?"

Ares blinked. "I haven't taken you to Henry yet, have I? Ah, then I am a beast," he confessed. He paused, and Nicole sighed for Renée.

He took her upstairs to the Surchatain's wing, nodding to the sentries. Then he opened the first door in the corridor. "Chatain?" He entered the chambers with Nicole behind him.

Henry was sitting at the window playing with toy soldiers, making them line up and march against each other. "Come, Ares, you be the enemy," Henry said, eyes on his toys.

"Not today. Today I shall be the hero, for I brought someone to see you," Ares said.

Henry looked up, and his face brightened. "Nicole! Ares, you got her back!" Nicole hurried to the window seat to embrace him. "Oh, Nicole, I'm so glad you're back. Ares was no fun at all while you were gone."

Nicole rocked him lovingly. "I am so glad to be back. I missed you and Ares so much." Ares watched them with a vague half-smile.

Henry nestled comfortably in her arms, then asked, "When will Sister be back?"

She looked up in concern to Ares, who knelt beside the window seat. "Chatain, we talked about this. Your sister is married to the Chatain Magnus. She may come back to visit us, we hope, but she won't be back to stay."

"You brought Nicole back," Henry said from her arms. "You can bring Sister back."

Ares looked disconcerted. Much as he always tried to be honest with Henry, he did not care to tell him this was something he could not do.

Evening came early, as clouds gathered for a springtime thunderstorm. While Ares rocked gently, Nicole closed her eyes, listening to the rain patter on the portico outside his chamber window. "This is wonderful, to be back with you," she sighed.

"Oh, yes," he whispered into her neck. "Yes, yes. . . ."

"I love the rain," she murmured, and at that, he started laughing. She opened her eyes indignantly. "What?"

"Forgive me, love. When you said that, I thought of the messengers who are cursing my name right now for having sent them out on a rainy night," he admitted.

"Since you are so preoccupied, perhaps we should continue this later," she said archly, attempting to push him away.

"I wish to continue now," he said, gripping her. She made as if to wriggle away from him, but he held her down. The more she struggled the more it aroused him, so that in a moment they were covered in sweat again.

The bell tolled, and they paused to listen, panting. "Seven," she relaxed, searching out his mouth with hers. "We've plenty of time—" At that they looked at each other, and in wordless mutual consent, got out of bed.

As Ares lazily donned his dress blacks, Nicole looked around forlornly. She had no more enthusiasm for wearing her father's dresses at the Surchatain's table, and had already worn the gown Renée had given her twice. Almost without realizing what she was doing, she prayed inwardly, *Lord God, I wish I had some better dresses to look nice for my husband.*

Ashamed to be praying over something so vain and trivial, she said out loud, "The Chataine has so many dresses left upstairs. I wish I could borrow something of hers to wear." Ares glanced at her and walked out.

Somewhat hurt, she put on the blue dress her father had made. She was arranging her hair when Ares opened the door and leaned his head in. "The Surchataine says you may help yourself to whatever you like of the Chataine's. Come pick something for tonight."

Nicole leaped up with a little cry and hugged his neck tightly. "I love you!"

"You said that once today, already," he noted in wonder. "But—come. I don't wish to be buttoning you at the table."

They went upstairs, where Nicole opened the door of the Chataine's apartments and went straight to the wardrobe. Running a hand over the dresses in excitement, she asked, "Which do you like?"

"Any. All of them. I don't care," he said from the doorway.

She turned. "Ares, you can come in! Renée's not here!"

"I know," he said. "But I just—can't." The longstanding inhibition was too strong. "Pick one."

She selected the green one, with its matching headpiece and shoes, because it brought out the red glints in her hair. These she carried out, kissing him at the door for good measure. "Oh, the joy of an affectionate wife," he murmured.

"That's bribery, my lord. Help me with this, please," she said, transferring the unwieldy burden of damask and taffeta to his arms. That is how the Commander of Lystra's army was seen to be carrying a formal gown downstairs like a chambermaid.

They appeared in the anteroom at the appropriate time, and Georges welcomed her warmly. He even commented on their immaculate appearance: "What a splendid couple you make!"

"Georges, you may accuse me of being anything but splendid," Ares said dryly.

"Oh, but you are, my lord," Nicole said, turning such lascivious eyes on his body that his breathing quickened. Georges motioned them to the doorway, and they entered with her hand atop his, all proper and decorous.

They greeted the table, and Thom kissed her hand warmly. "Welcome home, Lady Nicole."

"It is wonderful to be home. Thank you, Second Thom." She was glowing as she bowed to the Counselor, who nodded with a private wink.

Henry came to the table by leaping on Ares' back, as usual, but while there, he leaned over to Nicole puckered for a kiss. (After seeing them do it so much, he desired to try it.) She bestowed a generous one on him, so that Ares attempted to turn around: "Excuse me, but are you kissing behind my back?"

"Yes!" Henry shouted, and the table stifled their laughter as Georges announced, "Surchatain Cedric and Surchataine Elise."

After the formalities of bowing and being seated (with Henry's taking Renée's place at the table), Elise nodded to Nicole. "The gown looks lovely on you, dear."

"Thank you so much for allowing me to borrow it, Surchataine," Nicole said humbly. Cedric glanced at her with a slight frown, and Nicole felt as if she had said something wrong. Ares noticed it, too, and glanced at him.

When the dinner of cod, stewed pears, pea pods, and roast pheasant was served, Nicole sighed, "You can't imagine what a delight it is to sit down to a feast such as this."

"What did you eat at Eurus, dear?" the Counselor asked.

Nicole began, "Oh! Coarse barley bread—I could hardly choke it down—and bitter beer, or wine thick with dregs, and there were no servants at the table, but everyone just grabbed food by the handfuls, so that—"

"Enough! You shall not speak ill of Surchatain Ossian's hospitality," Cedric said irritably.

Nicole went white, whispering, "Forgive me, High Lord."

Ares looked at Cedric with something dangerous, unprecedented, in his face. The Counselor said hastily, "Let your rebuke fall on me, High Lord, for asking the question. We were earlier discussing the impact of the wheat smut on the provisions at Eurus, which is of great interest to us, considering the Chataine's presence there."

"Bah," Cedric waved it off in distinct ill humor.

No one spoke much after that, and Nicole could barely lift her head for the shame still weighing on her. Ares did not look at her, or at anyone, for that matter. The Counselor regarded the mask of his face from time to time, and Ares looked back blankly.

After dinner, Nicole went straight to Ares' quarters to change back into the blue dress. "I need to return the gown at once, before it gets soiled," she explained to him. "It may be best not to borrow another."

"You certainly shall. Surchataine Elise gave you leave," Ares said testily.

"But, the Surchatain—"

"I went to him first to ask, and he said, 'Don't bother me with such trifles.' Since he so clearly did not care, he had no business upbraiding you about anything," Ares said, growing more heated by the moment.

"Peace, my lord," she murmured, snuggling him, which never failed to calm him. He kissed her, and carried the gown back upstairs for her, but also insisted that she select a gown for tomorrow while she was there.

That evening, as they lay in bed, the rain beat furiously on the portico and the thunder rocked the skies. Nicole was exhausted from the long, eventful day, but Ares seemed restless. He pressed tightly against her one minute, then flopped on his back the next. She turned on her side away from him and fell right asleep.

Some time deep in the night, a loud thunderclap woke her. She started up, then reached beside her, where the bed was empty. Ares was not in bed, nor even in the room. She sat there for a moment, then lay back down. Confident that he would return, she went back to sleep. Upon waking some time later, she reached over to feel his chest expand and contract rhythmically. Sighing, she dropped off to sleep until morning.

Today, being the first of May, was May Day, celebrated with games and booths and all kinds of flirtatious behavior on the palace grounds. The whole town was invited to attend, and regular duties were suspended for most of the palace servants. The soldiers—clean, shaved, and dressed in brilliant jerkins emblazoned with Cedric's crest—demonstrated their prowess at a number of athletic endeavors, including archery, pugiling, and horsemanship, while pretty girls watched appreciatively.

Ares was out early, supervising the setting up of the games, so Nicole had to summon a maid to help her put on the rose-colored gown she had selected from the Chataine's wardrobe yesterday. (As it was an old gown that Renée clearly disdained, Nicole hoped that the Surchatain would not recognize it.)

Then she went out to the grounds to see all the entertainments: the jugglers, and the children dancing around the May pole, and the musicians and merchants—it was like a miniature fair! And she wished with all her heart that Renée were here to enjoy it with her.

Spotting Ares in the midst of a dispute between two merchants and a fire-swallower over certain prime space on the grounds, she edged forward to listen to him calmly and authoritatively settle the matter, directing that one here and the other one there and the fire-swallower he was going to personally dismember should he set anything ablaze. That was not likely, as the grounds were still wet from the drenching last night, but the sun was out in full glory today. Nicole carefully held her skirts out of the mud.

Ares turned and saw her, and it warmed her to see that look of softness that came over him whenever she caught him unaware. He approached to kiss her hands. "My love, where is your pouch?"

Immediately upon her questioning look, he added, "Which I forgot to tell you to bring. I left a pouch of silver pieces on the table in my quarters. Use it to buy what you like from the booths, and if that is not enough, I will produce more."

"Thank you, my lord," she grinned in delight, turning, but he caught her arm. "Nicole." She turned back, and he cautioned, "Do not allow Henry to wheedle you into buying candy for him. He makes himself sick on it, then comes to me and I am up half the night with him."

She curtsied, laughing, "Yes, my lord." Hurrying to his quarters, she found the small pouch heavy with silver pieces, then took it straightway to buy candy for herself.

Henry met her, complaining of Ares' neglect, so she walked with him from booth to booth to see what was interesting. She soon discovered that Henry's pouch carried a number of gold royals mixed in with silver pieces, so she carefully attended his transactions with merchants to make sure they did not accept a royal when a piece was due.

Hours later, laden with flags and toys, Henry stopped to watch the wrestling. Two shirtless men in breeches grappled with each other in the muddy ring until one gained the advantage, almost suffocating his opponent, and was declared the winner. He then received a medallion on a ribbon as his prize. In great excitement, Henry beat on a nearby soldier's leg: "Go get Ares!"

Moments later, the Commander appeared. He smiled wryly at Nicole before bowing to the Chatain. "You summoned me?"

"Ares, I want you to wrestle!" Henry exclaimed, pointing to a waiting opponent.

Ares, in his dress blacks, sighed. Since a direct refusal was likely to be counterproductive, he hedged, "As you wish, Chatain. But I can't do that and ride Karst as well. So which would you rather?"

"Karst! Ride Karst!" Henry cried, jumping up and down.

"When the equestrian events begin, Chatain," Ares said, casting a glance at Nicole, and she knew something special was in the works. Lystran soldiers were proud of their horsemanship, continuing in the tradition set by Surchatain Roman.

As it happened, the Chatain desired the equestrian events to begin without delay, so they did. Cedric and Elise sat in elevated stands overlooking a large field spread with hay (to give the horses traction in the mud). When Henry brought Nicole to join them, she bowed tentatively. Elise nodded; Cedric looked away. Spectators hastened to line the field, leaving a clear path to the stables.

The first event was the sled pull, in which the contestants' horses were harnessed to sleds loaded down with iron. The animal that could pull this burden the length of the course in the least time won a medallion for its owner. Watching the great beasts groan for the sake of a coin on a ribbon was not very entertaining to Nicole, but the spectators appreciated it. Ares did not participate in this.

The next event was the barrel race, in which two empty barrels were rolled out and set upright across from each other at one end of the field. At a signal, two riders dug in their heels, taking off from the starting line and racing toward the barrels. Each had to round his barrel from the outside in, which meant that if the horses were well matched, they might meet coming around the barrels to the inside. Collisions (though rare) were encouraged by the spectators, and winning required a fast, fearless horse. Contestants were weeded out through ten matches, until the winner received a medallion and cheers. Ares did not participate in this, either.

The third and final event was showmanship, and even merchants left their booths to watch this. Contestants rode out singly or in pairs to demonstrate their style and finesse. Nicole watched the prancing animals in delight. They reared and pawed the air; they went down on their knees, and one even rolled over like a dog (once the rider had dismounted). Nicole and Henry applauded, laughing.

Then Ares appeared on a white-gray stallion, and Henry jumped up, shouting, "Karst! Karst! Karst!" Other spectators picked up the chant like a drumbeat, and Nicole watched, entranced.

The horse was not large, as horses go, but his body was deep and broad, with a regal, arched neck. He seemed to play to the crowd, stepping high and flaring his tail. Ares trotted him around the field, showing off his unique gait. Then he wheeled and danced—the horse began dancing!—and the spectators cheered.

The horse snorted and turned as if to say, "Be quiet. You've seen nothing, yet," then began a sideways, diagonal trot from one end of the field to the other. Nicole's mouth dropped open. She had never seen a horse do that before.

Karst reared up, vertical to the ground. Ares perched easily on this tentative seat. Then the horse began hopping like a rabbit—once, twice, thrice, he hopped on his hind legs while his forelegs pawed the air. Nicole gasped and the audience cheered and clapped.

But now for the finale: Ares loped Karst around the field once in preparation, then pulled up in a stop. From a standing position, Karst reared and kicked out his back legs at the same time so that he was completely airborne, horizontal to the ground. In case anyone missed it, or did not believe it, Karst did it again. Finally, Ares rode him to the royal stands, where the great animal bowed his head to his foreleg as the people roared.

Henry was jumping up and down clapping, but Nicole sat in awe. Without waiting for the official judgment, Henry grabbed the showmanship medallion and leaned forward precariously to give it to Ares. He, in turn, made Karst rear up, extending the medallion to his wife. Nicole leaned over the railing to take it.

Karst wheeled on a victory circuit around the field, Ares waving to the crowd, and Elise murmured, "What a regal animal."

Yes, the animal was certainly regal, Nicole thought, but, he did what he was taught. It took a regal mind to train an animal to perform royally. Watching Ares at that moment, Nicole began to notice how—regal he was. How beautiful his horsemanship, how gracious his demeanor, how unflagging his loyalty. He behaved like royalty.

Karst completed his circuit back to the stands. "Let me ride with you, Ares!" Henry cried, trying to climb over the railing, but Ares did not respond. He was studying Nicole, trying to interpret the pensive look on her face.

A mounted sentry approached at a fast lope. "Surchatain!" he called, and everyone on the stands looked. Reining up before the stands, he gulped and said, "Surchatain, a messenger from Eurus has arrived with armed guards, demanding to speak with you personally."

"Give me your horse," Cedric said, leaving the stands.

As Ares reined around to accompany him, Nicole dropped the medallion and began climbing over the railing, skirts and all, to sit behind him on Karst. "No, Lady!" Ares said sharply, but he could not pull away or she would fall.

"My darling," she whispered in his ear from behind, "this is about the Chataine. You must let me hear."

He wrestled with the matter while Cedric mounted, but she wasn't about to get down. "I will let you off at the palace. Watch from the window. You must not be seen," he uttered.

"Yes, my lord," she said, squeezing his waist. He lifted her hand to kiss it, and then Karst burst into motion.

Clinging to Ares for dear life, she endured the bucking for the short distance to the rear portico door, near his chambers. He swept her down on one arm, then chased the Surchatain's mount around the side grounds. Once steady on her feet, she ran through the palace to the front foyer. Here, she climbed the narrow stone steps to the upper window, where the Counselor already stood.

He put an arm around her, and they watched the Surchatain and the Commander gallop into the courtyard and rein up before the Scyllan party—the messenger and six soldiers. "I am Surchatain Cedric. What say you?" His voice was audible throughout the courtyard.

The messenger matched his tone and volume: "I bear this message from Surchatain Ossian of Scylla: You have foisted used goods upon the Chatain Magnus, which he declines to keep. You may have your daughter back in exchange for the Lady Nicole. If you choose not to exchange, you may look for your daughter in the slave markets of Corona."

II

The slave markets of Corona—where the dregs of humanity, the barely human, trafficked in the bodies and souls of the defenseless. Captured soldiers fell on their swords rather than be taken there, and debtor parents shipped their children with strangers over the Sea to keep them out of the slavers' hands. For the Chataine, the child of privilege, to be enslaved was—unthinkable.

"It is as I feared," the Counselor said. "They had no intention of an alliance. But the insult to Tancred's pride must be answered." He turned to Nicole, weak-kneed beside him. "Can you be strong and extremely courageous for the sake of your sister, dear lady?"

"Yes," Nicole whispered.

"Then the time to be so has come." He nodded down to where Cedric was ordering a servant, "Bring Nicole."

The servant ran through the foyer looking for her; Ares, following, looked up whence she was descending. He met her at the bottom of the steps.

Placing a hand behind her head, he pressed his lips to her ear to whisper one sentence. Then other servants came in to take her, but Ares held up a prohibitive hand. "I will escort the lady out." His steely tone caused them to drop back a step.

Nicole exited on Ares' arm as if she were being presented at court. "Where is the exchange to take place?" he asked.

The messenger replied, "The Chataine is waiting at the halfway mark between here and Eurus. She will be sold to slavers this very evening unless the Lady Nicole arrives before sundown." They had ample time, as it was just now noon.

As Cedric had dismounted, Ares boosted Nicole into the messenger's saddle. Then he turned to mount Karst, and Cedric said, "No, Ares. Not you. Send another to make the exchange."

Ares turned in astonishment. "You doubt my loyalty?" he asked. Cedric looked uncomfortable. "You doubt that I will return the Chataine? I, who served under your father before you?" It was a shockingly bold answer to the Surchatain, whose response was even more telling: he turned and reentered the palace. Ares mounted Karst, who danced in place. The Scyllan messenger nodded, and the party set out.

They went at a fast lope, the hoofbeats ringing in Nicole's ears. Her skirts were wide enough to cover at least her knees while she rode, and the petticoats provided padding on the saddle. As before, she did not attempt to rein the horse at all, but let it follow the others. She looked across to Ares on Karst beside her, and saw the splendid animal snort with impatience to perform the impossible.

She tried not to think of where they were headed; she tried not to think at all, but listened to the grunts of the horses, the slapping of the leather, the drumming of the hooves. Karst tried to nose his way to the front, but Ares kept him abreast of Nicole's brown gelding. Karst shook his mane in displeasure, lifting his knees high.

They passed Willowring Lake, and she looked aside to the field of jonquils that she could not see. Clattering over the bridge into Scyllan territory, she thought of Renée in her humiliation, and she bowed her head over the saddlehorn.

They rode past the wheat fields blackened with smut, and she wondered what they would feed her in Eurus. Then she wondered how long they would feed her there. She looked to Ares riding beside her, and comforted herself with the words he had whispered in her ear.

As they continued northward in the afternoon, Nicole thought of Tancred's gifts she had left in the wardrobe, and ironically debated whether she could still have them. She really wanted the book. She tried to distract herself with the notion that he must love her inordinately to demand such an exchange, but could not make herself believe it. The Counselor was correct: this was a matter of pride, not affection, and Ossian's sons would derive great satisfaction from not only humiliating the Chataine of Lystra, but doing whatever they wished with the Commander's wife. Again, she sought comfort from Ares' whisper.

The sun descended, and she rode with no resistance to the horse's bobbing stride. But when they spotted the soldiers at the halfway point ahead, and the exchange became an imminent reality, she cried out in her heart to God. In reply, she heard Ares' whisper echo in her mind.

The arriving party reined up to the score of Scyllan soldiers with their captive. Ares called, "Chataine, are you well?" She was bent double over the saddle of her horse, weeping, but she managed to nod.

Ares turned to Nicole, his face expressionless, as he had already told her what she needed to hear. Quaking in the saddle, she took up the reins and kicked lightly with her heels. The gelding trotted forward until a Scyllan soldier reached out and took the bridle. He slapped the haunches of Renée's horse, causing it to bolt forward toward Ares. He caught the reins, drawing them over the horse's head as he spoke to her. She leaned from her saddle to embrace him tightly around the neck. He looked back at Nicole, and, holding both sets of reins, turned back toward Westford at a gallop.

The Scyllan soldiers watched until they were out of sight, then closed ranks around Nicole. And for the remainder of the trip to Eurus, Ares' whisper repeated itself in her mind like a lifeline of words. For this is what he had said: *"Wherever they put you, if you can reach a window, hang something out of it."*

The sun continued its descent; the hoofbeats sounded on. What few travelers they met coming or going leaped off the road to get out of the way, and more than one cart was overturned. Nicole, completely encased in this moving fortress, did not see all this, nor did she want to. She kept her head down, watching the horse's shoulder muscles flex and extend, flex and extend.

Twilight fell, and then it was dark. By the time they reached the gates of the palace at Eurus, Nicole was in a helpless stupor. Torchlight punctuated the darkness. She could hardly stand when they took her off the horse, and raised her head only when she heard Tancred speaking: "Greetings, Lady Nicole! What a pleasant surprise." She had no ability to respond. "So, the trench digger gave you up. Does he think to come rescue you? Oh, I wish he would try. We have trenches that need digging here, too."

He watched while her head sank down again, and chestnut hair fell over her shoulder. It was no fun bantering with someone too bruised to respond. "Bring her," he nodded, and a soldier led her stumbling after him. He who obeyed the orders assisted her sympathetically, seeing no reason to be brutal.

She was taken to Tancred's apartments, back to his bed-chamber. "Now, Lady," he murmured, attempting to embrace her, but Nicole turned her face and shoved him away. "You are mine now! Do you understand?" he shouted, shaking her. She did not respond. Then he said haughtily, "The dress is offensive to me. Remove it."

The tears poured down her face as she reached for the inaccessible row of buttons down the back. In a fit of pique, he seized the back of the gown and ripped out the whole row of buttons in one yank. The gown fell from her shoulders, and she stood weeping in linen bodice and bloomers.

Tancred paused, confounded at the sight. He had envisioned a dramatic scene of resistance and seduction, but this was just pathetic. Not depraved enough to take her by force, but not knowing how to redirect his fantasy, he went to the door and ordered the guard, "Take her to the tower."

The soldier, the same who had brought her in, entered and paused with embarrassment at her state. He glanced at Tancred, obviously wondering at this treatment of the woman he had presented to his parents as his betrothed. Perhaps shamed that the lowly soldier was demonstrating himself to be more honorable than the Chatain, Tancred gestured almost apologetically. "You will stay there the night, then we will deal with you in the morning."

So the soldier escorted her out through blessedly deserted corridors to a corner tower at the rear of the palace. With a torch in one hand and her arm in the other, he walked her up many narrow, winding steps. At the very top, he opened a door into a small, dank room. Nicole felt straw on the floor, but it was too dark to see anything beyond the circle of torchlight. He closed and barred the door behind her, sealing out the light, and she did not see his anxious expression as he withdrew.

She sank down where she was. With head bobbing feebly, she peered into the darkness for a window. She knew there must be one, because she felt a cold draft. She put her hands out to feel the wooden floor beneath the straw, and a stone fireplace in a portion of the curved wall. The embers were still warm. She pulled herself closer to the embers, as she was shivering with the cold. A moment later she got up to feel all around the circular room, as high as she could reach. She stumbled over a pallet, but there was no window. In despair, she sank down beside the fireplace again.

In a little while, she heard footsteps ascending, and saw a

feeble light through a crack of the door. It opened to the soldier, who brought in an armload of wood to rekindle the fire. Behind him, a maid set a trencher of brown bread and cup of water on the floor.

With the fire rekindled, the soldier said, "Watch the fire with care; the place is a tinder box." Then he and the maid left, taking their candle and barring the door on the outside.

First, Nicole drank the water and ate the bread. It had the consistency of brick, but she needed the nourishment. Then, by the firelight, she stood to look around the small circular room. There was a straw pallet and a blanket, and six feet above her head was a small barred window.

Nicole picked up the blanket, tied the cup in the corner to weight it, then threw it up at the window. It took four or five tries before the cup cleared the bars, but she finally succeeded in getting it to hang on the outside.

Then she pulled the pallet upright to rest against the wall and tied the lower corner of the blanket through a hole in the pallet. She tentatively let go to see if everything stayed in place. It did, and she sank beside the pallet to wait.

She stayed awake a long time, a very long time. Every time she started to nod off, she thought she heard something outside. But no one was there. The fire died down, the room grew cold, and Nicole sank into a deep, shivering sleep.

She did not hear the clunk of metal hitting the bars and falling away, twice. The third time, a small grappling hook landed perfectly between the bars and caught on the stone sill, where it was drawn tight. She did not hear the scrabbling on the wall outside that grew louder and louder. She did not see the hands grabbing the bars. "Nicole! Are you in there?" The hoarse whisper went unheard.

"Nicole! Nicole! Are you there?" Ares' whisper was louder, but he could not see down into the room. Directly below him, Nicole slept.

Finally, he shoved the cup back through the bars. It fell

clattering to the floor, bringing the blanket and pallet down with it. She started awake. "Nicole! Are you there?"

"Ares!" she cried softly, leaping up. "Yes, I am here!"

"Is anyone else there? Or guarding the door?" he asked.

Nicole scrambled on hands and knees to peer under the crack of the door, then returned to the window to report, "No."

"Are you hurt?" he asked.

"No, but I can't reach the window," she whispered.

"Are you chained?" he asked.

"No," she said.

"What is in the room?" he asked.

"Just the pallet, and blanket, and fireplace," she said, looking up to his hands. "But I can't reach the window!"

"Stand back," he said. His hands left the window, and she saw shadows of something else. There was the sound of muffled metal tools banging together, and bits of stone cascaded down the wall. Minutes later, one of the bars was removed and dangled inside the window. "Stand back," he warned, and the bar dropped with a thud to the wooden floor.

The end of a knotted rope was thrust through the opening. "Hold on to this. I will bring you up," he said. Nicole clasped the rope and let him pull her up to the window. She reached through to kiss him. "See if you can squeeze through," he said, all business.

"I am in my underwear, my lord," she murmured.

"Lady, I have seen you naked," he said dryly. "See if you can fit through the bars."

Grasping his shoulder, she pulled herself out to her waist, and gasped when she looked down. The ground was out of sight in the murky darkness. They had to be at least sixty feet up. He was suspended by the knotted rope twined around his legs, freeing his hands to work. The cloth-wrapped tools hung from his belt. "Your hips, now. Hold on to me and make sure you can get through," he urged her.

"Yes, I can," she said, when almost completely out.

"Good. Now ease back and I will let you down again."

"My lord?" she cried softly.

"Listen! When you get down to the floor, scoop out embers from the fireplace. Then quickly get back on the rope and let me pull you out again," he said.

"Yes, my lord," she breathed. Gingerly, she pushed herself backward over the rope, and he let her down again. Using the blanket, she brushed the glowing embers out of the fireplace onto the straw. It smoked for just an instant before bursting into flames. Then she grabbed the rope again, and he pulled her up as the flames consumed the floor beneath her.

She squeezed out through the window with smoke pouring out around her. "Now, hold on to my shoulders and climb onto my back. Wrap your legs around me," he instructed. Nicole did just as he said, clutching his neck. He coughed, then said in a tight voice, "Hold me under the arms —wrap your arms up under my shoulders. Good."

Grasping the rope, he loosed it from around his legs and let himself down bit by bit. Nicole clung tightly to his back, looking down at the ground and then up at the receding window, through which the light of flames was visible. She watched the ground come closer and closer, until she was able to alight from his back. A Scyllan uniform came around the corner at her, and she backed into Ares with a gasp. "Greetings, Lady Nicole," Thom's voice said.

Peering under the chain-mail hood, she saw it was indeed he. "Oh," she breathed out in relief. Ares picked her up to carry her. "I can walk, my lord," she said.

"Not through this, you won't," he replied, as he and Thom began sliding along the palace wall through mud and mire. They waited in the shadows until the cry rose: "Fire! Fire in the tower!" Holding Ares' neck, Nicole looked up at flames shooting out through the high tower window.

When the area was clear, they darted across the open field behind the palace toward the wall. The moment they reached it, Ares shifted her to his back again, then grasped a knotted rope hanging from the top of the wall. Directly above him was another Scyllan uniform, and its wearer was looking down.

Climbing up the knots, Ares brought himself up the rope hand over hand until the sentry leaned down to lift her from his back. She recognized him from his size alone: it was Oswald, and the Scyllan hauberk was too small on him.

"Greetings, Lady," he whispered. She hugged him, forgetting that she was in her underwear. Ares gained the top of the wall with Thom behind him, then they tossed the knotted rope down the outside. By now, the palace tower was completely ablaze, and the drawbridge was lowered for the residents to draw water from the moat to fight the fire. Even at the rear of the palace, they heard the echoed clanging of its opening.

The rescue party debated this opportunity. "It's safer to cross the drawbridge than risk swinging over the moat with her and falling in," Thom argued.

"She'll be noticed, Sir," Oswald pointed out.

"Let's see," suggested Ares, so they skulked along the top of the four-foot-wide wall toward the drawbridge swarming with people. Tom scanned warily for other scouts along the wall, but there were none that had not already been dealt with.

"A cloak," Ares said, looking down.

"That would help, Commander," Oswald agreed, but Ares nodded down. Below, people were pouring in over the drawbridge, armed with anything they had—shovels, blankets, and cloaks—that could smother fire.

"Ah." Oswald took the steps down from the wall on the inside near the drawbridge. He stood against the flow of people to stop one man carrying a cloak. "May I borrow this?" Oswald asked politely. The man shoved it on him, and Oswald brought it back up to the top of the wall, where Ares threw it around Nicole, covering her entirely. With his arm around her, the four of them descended the steps and pushed their way out over the drawbridge, unchallenged.

Once past the thick of the crowd, Ares picked her up again to pass through dark city streets. But with the fringes of sunrise on the horizon, and the alarm continually sounding from the palace, more and more street lamps were lit.

At this point, the four took to the main thoroughfare leading out of town. Anyone seeing the two Scyllan soldiers and the scarred man carrying the blanketed figure assumed they were taking out victims. But anyone who stopped them to ask questions received a brusque, "Stop yapping and go lend a hand!" from the imposing Oswald.

By the time the party arrived at the front gates, they were standing open for another day of business as usual. As it would be more difficult to explain their exit from the city with a victim, Ares hid with Nicole around the corner of a house while Oswald and Thom alerted the soldiers on duty: "All hands are ordered to the palace to put out the fire! Now!" This was immediately accepted, as black smoke filled the air. In moments the gates were deserted for the four to walk through.

They ran alongside the main road, and Ares had barely let out a whistle before a Lystran soldier appeared from the brush riding one horse and leading three others, including Karst. They quickly mounted, Ares placing Nicole in front of him on the hornless saddle with her legs draped to one side.

"Lash her to me," he said, and the fourth man brought out rope. With her still wrapped up in the cloak, he wound the rope around her and Ares, leaving his arms free, then he tied it off and Ares took up the reins around her, ordering, "Ride!" Nicole looked back at the city over his shoulder, where flames could be seen reaching to the sky. Then she gripped his coarse brown shirt as Karst bounded forward.

Ironically, the ride back was the worst part of the whole venture. Ares, who had ridden with Nicole to the halfway point yesterday, ridden back with the Chataine, and spent all night riding to Eurus after sleeping poorly the night before, was especially taxed on the return. One or the other of the men offered to carry her, but he merely shook his head. Meanwhile, they galloped on, mile after weary mile.

Despite the cloak, the ropes cut into her ribs and her shoulder, and she had to hold on to Ares anyway to keep from sliding out from under them. She felt the bounding of the great animal would surely dislocate her bones. Ares' head nodded from time to time, and the reins would begin to slide through his hands, then he would start awake and tighten his grip on her. But Karst never faltered.

When they were about two-thirds of the way along, Ares finally called a halt to rest. "One hour," he groaned, "no more. Thom, keep watch. . . ." Then he fell onto his back with Nicole still tied to him, and he was asleep. Nicole nestled down into his chest to sleep herself.

Some time later, Thom woke them. Ares blinked blearily, staggering to his feet, and Oswald helped him remount with her. As the afternoon waned into twilight, they pushed on. Once they got going again, Ares woke up some. He nuzzled her with his bearded cheek, and she did not mind that it scratched fiercely.

Night approached, lending her lights to illumine the road. Seeing the lights in the towers of Westford caused them to urge the horses on, and Nicole twisted in the ropes to sit up straighter. When Thom whistled and waved to the lookouts, the responding cheers were quite audible.

Then it was over the bridge and through the open gates into the cobbled courtyard. Hands rose to untie the ropes and let her down, and scores more slapped the backs of the returning rescue party. Ares was almost knocked off his feet.

With Nicole clutching the cloak tightly around herself, they entered the palace, and the Counselor came hurrying to greet them. "Commander, you're a bloodhound! Ah, Lady, how light it makes my heart to see you safe." He kissed her cheek, but seeing her dishabille, kept his hands to himself.

"Is the Chataine all right?" she asked feebly.

"She seemed well when the Commander brought her home last night, but has been in her apartments all day, and no one has seen her. She declined my request for an interview."

"She's coming to dinner, surely," Nicole said. "Unless dinner is over?" She was ravenous.

"You probably have just enough time to dress, Lady," he said, and the Commander nodded tiredly.

They went straight to his quarters to wash faces and hands as a servant rekindled the fire. While Ares doggedly put on his dress blacks, pausing over which arm went in which sleeve, Nicole sank before her trunk. She pulled out a dress her father made that she had not worn yet—it was an off-the-shoulder meadow-green gown with silk insets and taffeta petticoats. She kicked off the shredded rose slippers and put on a green silk pair. Then she brushed out her hair and fastened it with a clip trailing green ribbons.

Ares opened the door as the bell began to toll, and they arrived at the anteroom before the eighth strike had sounded. When Georges expressed delight at their appearance, they could do hardly more than blink at him. But when it was time to enter, she placed her hand atop Ares' and he escorted her in.

In the brighter light of the banquet hall, Ares looked at her. "After all that, you look as fresh as a morning glory."

"Thank you, my lord," she murmured, inclining her head. But she almost fell over when she tried to curtsy to the Counselor and the Chatain.

Henry jumped smack on Ares' back as usual, who staggered and groaned in his depletion. After a few minutes, Henry realized that his playmate was not altogether well, and let Ares hold him quietly as he studied his haggard face.

The ruling couple was announced; the guests bowed, and Ares was slow getting up from his knee. When they were seated, and Nicole saw Henry take Renée's place again, she protested, "Where is the Chataine?"

Cedric glanced at her as the wine was brought. "She has

brought enormous shame on me. I do not wish to see her face again, ever."

Ares opened his mouth but the Counselor intervened, "Ah, Surchatain, it was Magnus who dishonored you, not your daughter. The whole marriage was a ruse to spy us out and learn our weaknesses—once they had accomplished that, they had no more use of her. They had not a shred of evidence that she was 'used goods,'" he said distastefully. "She is the one who has been most injured in this." Cedric looked at him with a black, skeptical face, and Nicole kept very quiet.

"High Lord," Ares said wearily, "we have expended a great deal of effort and placed the Lady Nicole in grave danger to secure the Chataine's release. It would be a great comfort to us to see her at table tonight, where she belongs." His tone was respectful, without any hint that thanks were due.

"Well, it would not comfort me," Cedric said crisply, and the rest of the table just looked at him in his luxurious dress, with his shaved and perfumed face. Neither Ares nor Nicole noticed at this point the rope burns that scored her right shoulder, but they were an eloquent testimony to the sacrifice involved in rescuing the Chataine.

Glaring at his father, Henry demanded, "Bring my sister to the table! I want her here."

Cedric looked at his pursed lips and fiery gray eyes. There may have been some pride in his son's assertiveness, for he shrugged and lifted a finger to a servant. "Summon the Chataine, and give Henry his regular place beside me."

Ares leaned back and looked across at the Counselor, who nodded minutely. This interchange between father and son carried some import that Nicole did not understand at the time.

Moments later, the Chataine Renée entered, head down. The table stood to bow, but Nicole left her chair to embrace her. Renée threw her arms around her, weeping, and continued to weep as she sat at her place. Nicole looked distressed and Cedric looked irritated.

Ares sighed and said, "What I wouldn't give to have a bucket of cold water down my back right now."

Without so much as taking a breath, Renée started laughing instead, and the whole table laughed in relief. Then she murmured, "You saved my life."

"You are welcome, Chataine," he replied.

After one sip of wine, Ares had to prop his head up on his hand to stay upright. He ate the first course of smoked hake, but just stared at the heavy food following. In the middle of dinner, Henry left his chair to crawl into Ares' lap, who allowed him. Henry studied his watering eyes and asked, "Are you sick?"

"I am very tired, Chatain," Ares admitted.

"Do you want to eat, or do you want to go to bed?"

"I would rather go to bed, Chatain," Ares said.

"Then you can go," Henry said, climbing down.

"Thank you, Chatain." Ares glanced at the Surchatain, who did not contradict his son. So Ares got up and placed his linen napkin on the table. "I need Nicole to rest with me."

"She can go, too," Henry decreed. Nicole bent to kiss his cheek, which he gravely permitted. They bowed to the head of the table and departed the hall.

In his chambers, Nicole shucked off the dress and fell across the bed, but he paused at the door to tell the sentry, "Watch carefully who goes in and out this door while I am sleeping. I am going to be unconscious for a long time, but I will kill the next man who tries to take my wife away from me."

12

icole and Ares spent most of the next day in bed, leaving the chambers only to go to dinner. The day following, Nicole went up to Renée's apartments while Ares conferred with the Counselor.

At the Chataine's door, Nicole knocked quietly. "Go away!" Renée shouted.

"Must I, darling?" she asked through the door. In a moment it opened; Renée pulled her in by the hand and shut it again. Then Renée flounced back into the window seat with a goblet of wine. "Are you all right, dear Chataine?" Nicole asked softly.

"I've never imagined such humiliation. *Used goods*," she snorted. "Father won't even speak to me now."

"He shouldn't blame you. The Counselor said from the beginning that the wedding was a ruse. Magnus never had any intention of honoring his commitment to you," Nicole said.

"Yes, Carmine told me," Renée said impatiently. "He assured me over and over that it had nothing to do with any *personal* defect. But in Father's eyes, I am still tainted. He told Carmine that once word of this gets around the Continent, he won't be able to pawn me off on a stablehand." She raised

175

the goblet to her lips, looking out the window with fiercely wounded blue eyes.

"I can't imagine why the Counselor would repeat something like that to you," Nicole murmured, offended.

"He didn't. Eleanor told me," Renée said.

Nicole reached for her hand. "I am glad you are back, by whatever means. But . . . I wish you would tell me. . . . When I asked you if you were happy, before I signed the divorce petition. . . . You weren't, were you?"

"Oh!" Renée stood in a swirl of skirts to pace. "He was horrid! I hated him! I hated his hands, and his lips—he kissed like a leech. Ugh! I could hardly endure lying with him!"

"Why didn't you tell me this when I asked?" Nicole asked, distressed.

Now Renée looked bewildered. "Darling, didn't I say what I was supposed to say? I don't understand." Nicole blinked at her.

There was another knock on her door, and Renée shouted, "Go AWAY!"

Eleanor's voice said, "Chataine, Lord Preus and some other of your favorite merchants are here for a private viewing in the great hall. The Surchataine thought it might cheer you to pick out a few new things."

"Oh! What a splendid idea," Renée said, taking Nicole's hand. "Come. You must see the new summer fashions."

Nicole's heart sank. "I . . . promised Ares I would meet him. You go on." And Renée did, without a backward glance. Nicole continued to sit a moment, staring at the Chataine's bulging wardrobe, and picked herself up with a sigh.

She met up with Ares at the corridor off the foyer, and he put his hand at her back to walk with her to his chambers, smug and self-satisfied: "Well, we received a messenger from Eurus suing for peace. They wish to know on what terms we will leave them alone."

"Do you mean—they're not going to attack?" she asked.

She turned to him as they entered the room and he closed the door.

He laughed, "With half the palace burnt to the ground and famine looming? I think not. The Valley's wheat *is* tainted, by the way. So far, our farmers are reporting an infection rate of about fifty percent in their seed, but since we caught it so early, we will be able to replace the bad seed with that stored in the palace granaries. The farmers receiving it will have to turn over thirty percent of their crops instead of ten, but since they'll *have* crops, they're not complaining.

"And when the wheat seed runs out, the Counselor will start disbursing oats and barley. Regardless of what the rest of the Continent suffers, we won't have famine. We will have to dispatch soldiers to protect harvests, however, I'm sure." He poured a cup of wine for her and himself, unfastening his black jacket as he talked. She sat across from him at the rough-hewn table.

"So what of this peace treaty with Eurus?" she asked.

"Ah. The Counselor is drafting a righteous demand for compensation for the indignities inflicted upon you and the Chataine," Ares said in satisfaction.

"I want our dresses back," she said suddenly. "And the book. I want the book I left in the wardrobe."

"If it wasn't all burned up," he said cautiously.

"Do they know what happened to me?" she asked.

"I don't know what they know," he said, looking away.

"Ares," she said, and he looked at her reluctantly. "I do not want Tancred thinking himself responsible for my death in that tower."

He balked, then relented, "We will inform them that you managed to escape at great peril and by the sole providence of God, for which they had better be grateful, else we would come level what was left of the city." He finished on a considerably less conciliatory note. She nodded, staring at the cup in her hands.

"So . . . how is the Chataine?" he asked.

She sighed. "She seems well enough, though a little depressed. Her father still refuses to speak to her, and her future is rather—cloudy, at this point. To cheer her up, Surchataine Elise has invited some of her favorite merchants to a private showing in the great hall today." Nicole got up abruptly and turned to the window, but the odors from the stables drove her back a step. Still, she stood with her back to him, playing with the cross at her neck.

Ares was silent for several seconds, trying to interpret these actions. He ventured, "You . . . seem upset. Is it about the Chataine?" She shrugged, hanging her head. He came up to hold her from behind. "What is it?"

She caressed his arms. "I feel so selfish and petty," she admitted, staring down at the meadow-green dress she was wearing, again.

"Why?" he breathed into her hair, rocking her.

"I—I want to be presentable at table, but everyone laughs at my father's dresses, so I am reduced to borrowing the Chataine's, which the Surchatain disapproves of, so—so—"

"Why can't you buy your own dresses?" he asked.

She turned anxiously. "My lord, they must cost—six or seven royals a piece!"

"So? How many do you need?" he asked.

"Any would be more than I have now!" she exclaimed. "But—can you—?"

"I can afford to buy you dresses," he said, offended.

"Oh, Ares!" she hugged his neck in gratitude, which he received smugly. "How much can I spend?" she asked shyly.

"Get what you need," he said.

"My lord, please give me a figure, so I will know what is too much," she pleaded.

"I do not know what they cost, and I want you to have what you need," he insisted. "Keep track of the total cost, and I will pay it. They know I am good for it."

"Oh, Ares. Yes, you are good." She kissed his lips, and he stroked her, smiling.

"So when are they to come?" he asked.

"I think they are here already," she admitted.

"Then go on," he smiled. She kissed him again and flew out the door.

The merchants were indeed setting up their displays in the great hall—dresses, jewelry, furnishings, and novelties. Catching sight of Elise and Renée, Nicole approached them shyly and curtsied. "Surchataine, Chataine—may I have your permission to buy something so I will be presentable at table? After you have made selections, of course."

Their mouths dropped open. "Of course, darling!" Renée hugged her. "Oh, isn't this fun? Look here—which do you like?"

Nicole glanced over the gowns in nervous excitement. The near-finished dresses hung on display stands, awaiting selection and alteration to fit the royal wearer. "Oh, you select first, please. I don't want to pick anything you wanted," Nicole urged.

As Renée turned to examine the dresses, Elise sat in a nearby chair. She waved at Nicole, "I am not buying dresses today, dear." Nicole nodded, joining Renée among the dress stands.

While the Chataine selected several to try on, Nicole glanced at the Surchataine making eye contact with the woodworker. Nicole did not know his name, but he was a very handsome man. Elise rose from her seat to look at his carved furniture and candlesticks.

After depleting the available dresses by two-thirds, Renée waved, "The rest are yours, darling." The dressmaker's assistant accompanied the Chataine with her selections to a curtained-off area, where she would try them on.

Clasping her hands, Nicole inspected the leftovers. "They're all so beautiful," she murmured to the tailor at her elbow. Fingering a soft red gown with a train, she asked, "How much is this?"

"That one is a bargain at fifteen royals, my lady," he said, bowing. "You'll notice the beadwork on the neck and sleeves. Cap and shoes are included, of course." The jaunty red cap sported a feather in back.

Fifteen royals! Oh, I wish I knew how much I can spend! She was anxious not to break Ares' back paying for clothes, but she had no idea they would cost that much.

Then she remembered about Lady Rhea. If he had fifty royals that he was willing to throw away on her, then he could spare that amount for dresses. At fifteen royals a piece, she could get—she paused to count on her fingers—three.

"I would like to try this on, please," she said shyly, and he bowed again.

Continuing to look, she stopped in front of a beautiful peach-colored gown with cording on the bodice and cap. She could tell right away why Renée passed it up, as it was rather old-fashioned with a (relatively) high neck and simple lines. But the tailor's daughter discerned fine handiwork, so she asked, "And how much is this one?"

"Ten royals, Lady. It matches your perfect skin very nicely," he said.

"Thank you," she smiled at his salesmanship. But ten royals suited her just fine, as that left her with twenty-five.

At that moment Renée sent back a rejection that Nicole snapped up—it was black, very dramatic, with gold piping. Again, the lines were simple, without the exaggerated bustle and pouf Renée preferred. "And this?" she asked.

He paused. "That one is ten royals, Lady."

"Ten? Are you sure?" she asked. "It's so finely made—surely the gold thread is worth ten royals alone!"

"Ten royals," he said firmly, smiling at her appreciative nature. It was a refreshing change from the usual attitude of his demanding customers.

"If you insist," she sighed, and picked out one more, a dark green gown, for ten. These four she was very happy to try on.

As she was waiting for Renée to finish in the dressing area, Elise looked over. "Did you find something, dear Nicole? Do let me see how they look on you."

"Oh, I'd love to show you, Surchataine!" she breathed. Renée called her into the curtained area to see what she had, and they tried on dresses together, giggling.

Nicole came out first in the red dress, fingering the fitted sleeves. "Oh, darling, you look lovely," Elise said, and the woodworker winked at her. Nicole blushed at the attention. "That dress is my gift to you," Elise announced. "Put it on my bill," she instructed the tailor, who bowed.

"Oh, Surchataine, really? You are so kind!" Nicole cried, sweeping over to hug her. *Fifteen royals back!*

She tried on the peach gown, which clung softly to her curves. She curtsied before the Surchataine in it, who nodded her approval, and Renée eyed it. "You make even that tawdry thing look good. Do you really like that?"

"Yes, I do," Nicole admitted. "It won't need any alterations, and I like the way it feels. Ares will like it."

"Well, then, that is my gift to you. Put it on my bill," she told the tailor, who bowed again.

"You can't be serious!" Nicole exclaimed.

"For once, I am," Renée said, rejecting another dress. Nicole paused, trying to figure out how much she owed now. As far as she could figure, she had four dresses for twenty royals at this point.

She tried on the black dress, but Surchataine Elise was not to be found to view it. However, the tailor's assistant briefly left Renée to admire Nicole in the black, and make suggestions on minor alterations.

By the time Nicole tried on the green dress, the jeweler and rugmaker had joined the tailor and his assistant to watch her twirl exuberantly. "They're so beautiful! I've never had such beautiful things in my life! Oh! That's—" she stopped to catch her breath and count up what she owed on the dresses, with the tailor's help. She had thirty royals left—"I can get another one!"

She was skipping excitedly among the samples when the assistant brought out another dress Renée had rejected. "How does my lady like this?" she asked, spreading it on her arm.

Nicole gasped. It was a splendid creation of silk and lace, which Nicole knew to be rare and very expensive—so expensive that Robert did not even use it in his clothing. "It's exquisite, but I know I cannot afford that," she said levelly.

"Not at fifteen royals?" the tailor asked.

Nicole blinked at him. "You cannot possibly sell something like that for fifteen royals and still feed your family."

He bowed. "For you, it is fifteen royals, if you will tell anyone who asks that your tailor is Preus."

Nicole smiled, biting her lip. "Gladly, Lord Preus." She was ecstatic at having acquired five marvelous gowns for thirty-five royals. And since they required only minor alterations that the assistant could perform on the spot, she could get them today, if she waited.

After changing back into her old dress, she was giddy watching the assistant place the new dresses and accessories on a cotton sheet for wrapping. The red dress needed to be hemmed and the lace dress needed the neckline raised— originally created for Renée, it was much too revealing for the Commander's wife.

While waiting, Nicole began to look at the other wares offered. The merchants were eager to assist her, as Renée was still trying on dresses. Looking at the fine chests and tables, Nicole thought of Ares' chambers. "I shan't ask for a wardrobe, but I will need at least a rod to hang my dresses. How much is the hanging rod?" she turned to ask the woodworker. The other merchants looked around, but he was nowhere nearby.

"Oh. Well." Her eye caught the textiles, and she ran her hand over a large rug, woven in brilliant colors. Didn't Ares' stone floor cry out for a rug? "How much?" she asked.

"Seven royals, my lady," he replied, bowing.

"Taken," she said. She spotted a wool coverlet dyed in blue, the same hue of blue as was in the rug, and she said, "For this?"

"Three royals, lady," he replied.

"Put it with the rug," she instructed. All that amounted to forty-five royals. "I need to know how much the hanging rod is. Where is the woodworker?" she fretted.

Several people were becoming interested in the whereabouts of the woodworker when he abruptly appeared through a side door. "Oh, there you are. How much for the hanging rod?" Nicole asked, pointing.

"For such a lovely, gracious lady, one royal," he said, flushed.

"Really? One?" she asked, wondering why he looked so flustered. "Well, then—the candlesticks?" she asked, indicating a pair of large, ornately carved holders.

"One royal," he shrugged with a helpless laugh. He couldn't help glancing at the Surchataine as she entered through the main door and glided to her seat.

"Taken," Nicole said. She then turned to a wood-framed mirror and paused. Should she make Ares look at his scar so that she could satisfy her vanity? "I am finished buying," she said, turning away. Renée came out from the dressing area in yet another fabulous gown, complaining to Elise about the way it draped.

As Nicole was having the rug, the coverlet, the hanging rod, and the candlesticks placed with the dresses, Ares entered the hall, carrying a leather pouch. He bowed to the Surchataine and the Chataine and surveyed the merchandise in general before coming to Nicole's side. "Have you found anything, Lady?" he asked, catching her by the waist.

"Ares!" She turned and kissed him in joy.

"I take it that means yes," he sighed, reaching down for another kiss.

The assistant brought out the lace dress, which she laid on the pile to wrap in the cotton tarp with the others. "I have bought all this, Lord Commander!" Nicole exclaimed with a sweeping gesture.

Seeing all the merchandise, Ares straightened just slightly and murmured, "I had better go get a larger purse."

"This is my tailor, Lord Preus," she said grandly, and the tailor bowed. "We owe him thirty-five royals."

"Thirty-five," Ares repeated, opening the pouch. He counted out thirty-five royals into Lord Preus' palm, who bowed repeatedly in thanks.

"We owe ten royals to the textile master," Nicole said, and Ares paid him. "I know you don't like luxuries, but will you have the rug for me?" she asked, and he looked at her in some confusion.

"And two royals to the master woodworker," Nicole said. He wiped his sweating palm to receive the two coins Ares gave him. "And that is all," she said proudly.

"That—" Ares looked at the pile again. "Forty-seven royals? All this for forty-seven royals?"

She laughed in delight. "I cheated. One dress was a gift from the Surchataine, one was a gift from the Chataine, and Lord Preus cheated himself on another."

Ares still looked confused, but the jeweler approached, bowing. He observed, "Such a delightful, frugal wife deserves a reward, eh, my Lord Commander? You have not seen my wares."

"I don't need anything else, Ares," she whispered, touching the cross.

But he looked down on her. "Two weeks we've been

married, and you have no ring." He turned to the jeweler. "Show us your rings."

He opened his silk-lined boxes eagerly, and Renée drifted over to look. Ares leaned over the ladies' gold rings. "What do you like, my love?" he asked. She shook her head, afraid to look, afraid of what they cost. He looked at her. "I want you to pick something."

Regarding his scar, she thought how frivolous, how vain it was to decorate herself in the presence of a truly good man who could not buy anything to make himself look nice. She hung her head, ashamed. "I could not ask for anything lovelier than what you already gave me."

He glanced at her necklace, then looked down at the jewel case. "Something like this?" He lifted out a gold filigree ring with tendrils entwining a center gem. Renée pressed forward to look, and even Elise got up to see. Nicole stared in shock as Ares placed it on the ring finger of her left hand. "I say again: I will love you forever."

"I love you, Ares," she whispered, and flung her arms around him to kiss him again.

While she was holding his neck, the jeweler beamed, "That will be—"

"Wait," Ares said. Detaching Nicole, he told her, "The Chataine needs your help."

Renée looked at him blankly, then seemed to wake up. "Oh! Yes. Come, darling." She took Nicole's hand and began dragging her toward the changing area as Ares opened his pouch to pay the jeweler. And he never would tell her how much he paid for the ring.

Soldiers were enlisted to carry the bounty to the Commander's quarters, and a crowd gathered as Nicole directed them on the placement of the rug, the hanging rod, and the candlesticks. The chambermaids took great delight in the transformation of the bare room. As Nicole's dresses were hung on the rod and covered with the cotton sheet, from nowhere other little accessories appeared—candles for the holders, little curtains for the shuttered window, decorative feather pillows on the bed.

Gretchen, with the boldness of an indispensable servant, accosted the Commander: "What're ye thinking, making the lady sleep on a straw mattress! Get her a feather bed as is proper, Commander!"

That was the last straw for the old soldier. "Thank you, Gretchen; I am not sleeping on a feather bed. The dainty pillows here have robbed me of whatever credibility I possessed—thank you all; I thank you all from the bottom of my heart—now get out."

They left laughing and waving aprons at him. As he shut the door, Nicole was happily rearranging this and that. Standing over a bare corner, she said, "We can put the cradle here."

Ares froze where he stood, and she quickly amended, "When it's time. I can't know this early, of course."

He came toward her slowly; speechless, he touched her face, caressed her arm, then lowered his face to her neck, and she felt his trembling. He said, "I never allowed myself to hope." Nicole kissed him, and a thought seemed to cross his mind.

Crude wood shelving against one wall held his clothes; above them, his long sword hung from pegs in the wall. He removed the sword from its place and strapped it around his hip, saying, "I've something to show you."

"What?" she smiled in some concern, wondering why he needed his sword. Eventually, she was to learn that his putting on the sword was a signal that he was about to leave the palace.

He went to the door and ordered Karst and Misty saddled and brought to the courtyard. Taking her hand, he said, "We have to take Henry, too."

She nodded her agreement, and, holding her skirts, trotted

beside him up the great stairway toward the Surchatain's wing.

The moment they came within sight of the wing, Ares stiffened and drew his sword, flinging her behind him. She craned around him to see a lone mercenary lounging at the entry of the corridor. The two Lystran guards who were supposed to be there were nowhere in sight.

Before the mercenary even saw him clearly, Ares had the point of his blade at his throat, whistling to summon other soldiers. As the man flattened himself against the wall in terror, Nicole recognized him. He was in the hire of one of the merchants—she did not know which—who brought their wares to the private showing today.

Surchataine Elise appeared from her chambers and hurried down the corridor. "Peace, Commander, all is well," she said.

"Who is this? Where are my soldiers?" he asked in alarm.

"He is here at my bidding, as I sent the two on an errand," the Surchataine explained. Turning to the petrified man, she said, "Go down and pack up the merchandise I ordered. I will send my maids for it." He looked confused but totally disinclined to question anything she said. Sliding out cautiously from behind the point of Ares' blade, he ran downstairs.

Disturbed, Ares sheathed his sword. "Surchataine, if you employ the sentries on errands, they are to replace themselves. They know that the corridor must always be guarded." To the soldiers who came running in response to his whistle, Ares began, "I want to know who—"

"Commander, it is of no consequence. You will let it be," the Surchataine said.

He looked at her, then inclined his head. She turned in a sweep of taffeta to go back to her chambers. Ares chewed his lip and uttered, "You will see that this corridor is never left unguarded, regardless of her order." The soldiers saluted.

He and Nicole entered the Chatain's chambers, where Henry sat listlessly among a great pile of toys. Nicole suddenly felt sorry for him, so lonely and bored in the midst of so much wealth. Upon seeing them, his face lit up and he scrambled on all fours toward them, roaring like a lion. Ares caught him under the shoulders and tossed him in the air as he laughed himself breathless. Then Ares hung him upside down to tell him, "We are going to the abbey today, Chatain."

"Let me down! Let me down!" Henry exclaimed, clutching Ares' knees, so Ares let go of his legs. Henry landed on the carpeted floor and slithered underneath his massive feather bed. He emerged lugging a tied sack, which he opened to throw a few more toys inside, although it was already almost full. Then he hoisted the sack over his shoulder and said, "I am ready."

"Very good," Ares said regally, placing a hand on his head. Henry grasped Nicole's hand, and they exited into the corridor. Ares paused beside the stiff-backed sentries: "I am taking the Chatain to visit the abbey, if the Surchataine should inquire." They saluted.

In the front courtyard, they found Karst and the little white mare all saddled and ready. Nicole fell on her with delight, hugging her neck and stroking the clean, crimped mane. Karst snorted, nosing her, and Ares turned him by the bridle to mount.

"Mind your own business, jealous beast," he chided. A soldier lifted Henry, clutching the sack, to sit in front of him, and another soldier got down on hands and knees for Nicole to reach the sidesaddle. They started out of the courtyard at a rolling walk and took the main road south, toward the fortress on the hill.

"Do you go to the abbey often?" she asked.

"Oh, yes," Ares said. "Henry and I go at least once a month, to take our offerings for the care of the orphans. It does everyone good." Nicole smiled at Henry, watching the outside world from Karst's great back. *Ares will be a good father*, she thought.

"You were there as a boy," Henry reminded him, and Nicole looked inquiring.

"Yes. After my father was killed," Ares said.

"Oh, I'm sorry. How did he die?" she asked.

"Defending me in the attack in which I was slashed," he said.

Nicole paused. "But . . . my lord said that the slashing was accidental."

"Yes, it was. But when he saw me in trouble, he got in the midst of it, and. . . . I was brought to the abbey, and raised here until I was old enough to serve as errand boy in the army," he said.

Nicole studied him, and he elaborated on the history: "The abbey was built during the reign of Surchatain Ariel, and endowed by a perpetual royal stipend. Talus ended the stipend when—" He suddenly stopped talking.

"When what?" Nicole asked. The horses ambled easily up the switchback toward the fortress.

"When he came to the throne," Ares said.

Something seemed askew. "Why wouldn't he continue the stipend his father set?" she asked.

"Talus wasn't Ariel's son; that was Bobadil."

"Yes, I know: it was Roman, then Ariel, then Bobadil, then Talus, then Cedric. What I meant was, why wouldn't Talus honor the family stipend?" she asked.

"You know a great deal of Lystran history," he observed.

"I read the Annals," she said loftily, perceiving his change of subjects. But she did not pursue the matter.

When they arrived at the iron gates, Ares called out, "Ho! Sister Agnes!" ringing the bell at the gates. The sister came, eventually, but not before hordes of children rushed the gates, and little hands reached up to turn the great key in the lock.

"Children!" the sister chided as they swung the gates

open. Surrounded by little bodies, Ares slid off Karst, who stood as still as the fortress itself in the midst of so many little feet. Ares sank to his knees to receive the welcoming kisses and hugs of the children, not a one of whom saw anything alarming about his face.

Dismounting from Misty unaided, Nicole watched Sister Agnes take the sack of toys from Henry and lift him down from Karst. Several of the children greeted him as well, and, after the requisite moment of shyness, he was running and rolling in the dirt with the roughest of them.

The children ranged from toddlers to nearly grown, and were all dressed as she once had been, in cast-off, well-mended clothes. Nicole watched Sister Agnes hand off the sack of toys to a subordinate for later distribution. Then Nicole looked down at a little girl who was staring up at her in wordless awe.

She knelt. "Hello. I am Nicole. What is your name?" she asked. The child was too stricken to reply, and Nicole wished she had something to give her. On a thought, she pulled one of the green ribbons from her hair clip and said, "Would you like me to put it in your hair for you?"

The child's eyes widened, and Nicole gathered up the thin blond tresses as best she could without a brush, then tied the ribbon on the ponytail. The child turned to walk away, feeling the ribbon in wonder.

But one of the nuns stopped her and began to take the ribbon out of her hair. The child threw a screaming fit and Nicole rushed to her defense: "Leave it! I gave it to her!"

"Lady, we do not allow the children to receive gifts from strangers. Then they expect every stranger to give them a gift," the nun said severely.

Nicole was livid, but before she could reply, Sister Agnes approached. "Ah, dear Angela, let us allow small gifts of the heart." The chastised nun relinquished the ribbon, and the child clutched it.

From behind Sister Agnes, Ares said, "This is not a stranger, anyway. Sister, this is my wife, the Lady Nicole."

Sister Agnes uttered a small cry of delight, clasping Nicole's hand in both of hers. "Oh, what little faith I have, to be always so amazed at the gifts of God. The years of prayer have had their effect, Commander."

"More than you know," he murmured, looking at Nicole, and she lowered her eyes. "So. . . ." He pulled out his pouch and emptied it into the nun's hands—at least thirty royals.

Receiving the gift, Sister Agnes said, "The Lord bless you and keep you; the Lord make his face to shine upon you, and be gracious to you; the Lord lift up his countenance upon you, and give you peace."

"Amen," Ares said. "Thank you, Sister."

They stayed to play with the children until twilight descended and they heard the bells faintly toll six. Then they remounted to return to the palace. By the time they rode through the palace gates, Henry was asleep in Ares' arms. The evening call was raised in the courtyard; all merchants and townspeople not specifically invited for dinner had to leave the palace environs before the gates were shut for the evening.

As Ares carried Henry into the foyer, he turned to Nicole. "I'll take him up. Will you ask a maid to send up Hillary to bathe him?"

"Yes, my lord," she smiled, reaching to kiss him over the sleeping Henry.

"I saw that," Henry said, peeking at them, so Ares turned him upside down to carry him up the steps.

Smiling, Nicole turned to look for a servant. But they all must have been occupied with dinner or attending someone, as she saw not a one nearby. Unwilling to take a sentry from his post to look for a maid, she went looking herself, down one corridor by the kitchen and up another.

She found herself in the little-used corridor that her father had stayed in overnight. Turning a corner, she saw a maid closing a door with a gasp and running white-faced toward her. Nicole caught her arm, and the maid spun her around trying to get free. "Stop! What is wrong?" Nicole asked.

"Nothing! Nothing!" the girl cried. "I saw nothing!"

This was evidently untrue, but Nicole said, "Well, then, go find Hillary and send her upstairs to bathe Henry."

"Yes, my lady!" the girl cried, and Nicole released her, wondering.

While she was standing there with her back to the door the maid had closed so urgently, it opened and closed. Before Nicole could turn around, the Surchataine appeared at her side. "My lady!" Nicole said, curtsying in surprise.

The door behind her opened again, and the Surchataine made a furtive gesture. Then she looked at Nicole, whose heart was beating in her throat. She had the choice to turn around and see who was there, or not.

"Excuse me, Surchataine; I must go dress for dinner," Nicole said softly. The Surchataine nodded, and Nicole walked straight out of the corridor, not looking to her left, or her right, or behind.

13

$\mathcal{N}$icole determined to put the incident firmly out of her mind, which she found easy to do upon entering her chambers—now, for the first time, she considered these chambers hers as well as Ares'. Rejoicing in the beauty of the new textiles surrounding her, she lit the candles, stoked the fire, and pulled out the tub to bathe for dinner.

By the time Ares came back, she was sitting on one of the little feather pillows, draped in a large towel, drying her hair before the fireplace. He paused at the sight: "Ahh, I am a happy man."

"When your personal living space has been so ruthlessly violated?" she asked, grinning at him as she threw back her hair.

"Invaded, conquered, and enslaved," he sighed, kneeling to kiss her bare knees. Then he parted them, but she stood.

"Your attentions will have to wait till after dinner, my lord," she said aloofly. "I have no intention of being late tonight."

"You are heartless," he grinned. While he bathed and shaved, she dressed in the black gown. This she selected not only because it was strikingly different from anything she had

seen at the palace yet, but because it would complement Ares'
dress blacks.

As he shrugged on his jacket, she smoothed the gathered
back of the dress. "Is it straight? Not bunched to one side?"

"As far as I can tell," he said slowly.

She brushed her hair out and put on the simple black and
gold headband, held in place with combs. "Is it adequate?
Does the hair fall evenly behind it?" she asked anxiously.

"You need a mirror," he said.

"No, just tell me if it looks acceptable," she said.

"You look—indescribable. I cannot believe you are my
wife," he said softly.

"Indescribably good or indescribably bad?" she asked
with perfect seriousness, and he just laughed. He reached out
to her, feeling the softness of the dress, and pulled her to him.

The bell began to toll the eighth hour, and he said, "I am
beginning to hate that bell tower, actually."

She smiled. "Tonight, I welcome it." She lifted her hand
and he turned it palm up to kiss it.

When they arrived at table, Nicole greeted everyone with
a glowing smile. Numerous eyes studied her gown, and she
tossed her head in unconcern: *Let's see what the gossipers
make of this.* Thom kissed her hand warmly, and she nodded
to Deirdre, curtsying beside him.

For the first time, Nicole noticed the plainness of
Deirdre's dress, and she empathized deeply. Nicole looked
past her to the man seated at Deirdre's right, whom she knew
to be the palace doctor, Wigzell. But as he seldom gave an
opinion without being asked, she seldom heard from him.

Upon arriving, Renée appraised Nicole critically a moment, turning her around, then adjusted the gown's shoulders
and headband. "Perfect," she pronounced. "A month from now
you will see everyone wearing black."

When Nicole curtsied to the Counselor, he said, "Dear
Lady, you even make *him* look elegant!"

"Like a gargoyle wearing a diamond necklace," Ares sighed, kissing her hand, "or a carthorse in jonquils." And she laughed.

Henry landed on his back, as usual, then leaned over to kiss Nicole, which had become his new ritual. She hugged him, and he petted her hair. Ares looked over his shoulder in feigned jealousy, demanding, as he was supposed to, "What is going on behind my back?" Henry giggled.

They bowed to Cedric and Elise, then all were seated. Cedric waved for the wine steward, but he was not there. Everyone looked toward the anteroom, where there seemed to be a small commotion.

Then the wine steward came flying out with his pitcher. "Forgive me, High Lord! Forgive me!" he cried. "The silly girl dropped the pitcher, and we had to get another!" As he was practically frantic in remorse, Cedric merely grunted and waved.

"What's going on?" Renée asked the steward. "All the servants are abuzz, but I can't get a word out of Eleanor."

"Forgive me, Chataine. I do not know anything except wines," he said miserably. This he poured with shaking hands.

During the first course of oyster stew, the Counselor said, "The men are making excellent progress on the waterway. You should see it, Surchatain. You also, Commander."

Cedric grunted, and Ares shook his head absently. "I've been so busy trenching that I haven't given a thought to the waterway." Then he looked up in wonder at his own comment.

Renée looked at Ares as if she were going to burst out laughing; Carmine raised his spoon precisely to his lips and murmured, "Congratulations, Commander. You've made the unanswerable observation." Nicole smiled, unflappable.

Cedric glanced at her once or twice, then said, "I don't remember that dress. When did Renée get that?"

Nicole said proudly, "It is not the Chataine's dress, High Lord. My husband bought it for me today."

"Oh. Really?" he said. "Then I must be paying him too much."

She smiled brilliantly on him. "Oh, no, High Lord. I am sure Chatain Henry will tell you that he's worth every piece."

Henry looked up importantly at the mention of his name, and Cedric did not reply. As Carmine's gaze rested on her momentarily, she returned it. For her sake, it disturbed him that she was not afraid of the Surchatain anymore.

Renée, who had been carefully evaluating this conversation, then said, "Nicole, darling, I know you bought several lovely gowns today—that being one of them—but I have scores of dresses I simply don't care for anymore. Will you be so good as to take them off my hands? If they're not adequate for dinner attire, you can always rip them up for rags," she said tightly, glancing at her father.

"Are you serious?" Nicole asked in disbelief.

"Utterly, darling," Renée announced.

"Yes, I'd love them! Thank you!" Nicole exclaimed. Renée smiled, especially as Cedric was grinding his teeth.

After dinner, Ares and Nicole went walking in the rose garden. Many of the varieties were fully opened now, and the palace gardener was skilled in coaxing every possible bloom from every resident bush. With fingers interlocked, the lovers strolled down the pebbled path, inhaling mingled fragrances. In a dark corner out of reach of the globed candlelight, Ares pulled her close to pet her. She yielded to his hands and lips, closing her eyes. His hand dropped to feel her abdomen, lately a little fuller than it had been. In increasing excitement, he pressed her harder to him.

Suddenly he pulled back and said, "Why had Tancred stripped you? What did he do to you?"

She blinked. "He . . . nothing. His mother had said how much she hated our dresses, and his father had said, 'If they are displeasing, one can always remove them.' I think Tancred was simply trying to make a point in removing the dress."

In the darkness, she felt him pause, debating the veracity of that. "My lord, Tancred did not molest me," she insisted. He did not respond, and she said heatedly, "If you are going to doubt me when I tell you the truth, then you should have signed the petition of divorce."

He exhaled, "Never. Forgive me. God forbid I should become a monster to you." She reached up to stroke his hair and he delved into her lips.

Early the next morning, she felt the mattress shift when he rose from bed. He was usually up far earlier than she, often returning hours later with breakfast for her. She smiled to herself, and went back to sleep. But . . . her sleep was not restful. She was . . . uncomfortable. Gradually, she came to, trying to make sense of what she was feeling.

She sat up groggily, and then doubled over with the cramps. "Oh, no. Oh . . . no!" She twisted to see the large bloodstains on her bloomers and the linen sheet. She stared at the blood, disappointment welling up inside her, then she burst into tears.

She sat there crying with the pain and the disappointment until the door opened and Ares entered, carrying a tray. Seeing her, he set the tray down so abruptly that the bottle toppled. "Lady!" he choked out, kneeling to take her hands. "Nicole!"

"I'm not—I'm not—" she sobbed, then shifted so he could see the blood for himself. "I'm such a mess," she moaned.

"Oh, my love," he said, kissing her hands in comprehension and relief. "No matter. It's no matter, darling. Here—" He quickly wheeled the tub in place under the water, then lifted her by the hands. "Come. We'll clean you up. Don't cry, love."

She still sobbed, leaning into him. "I wanted to give you a son," she whispered.

He clenched her to him. "Show mercy, Lady," he said levelly, and she looked at him, all teary. "Please, Lady, give me some time to enjoy you before you get all great and bloated. Heaven knows I've already been deprived enough for one lifetime." She laughed wetly, and he whispered, "God will decide when I should have a son, or a daughter, or both, or none. Come."

Ares stripped her of her soiled underwear, then helped her stand in the tub under the flow of warm water. She lifted her face to wash away the tears while he tenderly bathed her. He stood outside the tub, but so close to the flow of water that he got thoroughly soaked, from his hair to his cotton breeches.

He washed her with scented soap and rinsed her with water, cupping his hands to rinse in all the hard-to-reach places. She stroked his bristly face and kissed his scar. He held her under the flow and comforted her with kisses while the water ran down between them.

The door to his chambers banged open and two soldiers appeared. Nicole cried out and Ares wheeled. The soldiers advanced in something of a blind panic until Ares held up a hand, uttering, "Explain yourselves before you die." His voice, so low and precise, had its effect in stopping them.

"Pardon, Commander, pardon!" one cried. "The Surchatain summons her for trial, and we go to the block unless she is brought before him this moment!" Cringing behind Ares, she was sobbing in fear and shame.

"Get the bed sheet and turn your backs," Ares said. "I will escort her out myself." When they hesitated, he said, "Do it or die by *my* hand!"

One grabbed up the top sheet and thrust it at him, then they dropped back a step. Ares wrapped her in the sheet and cradled her as she shakily stepped out of the tub and crossed the room into the corridor, followed by the two sentries. Servants and soldiers lined the corridor, wringing their hands or staring with eyes full of sympathy as Ares, with a face of stone, escorted his shaking wife into the great hall.

At the sight of all the people gathered who turned to look,

Nicole gasped and went limp. "Be strong, Lady. I will not leave you alone," Ares said in her ear. She nodded, and shakily began walking up the center aisle through the crowd toward the Surchatain seated on his throne, a great, long distance away.

They were quite a sight—Ares in his breeches and Nicole in a sheet, both soaking wet. He kept his arms around her, covering as much of her as possible while they made the long walk.

As soon as the Counselor, standing beside the Surchatain, saw them, he hissed at a servant, who ran out. The couple reached the dais before the throne and bowed, then Ares stepped in front of his trembling wife. "We have come promptly in obedience to your summons, Surchatain, but as you can see, my wife is not presentable to your eyes. I request that you allow her to dress and then return."

"This will only take a moment, Commander. Step aside," Cedric waved.

Ares stood his ground. Nicole, behind him, hung her head so that water dripped from her long hair, soaking the red carpet beneath her. "I know," Ares said in a gravelly voice, "that my lord is kind and gracious enough to allow—" At that moment, the Counselor's servant ran up with Carmine's own robe, which the Counselor handed to Ares.

He turned his back on Cedric to place the robe on his wife's shoulders. She thrust her arms into the sleeves and tied the belt tight. Its fur trim dragged the floor, and the dagging on the sleeves hid her hands, but at least she was covered. The sodden sheet dropped to her feet. Ares stepped to her side, eyeing Cedric, who waved at the Counselor.

Carmine began gently, "Lady Nicole, I apologize for the abruptness of your summons. This involves a grave question regarding Surchataine Elise. It is my understanding that you saw her in the lower corridor last night before dinner. Is that correct?"

"Yes, my Lord Counselor," she said in a quavering voice. Ares watched intently, wiping away water that dripped from his hair into his eyes.

"Please tell me exactly what you saw," Carmine said.

She gathered her wet hair out of her face, trying to think. "I—had come down looking for a servant to summon Hillary to bathe the Chatain for dinner. I saw one girl come out of a room, and I told her to get Hillary. While my back was turned, the Surchataine came out of one of the rooms—I do not know which one it was. I—bowed to her and excused myself to go get ready."

"Did you see anyone else?" Carmine asked.

"No, my lord," Nicole replied firmly. Cedric shifted impatiently, as if disbelieving.

Carmine glanced at him. "Did you hear anyone else?"

"No, I heard no one else speak," she said.

Carmine started to ask another question based on what she had just said, but Cedric interrupted, motioning, "Bring the maid."

Nicole's heart sank as the maid she had seen in the corridor last night was brought in a state of terror to stand before the Surchatain. Blubbering uncontrollably, she sank to the carpet before a sentry lifted her by the arm.

As distressing as the sight was, it strengthened Nicole. She was the Commander's wife. She would not blubber and cower. Straightening, she glanced at Ares beside her, and he looked back.

"Lila, dear, you must say again what you saw last night," the Counselor said firmly.

"Oh, sirs, have mercy. I didn't mean to. I didn't want to," she wailed.

"Stop that carrying on and speak!" Cedric ordered.

She gulped, then poured forth: "I went to shift the bottles as I always do, as is my task, and one had its cork split and needed a new one, and I went looking for the spares, and opened up the room looking, and saw—ohh!" She burst out in tears again, unable to continue.

Cedric rose up in anger, but Nicole took the girl's hand and said, "Look at me! I am in a worse state than you. Be strong and speak."

The girl regarded her, nodding, and then dropped her head to say miserably, "I saw the Surchataine in the embrace of a man, and he was not the High Lord." An awful stillness fell on the hall.

"Who was he?" Cedric asked, pale with anger.

"I do not know, High Lord; I did not see him clearly!" she pleaded.

"Then what?" Cedric asked, reseating himself.

"I ran from the room and the Lady Nicole stopped me," the girl said, resigned.

"What did she say?" Cedric asked, waving away his Counselor.

"She said, go find Hillary to bathe the Chatain, and I ran off and did that," the girl said.

"Did you tell her what you had seen?" Cedric asked.

"No, High Lord, sir, I just ran," she said.

"But you were upset," he observed.

"Oh! I was beside myself, High Lord!" she cried.

Cedric turned his attention to Nicole. "You did not notice her state?"

"I do not know the girl, Surchatain. For all I knew, she might have seen a mouse," Nicole said coolly, in full control.

"And it did not strike you as strange that the Surchataine should be in that area of the palace?" he pressed.

"The Surchataine does not answer to me for her whereabouts, High Lord. I presume she can go wherever in the palace she wishes," Nicole replied.

"What did the Surchataine say when she came out?" he demanded.

"Nothing, Surchatain," she replied.

"Nothing? Not a word? Not to you or anyone?" he pressed.

Perceiving that he was trying to maneuver her into incriminating his wife, Nicole said, "She said nothing. I am the one who spoke. I said, 'Excuse me, Surchataine, I must go get ready for dinner.' She nodded, I left, and that was all."

Cedric looked dissatisfied, and Ares gripped his wife's hand. She felt the approval in his fingers, and squeezed back. "You must have seen him!" Cedric shouted at her.

"But I did not, High Lord," she said loudly in reply.

"Bah!" he waved her away, and in great relief she fell into Ares as they stepped aside. He covered her with his arms and fervently kissed her wet hair. But Cedric ordered, "Bring the Surchataine."

From the safety of Ares' muscled arms, Nicole looked over her shoulder at Elise, escorted between two soldiers to come stand before her husband. He sat rubbing his face, looking at her, then demanded, "Who is this man you were with?"

Elise raised her head slightly, but made no reply. "Who were you with?" Cedric shouted again, his voice booming across the hall. Again, she was silent. "You would do well to confess, for I already have two witnesses against you," he told her. "Nicole and the maid."

"Tha—!" Nicole opened her mouth to dispute him, the Surchatain, and Ares clapped a hand over her face to silence her. But the Surchataine blinked, understanding that Nicole had not betrayed her, and spoke not a word.

"You shall be put to death," Cedric decreed.

Gasps resounded across the hall. The Counselor came forward to drop on his knees before the Surchatain. "High Lord, I beg your gracious indulgence to hear your loyal Counselor. This is a grave matter, to be sure. There may be reason indeed, much as it grieves us, to doubt the fidelity of the Surchataine. But what shall the rest of the Continent say to hear that the great Surchatain of Lystra put his wife to death on the word of a chambermaid? All the respect that they have for my lord now, in routing the advances of Ossian and redeeming the province from famine, shall be obliterated. I beg my lord to resist such a course, for the sake of the future reign of your son, the Chatain Henry."

Cedric turned his eyes away from the beautiful Elise, and, by chance, set them instead on Ares' wife, who was watching from under mounds of damp chestnut hair, with bare toes peeking out from the fur lining of the luxurious wrap. Then he looked at Ares, holding her, and set his jaw. Cedric waved. "Banish her. Send her out to find her true love," he said sardonically.

The crowd let down in relief; Carmine, still on his knees, uttered, "Thank you, thank you, Surchatain, for displaying the gracious wisdom we have come to expect from so great a ruler. Thank you, High Lord."

The crowd was dismissed, and Ares turned with Nicole in hand to plow his way back to their chambers. He bolted the door this time and began throwing on his dress blacks. Nicole stood helplessly in the robe. "I cannot dress, my lord," she murmured. He glanced up at her once, then again, then threw open the door to shout down the corridor, "Gretchen! Bring menstrual rags!" Nicole buried her head in embarrassment, but Ares saw nothing shameful about normal bodily functions.

When Gretchen brought the rags, Nicole handed her the Counselor's gorgeous robe. "Can you clean it, Gretchen? Please tell me that you can clean it."

"We'll try, Lady," she shrugged.

Ares kissed her quickly on the way out. "I must go see to the safe conduct of the Surchataine—of Elise," he corrected himself.

With Gretchen's help, Nicole dressed in the red gown that Elise had bought for her yesterday. The maid cooed and chattered the whole time, and Nicole listened, because she was appreciative of her help. Then another maid came to the door to tell her that the Chataine summoned, so Nicole went up to her apartments.

She found a flurry of activity—maids were coming and going with dresses, accessories, jewelry, and furnishings. Nicole made her way around them to where Renée stood, appraising a fabulous gown that Nicole recognized as the Surchataine's. "Darling, what is all this?" Nicole asked.

"Oh, good. Here you are. Here—I want you to have those." Renée gestured at a large pile of dresses on the floor.

"What—?" gasped Nicole. "You said a few dresses! These are far too many!"

Renée tossed off to a servant, "Summon Preus to alter this for me. Elise had no bust at all." Turning to Nicole, she said, "You don't think I'd hand over all of Elise's things to a new stepmother, do you, darling? Since I get these, you may have my old ones."

"But—darling—" Nicole stammered. "What will your father say?"

"He doesn't know what she has!" Renée laughed. "And he's not going to come take anything I have. Oh, I'm leaving a few things for dear stepmother, whoever that will be. But not much. Let him buy her new things." To another servant, she ordered, "Take all this down to Lady Nicole's chambers."

Stunned, Nicole glanced at the servant who enlisted the help of another, then said, "But, darling, didn't Elise take anything?"

"The clothes on her back," Renée said flatly. "If she's going to be so foolishly indiscreet, that's all she deserves." Lowering the dress, she added, "I heard you would not testify against her at the trial."

Nicole shook her head. "I could not. I . . . couldn't." She stood apart then, watching Renée plunder her ex-stepmother's chambers with cool efficiency. Then she went out, somewhat depressed.

Outside the Chataine's apartments, the Counselor met up with her. "I thought I might find you here, dear Lady."

Nicole curtsied to him, taking his hand to kiss it. His fingers were delicate, almost like a woman's. "I cannot thank you enough for the kindness you showed me today. I desperately hope Gretchen can clean your robe."

"Think nothing of it. Please—let's talk." He gestured to his chambers down the hall.

Walking with him, Nicole wondered, "Why are the Chataine's apartments in this corridor, and not the Surchatain's wing? Henry's are."

"Ah, but Henry is the Surchataine's child, and Renée is not. When the new one comes, he may be moved as well. And that we must discuss. Come," he said, as the sentry opened the door to his receiving room.

When he had shut the door, Nicole asked, "What will become of Elise?"

"The Commander is now escorting her to meet with her lover just north of the border, in Scylla. It is Yael, the woodworker, is it not?" he asked, gesturing her to sit as he poured wine into a pair of gold goblets.

She accepted the wine and the seat. "I do not know, my lord. I truly do not. I never saw who it was in the room with her."

"But you knew someone was there," he observed, sitting himself.

"There may have been. I still am unsure of that," she said dubiously. Sipping the wine, she saw that his windows were paned with glass, as very few in the palace were. She noticed again, with greater acuity, that his clothes and furnishings rivaled those of the Surchatain himself.

"Well. That is a closed chapter. On to the next," he sighed, then studied her. Nicole looked back at his smooth features and coifed hair. "And you are not pregnant," he added.

Nicole almost choked on the wine. Flustered, she sputtered, "The conduit of information here is—is hardly to be believed."

"Forgive my bluntness. But you have gained another month of grace for the Commander," he said.

"What?" she blinked.

"The day you turn up pregnant, his neck will go on the block, one way or another," he said.

"What?" she gasped.

He stood. "I have something to show you. But you must tell no one, not even Ares."

"You can't be seriously telling me to keep secrets from my husband," she said, standing as well.

"Listen! The days are evil, Lady. I do not know how long I myself will survive. But you must know the truth, as your husband is in denial." He went to a large old book sitting on a table by itself, and opened it.

"You can't be—!" she broke off as a sentry pounded on the door.

"The Surchatain summons, Counselor!" he shouted.

The Counselor closed the book. "We will talk of this later, Lady."

14

As Nicole and Carmine entered the corridor behind the sentry, she asked, "Has anyone talked to Chatain Henry about what has happened?"

He turned to her on his way downstairs. "I don't know. Perhaps you should." He gestured toward Henry's quarters in the Surchatain's wing.

She did not know if she should, but she decided that she would. She passed by the sentries unchallenged and knocked on Henry's door. There may have been a quiet "Enter," but she was unsure. She opened it anyway.

Henry was by himself at the window, as usual, playing with his toys. He did not look up as she approached the brocaded window seat. "May I sit with you?" she asked.

"You may," he said, then scooped toys off the seat to make room for her.

She watched him a moment, then looked out his window. He had a fine view of the Passage and the fields beyond. While scanning the far-off fields, she broached, "Did you know that your mother has gone away, Chatain?"

He shifted, repositioning his soldiers. "Father sent her away."

"I'm sorry, Henry," she whispered.

He looked at her with his serious gray eyes. "When Ares sends you away, can I have you?"

She opened her mouth in mild shock. "Chatain, the Commander will not send me away."

He looked back to his soldiers, meticulously lining them up all along the windowsill. "Father sends his wives away."

"But Ares is stuck with me!" she laughed.

He abandoned the soldiers to crawl into her lap. "When you have a baby, will Ares send me away?"

"Chatain, wherever do you get such ideas?" she asked, distressed.

"Hillary says that Ares will love his own child more than me," he said.

Now she began to get a glimmer of what the Counselor meant. She hugged Henry tightly. "Ares and I will always love you, regardless of how many children we have. You have seen how faithful he is."

"Hillary says he takes care of me because he has to," Henry murmured.

She snapped, "Hillary talks too much. Yes, Ares is your guardian, but he does many things that he does not have to do. Would he take you with him to the abbey if he did not love you? Would he carry you on his shoulder and hang you upside down?" she demanded. Henry giggled, snuggling down in her lap.

She sat there with him a long time, holding him and watching the sun track westward across the sky. They didn't say much, for he asked no more questions, but just lay in her arms. And she thought wryly, *In some ways he is much like his guardian.*

As if reading her thoughts, Henry suddenly said, "My father's uncle was his guardian. He saved his life."

Nicole paused, trying to decipher this revelation. "Your great-uncle was your father's guardian?"

"No! My father's uncle was *Ares'* guardian," Henry said, exasperated. "He saved Ares' life when he was hurt."

"You mean, when he got slashed?" Nicole asked.

"Yes. My father's uncle Reynard saved his life. Ares loved him just like I love Ares." Henry reached up to play with her hair as he said this.

Nicole was contemplating this when the door opened and a sentry leaned in. "Lady, the Commander desires your presence."

She gently removed Henry from her lap. "Excuse me, Chatain. I will see you at dinner shortly."

He looked up to say, "*I* would never send you away."

She smiled, "Then we are all of one mind," and curtsied before leaving him.

Ares was waiting at the foot of the stairs, watching as she descended. He was windblown and a little agitated. He extended a hand to guide her off the stairs and draw her close to his side. "Did you see the Sur—Elise off?" she whispered.

"Yes. Her lover was waiting for her," he muttered on their way to their chambers. "I had no idea . . . she was unhappy with him—Cedric. She never showed it." He shook his head at the mystery of women, then opened the door and pulled back in astonishment. "What the—!"

Nicole looked at the dresses piled on the bed and floor. "Oh! I forgot! They are from the Chataine!" she laughed. She threw herself into sorting through them. "Oh, this is impossible! There must be thirty gowns here!" The obvious course becoming plain, she opened the door to tell the sentry, "Summon Thom's wife Deirdre."

Turning back around, she saw Ares transfixed with a look of horror. In alarm, she came to his side, and saw another item that Renée had sent down: a large, finely silvered mirror. For the first time in years, Ares saw his true appearance, and it appalled him. Caught in the human fascination with the grotesque, he could not look away.

Nicole seized the mirror and carried it out into the corridor. Ares sat limply at the table. When Deirdre appeared at the door and curtsied, Nicole was rather abrupt: "Here. I want you to have some things."

"My lady?" Deirdre murmured.

Nicole lifted the top seven or eight dresses, with caps, slippers and other accessories tied into the bodices. Staggering under the load, she thrust them on Deirdre. "These are yours. Call someone to help you with them. And take the mirror in the corridor, too."

"Why—why—thank you—" Deirdre said from somewhere underneath the mountain of fabric.

"I'm sorry," Nicole said, glancing at Ares sitting wordlessly at the table. "Take these now, and I'll send more later. Be sure to take the mirror."

"Thank you, Lady!" Deirdre said, muffled. Nicole nodded and closed the door.

Heart pounding, she sat across from Ares and took his hand, regarding the paleness under his brown complexion. He blinked, turning his scar away from her. "How can you stand to look at that?" he whispered. She opened her mouth helplessly. "Rhea was right. I should wear a hood all the time," he groaned. "It's—it's hideous. *I'm* hideous—"

"Stop it! I won't hear it! It's not what you are! It's just— there, and people get used to it, and—others are worse. Heavens, have you ever seen Merle?" she cried. He stared at her, and she sat on his lap, leaning over to kiss the scar.

He turned his head in revulsion. "Don't!"

"Why not? You let me before! What is different now?" she pleaded. "Oh, Ares," she breathed. "It's just—a scar. It's not like—a hateful heart, or a lying mouth, or lustful eyes— those things are horrible. It's just a . . . scar."

He gazed at her searchingly, then lowered his eyes in dismay. "It is not right for a beautiful woman to be yoked with a monster."

"That is why I would never marry Tancred, or Magnus, or . . . Cedric," she said coldly, and he looked at her. "That is why I love only you," she insisted.

Some color began to return to his face, and he encircled her with his arms, leaning his head on her chest. "I don't understand why you choose to be blind," he said softly, then he stirred. "I am being a fool. You need the mirror. We can keep it covered, and—"

"No," she said.

"Lady, truly, it is well. I had my shock, but, in truth, it was the gray hair that frightened me!" he said, brushing back the hair at his temples, where a few strands of gray were scattered among the dark brown. "But we can put it in the corner, there—"

"If you bring it back in here, I shall smash it," she said calmly.

He sighed, then played with her skirt, murmuring, "How long must you . . . wear the rags?"

"About three days," she said.

"Now I am suffering," he groaned.

Before dinner, she sent a few more dresses to Deirdre, one to Eleanor, and one to Gretchen. Nicole was blithely unaware of the uproar she caused in giving formal gowns to servants. All she knew was that they had been kind to her, and all girls liked pretty dresses.

So it was understandable if Cedric's head was swimming that evening, for not only did Renée appear at dinner in one of Elise's gowns, but Nicole and Deirdre showed up in the Chataine's erstwhile dresses, and even Eleanor managed to sweep downstairs in suspiciously formal petticoats.

As it turned out, Cedric never noticed, for he had his own diversions. At entrances, Georges announced: "Surchatain Cedric and his guest, the Lady Hathor." Eyebrows went up all around the table as the guests turned to bow to the Surchatain escorting in the first candidate to replace Elise.

211

She was a pretty, bouncy, blond woman with a large bosom heaving precariously atop plunging décolletage. Unfortunately, she was also possessed of an unsophisticated air that turned the courtiers into circling wolves.

Renée took one look at her and almost burst out laughing. Nicole watched the reactions with intense interest, knowing that she herself had come to the court with even less sophistication, but had been received far more kindly. She wanted to know why.

After they were seated, Cedric made introductions: "Lady Hathor, this is my son, the Chatain Henry."

He barely glanced at her, murmuring, "Welcome, Lady," according to etiquette.

"Oh, what a darling child! How old are you, darling?" the lady cooed, leaning toward him. Ares, in the line of sight of her breasts, quickly found somewhere else to look. Renée sniggered.

Henry heard her and grew interested. "Seven, Lady," he replied politely, watching.

Cedric fought for control of the situation. "This is my daughter, the Chataine Renée."

"Welcome to our humble table, Lady," Renée beamed at her. "Who is your tailor?"

"Why, Milford, of course," the lady replied.

"You should have him hanged," Renée said gaily, and the poor Lady Hathor produced a high-pitched, grating laugh.

"This is Counselor Carmine," Cedric said desperately.

The Counselor inclined his head and the lady cooed, "Oh, what a handsome man."

"Second only to the Surchatain himself, Lady." The Counselor covered her faux pas himself, and Nicole admired his grace all over again.

"And this is the Commander Ares," Cedric finished.

She looked at him and started. "What happened to you?" Even Cedric flinched at the question.

"I made a misstep, Lady," Ares said sympathetically, forecasting her fate.

Dinner began with polite, easy conversation, as Cedric was determined to salvage the evening for his pride's sake. Hathor kept glancing at Nicole, not knowing the status of the lady seated next to the Commander. Nicole could almost read the question in her eyes: Was she a rival or a person of no consequence?—for those were the only two categories of females at this table.

Nicole tried to put her mind at ease by resting the hand with her wedding ring on the table, or placing it on Ares' arm, or behaving in an overly familiar manner with him. He, not knowing the reason for her attention, relished it nonetheless.

At one point, Ares extended his empty goblet over the back of Nicole's chair for the steward to refill. Ares was able to do this because of his status and the nature of his work. The Counselor had equal status, but he did not drill soldiers in the hot sun all day. Thom did, but he was not Commander.

So no one was offended that Ares demanded, and received, more liquid with the evening meal, even though Giles was notoriously stingy with the allotment for dinner. The wine steward hastened over to refill the Commander's goblet.

A few minutes later the Lady Hathor extended her wine goblet behind the Surchatain's chair for a refill. Renée almost spewed her mouthful and Henry giggled. The table looked on in wonder, and even Ares paused to see what Cedric would do. The wine steward was frozen, watching the Surchatain.

Admirably, he chose to make the best of it. "Refills for everyone, good steward," he nodded.

The steward refilled the lady's cup, then hurried around the table to satisfy the demand. A second cask had to be opened that evening, and everyone became noticeably more relaxed. "Darling, you must see this," Renée said, removing a letter from her bodice to thrust at Nicole.

"What? What is it?" Nicole asked eagerly, taking it. Ares looked over.

"A proposal from a nobleman of Calle Valley we met at the Fair—Lord Lieterstad. Do you remember him? I don't, but he seemed to remember me," Renée said, while Carmine listened. "He goes on and on with the sweetest drivel. Such a patsy. But he's very rich."

Ares leaned over to read the letter, and Nicole pretended to be offended, raising her shoulder to block him. But it was a bare, pretty shoulder, so Ares, being deprived, kissed the shoulder while reading over it. As Nicole was engrossed in the letter, she let him rest his lips on her skin before turning to him. "It sounds promising. Shall you check him out?"

"Yes." Ares took the letter and handed it over to the Counselor, who had been patiently waiting to see it. "I'll send two scouts out tomorrow." Carmine read it, then nodded his assent, returning the letter to Renée. Ares, meanwhile, leaned close to his wife.

Watching all this, Hathor blinked, "Who are you?"

Nicole, unaware that the lady was addressing her, was attending to Ares' lips at her ear—or her neck—it was hard to tell under all that hair. So Renée generously replied, "The Lady Nicole. She loves to drive all the men mad."

Ares and Nicole both stared at Renée, who was smirking. Ares burst out in appreciative laughter: "True, true!" while Nicole, red-faced, insisted to Hathor, "He is my husband."

As the lady looked disbelieving, Renée chided, "Dear Nicole, hasn't the Commander suffered enough? You should cast your net for bigger fish," she said, pointedly eyeing her father for the sole purpose of needling his guest.

"That could be arranged," Cedric said, and a leaden stillness fell around the table.

Renée's breathing deepened in anger. "That is not amusing, you beast."

"I am no jester," he replied. Nicole ducked her pale face;

Ares stared off in masked thought; and Hathor let loose one of her screeching, nervous laughs.

After dinner there was dancing, but no picking of the leaves tonight. As all were leaving the table to partner up, Ares stood over Nicole's chair in such an aggressive manner than even Thom felt compelled to bow upon approaching: "Lady Nicole, I thank you, and my wife adores you."

"Why?" she blinked.

"The dresses," Ares reminded her, relaxing.

"Oh, yes, of course!" she said, turning in the chair. He pulled it out for her so she could appraise Deirdre full-length in a tawny taffeta gown—something Nicole had been too preoccupied to notice earlier in the evening. "Darling, you look like royalty," Nicole pronounced.

"Thank you, Lady." Deirdre curtsied, glancing nervously at Cedric's watching.

Ares placed Nicole's hand on his to lead her out on the floor. Tonight, she was eager for her second dance lesson, knowing that everyone else would be watching the unfortunate Hathor, who sealed her fate by proving herself inept on the floor.

When Ares took Nicole's hand tonight, and placed his arm around her waist, she knew what to do without watching her feet. He turned once, and she followed; he turned again, and she flowed with him.

Now she understood why Renée was so particular about her dresses: they were crucial tools for dancing. The best dresses provided balance, roominess, and ease of movement in turns, as well as dramatic visual flair. Even more important, however, was having a strong, graceful partner, and Ares was flawless in his leading.

Nicole was enjoying herself so much that she was unaware of the eyes of the courtiers on them, and the whispered comment that the two did go well together, didn't they?

And Ares did suffer that night, pouting over his deprivation like a spoiled child.

Over the next several days, the dinner guests suffered through Cedric's attempts to find a replacement Surchataine. Once the position was advertised, so to speak, hopefuls came from as far away as Eurus and Crescent Hollow.

After being verified by an unbiased source as beautiful, the aspirants received an invitation to interview with the household steward Giles, then the Counselor, then the Surchatain, with the possibility of elimination after any interview. If a woman survived all three interviews, she was scheduled as a dinner guest.

The night after Hathor's debacle, the Surchatain's guest was Lady Estelle. She was a petite, dark-haired beauty who looked stunning in red. Henry liked her right away, and Renée refrained from pouncing with bared claws.

The Counselor was strongly in her favor, pointing out to the Surchatain in front of his guests her fluency in literature and poetry. "If it would please the Surchatain, allow her to recite for his guests the lines she so delightfully rendered earlier," Carmine requested.

She glanced at Cedric for permission, who nodded. Then in a soft, entrancing voice, she recited:

> "The voice of my beloved!
> Behold, he comes,
> leaping upon the mountains,
> bounding over the hills.
>
> "My beloved is like a gazelle,
> or a young stag.
> Behold, there he stands
> behind our wall,
> gazing in at the windows,
> looking through the lattice.

"My beloved speaks and says to me:
'Arise, my love, my fair one,
and come away;
for lo, the winter is past,
the rain is over and gone.
The flowers appear on the earth,
the time of singing has come. . . .

"'Arise, my love, my fair one,
and come away.
O my dove, in the clefts of the rock,
in the covert of the cliff,
let me see your face,
let me hear your voice—'"

The guests were rapt, listening, and Ares' hand had slipped beneath the table to grip Nicole's, when Cedric snickered. The lady faltered, and tried to resume, but then the Surchatain snorted, shifting. She fell silent. "That's the most beautiful thing I've ever heard," Nicole said in defiance of his rudeness.

"Um, yes, well . . . I suppose I'm not one for poetry, and such," he somewhat apologized. Having been so thoroughly humiliated, the lady spoke not another word, and was not seen at court again.

The next night there was another lady who was bright and vivacious, but since she was not as charming as Estelle or as tacky as Hathor, the guests were not much impressed. Henry virtually ignored her, which spelled her doom.

For the following evening, Carmine had found a captivating woman who could have passed for the younger sister of Elise. She was more than beautiful; she had a certain fire and spirit in her manner that impressed Nicole and enabled Renée to treat her as an equal. "Lady Ingrid, your father is a vintner, is he not?" Carmine asked leadingly.

In reply, she picked up the goblet and tasted the table wine. "This is from last year's crop in the northern Valley, which was adequate, but not the best. My father can supply you with casks from three years ago—I'm sure you heard about the vintage. It was so excellent that when Ossian tasted it, he agreed to keep his soldiers out of the Valley to preserve the vines. So we bought the Valley's freedom with a few hundred casks of wine per annum."

"Well done, Lady," Ares murmured, appreciating the achievement.

"Thank you, sir," she replied without a glance at his scar.

"The Lady is also an accomplished horsewoman," Carmine added.

"Ares can make his horse dance!" Henry told her.

"Ah, but does he capriole?" she asked, with lifted brow.

"Indeed, he does, Lady," Ares replied in like banter.

"Oh, show her, Ares! Tomorrow! Will you show her what Karst can do?" Nicole asked excitedly.

Everyone looked at the Surchatain for his permission. He grunted noncommittally, leaning back with his goblet in his hand. "You don't like me much, do you?" the lady asked.

"You look too much like Elise," he said, and that was the end of her. Carmine looked at Ares, and Nicole looked at Renée, and they all began to understand that Cedric was not serious about finding a replacement among the applicants.

Ares noticed immediately when Nicole dispensed with the rags, and that evening, he crawled into bed with definite expectations. But Nicole, remembering what the Counselor had said, tried to dissuade him, playing with him to put it off. He tolerated that for a while, but in his hunger, he was soon pressing her to remove her undergarments. When she balked, he did it himself, but as soon as he was on top of her, she clamped her knees together.

He pushed himself up on the maddeningly unstable mattress, breathing heavily while he thought about this new situation. "Why are you denying me now, Lady? Should I wear a hood, after all?"

"No, Ares," she moaned. "I—I'm afraid."

"Oh, my love," he whispered, lowering himself again. "I'll never hurt you. If I get too rough, tell me. I know how to be gentle."

"No, Ares, that's not it." She turned her head to the side, wondering how to make him understand. He would not like what she had to say. "Ares, the—the Counselor told me that for me to get pregnant would place your life in great danger. I believe—"

"The Counselor—!" he gritted his teeth. "The Counselor is a eunuch, and he does not want me to enjoy what he cannot have! If you listen to him, then we have no marriage!" he hissed.

She stiffened, so he nestled down on her, close to her ear. "Listen, my love. It makes no difference whether I have an heir or not—my path is still strewn with dangers I cannot avoid. If I had chosen to walk in fear, I never would have asked for your hand. But I did, and you gave it, knowing that the Commander will have enemies. I ask you not to withhold what you promised me. You are my joy," he pleaded.

"Ares," she whispered, overcome. What could she do but yield?—with tears in her eyes. As he set to, she gripped his back, feeling his strength, and waves of bittersweet longing washed over her like the tide over the rocky shore.

Drained and happy, he rolled on his back to fall asleep. But before he did, while he was just barely awake, she lay on his chest to seek reassurance. "Ares, tell me it will be all right. Tell me we will be together," she whispered.

"I will love you beyond death," he mumbled, and she knew that, once again, the Counselor had told her the truth.

15

Surchatain Cedric continued to entertain prospective mates at dinner, but the Counselor no longer conducted interviews, and no one at table believed that any of these women would ever sit on the throne. Some were entertaining, some annoying; all were quite beautiful, but all somehow fell short of Cedric's expectations. Over their heads, the Commander and the Counselor talked of other, more pressing matters.

Carmine knew right away that Ares had told Nicole of his physical state; one look at her downcast eyes at dinner revealed that much. Even Ares looked a little guilty after the fact. But Carmine nodded at her, "It is all right. It was my choice."

Nicole looked at him in dismay. Thom glanced over without any idea of what they were talking about. "I was given the choice of submitting in order to keep my position," Carmine said in a low voice as the lady of the evening prattled on about something or other to Cedric.

"The Surchatain believed it an advisable procedure, to keep me in line. I . . . cared more for the post than anything, so. . . . I have been well compensated." Nicole, not entirely believing him, cast a dark glance at the head of the table.

"Not him," Carmine said in a bare whisper. "It was at the hand of his father, Talus."

Renée, in a rare show of pure affection, draped her arm around his shoulder and kissed his cheek. Cedric, seeing it, smiled unpleasantly. "It's good to know I can trust one man around you, Chataine." She removed her arm to forestall further comments directed at her friend, and even refrained from a tart reply.

Cedric suddenly turned irately on the Commander. "You kissed her, though."

"Excuse me, Surchatain?" Ares said, bringing his napkin up to his mouth in surprise.

"When she was leaving for Eurus, you held her and kissed her!" he said, gathering steam, and his lady guest looked on in disgust. Perplexed at the accusation, Ares was at a loss for words.

"High Lord, a hundred people watched him kneel before her and kiss her hand. She hugged him goodbye like a favorite pet," Carmine said dryly.

"Exactly so, Surchatain," chimed in Giles, and a score of heads nodded.

"You idiot," Renée said under her breath.

"What did you say?" her father demanded.

"I said, 'I did it,' Father," she clarified.

"Well . . . watch yourself," Cedric snapped at Ares, who inclined his head.

Carmine glanced at Nicole before taking the bowl of custard the servant offered. To Ares, he said, "The waterway trenching goes well, better than I had hoped. But the soldiers are complaining of the digging."

Ares looked irritated. "Peacetime arrogance. Thom, see if they would rather be bleeding on a battlefield somewhere. I can arrange to sell their services, if they wish."

Thom smiled wryly. "More than a few of them think we

ought to be fighting to regain territory lost to Scylla." Ares snorted, but his Second continued, "They've heard of the crop failures, and think the Scyllan armies will be so weakened by wintertime that they won't be able to withstand us."

"Boys who have never been in battle want to conquer the world," Ares said bitterly. "God help us if any of them come to power." Thom conceded this with raised brows. "What is the status of our crops?" Ares asked the Counselor.

"Actually, that has been delegated to Giles," Carmine replied, looking down the table.

"Oh, yes, the seed disbursement," Giles, next to Renée, said importantly. "We've found a distressing amount of infected seed, but I doubt any of it's gone to planting. We'll be lean of wheat until the summer harvest comes in, but we'll have no famine, by God's grace."

"Our lives are by God's grace alone," Ares said, taking Nicole's hand under the table, and she felt a sharp pain in her chest.

Still, she did not refuse him that night, or ever.

The following day, the arrival of a convoy from Eurus caused a great stir at the palace. Every official and numerous servants crowded into the courtyard to inspect the cartloads. The leading delegate from Eurus bowed to the ground before Cedric. "High Lord, Surchatain Ossian of Eurus implores that you receive these gifts from his hand in compensation for the indignities suffered by your ladies.

"First, as directed, the divorce decree from the Chatain Magnus and compensation in the amount of three thousand royals." He gestured to a box on the first cart, which opened to reveal the breathtaking sum of gold. Meanwhile, Carmine accepted a sealed scroll from his hand.

Cedric turned irately to his Counselor. "Three thousand royals! Is that all you demanded of them?"

"As a first installment, High Lord," the Counselor replied, scanning the divorce decree. "We saw no reason to break the backs of peasants facing famine." Cedric waved angrily, and the box was taken to the palace treasury under the watchful eye of Giles.

"Second, Surchatain, we abjectly plead for the Chataine Renée to receive these gifts and letter of apology from Chatain Magnus," the courier said. Bowing again, he extended a sealed letter toward her. When she took it, he stepped back and directed the opening of another trunk.

Renée inspected the trunk before looking at the letter. Atop a coverlet of silk were jewels—the heavy cross necklace, pearl earrings, gold rings—which she deposited on Eleanor, with the instruction, "Take them up to my apartments."

"No, to the treasury," Cedric contradicted her.

She wheeled on him. "I think not!"

"As compensation for our troubles in retrieving you, Chataine," he said hastily.

"*Your* troubles! I don't remember anyone calling *you* 'used goods'!" she cried. Under the stares of his entire court, Cedric gave in. With a scowl at the trunkloads that were of no use to him, he withdrew.

Businesslike, the Chataine returned to the trunk. Beneath the silk were folded the fabulous gown she had been married in and three others. Renée took the wedding gown, also directing that it be taken upstairs. But she turned her nose up at the others: "Nicole, darling, the rest are yours."

As an afterthought, the Chataine opened the letter from Magnus, read it, laughed hysterically, then left it lying on the cobbled driveway as she reentered the palace.

Somewhat flustered, the messenger continued: "Also, a letter and gifts from the Chatain Tancred to the Lady Nicole." He bowed again, extending the sealed letter to her.

With Ares standing over her, she opened it and read: "From the Chatain Tancred to the Lady Nicole: To hear that you were alive and well after the terrible fire that destroyed the tower wing brought tears to my eyes. And somehow, I cannot stop weeping. I erred greatly in putting you there—it was stupid pride, and pique. I should have placed you immediately in the most lavish quarters, and dressed you in the softest furs, and placed a diadem on your head. And you would have been a Chataine instead of a trench digger's wife, with luxuries and comfort and position. But as you have so chosen, that shall never be."

Nicole blinked, shrugged, and handed the letter to Ares, who found satisfaction in ripping it into shreds. She then turned to the trunks, two of them. And what she found were first, the book she had requested, second, the jeweled bracelet, and third, all the dresses that she and Renée had brought with them to Eurus—ten of them.

Ares slumped in despair. "More dresses." For his quarters already looked like a tailor's shop, with numerous gowns hanging on rods and stuffed in every corner. He was having difficulty finding his own clothes among the silk and damask.

"Oh, dear," she murmured over the gowns. She began going through them while Ares watched glumly. Then she looked up at Giles' wife Genevieve gazing at the dresses in pathetic longing. "Genevieve," Nicole said, and she started. "Here. This would look lovely on you. Take this one, and this. Thom, where is Deirdre?"

As Genevieve embraced the gowns with a little cry of joy, Thom moaned, "Oh, Lady, she has plenty. Truly. I beg of you, no more."

"Will she agree with you?" Nicole said coolly, and he gulped and sent for her.

Meanwhile, Nicole became the most popular person at the palace. A crowd gathered around the cart as she gave a gown to Georges' wife, and another to a courtier she hardly knew. Deirdre appeared, who restrained herself to taking only two. Then Nicole looked up at Lady Rhea, watching silently. "Lady Rhea, do you like this one?" she asked, shaking out a red dress with frilled layers.

The lady hesitated, as if expecting an insult or rebuff. Ares watched without comment. Nicole made it easy for her: "If you do, it's yours."

It was not the kind of gift anyone could refuse. Rhea gathered up the dress, curtsying briefly as she murmured, "I thank the Lady." Then she quickly walked away from the hundred or so who knew every taunt and insult she had ever tossed at Ares.

He leaned over to whisper to Nicole, "You are brutal in your vengeance, Lady. I shall be careful not to offend you."

Many other women were pressing around the cart now, some with their hands on the garments, claiming this or that. "Stop. Get back!" Nicole said, but they did not hear her.

Ares whistled shrilly, and they all got very quiet. "Ladies, you are requested to step away from the cart," he said, which they did, promptly.

With things getting out of hand, Nicole gestured to a soldier. "Take the rest of these things to my chambers—" At Ares' look, she promised, "I will go through what I have and weed more out. I promise, my lord." He looked gravely placated, and his eye fell on the jeweled bracelet she had unconsciously put on her wrist.

Nicole took it off and pressed it into his hand, kissing his fingers. "Will you take it to the abbey for me, Commander? And while you are there, ask Sister Agnes to pray for your life, for me?"

His face melted, and he kissed her there on the palace steps. He then saw the book she was clutching in her other hand. "I am keeping this," she uttered, and he grinned.

Turning back to the remaining dresses (including the ones from Magnus that Renée had rejected), Nicole spotted a kitchen maid hanging back from the crowd. She was a young girl with a hardened, disillusioned face, watching without any hope whatsoever of sharing in the pretty things.

"Come here," Nicole said, extending her hand. Reluctantly, the girl came forward under all the envious eyes. "Pick one," Nicole said. "Whichever dress you like."

The girl glanced at them, then looked down. "I've no use for such things. I'll never be able to wear them," she mumbled.

Nicole appraised her, and said, "Exactly one month ago I was wearing linsey-woolsey hand-me-downs from the miller's children, with rags for shoes. I ran goats with the goatherd and dug clams from the sand to sell for a few pieces. I harvested vegetables with my own hands and bathed—occasionally—in the surf. If you had told me then that I would be giving away court dresses because I had too many, I would have laughed in your face."

The girl hung her head, sighing. "Your things are very beautiful. Sometimes, when a soldier comes to call, I would like to have something nice to wear, but these—I'd look ridiculous in these. Like a pig putting on airs."

Nicole blinked. "I understand. I have something that may suit you better. Come." While the soldiers trailed her, rolling their eyes over their burden of finery, Nicole took the maid to her chambers and opened the trunk with her father's dresses. The girl found them wonderful, so Nicole gave her several of them—but not the linen traveling dress she had been wearing when the Commander fell for her.

It took a few more hours for Nicole to weed her garden of gowns, but this was as good a time as any to do it, for Ares had to not only take her gift to the abbey, but attempt to address the numerous responsibilities he had let slide over the past few weeks.

With six dresses still to give away, Nicole began to think more like a courtier. She sent one dress to Merle to quiet her fierce tongue, and one to the kitchen mistress to ensure that Ares could get whatever refreshment he needed in the midst of a long, hot day.

She sent another to the scabbard maker's daughter, a

commoner who was trying to catch the eye of one of Ares' better lieutenants. (None of these recipients considered herself unworthy of fine dresses, by the way.) The rest Nicole packed away in her father's trunk as emergency bribes. Then she pulled out all of Ares' things, making sure they were neat, prominent, and easily accessible above her wardrobe. That done, she went upstairs to see how the Chataine was faring.

Renée's apartments were overflowing with lavish furnishings she had purloined from the Surchataine's chambers, to the point that she was actually pressed for space. "Darling! I'm so glad you're here. Why don't you take this, and this—?"

"Absolutely not, darling," Nicole said firmly. "Ares would have a fit. There's not room, anyway, with all the other things you've given me."

In delicate exhaustion, Renée flopped down on a brocaded daybed, patting the seat. "Sit with me, and I will just have to decide what to do with it all later." Nicole readily joined her.

Toying with the pearls dangling from her ears, Renée said, "The scouts came back with word that Lord Lieterstad is not only wealthy—he owns hundreds of acres in the Valley—but he is a close friend of Surchatain Verschoyle. Father has sent him an invitation to visit."

"Wonderful!" said Nicole.

Renée did not look greatly excited. "I know that Father wanted to invite the Surchatain himself, but . . . he just announced his engagement. We don't know the woman."

Nicole pulled up her feet, wiggling her toes in her soft leather shoes. "It seems to me you would be happier with a rich lord than a Surchatain. You'd have more freedom, and less scrutiny, you know." Renée was silent, and Nicole went on, "I cannot imagine living with the kind of pressure that Elise had on her. Do you wonder if that's why she—did what she did?"

As Renée's thoughts did not include Elise, she responded with what was on her mind: "Since I am 'used goods,' I had almost despaired of finding anyone to suit Father."

Nicole did not say anything at first. "Then marry for love," she said softly.

Renée eyed her, and Nicole could almost see what she was thinking. The Chataine had defied her father about many things, becoming more openly rebellious all the time, but this —it was her paramount duty to her father to marry well. Nicole herself had married Ares in obedience to that duty, as she understood it. It was just serendipitous that she had grown to love him so.

Confronted with her own hypocrisy, Nicole bit her lip. "Forgive me, Chataine—I spoke without thinking. You would grace the life of any man, royal or not, and it is quite possible to marry for duty and be happy. I certainly am."

Renée sighed. "You and Ares were destined for each other. Everyone can see that, and it makes Father livid."

"Why?" Nicole asked in alarm.

"He's jealous, I suppose," Renée said derisively. "Don't let it worry you. What can he do? Ares is his Commander."

Eleanor entered. "Oh, hello, Lady Nicole!"

Nicole smiled at her and Renée said, "Is there something you want?"

"Oh, yes, Chataine. Lord Preus is here with your gowns, and requests you to try them on," Eleanor curtsied.

"I'll be right down," Renée said listlessly.

Nicole got up. "Then I'll be off. I can't wait to see what you're wearing tonight." On leaving, Eleanor hiked her skirt just a few inches so that Nicole could see her bright chartreuse petticoats, and Nicole laughed in delight.

From there, she went to the Chatain's quarters. She knocked, and heard nothing, but looked in just the same. And there was Henry, at his windowsill with his soldiers, as usual. "Hello, Chatain. May I sit with you?" she asked.

He did not reply. "Henry?" she repeated. He said nothing.

She studied him in concern, then it dawned on her that he was engrossed in what he was doing. He had soldiers all lined up along the broad windowsill, and one lone soldier standing on a block before them. There was a large wooden eagle at one end of the sill, which Henry picked up. This he made to speak: "I sentence you to die!"

The soldier on the block he made to lie face down, then he brought over another soldier with a sword. The eagle said, "Chop off his head!" and the executioner raised his sword, which he brought down again and again on the prone soldier. With a groan of death, he rolled off the block. Nicole watched without a word.

"Good. He is dead," said the eagle, which then turned its back. But the man he thought to be dead roused himself slowly, as if badly hurt. Then with a hoarse cry, he fell on the eagle and killed it. Then all the soldiers gathered round him, some falling down on the way, and cheered, "Hurrah! Hurrah!" They lifted the body of the eagle and threw it off the sill onto the floor, where its beak broke. Then Henry looked up at her, and Nicole slowly sat.

"Who is that?" she asked, pointing to the man who had killed the eagle.

Henry did not answer, but began rocking on the cushioned seat. "Ares told me that when Reynard died, he cried so hard that he bled from his scar." Reynard—Cedric's uncle who had saved Ares' life.

"How did Reynard die?" she asked softly.

"In battle a long time ago," Henry said. He began gathering his soldiers to line them up again. Then he stood the man on the block again, and brought up the eagle from the floor. This time the eagle said, "You are sentenced to die— you and your child. Bring the child!"

Nicole's hands went clammy as he brought over a small figure that he placed with the lone soldier. This time, the executioner killed the child, but the soldier survived to kill the eagle. All the other soldiers rejoiced, but the lone soldier cried over the body of his child, and Henry shed tears.

A third time Henry gathered the soldiers, and this time the eagle said, "You will die as your father died. I will not spare your life again, but you and your child will die." This time the eagle killed them both, and the brave soldier did not rise, and the eagle scattered all the rest of the soldiers, killing them and eating them. As Henry made the eagle swoop among the carnage, he was crying bitterly.

Nicole stopped the game, gathering Henry tightly in her arms as he shuddered with sobs. "Shh. Shh," she urged, rocking him. "Chatain, why such gruesome play?"

He lay in her arms until he was all cried out, then he stared through the window with glassy eyes. "I shall cry when Ares dies," he said.

"Why should Ares die?" she whispered.

His answer confirmed her worst fears: "Father said that when Ares has a child, he must die."

"Why, Chatain?" she choked out.

"Because he will love his child more than me," Henry said.

"I told you that is not so," she said.

"That is what I told Father, but he did not care. He said Ares must not have an heir," Henry said, his face white.

Nicole studied him, then began setting up the soldiers herself. "Here. You be the eagle. I will be the soldier."

With the soldier standing on the block, the eagle said, "You and your child must die!"

"No, Lord Eagle," said the soldier. "I and my wife and child are no threat to you. Let us go in peace and you may rule forever, if it please you."

"No! You may not leave! You might come back with an army!" the eagle said.

"Where is Lord Henry?" the soldier suddenly asked. "Let

him decide our case. Lord Henry, where are you?"

Henry grabbed a soldier off the line. "Here I am, Ares!"

"Lord Henry, will you give us your leave to go in peace? I swear we will not come against you with an army."

Lord Henry hesitated. "But I don't want you to go, Ares," he pleaded.

"Then we will stay and serve you. Why should Lord Eagle put us to death? You give the command, and we will stay and serve you."

Lord Henry turned to the eagle. "Ares shall not die! YOU shall die!" And Henry picked up the eagle and threw it out the window.

Nicole gasped, looking down to make sure the wooden eagle had not actually killed someone on the ground below. Fortunately, it had shattered harmlessly on the roof of the portico.

She and Henry looked at each other. "I shall not permit Ares to die," he said, a childish tower of strength.

Nicole gathered him up and he kissed her cheek. Hillary entered, pausing with a warm smile: "Why, hello, Lady Nicole. What a nice thing you do to come play with the Chatain. I'd leave you be, but Chatain Henry must needs be bathed for dinner. But thank ye for coming to see him, Lady." She was smiling and bobbing the whole speech through.

She wants a dress, Nicole thought as she excused herself from Henry. She nodded to Hillary and paused at the door to glance back at Henry. He was looking down at his enemy the eagle, smashed to bits on the portico roof.

In the corridor, Nicole stopped to ask a sentry, "Do you know where the Counselor is?"

"He is in his chambers, Lady Nicole," he replied.

She went to the Counselor's door and knocked. Hearing him call, "Enter!" she did. He and Giles, sitting at the table over an open ledger, looked up in mild surprise to see her.

The steward rose to take her hand and kiss it: "Lady, it

was such a generous thing of you to give my dear Genevieve the gowns, and let it not cross your mind that the Surchatain said they were to go to the treasury."

"The gowns?" Nicole said, her heart stopping.

"Yes, but as I said, give it no thought," he insisted.

Carmine sat back in his chair with a tired sigh. "Giles, I think we're done for the day. We will resume tomorrow morning."

"Certainly, Counselor." Giles bowed to him and to her. "Again, thank you, dear lady; so courageous of you," he said, and left, closing the door smoothly behind him.

Nicole stood where she was a few moments. "The Chataine gave those dresses to me, and the Surchatain said not a word about them!" she said anxiously.

Carmine laced his hands behind his head, stretching tiredly. "Giles likes to see as much income as possible funneled to the treasury, and nothing going out. If the Surchatain mentions it, I will make him aware that Giles told you not to give it a thought. But I do not believe the Surchatain will make an issue of it. Please sit." He gestured toward the chair Giles had vacated, and Nicole took it.

Still mulling over the possibility that she had given away treasury property, Nicole was slow to speak. "I do envy him," Carmine said softly.

"Excuse me?" she said, giving him her attention.

"Ares and I had a standing joke that, maimed as we were, we'd never be married. Once, when we were both very drunk, I asked him if he'd ever trade scars with me, were it possible. He didn't think about it three seconds. 'Never,' he said. 'I might find a beautiful blind woman.' He has, and . . . I envy him." Nicole lowered her eyes. "But you have not come to hear all this. What can I do for you?"

"Why have you been so kind to me? I had nothing to give you, but from the very first, you have been nothing but kind. Why?"

He sat up with a rather rueful expression. "You're forgetting that I used you quite shamelessly in gathering information about our Scyllan neighbors."

"That was different. I wanted to help."

"So how may I reciprocate?" he asked again.

She shook her head, and he watched the chestnut hair fall across her shoulder to the crook in her arm. "You started to show me something about Ares in a book—something you said I should know. I want to see that now."

He nodded pensively. "You should know, definitely. But I have come to realize that it is not my place to tell you about it. You must ask Ares."

16

Reluctantly, Nicole did not press the Counselor to show her the book because she knew that, once again, he was right. So she asked him instead, "What do you think of the match with Lord Lieterstad? Will it be good for the Chataine?"

"It will be good for the Surchatain," Carmine admitted. "But it will not thrill our dear Chataine. Lord Lieterstad is older than Ares and twice as ugly."

"Oh," Nicole said, drooping. "I so wanted to see her in love."

Carmine nodded, studying his hands, and there was something unreadable in his face. She regarded him, wondering what she had said wrong, then recognized the look —it was the same look as was on Ares' face after he had seen himself in the mirror, and the full extent of his deformity had sunk in. It was the apprehension of one's own irrevocable deficiency. "Counselor, I—I am sorry. I did not mean to—" she floundered.

"You've not wounded me, dear lady," he assured her, but he did not say he was not wounded.

The bell began tolling, and he rose, offering his hand. "I believe that strikes our dinner hour."

"Already?" she started. Accepting his hand, she hurried to the stairway, and he had to step briskly to keep apace of her. When, descending the stairs, they saw Ares looking anxiously around the foyer, he released her hand.

He saw them coming down the stairs together, and his look was cool. So she reached up to kiss him, pressing her body to his, and the Counselor said, "Lady Nicole was inquiring after our appraisal of Lord Lieterstad." Satisfied, Ares kissed her hand, and the three of them entered the banquet hall together.

Nicole received very warm greetings from the table as she curtsied, and Ares asked her, "When do you think you might have time to clear out a few of the dresses?"

Her heart sank, but she replied, "I will make time first thing tomorrow, my lord." That would give her the opportunity to send a token few to the treasury, at any rate.

He glanced down at the gown she was wearing now—in the style she favored, it was simpler and more modest than most of the Chataine's, with translucent sleeves and folds of lilac silk at the neckline. But the silk puckered in such a way that when standing directly over her, he could look down and see the filigree cross nestled between her breasts.

Confident that no other man would ever get close enough to enjoy such a view, he whispered, "Keep this one."

"The Chatain Henry and Chataine Renée," Georges announced, and the table turned to bow. Nicole glanced at the seating, and saw that the Counselor had indeed traded places with the Chataine, giving up his seat around the corner on the Surchataine's left.

"The Chataine has been asserting herself," Carmine murmured humorously to Nicole, and she smiled in appreciation of his tolerance.

Henry rushed at Ares with his usual roar, but Ares was ready for him tonight, with outstretched arms. Henry landed on him with such force that only his solid stance kept him from crashing backward into the table. With Henry's arms and legs wrapped tightly around him, Ares was a little hampered in bowing to the Chataine, but he managed. Then he turned to face his chair with the burden still clamped on him, resisting Ares' efforts to pry him loose.

"Is this a new game, Chatain?" he asked bemusedly. Henry whispered something in his ear, and Ares replied, "That will not come to pass."

Georges announced, "Surchatain Cedric and his guest, the Lady Vola." Ares abruptly put Henry on his feet, setting off an undercurrent of intense, isolated reactions as Cedric entered with the lady and the dinner guests bowed.

Nicole scrutinized the woman, who had a relaxed, pleasant manner in taking her place at the head of the table. She was beautiful (as required), but conspicuously older than the other candidates, and she wore a great deal of makeup. There was nothing to be faulted in her gown, which was definitely Lord Preus' handiwork.

But Ares was gazing wide-eyed at Thom, who was muttering distractedly under his breath. Carmine looked mystified and Renée alert. Looking down the table, Nicole saw Genevieve pinching Giles in anger and several gentlemen earnestly trying to hide their faces.

Nicole blinked at Ares, who looked back at her helplessly. Cedric began making introductions, and everyone greeted the lady tentatively until they should figure out what was going on.

But when he came to Ares, the lady smiled broadly. "Good evening, Ares. He and I are old friends, Surchatain, though it has been too many years since he came to me on business. Now, whenever I see him, he only yanks away my customers. Is that nice of you, dear Ares?" she chastised him sweetly. He opened his mouth without being able to produce any reply at all.

With a glance at the speechless Commander, Carmine

asked in friendly interest, "What is your business, Lady Vola?"

"I am a chandler, sir, the finest, and I have not seen you in my shop," she said almost in rebuke.

"I regret that it is not my business to buy candles for the palace, Lady," Carmine said guardedly, and Nicole looked at Ares again. It certainly was not his business, either, nor would he concern himself with her customers. She watched him working his jaw and biting his lip as he stared down at the table.

"Ares, I heard you were married. Would this lovely girl be your wife?" Lady Vola asked with a radiant smile. Ares was still unsuccessful in producing anything of volume, but he did nod. "How sweet. It is wonderful to watch such a man ride, isn't it, dear? Such rhythm and grace. Such bridled strength."

Ares was pale and Nicole's mouth dropped open upon deciphering the subtext of her message. Nicole sat trembling in anger while the woman smiled on her with impunity.

Then Nicole stirred and smiled in return: "Yes, but it's so sad to think of him wasting his ability on the old nags he's ridden in the past."

The woman's smile froze; Thom ducked his head to choke back laughter; Carmine stared at Nicole in admiration and Renée, comprehending all, gazed at her in delight. "He's good on Karst," Cedric admitted, and then looked up, surprised that the dinner guests found his comment so extraordinarily amusing.

"*Dear* Lady Vola," Renée began, flinging her blond ponytail like a battle standard, "Judging from your immaculate dress, I would certainly say you are a woman of stature. But I have not seen you at court functions, and I thought I knew all the merchants of Westford. I certainly thought I had done business with them all, hadn't I, Father?"

"That's certain," he grunted.

Renée gave a ringing laugh, and Nicole, watching calmly, drank from the goblet the steward had just filled, then let her hand rest on its base. Ares' hand crept tentatively toward hers; she folded her hands in her lap. He closed his eyes in pain. "So, I am consumed with curiosity to know how my father found you!" Renée broached brightly.

"We were introduced by a mutual friend—Lord Giles," Vola nodded.

Steward—not Lord—Giles nodded sickly, and Genevieve stared straight ahead in stony fury. "Well, of course, silly me. Lord Giles buys the candles, doesn't he?" Renée asked, savaging poor Giles with the undeserved title.

Everyone looked at Giles, who was forced to admit, "The candles are bought through the wholesaler Petry," which half the table knew. "But we buy from Lady Vola on special occasions," he said desperately.

"Special occasions?" Renée laughed. "Oh, I love special occasions! For which occasions did we patronize the lady's business, Lord Giles?"

He was sweating profusely. Ares watched, resting his head on his hand while his scar throbbed. Nicole sat quietly attending to the torture of Giles. "We—" Blinking rapidly, Giles passed a hand over his dripping brow. "It must have been—last Christmas."

"And which candles were purchased for Christmas?" Renée purred over her goblet. "The tapers for the table? The votives for the globes? The scented candles for the garderobes? Or the decorative candles for the tree?"

Giles, strangling on his own rope, was unable to answer. So Renée turned to the lady. "Dear Giles has so many accounts to keep straight, he just can't remember them all. Perhaps you can tell us which candles you supplied for Christmas, Lady Vola."

"I specialize in decorative candles," Vola admitted.

"And these are what you supplied us?" Renée asked.

"Probably. I can't remember," Vola shrugged.

"You can't remember your last order from the palace? With the volume of business we provide? And the opportunity to be introduced to the Surchatain?" Renée asked, wide-eyed. Cedric had been scowling at his daughter, but after the last question, he began to pay attention.

"Yes, it must have been the decorative candles," Vola sighed somewhat impatiently.

"For the tree," Renée prompted. Every Christmas, the palace erected a giant fir in the foyer, decorated with candles, candies, and toys.

"Yes, for the tree," Vola said, rolling her eyes.

The Chataine took a sip from her goblet as the table waited for the death blow. "We buy the decorative candles for the tree from the abbey orphans. Everyone contributes something for the candles, from the kitchen maids to the Surchatain," Renée said. "You never sold us candles, and you never rode Ares," she finished in guttural savagery.

Cedric blinked several times as it dawned on him that the guest who sat in the Surchataine's chair was the most popular, longest-established prostitute in Westford.

To her credit, the lady sat unbowed under the table's glare. Only Ares did not look at her. He glanced up at Renée before lowering his eyes to the table again. "Georges!" Cedric called.

The dinner master appeared, bowing. "Surchatain?"

"Georges, give the lady her wages for the evening and see her out," Cedric said heavily. The lady dropped her napkin to the floor and walked out proudly, without a backward glance. The table sat in silence. Then Cedric turned to the wine steward at his elbow. "Another round for everyone," Cedric gestured, and the steward was quick to comply.

Only then did Cedric get testy: "Giles, what were you thinking?"

"I didn't know, High Lord! She was so—charming and

well dressed!" he pleaded nervously. Genevieve looked fit to be tied.

"Bah!" Cedric waved, then glanced at Ares and Nicole, both downcast. "That's what you get for marrying a soldier, Nicole. There's not a one of 'em that's a virgin after the age of twelve," he snorted. She did not reply.

This seemed to irritate Cedric so that he snapped, "How many bastards have you fathered, Ares?"

Several people gasped at the question and Carmine began, "High Lord, this—"

"I know you haven't sired any, Counselor! I was asking him!" Cedric said.

"None, Surchatain," Ares said without inflection.

"Huh. You're sure?" Cedric pressed.

"Yes," Ares said.

"Huh," Cedric said, leaning back. He waved for the first course to be served, but no one showed much interest in the food. Ares merely stared at the onion soup. The Counselor sat upright, eyes fixed on the middle distance. Renée was glaring at her father.

Looking around, Henry piped up in a small voice, "What's a bastard?"

As Cedric ignored him, Ares leaned forward and said quietly, "It's a child whose mother and father are not married, Chatain."

"So . . . you don't have any children, Ares?" Henry asked.

"No, Chatain," he answered.

"Are you going to?" Henry asked.

Cedric looked up for the answer, as did everyone within earshot. Ares said, "Whatever God wills."

As to a simpleton, Cedric observed, "I think you had better be more concerned about what *I* will, Ares."

The main course of venison pie came around, with pastry cut in fanciful shapes of animals, birds, and flowers. While the guests ate in dead silence, Cedric glanced around. Then he observed, "Whatever are you paying these people, Giles? I've never seen more extravagant clothes in my life."

Carmine shot a warning look at Giles and said, "I believe that is due to your daughter's generosity in distributing some of her old gowns among the ladies, High Lord. I understand that she was anxious for your courtiers to put on a good appearance for the candidates who may be coming to dinner. Did you decide whether to interview Ossian's niece?"

Cedric shrugged. "I hear she has the face of a horse." Almost despondently, he let his eyes rest on Nicole—her clear skin, her delicate features, her luxuriant hair. He tilted his head, observing how she favored little caps that held her hair back from her face but let it flow unhindered down her back. No fussy braids or elaborate, puffy styles. "Let your hair down," he said suddenly.

The whole table looked at him in shock, and Nicole stared in panic. "Everyone," he amended. "It's the new style, isn't it? All the ladies may unbind their hair for tonight."

No one dared move at first—he might as well have asked them to disrobe. Then Renée spat sarcastically, "Oh, yes, let's!" With a furious jerk, she ripped the clip out of her hair and shook her head, mussing the hair for good effect. "There! How's that?" she shouted, jumping up. "Let all your ladies look like the woman you just threw out tonight, so that tomorrow it will be all over Westford that the palace courtiers are whores!"

Cedric jumped up in a rage, drawing back his hand to slap her. As Carmine pulled her out of range, Ares grabbed the Surchatain's wrist. No one could believe it, least of all Cedric. "Strike the one you are really angry at," Ares said, and Cedric did. With his other hand, he slapped Ares directly on his scar, hard.

Henry screamed and threw himself on his father with balled fists. Ares lifted the little avenger under the arms and sat with him on his lap while blood seeped from the scar.

Renée sat weeping and disheveled, and Henry sat crying on Ares' lap, trying to staunch the flow of blood with a napkin.

While the rest of the table sat agape, Cedric collected himself and sat down. He looked distractedly at his weeping children, his bleeding Commander, and Nicole with her cap in place. "Ah, forgive me," he muttered. "Ares, thank you for stopping me from doing something foolish."

Too late, more than one person thought. "Steward, more wine all around," Cedric ordered, although most goblets were still full. After a hasty dessert of pudding, Cedric dismissed his guests with a wave. No one wanted entertainment; no one wanted to dance.

"Ares, come put me to bed," Henry said shakily.

Ares turned to Nicole without looking in her eyes. "I will be in shortly," he said, and she nodded.

At the door of their chambers, she paused. She was tired of this room, tired of the palace, tired of the capricious Surchatain. She was homesick for the Sea at night, for moonlight on the water, salt spray in her face, and the beach at low tide.

Well, she had no beach here, but—She turned to the sentry at the door, who blinked to make the point that he was not watching her, specifically. "Please tell the Commander that I am in the orchard," she said, and he nodded.

Removing a globed candle from its stand, she made her way across the palace and out the far door, then down the pebbled path toward the fruit orchard. The trees were not the Sea, but they welcomed her with small showers of spent blossoms. Nicole glanced back on the path at the soldier who was trying to be discreet about keeping her in sight. She sighed. Eyes everywhere.

At the edge of the orchard, she sat under a tree with the candle in sight of the palace. She was not trying to hide, nor be difficult; she just wanted to breathe. She raised her face to the new leaves, and the stars, and the waning moon. She closed her eyes, resting in the peacefulness of night. Minutes later, hearing footsteps on the path, she turned her head and sat up in mild alarm. It was not Ares approaching.

It was a soldier, who bowed. "My lady, the Commander requests to know whether you desire his company or wish to be left alone here."

As she had to think about that for a moment, she appreciated his asking. "Please ask the Commander to join me, if it please him." The soldier bowed and turned to trot back up the path.

Shortly, she heard footsteps that were definitely Ares'. It was a fast, balanced stride. Yes, of rhythm, grace, and bridled strength. She exhaled and covered her eyes upon remembering the woman's words. "May I sit, Lady?" Ares' voice was low and gravelly.

"Please, Commander," she said, gathering her skirts. As he lowered himself to the ground, she asked, "Is Henry well?"

"He is angry and frightened, and I am not succeeding in comforting him," he said dully.

Then Nicole gently turned his cheek to look at his scar. Since she could not tell in the candlelight, she asked, "Are you still bleeding?"

"Not much, I don't think," he said hastily. "It will stop of its own." He was still carrying a napkin with which he daubed at the scar.

She nodded. "It was very good of you, Ares. You are a good man."

He exhaled, leaning as close to her shoulder as he could without touching it. "Nicole, my love. . . . I have no excuse for going to her. I was young. That sounds like an excuse," he realized.

She looked away, silent for a moment. "The Surchatain is right; I did not expect you to be a virgin. I was just—surprised to hear a strange woman describe your lovemaking so accurately."

"I caused you terrible humiliation. I am so sorry," he whispered. "I would give anything to make it right."

She debated her choice of words. "Then tell me why the Surchatain will kill you if you produce an heir."

He paused. "Is that what the Counselor told you?"

"No, Henry," she said.

"Henry is a child," he pointed out.

"Henry understands quite clearly what his father said. Why do you think he is so angry and frightened?" she asked. He was silent, and she nodded. "So you will do anything to make it right except tell me the truth. Of course, you expected that of me before you would propose."

Ares drew a deep breath. "Cedric's uncle Reynard rescued me when my father was killed, and I became something of a son to him, as he had no heirs of his own. So Cedric has always seen me as a rival to the throne, although I have no ambitions to that end. I only want to serve."

"Who was your father?"

"His name was Erlend," he said.

"And your mother?" she asked.

"She died in childbirth. It was a difficult birth. I don't remember her name," he said.

"Was your father or your mother related in any way to Cedric and Reynard?" she asked.

"No," he said.

"So you have no blood claim at all to the throne?"

"I am related in no way to the ruling family," he said.

She considered all this as his fingers sifted through the wilted blossoms littering the ground. Despite the protection of the globe, the candle flame flickered in the brisk night breeze. "The Surchatain scares me. He is becoming almost irrational."

"As long as he vents his anger on me, no one else need worry," he said.

"Ares! You are saying I shouldn't worry that he wants to kill you!"

"He will not kill me. He needs me, and he knows it."

"I don't like the way he looks at me," she said.

"Neither do I. But he cannot take you from me. He cannot rescind his own word, and he gave permission for us to marry. That is the law he swore to uphold, and he can be deposed for defying the law."

"Unless he changes the law," she observed.

He shook his head in the darkness, and she could not read his face. But she could see the blood still trickling down his jaw. When she reached up to his face, he hastily wiped it with the napkin.

He leaned up against the tree without touching her, although he was close enough for her to sense his anxiety. "I only went to her a few times. It was depressing—I knew God had something better for me. But I was foolish, and impatient. Had I known the humiliation it would cause you tonight. . . . Nicole, please forgive me. I did not know."

She looked at him in the bare candlelight, the scar a chasm in his somber face. She had no intention of holding his youthful indiscretions over his head. What troubled her was the impression that he was still not being completely forthright about his relationship to Cedric.

A child of the Chatain's great-uncle's ward was simply no threat to the throne, legally speaking. If that's all it was, Cedric had no sane reason for these continual death threats, especially considering Ares' record of service.

So Nicole was faced with the age-old dilemma of woman: whether to trust the man or not when his motives were cloudy. Whether to continue to love unreservedly when she saw his stumbling with her heart in his hands.

For Nicole, there was no other way. She leaned forward to kiss him, and he tried to make sure his face was not bloody before he embraced her. He dropped the napkin to press his hands on the silk, and she murmured, "Shall we ride, my lord?"

"There was never any horsewoman who could bring a beast to its knees as you do, Lady," he confessed. She started to lie back on the ground, but he lifted her. "Not here. There are watchers," he whispered, and took her hand to lead her back up the path.

Late in the night, when Nicole was sleeping on her side with Ares pressed up against her back as usual, they were startled awake by a pounding on the door: "Commander! The Surchatain summons! Commander!"

Nicole raised up with a cry, but Ares calmly went feeling for his breeches in the dark. Since he had the door bolted, the sentries had no choice but to wait outside. "I am coming!" he called to them, pulling on his pants. Nicole grasped his hand in fear, but he said, "Shh! It may be nothing. I'll send you word. Bolt the door behind me."

He opened the door into the candlelit corridor and glanced back at her as a reminder. Once he had left, she scrambled up and slid the bolt across, then rekindled the fire with trembling hands. She lay back down in bed to wait, wide-eyed and alert to every footfall in the corridor outside.

She waited for a long time, jerking awake whenever she started to drift off. Then all at once there was a soft knock. "Nicole? It's Ares."

She slid back the bolt and reached up to him in relief as he entered and rebolted the door. "What was it?" she whispered.

"He—" Ares laughed a little incredulously. "Ah, he got up me and the Counselor to tell us he wanted to attack Eurus. That is, he wanted me to lead an attack on Eurus.

"So the Counselor had to tell him we couldn't; we had accepted the first payment of three thousand royals from Ossian to assure that we wouldn't attack Eurus. It took a bit of explaining to get him to understand how much we would alienate our allies on the Continent to accept tribute and then attack anyway."

He shed his breeches and crawled back into bed, leading her by the hand. Nicole hardly noticed his slipping her bloomers off her hips.

As he contentedly set about his business, she asked, "Why does he want to start a war with Eurus?"

"He's bored," Ares muttered, not bored himself at present.

Either that, or he wanted his Commander out on a battlefield where he was likely to get killed.

17

Ares was up hours before Nicole—the more tension in the palace, the more she tended to seek refuge in sleep. She did not know any other reason she should feel so tired. She was appreciative to the maid for bringing breakfast as well as a bit of news: Lord Lieterstad would be arriving in time for dinner tonight. Rumor had it that he was bringing a large entourage and cartloads of food and gifts.

As soon as Nicole had dressed, she set about weeding enough gowns from her collection to leave conspicuously empty areas in Ares' formerly stark quarters. She sent four gowns to the treasury, and solicited the maid's help in packing four more in her father's trunk. That was all she could do for now, not knowing anyone else who should receive one. Deliberately, Nicole rejected the thought of sending a gown to Hillary. Nicole would not be bullied into giving them away.

As it was by now late morning, Nicole went up to the Chataine's apartments to see if she was up yet. And she was, barely. While Eleanor helped her dress, Renée directed Nicole to sit on the exquisite daybed. "I've come to a decision, darling. I wanted you to be the first to hear it," Renée said.

Nicole felt warmed and honored. "Oh, do tell me!"

"I've decided to accept Lord Lieterstad. It will make Father happy, which will make him ease up on poor Ares. With any luck, the lord will dote on me as Ares does you, so I shall certainly be happy. I will have to live in Crescent Hollow, but I will be well provided for, and I shall send a carriage for you to come visit me. At any rate, it's time I grew up—heavens, I will turn twenty in a few months. I can't live here forever. There's nothing to keep me here." The despondence in her voice reflected nothing of what Nicole wanted to hear in an announcement of betrothal.

"Oh, darling." Nicole stood to embrace her. "Just—wait and see what happens. He may be perfectly delightful."

Renée looked downcast. "Did you . . . love Ares when you married him?"

"No," Nicole said promptly. "I was too frightened—everything happened too fast! I did not know I loved him until after I had signed the divorce petition, and thought about what it would be like to never see him again."

"Then, if Lieterstad loves me, I shall fall in love with him, too," Renée said.

"I hope so. I pray so," Nicole said.

"No matter." Renée dismissed Eleanor with a wave, then picked up a gold goblet of spring wine. "I won't think about all that now. I will just enjoy myself. We shall have the most lavish banquets—oh, darling, have you heard about his banquets? They say they've no match on the Continent."

"I've heard he's bringing a great deal of people and food," Nicole admitted.

"And musicians for the dancing—now you shall really appreciate those gowns, for Lord Preus is the master of the dance gown," Renée said.

Nicole winced. "And Ares is such a lovely dancer, but I only know that one dance! I will humiliate myself and everyone around me."

Renée set the goblet down with a thump. "No, you shall

not! I'm going to teach you everything. Come." She seized Nicole's hand and took her downstairs to the great hall, empty but for the maids cleaning and refilling the chandeliers. "Have Ardis bring his viele," she ordered a maid, who got up from her knees to comply.

"Now," Renée said, "I shall lead. First, you must know the basic quadrille, and then I will show you the variations they favor in Crescent Hollow." Renée took Nicole's hand and walked her through the steps, counting beats.

When the musician appeared with his instrument, they did the steps to the music, over and over, faster and faster, until Nicole could dance it well enough to require another couple to complete the quadrille. So the Chataine drafted two male servants who were known to be exceptional dancers, and with delight they abandoned their chores to assist in the lessons.

With many missteps and startovers (caused mostly by Nicole), the learning was great fun, and the girls laughed so much that numerous courtiers and servants peeked around corners to watch.

From there, Renée covered variations of the quadrille, which Nicole found easy to master. Renée then took her through another paired dance that was more complex than the first Nicole had learned with Ares.

Renée placed the hands of the blissful servant on Nicole for the dance, instructing, "Now the trick with this one is that you must not let your partner hold you too close. They're always trying to press up against you"—Renée demonstrated by shoving the man close to Nicole—"but if you let him do that here, he's going to stomp on your feet. Keep him this far away"—again demonstrating, pulling him away—"by elbowing him in the throat, if necessary. Here." She showed Nicole how, and the servant drew back, coughing.

"Keep the beast in line," Renée said imperiously, and Nicole laughed. They practiced that one until they were quite winded.

They plopped into dining chairs to rest, and Renée dismissed the servants, who bowed and kissed the ladies' hands in gratitude before departing. Nicole said, "Oh, I wish Ares weren't so busy today, so I could practice with him!"

"No need. If you do it just like I showed you, you'll look lovely together, because I taught him everything he knows," Renée said smugly.

"You did?" Nicole exclaimed.

"Oh, yes. The dancing master was never here long enough to practice as much as I wanted, so I dragged Ares out onto the floor for hours on end. Him and Carmine. They whined pathetically about their duties—particularly Ares—so I shut him up about that."

"How?" Nicole asked.

Renée looked over with mischievous, slitted eyes. "I taught Ares how to kiss, too." Nicole was silent, and Renée laughed deep in her throat. "Soldiers are such horrid kissers— all drooling, gaping mouths. I taught Ares how to kiss pleasantly, how to use the tongue, how to use the hands, and how not to."

"Renée—darling—" Nicole said, a tight knot forming in her stomach. "That's—not good. Then he would think—that you wanted—"

Renée laughed again, and the sound was becoming harsh to Nicole's ears. "Oh, it was nothing, darling. Just play. I told you, he was my patsy."

Nicole was distressed, floundering, torn. The Chataine leaned over to put a sympathetic hand on hers. "I've offended you. I'm sorry, darling. Forget it. Let's grab a bottle and see what Merle knows."

"Another time, darling," Nicole said weakly. Renée patted her hand and swept out toward the kitchen corridor. Nicole stood, feeling light-headed. She went out to the foot of the foyer stairs and gathered her skirts to ascend, then stopped to wonder where she was going.

Hillary, with an armload of the Chatain's clean laundry, paused at the foot of the stairs before ascending. "Did she tell you?" she whispered in a rasp. Nicole blinked at her. "Did she tell you about the soldier she used to meet in the orchard and the rose garden? Eh? Did you ask, 'Now, what soldier could you meet with under the Surchatain's nose, who was not afraid of getting gelded,' eh?"

Nicole froze in horror as Hillary brushed past her up the stairs, muttering, "She has dresses enough to send to the treasury, eh? And give to that nobody Erin."

Meanwhile, Nicole was reeling at the foot of the stairs. What soldier indeed had the Chataine fallen in love with? What rumors could reach the Surchatain's ears so that he summoned this soldier, and Ares not know of it? What soldier could escape punishment for such a transgression?

Suddenly other things became clear. For Ares to have a child by a commoner was indeed no threat to Henry's ascension to the throne. But should Ares produce a child *by the Chataine*—that was quite a different matter. And what father would not be surly to the soldier who handled his daughter with impunity?

Nicole lifted her skirts with shaking hands to ascend the stairs. Why would Ares bother marrying her, then? Because he and Renée both knew the Chataine must be married off soon? And it appeared to Nicole that the true patsy in all this was she herself.

"The Counselor will tell me," she whispered desperately. "He will tell me the truth." With renewed resolve, she gripped the balustrade to make her way up the long staircase. She hurried to the Counselor's chambers and knocked anxiously at his door.

When there was no answer, she turned to the sentry down the corridor. "Where is the Counselor?" she asked.

"I am not certain, Lady. You may wait for him in his chambers and I will find him," he offered.

"Yes." Nicole entered, agitated, and began pacing as she waited. "He will tell me the truth," she repeated, then looked at the large book on the stand.

Nicole went over and opened the book, which was bound by leather cording, so that pages could be added or removed. It was a list of names—page after page of names in no discernible order.

After studying it for a moment, Nicole gathered it was a genealogy. She searched the pages for *Ares* or *Erlend*, but found neither. Nor could she tell how the names were arranged, as crowded as the entries were. So she closed the book with a sigh of frustration, lifting her eyes to the wall above it.

There was a framed parchment hanging on the wall that she listlessly regarded. It was the royal proclamation announcing the appointment of Carmine of Westford as Lord Counselor under Surchatain Cedric, signed and sealed by Cedric. Nicole looked at the date. It was dated six years ago. Signed by Surchatain Cedric.

But Carmine had told her he had served under Talus, and had been castrated under Talus to keep his post. She backed away from the certificate. "No. There is a mistake. I have misunderstood him. Perhaps he was an apprentice—" But even she knew there was no apprenticeship, no junior counselor rank. One was a Counselor or not. And he had lied to her about serving under Talus.

Head swimming, she left his chambers and found her way to the head of the stairs, where she clung to the column topping the balustrade. Here, she watched servants come and go, and soldiers come and go, and the business of the palace being transacted with alacrity and efficiency. She watched Giles complete a purchase of bed linens and the maids carry out copper pots to be cleaned. She saw messengers come in with sealed letters for the Surchatain, and she saw the Counselor ascend the stairs.

At the top of the stairs, he greeted her, "Lady Nicole, were you looking for me?"

"No, Counselor," she whispered.

His brows gathered in mild concern. "Are you well? You look pale."

"I am well, Counselor. Thank you," she said.

"Perhaps you should rest for tonight, my dear. I hear it's going to be a rather extravagant affair," he said, and she nodded.

She made her way down the stairs to Ares' chambers. She lay down on the straw bed and closed her eyes, then knew nothing more until a maid awakened her hours later. "Lady, come! Lord Lieterstad's party is here, and you won't believe your eyes!"

Nicole lifted up, groggy and leaden. She used the garderobe and bathed her hands and face, then came out without caring about the state of her dress, or her hair, or whether her cap was on straight or not. Then she entered the great hall with a throng of people.

Long rows of tables spanned the room, laden with a quantity of food that Nicole had never seen in one place in her life. People were gathering handfuls of delicacies off the serving tables, yet making hardly a dent in the feast. Forty or fifty casks with spigots were resting on their sides, already being tapped. There was so much laughing and talking that the musicians in the corner were completely drowned out.

More and more people were pouring into the hall all the time. And in the center of the tables, Nicole spotted Lord Lieterstad himself with his arm around Cedric's shoulders, gesturing and laughing. Even from this distance, Nicole could see that he was gray, obese, crude—and richer than Cedric. Renée was presented to him, and he embraced her with the sloppy, overbearing kind of kiss she hated. Thus the banquet was inaugurated, and gathered steam from there.

Nicole was elbowed out of the great hall by the sheer

number of people trying to get in, including soldiers. To get out of the way, she climbed the staircase to watch from the second floor. This was prudent, for the celebrating soon spilled out of the great hall into the foyer, courtyard, and every other open space.

A great number of people were eating, but an even greater number were drinking, and in great quantities—Lieterstad had apparently brought a hundred casks or more of pure Valley wine. The casks just kept coming and coming, and were set up on the steps, on the hearth, anywhere there was a raised place to set them.

The fest—for it could no longer be called a banquet—got louder and more boisterous. Nicole watched Lady Rhea drunkenly twirling in the red dress. A soldier pulled the cap off her head and kissed her, and she clutched his head in blatant lust. Nicole looked elsewhere.

At that point she began to notice the number of soldiers who were as drunk and disorderly as the invited guests. Then she saw Ares tearing through the foyer in rage. He grabbed one soldier, evidently demanding that he return to his post. The poor fellow saluted, then swayed on his feet and sank to his knees. Then a trio of soldiers lurched out of the great hall, arm in arm. Ares seized one and shook him like a rag doll. The other two burst into fits of laughter.

Ares shoved them away, looking through the crowd. Renée emerged from the banquet hall to head straight for him. He spotted her and clasped her hands as she said something in his ear. Then she reached up to kiss him passionately, and he replied earnestly to her.

They parted in the foyer: she returned to the banquet room while he went down the opposite corridor. And Nicole remembered the times she had awakened to find Ares not in bed. And how Renée had bragged about meeting her lover in the rose garden, in the orchards, in her chambers—

She raised her eyes to the chandelier in the ceiling,

thinking how nice the stars would look right now. So she descended the stairs and pushed her way through the foyer to get out into the courtyard. It was just as crowded here, with drunken revelers rolling on the steps or throwing up in the gutters. A stranger grabbed her arm, and she wrenched free only to stumble into a couple making love on a stone bench.

Nicole looked up at the walls, deserted of sentries, with the palace gates standing open in the night. So she walked through the gates, and down the south road. And she kept walking until the lights and clamor in the palace were a distant blur. Then she turned and said, "No more games. I am weary of your games, and will play no more."

She walked along the dark, deserted road, confident that the Lystran Commander kept it purged of wolves or robbers. Head down, she trudged up the switchback, step after step, until her legs ached. In a while the abbey fortress loomed ahead in the darkness, and a while later, she had reached its gates.

Nicole rang the bell again and again; finally, a wavering candlelight appeared, and a woman's voice called, "Who is there?"

"I need refuge," Nicole said, leaning her face against the bars. "Please let me in. I have nowhere else to go."

The nun opened the gate for her, and showed her to a tiny room with a pallet and a washbasin. Nicole thanked her, then removed the Chataine's gown, lay down on the pallet, and went to sleep—a deep, dreamless, depressed sleep.

Very early in the morning, a nun woke her: "Sister Agnes wishes to see you."

"Yes. Certainly," Nicole mumbled, getting up. The nun handed her a shapeless, course brown dress with a rope for a belt, a scarf for her head, and sandals for her feet. Then another nun took the gown, cap, and beaded shoes away while the first led Nicole into the corridor.

They walked down bare, narrow passages to a small room

where Sister Agnes sat at a table with a candle and ledger before her. "Good morning, child. I was told you came to the gate last night. What is your need?"

Apparently, Sister Agnes did not remember her; it seemed that her eyesight was not very good—the ledger was written in very large figures. "Sister," Nicole curtsied. "First, thank you for giving me shelter, for that is what I need. I am a willing worker, and will do whatever you require to earn my keep. I just ask that you let me stay, and not betray my whereabouts to anyone who comes searching."

"And what shall we call you, my child?" the Sister asked.

"Whatever you shall choose," Nicole murmured.

"Sister Elizabeth," Sister Agnes nodded to the nun who had brought her, "give Sarah her chores."

"Thank you," Nicole curtsied again.

On her way out, the sister said, "Child," and Nicole turned. "I will hold your garments for whenever you are ready to return to your life in the palace."

"Keep them, Sister," Nicole murmured.

Sister Elizabeth took her out past the children's ward and playground, explaining, "If you are here long enough, you will be allowed to care for the children. But not now. They are our greatest treasure." Nicole nodded, thinking about Henry, and she felt a little pain.

Then the sister showed her their candle-making shop, and kitchen, and chapel. Exiting the south side of the fortress, Sister Elizabeth showed her the vegetable garden that would henceforth be her responsibility. But what Nicole saw in the distance, when she looked up, was the Sea. And her heart soared in joy.

So began her new life. It was very regimented—early morning prayers and Scripture reading, to which she was summoned by a loud rap on her door. There were no elaborate dresses nor makeup, no braids nor jewelry but the filigree cross that still hung around her neck—she had taken off the wedding ring and placed it on the chain as well.

Each morning, after splashing her face and hands in the basin, she joined the other twenty-three sisters in proceeding to the rough benches in the chapel, where they listened to Sister Agnes read from the Holy Canon.

Then, without speaking, they gathered in the kitchen room for a simple breakfast, usually of bread and water. Again, there was no speaking, and it took a long time for Nicole to be able to distinguish individual sisters—silent, in their identical robes, there was no telling them apart. This she found strangely comforting, for she wanted nothing more than to hide among them, safe from treachery, heartache, and lies.

After breakfast Nicole was given gardening tools to work over the vegetable garden in progress, in which was growing carrots, chard, beans, and peas. It was a large plot, actually, about twenty by fifty feet. She had to weed the rows, water them, and harvest ripe vegetables.

The watering was the most laborious of the tasks, as she had to carry water in a bucket from the well on the other side of the abbey, past a cemetery plot with solemn stone markers. Fill the bucket, troop to the garden, empty the bucket, then troop back again many times over.

A bell was rung for lunch, and the sisters gathered again in the kitchen room for another simple meal, maybe of porridge or stew. At this time, Nicole could hear the children in the adjoining room whispering and giggling over their modest meal, and she longed to join them. Perhaps later, she would be allowed.

Following the meal, Sister Elizabeth showed Nicole her task for the afternoon, usually chopping wood or hauling water for the others who were doing laundry, cleaning, cooking, or candle-making. Elizabeth was a sweet, rather absent-minded woman who explained everything so haphazardly that Nicole had to fill in considerable blanks: "Take this over here, and, get the bucket off the shelf—no, the other shelf—no, the other bucket—" But Nicole had been self-sufficient long enough to figure out what to do.

The bell for the evening meal called them all back into the kitchen, where they would have a special treat of whatever vegetables Nicole had harvested that morning. At dinner, they were allowed the privilege of conversation, to which Nicole had nothing to contribute. She only listened, and listened so quietly that they almost forgot she was there. The conversation was less interesting than palace talk, as it was considerably less bloody, especially without the Chataine.

Following were prayers and Scripture reading until the evening bell, then a sponge bath and bed. Over the next few days, Nicole's long hair became heavy and greasy. With no sea water nor underground stream to wash it in, a great deal of it was cut off at her request. As there was no one to admire it, what did she need long hair for? Tub baths came once a week, at most.

The days passed in quiet work, and the nights in sound sleep. Such a drastic change from the luxury of palace life would have maddened others, but for Nicole, it was a necessary retreat to the simplicity and gentleness of the life she had left behind in Prie Mer.

After lining up to receive her meager portion at her first meal, she understood that no servers would attend her here, and she did not mind. She was weary of the finery, the gossip, the tension in Westford. Here, it was possible to put out of her mind the memory of Ares' kissing Renée; Nicole could pretend it never happened.

Once she got used to sleeping on a pallet again, she lost sleep over nothing, as tired as she was at the end of the day. The vegetable garden nourished her body and the Scripture reading nourished her soul. When she tired over the shovel or hoe, she could always look out to the Sea, and no one laughed at her clothes.

The only difficulty was that she was still unwilling to tell them anything about herself, and that offended them. She knew that scouts from the palace had come asking about Nicole of Prie Mer, but Sister Agnes had told them, "Our only new arrival has been Sarah."

At dinner, one of the nuns had asked her, "Are you this Nicole they are searching for?"

She had replied, "I am not who I once was."

Scrutinizing her, the sister caught a glimpse of the gold chain around her neck, and reached out as if to take it. Nicole caught her hand in surprise. "Jewelry is not allowed here. You must remove it," the sister said.

"Remove your hand or I will break it, dear sister," Nicole said sweetly. Sister Agnes was appealed to, who rendered the unpopular judgment to let the novice be.

Fitting in was made a little easier when Nicole discovered that leverage was as useful in an abbey as a palace. When she saw one nun stealing candy from a child's bag, she paused in the corridor long enough so that the guilty sister would know she had been seen, and by whom. This sister became one of Nicole's staunchest defenders.

To another nun who had a tart, bitter tongue, Nicole leaned over sweetly to whisper at dinner, "I learned conversational skills from a laundress who would rip you to shreds in seconds, so if you mimic dear Elizabeth one more time behind her back, I shall entertain the table with what I saw you doing in the wash tub last night." The poor sister then attained a new level of self-control, at least around Nicole.

A few of the nuns were extremely curious about "Sarah," several were quite jealous, and a majority thought that she should not be allowed to stay unless she took vows to enter the order. For the most part, Nicole kept her head down and her mouth closed, looking out to the Sea whenever she needed its broadness and peace.

There was another source of peace even richer and deeper. The reading of the Holy Canon gave her a great deal to think about as she weeded row upon row of carrots. When she heard, "Bless those who curse you, pray for those who abuse you," she knew that applied even more to those who did it unintentionally. For she held no ill will against the Commander, and the Chataine, and the Counselor because of the games they played; that was their way of life. Just not hers.

In the scant moments of rest, when she lay down on the pallet at the close of day, she did miss him. She missed his warmth, and tenderness, and lust for her. Sometimes she dreamed of him, and upon first waking, would reach over expecting to feel him beside her. But when she came full awake with the emptiness of his absence, she wished that she had never come to Westford, never known his embrace.

Once, she even thought, *I should have married Tancred.* But that fleeting thought never merited a second. At times she would feel the hardness of her abdomen, but did not speculate on anything. And, she did pray the Lord God's peace on the man she married. She prayed for them all, but she did not want to go back. The thought of the beautiful Chataine riding her stallion was too painful.

The days followed in such rapid succession that she lost track of them. The morning hours in the garden grew warm, and the nights lost all chill, so that Nicole woke once or twice perspiring on her pallet. But she just bathed herself with water and lay down again.

Then at one morning devotional, Nicole heard these words read:

> One thing have I asked of the Lord,
>   that will I seek after;
> that I may dwell in the house of the Lord
>   all the days of my life,
> to behold the beauty of the Lord,
>   and to inquire in his temple.

> For he will hide me in his shelter
>> in the day of trouble;
> he will conceal me under the cover
>> of his tent,
> he will set me high upon a rock.

The words were so beautiful, so applicable, that Nicole believed them to be a sign. So she asked Sister Agnes for permission to take beginning vows, and to send the gown back to the palace. The sister agreed.

But almost immediately, contradictory signs appeared. The very next day these words were read at the morning devotional:

> Be gracious to me, O Lord, for I am in distress;
>> my eye is wasted from grief,
>> my soul and my body also.
> For my life is spent with sorrow,
>> and my years with sighing;
> my strength fails because of my misery,
>> and my bones waste away.

On hearing that, Nicole thought of Ares. He came to her mind very vividly, and she wondered what he was praying, because she knew he prayed. Then she began to feel guilty that she had not even told him she was alive and well. She had demanded that Tancred be given that message, when Tancred had loved her less. Wasn't it cruel of her to not let Ares know?

She tried to tell herself he did not care, but she knew that he did. No matter how much he loved the Chataine, he still cared for her. Pondering what great effort he had exerted to rescue her from the tower at Eurus made Nicole so drawn and anxious that the other nuns took notice. Sister Agnes held off on her request to take vows, and did nothing with the palace garments.

And then one morning, Nicole was out working in the garden, hoeing the rows, when she looked up and saw an eagle circling the cliff. It reminded her of Henry's wretched game with the soldier and the eagle, and she dropped the hoe. Henry! How could she forget Henry? He had done nothing to deserve desertion. How was Henry faring?

That night, she was so restless that she could not sleep. And in the morning, she arose early to accost Sister Agnes before her reading of the Scriptures: "Dear Sister, I am not ready to go back, but . . . I must see Chatain Henry. Is it possible for me to speak with him?"

"I will see if the Commander will bring him," the Sister said.

Nicole panicked. "Just—Henry, Sister. I wish to speak with no one else."

"We will try to arrange it, child, but the Chatain cannot come without his guardian," Agnes said.

"I understand," Nicole nodded, and fidgeted anxiously throughout the devotional.

Some hours later, she was harvesting chard from her garden when one of the sisters approached. "Sarah, you have a visitor."

Nicole turned quickly to see Henry looking at her quizzically. The sight of him pierced her heart, and she fell on her knees to embrace him, crying, "Oh, Henry, I've missed you so!"

"Nicole?" he said dubiously. She took the scarf from her hair, nodding and crying. "What are you doing here?" he asked with grown-up logic and seriousness.

"Leave us, please," she said to the sister, who withdrew hesitantly. "Oh, Henry. I was scared and upset. I ran away the night of Lord Lieterstad's banquet."

"Oh," he said.

"Henry, please forgive me. Tell me how you are," she pleaded.

"I am well," he said almost formally.

Her heart shattered at his indifference. "Henry, how are things with your Father?"

"Father is fine. He's doing much better now that you're gone," Henry said.

"Why is that?" she asked weakly.

"Because of Ares," he said.

Nicole inhaled, squeezing his small hands. "Henry, please —tell me everything from the beginning. What happened after Lord Lieterstad's fest?"

"Well, so many people were being bad that Ares was throwing them in prison, and then he couldn't find you, and the next morning nobody could find you, so Ares said that Lord Lieterstad or somebody with him had taken you away. And the lord said that he didn't, and there was a big fight and Ares threw him out and so sister didn't go to live with him.

"And then Ares sent scouts out looking for you, but nobody could find you, and he offered a thousand royals for your safe return, and people were bringing all kinds of girls to the palace, but none of them was you. And then Ares got so— sad; he's been so sad, and people say he's going to kill himself, and so Father is happy that he won't have to."

Nicole looked down at the tears dropping from her face to the fresh chard. "Henry, how long has it been since the fest?" she whispered.

"Um, about a month, I guess."

"A month!" she groaned. "I have been very foolish. Will you forgive me?"

"Will you come back?" he asked.

"Do you want me to?" she asked.

"Yes!" he said, jumping up. "Oh, Ares will be so happy!"

"I don't know about that," she murmured. "Is he here with you?"

"Yes! I'll go get him—"

"Wait! Henry, just—will you go wait with him? Tell him

to wait, but don't tell him why, and then I will come to you. Please, Chatain?" she asked.

He snickered. "It will be a surprise!"

"For all of us," she said, having no idea how he might react. "Go. I'll be right there."

18

When Nicole rushed into Sister Agnes' little cubicle to request her palace clothes, she had them ready for her. Clutching them, Nicole paused. She did not want to meet Ares filthy and smelly as she was, but just drawing a bath would take hours.

So Nicole brazenly interrupted the sisters in their washing of clothes, and commandeered the tub. They shrieked and fussed at her as she stripped and sat among robes and bloomers, but she did not care. She could hardly believe that she had been hiding here longer than she had been married before she had come here. Scrubbing her head, she realized she had run from the wedding after all, just a few weeks later.

As she stepped out to dry herself with someone's clean robe, she asked one of the sisters who watched incredulously, "Help me dress, please."

The sister snapped, "What, are we servants now?"

"Would you like to get rid of me?" Nicole asked. So the sister helped her with the petticoats and fastened her buttons. Nicole dried her hair as best she could on someone else's clean robe, but it was still wet as she affixed the cap. The hair fell just below her shoulders, and she winced, considering how long it used to be. The wedding ring she slipped back onto her ring finger. He could remove it if he wished, but for now they were still married.

Nicole was shaking as she walked the corridor toward the front of the abbey. The nuns gathered to watch, some disdainful, others happy for her. Nicole tried to smile at them, because if Ares rejected her, she would have to crawl back here on her knees. If he wanted her back, she still had to confront the lies she had been told. She continued to shake badly until she realized, no, there was a third option: she could always go home to Prie Mer. And with the memory of the Sea in her heart, she calmed.

Sister Elizabeth opened the door into the yard and Nicole stepped out, but Ares was looking toward the side yard whence Henry had appeared in great excitement to tell him to be still and wait. As she approached, his head snapped in her direction, and he straightened. She saw how drawn and tired he looked. Curtsying, she said, "My Lord Commander."

"Lady," he nodded.

For a few moments, nothing more was said. Henry looked between them in absolute disgust that they weren't falling into each other's arms. Nicole swallowed, then said, "Forgive my absence, my lord. Forgive my failure to send word to you."

"I knew you were here," he said. "I did not know why."

She looked around at the wide-eyed children and listening nuns. "May we—" she turned to Sister Agnes. "May we have a private room to converse?"

"Step out of the gate, and we will keep Henry here for you," the sister suggested.

"Put me on Karst," Henry demanded.

Ares opened the gate and extended his hand, and Nicole stepped through. They walked twenty paces down the road while a score of little faces pressed against the gate. He turned to her, folding his hands, and waited. In that stance, he was such an imposing figure, hard and unyielding. But if they were to stay married, she must not be cowed in her demand for the truth.

Nicole inhaled and began, "When we were on our way to Eurus, Renée told me that she had been in love with a soldier. They were lovers. Her father got wind of it, and sent for him, and he disappeared. Then, the day of Lord Lieterstad's fest, she was teaching me how to dance. She said she taught you to dance. She said she . . . taught you how to kiss. And then, Hillary said . . . you were that soldier. And, I saw you kiss the Chataine in the foyer, and I knew that you still loved each other, and there was no place for me."

His eyes filled with tears, and he looked off into the trees. He cleared his throat, then said, "She taught me to dance. She taught me to kiss. I was her patsy, her plaything. But we were not lovers. We were never lovers."

In a flash, she saw two things: first, his willingness to be her plaything when they had just met—how little she knew what he meant at the time! And second, his desperation to be married. The torture of desire was endurable only for so long. His words rang true.

But, mindful of how many plausible lies she had been told, she said, "I do not believe you, Ares. The only way it makes sense for the Surchatain to want you dead is if you father a child by his daughter. Not by me."

Blinking rapidly, he dropped his head. "If you come back with me to the palace, I will prove it to you," he whispered.

"I will do that," she said. He extended his hand for hers, and she gave it. But when he turned it palm up and paused in surprise over the blisters, she withdrew it. He seized her hand again and pressed his lips to the blistered palm, and she had to sternly remind herself that he still had much to prove.

He turned back to the gate, which was opened for Henry and Karst. Nicole embraced Sister Agnes, thanking her, but Ares was more subdued in his thanks. He lifted Nicole onto Karst behind Henry, and took the reins to run alongside as

Karst trotted. Henry thought it great fun to see how fast he could make Karst go, so that Ares would lose hold of the reins. But Karst snorted at that idea and kept his own head. Meanwhile, Ares kept tripping, as he was trying to look up at Nicole while he ran.

There was astonished murmuring as they entered the cobbled court and brushed through the crowd to the palace steps. Tossing Karst's reins to a servant, Ares gave swift instructions for Henry to be taken upstairs and the Chataine to be summoned to the Counselor's chambers.

Told that the Counselor was in conference in the Surchatain's receiving room, Ares said, "Wait for him to come out, then tell him we are all waiting in his chambers."

The soldier saluted, then said, "Welcome home, Lady." She smiled, unconvinced.

Gripping her hand, Ares led her upstairs, bypassing courtiers who greeted her. She tried to acknowledge them, but he escorted her directly into the Counselor's receiving room and shut the door, gesturing to a chair. Then he stood back, crossed his arms, and waited. She sat staring at the floor.

After a moment, he observed, "You cut your hair."

"I did not have running water to keep it clean," she said.

"I like it," he said, slightly choked.

"I thank you," she replied.

They resumed their burden of silence, unwieldy when so much was waiting to be said. She twisted her wedding ring around and around on her finger, trying to ignore how much she wanted to feel his arms around her. As she did feel his eyes, she did not trust herself to lift her head.

The door burst open and Renée appeared. "Darling!" she cried, flinging herself toward Nicole, but waiting until she stood to embrace her. Nicole held her calmly, looking at Ares over her shoulder, and he lifted his chin. "Darling, where have you been?" Renée asked.

"The abbey," Nicole replied.

"The abbey! Why were you at the abbey?"

Ares cut to the chase: "Chataine, we have some matters to clear up. You told Nicole that you had made love to a soldier. Hillary told her that soldier was me. Now you have to tell Nicole the truth."

Renée flung up her arms in exasperation at Nicole. "That wasn't Ares! How could you think that?"

Nicole looked off without speaking. Ares told Renée, "Tell her what you said to me in the foyer on the night Lieterstad was here, and what I said to you."

Renée looked pensive, and Ares lowered his chin at her. She sighed, "I told you I was going to marry Lieterstad even though I hated him because he was old and fat and I would miss you terribly."

"And then you did what?" he prompted.

"I kissed you," she shrugged.

"Now tell Nicole exactly what I told you," he said.

Renée crossed her arms, pouting, "You said, 'I'll miss you, too. Now stop kissing me,' or something just as rude."

"This is pointless. Why shouldn't she kiss you if she wants? I will not interfere." Nicole turned toward the door, but Ares blocked her path.

"Chataine, tell her who your lover was," he insisted, beads of sweat on his forehead.

Renée clamped her mouth shut and the door opened as Carmine entered. "Nicole! You are back! Welcome home, dear lady!"

"Thank you," she said coldly.

Carmine looked at Ares, who said, "We have some matters to untangle. My wife has been told that the Chataine and I are lovers."

"Oh." Carmine dropped his head.

"She must be told the truth," Ares repeated.

Nicole burst out, "I am sorry, but—I don't believe a word any of you says! Not about your lover [gesturing to Renée], or your threat to Cedric [at Ares], or your post! [indicating Carmine] I am here only as long as Henry wants me to be, and the rest of you can play with each other to your heart's content!"

As she reached around Carmine to put her hand on the latch, he said, "I was her lover."

The shock of it caused Nicole's hand to squeeze the door handle. She slowly turned while her hand was still attached to it. "She—" Carmine gestured, "played with both of us—Ares and me. We were both her toys, her pets. And we both loved her madly, but—Ares kept himself under control. I did not. I —succumbed. When Cedric found out about it, as inevitably he would, he—dealt with it." Carmine spread his hands over his loins.

"When did this happen?" Nicole asked.

"About a year ago," Carmine admitted while Renée hung her head.

"Yet he kept you as Counselor?" Nicole asked in disbelief.

"I am an excellent Counselor," Carmine laughed dryly. "One thing you must understand about Cedric—he keeps exceptional people even though they may be dangerous. He just makes sure they are—sufficiently harnessed." Renée came over to place her arms around his neck, and he kissed her face.

Nicole looked at Ares. "Case in point," the Counselor said, nodding toward him. "The superlative soldier. Quick, strong, courageous—head and shoulders above the rest. Moreover, a master strategist. Incisive reasoning. Decisive in action. All very dangerous qualities in a Commander, for without blood loyalty, those qualities also make him an excellent usurper."

"All the more reason for the Surchatain to kill you," Nicole said to Ares.

He shifted his gaze to Renée, and the Counselor patted her back. "Darling, you must wait outside now."

"Why?" Renée said, offended, as she lifted her head from his shoulder.

"We have one more matter to cover with dear Nicole, which Ares wishes to keep private," Carmine said. Renée glanced down her nose at Ares and swept out.

After the door had closed, Carmine walked over to the book on the stand and opened it. "Here, Nicole." She came to stand by his side.

"This is the book of families of Westford. They are listed in alphabetical order of the patriarch's name—the first person in the family line to have lived in Westford. Unfortunately, the book is only fragmentary, but it is a great help in establishing estates and such. Here is my grandfather Aschner, my father Maxon, and myself. It will end there," he noted heavily.

Nicole looked at the listing in black ink, with sidebars to siblings, and wives in parentheses. "Here," he said, flipping pages, "is the listing for Ares." She bent over the book to see, in the E's, the listing of "Erlend" followed by "Ares." "Nicole" was in parentheses by his name, and she felt strangely warm to see it. His listing also ended there.

"Here is the listing for Cedric," he said, turning a great portion of the book to the T's. There she saw "Talus," and a sidebar to "Reynard" and "Ellis," then "Cedric" below "Talus." Here it got complicated, with Cedric's wives in parentheses, "Renée" squeezed in beneath "Cedric" and "(Vivian)," and "Henry" beneath "Cedric" and "(Elise)." There was also a sidebar from "Cedric" to "Lute," but there was no indication of Roman's line.

Nicole began, "But, I thought he was—"

"Descended from Roman? Of course. Let's look," Carmine said, flipping back to the E's. "Here is what we have." Nicole bent to see the listing of "Eudymon," then "Roman," "Ariel," and "Bobadil," with their wives. Beside Bobadil's name, there were sidebars to "Hume" and "Toal." And that was all.

"I don't understand," she said.

"Look closer, beneath Bobadil," he instructed. "Do you see something that might have been written there at one time . . . ?"

Nicole peered down at the page. "Yes! There are letters that have been blotted out. There is a C?—no. That's an E. It's E-R-L—" She gasped and looked up at Ares, who shifted.

"That is correct. Erlend. Ares' father. Your husband is the great-grandson of Ariel and the great-great-grandson of Roman of Westford," Carmine said.

Nicole exclaimed, "Then where did Talus come from?"

"Talus was Commander of the army under Bobadil. When Bobadil lost much of Lystra, he lost his life, as well. Talus murdered him and usurped the throne," Carmine replied.

Nicole stared at Ares, who was watching her without expression. Carmine continued, "But Bobadil left heirs. Talus killed Bobadil's younger brothers Hume and Toal, so Bobadil's son fled with his grandson, but Talus caught up with them in a tavern. He killed Erlend, and struck at the boy, who wrenched away so that the blade missed his throat and slashed his face instead. Talus' brother Reynard had been following him, and found him poised for the kill.

"Reynard, who was a better man than Talus, convinced him to spare the boy's life—he gave his own life in surety for the boy. 'I will raise him to be loyal to you,' he said. So they drilled it into the boy that he was slashed by accident, that his father Erlend was a newcomer to Westford.

"By the time Reynard died, the boy had grown into the most promising lieutenant the army had seen in years. But Talus would not risk his living another day—would not risk Roman's only surviving descendant producing an heir. So the day after Reynard died, Talus brought out the young man to be beheaded on the block. But he almost had a rebellion among the soldiers when they saw what was transpiring.

"While the young man stood by the block, Talus asked

him, 'Who is your father?' 'Erlend,' the young man answered. 'And how did you get slashed?' 'By drunken soldiers,' the young man said. The army, knowing nothing more, saw no reason for his execution, so Talus kept him alive, but advised his son Cedric to keep him firmly under his thumb."

"But—how can a usurper rule, under the Law of Roman?" Nicole asked.

"By treachery and deception. Talus told his officials that they were set upon by Selecan assassins, and they chose to believe him. They foolishly allowed him to be regent for the Chatain Ares. But one by one, Bobadil's officials met untimely deaths, and gradually the positions of Talus and Ares were shifted. Only Reynard stood between the boy and the block. Moreover, Talus was well on his way to overthrowing the Law of Roman when he died," Carmine related.

"Who killed him?" Nicole asked.

"The Lord of heaven," Carmine replied. "Talus died of a fever. Cedric said it originated in an infected toe."

"Did Talus kill his own brother Reynard?" Nicole asked.

"No. Reynard died defending his country against Qarqarian invaders. Ares fought in the same battle," the Counselor said, inclining his head toward the Commander, still mute.

Nicole glanced at her husband, then looked back at Carmine. "How do you know all this?"

"From Surchatain Cedric himself," Carmine uttered. "After I had found the blotted-out name in the book."

Nicole turned to Ares. "Why wouldn't you tell me this?" she whispered.

"My love," he said softly, "there is no place I could have told you free of ears—not even in my own quarters. And once you knew. . . . The only way I have preserved my life is by keeping the deception alive."

"But—you always knew who you were," she said.

"I always knew," he admitted.

She gazed at the book. "That is why Cedric cannot allow Roman's heir to have a child." She put a hand to her abdomen. "How long has it been since Lord Lieterstad's fest?"

"Three weeks," said Ares. "Twenty black, miserable days."

Nicole inched toward him. "If you knew where I was, why didn't you come for me? Why did you send scouts and offer a reward?"

"I found you after the scouts reported that Sarah, with long, beautiful, red-brown hair, had come to the abbey the night Lieterstad was here. I offered the reward hoping one of the nuns would get greedy and bring you. But God forbid I invade His territory to bring you out by force," he said.

Nicole looked at him—his smoky eyes, his dark hair, his full lips—and reached out to him. He covered the distance between them in two steps to grab her up and bury his face in her neck. "I wish you had told me," she said with tears.

He hushed her with his mouth, and the Counselor turned away. Ares, with his arm tightly around her, led her out of his chambers down the staircase. Courtiers and servants appeared from out of the walls to extend their welcome and good wishes, but Nicole hardly saw them for flying down the stairs and corridor.

When Ares opened the door to his chambers, she saw with an aching heart that he had left everything in place, even the annoying dresses, to await her return. Except there was a pallet on the floor beside the bed.

She turned to him, laughing, and he caught her face. "The sweetest sound in the world," he said, his voice catching, but as she pointed down to the pallet, he ruefully explained, "I could hardly sleep on that bed while you were here; I surely couldn't while you were gone."

She kissed him deeply, then laughed in her throat. Imperially, he raised his face in inquiry. She admitted, "I should be grateful to the Chataine. She taught you well." He dropped his reddening face, and she pressed her lips gently to his scar. "Oh, Ares, I am sorry. I was wrong to stay away for so long."

He kissed down her face to her neck. "It was ordained. I had not yet weakened to the point of telling you the truth. You were not to be returned to me until I resolved to speak the truth."

"Ares, what happened with Lord Lieterstad?" she asked.

He snorted, rolling his eyes. "What a disgraceful scene—so much wine, everyone drunk—my army fell apart in a matter of hours. I never realized until then that Lieterstad was a greater threat to our security than Ossian! Without sentries, people began looting the palace, harassing the maids—I finally had to lock the women up, including the Chataine, to keep them safe from two-legged wolves. Then I could not find you—" he broke off, momentarily overcome, and Nicole breathed repeated apologies into his brocade jacket.

He straightened. "When, by the next morning, you were not to be found in the palace environs, I had concluded that someone of Lieterstad's party had taken you. So, while they were hung over and deathly sick, I made threats and pronouncements and threw them out into the street. I broke open all the casks and threw the food out to the beggars. As soon as I had sober scouts, I sent them out. And by the end of the day I had the report from the abbey.

"I put out the reward and waited; I approached Sister Agnes and asked for you. She said, 'If Sarah is here because of her own sin, then God will make that plain to her. If she is here because of your sin, then God must make that plain to you.'

"So I came back and pleaded with God, and He confronted me with the fact that I had not been truthful to you. I had not *lied,* but I had not told you the truth. And every day when I asked for you, He showed me my sin in reply.

"When at last He brought me to my knees this morning,

and I resolved to tell you the truth, not five minutes later the messenger came from the abbey with the request to bring Henry. And when I saw you, and the first words out of your mouth were a plea for the truth—" he stopped, again overcome, and she held him tightly. "God is merciless. He routed me thoroughly," Ares whispered.

Nicole held his face down to hers to comfort him. Then a thought crossed her mind, and she asked uneasily, "Was the Surchatain very angry over your treatment of Lord Lieterstad?" The failure of that marriage alliance might easily be blamed on Nicole herself.

Ares laughed dryly. "He was quite pleased. He could not turn Lieterstad down without insulting him, but he did not want his daughter in the midst of such decadence. Even Cedric has that much sense. Lieterstad left humble as a lamb, knowing only that he did something unforgivable while drunk out of his mind."

"Oh." She caressed his black dress jacket and waited. He kissed her and held her, but that was all, and she wondered why he wasn't fumbling with clothes. In scant minutes, she got her answer. A sentry pounded on the door: "The Surchatain summons the Lady Nicole, Commander."

This is what he had been expecting. Opening the door, he said, "I will escort her." The sentry saluted, but followed them as Ares took her back up the stairs to the Surchatain's wing. At the door of his receiving room, Nicole was shown inside while Ares was blocked from entering. She glanced back at him in surprise, but the door was shut between them.

She turned around as the Surchatain emerged from his inner chambers. "Hello, Nicole," he said mildly, and she curtsied. He was fresh and perfumed as always, with his curling hair and ruddy cheeks, and Nicole suddenly saw why Ares resisted luxury. It softened a man's body and conscience. Cedric sat, studying her with some indecision. "Why did you come back?" he asked.

"Oh, that was such a silly misunderstanding, Surchatain. Lord Lieterstad's fest was so wild I got frightened and ran to the abbey. Ares thought I was running from him and waited for me to come back, while I was waiting for him to come get me. I feel very foolish now," she ended quite truthfully.

"Ah. I see." He sat at the table littered with parchments. She remained standing. "He was very upset," he added.

"I am sorry to have caused so much trouble," she said.

"So the only way he could get you back was to tell you he is descended from royalty," Cedric said. Nicole did not react, other than to look slightly bemused. "I wish he had been content to be Commander. He was very good at it," Cedric admitted, rubbing his face, and Nicole began to tremble at his use of the past tense.

"Are you pregnant?" he asked suddenly.

"Not that I know of, High Lord," she replied.

"Well, here is the most I can do for him. I will marry you, and Ares can keep his post. But don't expect to have any authority as Surchataine—you will be just a figurehead. You are good for Henry, though. And don't expect that you can continue to sleep with Ares behind my back, because then I will certainly execute you both. And don't expect to sleep with me every night in my chambers. I will have occasional guests," he warned her.

Somehow, she knew this moment had been coming. She had been preparing for it ever since her first day in the palace, when she looked at the lion and the cross on Roman's banner and knew they belonged to her. She knew it in the tower at Eurus, waiting for an impossible rescue that came to pass. She knew it in the abbey, where the simplicity and quiet and Scripture fortified her, and her refusal to give up the necklace signified her refusal to give up on Ares. All this she realized only now.

"You do not want me. You just do not want Ares to have me," she said.

"That's quite right," he agreed. "Although I won't object to having you in my bed."

"I will not marry you," she said.

He looked up at her, pursing his lips in surprise and aggravation. "Don't tell me he's persuaded you that you will be Surchataine with him, has he? I did want to keep him. Oh, well, he's brought Thom along well enough, so I suppose now's as good a time as any to find him guilty of treason. The only way you can save his life is by doing what I ask."

"I do not believe you. I believe that you will execute him regardless of what I do," Nicole replied.

"I had hoped you were a little more trusting," he said ruefully. "You must understand that Ares has been under the blade all his life, even though Reynard bought him a reprieve. Ares has been most useful to me, but under no circumstance will I let him out from under that shadow, for Henry's sake. By law, the only way for Ares to regain the throne of his ancestor is for me and Henry to die. How could I permit that?

"But just to show you that I am not a monster, I will not force you to marry me. You can marry Lieterstad, and live in luxury the rest of your life. Actually, that probably would be preferable, as it would remove both you and Ares from temptation."

Nicole replied, "I will not marry Lieterstad, because I am already married. You gave us leave to marry, and your seal is on our marriage decree. It is not lawful for you to break your word."

Cedric only laughed, "Faith, you're maddening. I don't think I'd want you after all. But thank you for reminding me." He stepped to the door and told the sentry, "Come in. Ares, you wait there."

Once the sentry was inside with the door shut, Cedric said, "Instruct him to give up his signet, and go with him to get it. I know he's got it hidden somewhere in his quarters. When he opens his hiding place, clear everything out of it and bring it all to me. Have Ares put in prison." With a troubled face, the sentry saluted and left.

Nicole turned to the Surchatain to request, "Put me there with him."

"It is not a pleasant place, Lady," he smiled grimly. "Besides which, there is no way in heaven or earth I will give him the consolation of your presence for another moment before he dies tomorrow."

19

edric offered her a chair to wait, and she sat, wondering if she shouldn't have remained at the abbey, to prolong Ares' life. But that was no solution. The crisis was ordained.

Some time later the sentry returned. With him were two other soldiers bearing heavy leather satchels. "What's all this?" Cedric exclaimed.

"The contents of the Commander's hiding place, High Lord," the first man said, bowing. "We figure he had close to a thousand royals stashed away."

"Where did he get that?" Cedric demanded.

"He saved his salary, Surchatain. No one ever saw him spend any of it, except for gifts to the abbey. And dresses," the sentry replied, nodding down at Nicole. She reflected on the fact that he had offered everything he had to redeem her out of the abbey. And those thousand royals compared to the fifty he had offered for Lady Rhea spoke volumes about whom he valued more.

"Excellent. Put it there," Cedric nodded to a corner, and the satchels were stashed atop each other. "Now what else do you have?"

"Your signet, High Lord." The sentry handed over the

ring on the chain. "And this." He extended the parchment scroll tied up with the bodice ribbon.

Cedric untied it and glanced over the certificate of marriage. Then he tossed it on the embers of the hearth, where it burst into flame. Nicole reached for it with a little cry, but in moments it was ashes. "There. You see how easy it is? You are now free to marry anyone I choose," Cedric said.

Nicole clenched her fists in anger, then calmed. Now, more than ever, she must keep her head. "You let Elise go. Let us go—banish us—and we will not trouble you," she said.

He laughed in derision. "Let him go so he can gather an army against me?" Nicole saw an uncomfortable resemblance here to Henry's game with toy soldiers. But then she thought, there may be hope in that.

"You tire me. Take her," he nodded to the sentry.

He paused. "Where to, Surchatain?"

Cedric shrugged, "She can go about as she wishes, except not to leave the palace."

The soldier bowed, then opened the door for Nicole to exit. He walked with her to the head of the stairs, where he conspicuously paused. Seeing the hesitation on his face, Nicole requested, "Take me to Ares. Please."

"The Commander asked to see you, and the Surchatain did not forbid that, did he?" the soldier considered.

"No," she said lightly. "No, he did not."

"It can only be for a moment," he said sternly.

"I understand that," she said meekly, looking up at him.

With a grunt, he gestured her down the stairs. Then he took her down a lower corridor to a locked and guarded door. He nodded at the sentry there, who unlocked the door with a large key on his belt. Then the soldier took her down a long, dank flight of steps lit by smoking torches. Nicole coughed, and the sound bounced off the cavern walls into which they descended. She heard dripping water, and foul, stagnant odors rose around her.

At the bottom of the steps, the sentry motioned her to the first cell in a long corridor of cells. Another guard brought out a key to open the barred door, and she looked in at Ares, resting against the wall, blinking in the torchlight. "Don't come in!" he warned, and she paused in dismay on the threshold of the cell. Then she peered down at the excrement, mud, and rat droppings in which he stood.

Ares made his way to the doorway as she reached out to him impatiently. While the guard stood close by, he took her in his arms to kiss her and caress her. "Oh, my love," he sighed. "Tell our child about me. Tell him how much his father loved his mother."

"Ares, don't say that," she said, fighting the tears. "You will live."

He kissed her lips and her face, seeming as insatiable as he was on their wedding night. Then, as the guard shifted uncomfortably, Ares put his lips to her ear. "I do not know what will happen tomorrow, but I am certain there will be bloodshed. You must get Henry and Renée to the abbey at once. There is a secret exit in the Surchatain's chambers— Henry knows of it. Get them to safety, my love," he whispered.

"Yes, my lord," she whispered.

Ares released her to the guard with a nod of thanks. He locked his Commander back in the stinking hole, then escorted her back up the steep, slippery steps. Nicole was thinking hard the whole time. If she succeeded in getting Henry to the abbey, he would not be able to intervene and save Ares from execution. Since Nicole had promised she would get them out, she had to make good on her word. But perhaps there was something else she could do for Ares. . . .

At the top of the steps, as the soldier released her into the lower corridor, she turned to him to say, "Did you know that Ares is the great-great-grandson of Surchatain Roman? The Counselor showed me from the book of families." The soldier and the guard at the door both stared at her. "Ask the Counselor," she shrugged. The winter of deception was over.

As the bell tolled seven, Nicole went to Ares' quarters to bathe and change. (The harsh soap that the nuns used to wash clothes smelled almost as bad as sweat.) She bolted the door from the inside, noting the stone still on the floor, exposing the empty hiding place. She pulled his tub out under the water flow, then ripped a few buttons off the dress rather than call for assistance. Tonight, she trusted no one.

Once bathed, she dressed in the old-fashioned peach gown from Lord Preus, as it was easy to put on and easy to move around in. Also, it would give less offense to the nuns than some of the Chataine's gowns. (Surprisingly, it was also rather loose on her.) While waiting for the bell to toll eight, she twisted the wedding ring on her finger and deliberated a plan of action. Then she wondered if she would be invited to the Surchatain's table at all tonight.

Before the dinner bell tolled, she went to the anteroom where the courtiers were waiting. At that time she was able to properly greet all those who had tried to speak to her earlier. Everyone wanted to know why she had been at the abbey all this time, but no one ventured to ask. "Everyone may enter now," Georges announced.

Thom, however, drew close to Nicole to mutter, "Why has the Surchatain put the Commander in prison?"

"The Commander's in prison?" Deirdre shrieked, and a host of courtiers hushed. No one went into the banquet hall yet.

Nicole paused with suspended breath. Telling a few lowly soldiers was one thing—what was she to say to a roomful of courtiers who ate with the Surchatain? She opened her mouth and said, "Commander Ares is to be tried for treason, and will be found guilty, and be executed, and you have been selected to replace him, Thom."

"What treason?" Thom asked, barely audible.

"Please be seated now," Georges directed the guests in a high, anxious voice.

"Ares is Surchatain Roman's last living descendant, and Surchatain Cedric will not allow him to produce an heir," Nicole replied.

Thom's mouth continued to hang open. "The Commander is . . . ?"

"Roman's great-great-grandson. The Counselor showed me the names in the book of families he keeps in his chambers," Nicole said.

"Everyone enter now, please!" Georges pleaded, imagining the Surchatain entering to an empty table.

There seemed to be a general hesitation. Thom stood fixed in place, eyes on the wall, then he took Deirdre's hand to stride into the banquet hall. The others began following. Nicole turned to Georges. "Am I eating at this table tonight, sir?"

"Yes, of course, Lady Nicole. Welcome home," he said almost desperately.

She stood behind her usual seat, and waited with the others in heavy silence until Georges announced, "Counselor Carmine."

He entered, immediately perceiving the oppressive atmosphere at the table, and looked at Nicole. "Ares is in prison," she whispered. Since Ares' place to her left was set as usual, a tiny inner voice told her that the Surchatain would relent, and bring him to the table where he belonged, and forget this bloody business of ascension. But she was unbelieving.

"Chatain Henry and Chataine Renée," Georges announced. The table turned to bow as they entered, Henry skipping ahead of his sister.

But seeing Ares' place vacant, he balled his fists with a roar of frustration. "Now you are here, and he is not! Where is Ares?" he bellowed in his childish voice.

Nicole felt a surge of pity, knowing how empty his days were, how he hung on those moments of play with his guardian, his toy. But everyone was looking to her to answer Henry, even the Counselor.

"You must ask your father, Chatain," she replied. Renée looked at Carmine in alarm, and he leaned over to whisper in her ear. Henry, however, crossed his arms and set his face to wait sternly for his father to give an account of Ares' absence.

"Surchatain Cedric and his guest, the Lady Tegge," Georges announced.

The table turned to bow, but Henry hardly waited for his father to be seated before demanding, "Where is Ares?"

"My son, the Chatain Henry," Cedric introduced him wryly to the Lady Tegge, who was a pert, pretty thing with a somewhat vacuous expression.

"Where is Ares?" Henry repeated.

Cedric sighed. "Ares is getting ready for a special ceremony tomorrow."

Henry's face brightened. "A surprise?"

"Oh, yes," Cedric said, motioning for the wine steward.

Henry sat contemplating the delightful possibilities while the steward filled the goblets of ashen, motionless courtiers. "Will he receive a medallion?" Henry asked.

"He will certainly receive something on his neck," Cedric said, and Henry bounced in anticipation.

Appalled, Carmine opened his mouth, then shut it. There were some breaches that not even the most skilled mediator could repair.

When the first course of eels was served, Henry took his portion to sit in the Commander's chair. "I am Ares tonight," he announced, leaning toward Nicole with his lips puckered. She kissed him primly on his mouth, then held his head with her heart aching. "I am happy you're back," he said, scooping the slimy entree into his mouth with his fingers.

"Then we will keep her for you, for when you are older,"

Cedric said. Henry grinned up at her, and she knew he did not understand.

A sentry entered, head down in his effort to pass unnoticed by the Surchatain, and bent to speak briefly in Thom's ear. Nicole glanced down at the scum clinging to the man's boots, and knew he had come from the prison.

Thom listened, then waved him away with a casual gesture, nothing special, all routine. As Cedric did not address him, the sentry slipped out again. Carmine looked at Thom, and the Second delivered a mute promise to relay the information as soon as it was feasible.

Hampered by matters so far over her head as to be out of sight, the Lady Tegge was confounded by the eels, as well. She had the presence of mind to keep her mouth shut, however, and no one ventured to speak to her. Cedric glanced at his uncharacteristically quiet daughter and said, "I must apologize for the dullness of our table, tonight, Lady Tegge. Georges! Summon the musicians!"

So as veal medallions with onions were served, the musicians played ghastly, happy tunes for the table in their death watch. Henry, humming along, abandoned his charade of Ares to climb into Nicole's lap. Since she could hardly eat anything, she accepted him.

The Lady Tegge finally chose to open her mouth and remove all speculation about her mental adroitness by asking Nicole, "Are you his mother?"

Carmine blinked in distress and Renée looked up, ready to finish off the woman with one swift comment, but Nicole replied, "I am Commander Ares' wife. My husband is Henry's guardian, and loves him very much."

"Oh. He's the one you're planning a special ceremony for, is that right?" the lady said to Cedric. As Henry nodded contentedly in Nicole's lap, even Cedric found himself without a facile reply.

At the conclusion of the wretched dinner, Cedric and the

Lady Tegge left the table, and Nicole sidled to the door of the banquet hall to watch them ascend the stairway together—to his quarters, no doubt. Nicole turned back to the table in anxious thought. She should have gone to fetch Henry and Renée immediately upon leaving the prison, without waiting for dinner. Now how would they get past Cedric and his guest to the secret exit?

Nicole looked at the courtiers who drifted away from the table slowly, as if fearing they might miss something. Then her eyes landed on Thom, Ares' faithful Second. He would help her.

As she approached him, his eyes darted up in alarm. "Thom, I need your help," she whispered.

"Lady, don't ask," he said abruptly, stunning her. "There is . . . what comes to pass is of God's hand, lady. Don't ask me." He took his wife's hand and strode away.

Nicole looked after him. *So it sits well with you to be Commander? I will remember that, you traitor.* She looked at Carmine, wondering what he, too, had to gain from Ares' death. Less competition? Now, he was the only one to carry the royal seal besides the Surchatain himself.

Henry pulled on her hand. "Nicole, will you put me to bed?"

"Yes, darling, I will. Come."

They went up the stairway to the Surchatain's wing, bypassing the pair of sentries at the entrance. She glanced at the second pair of sentries outside the Surchatain's door, and felt her stomach knot. Before dinner, she might have had a chance to get Henry and Renée into the Surchatain's chambers unnoticed, but now—it was impossible.

Then again, she realized that had they been missing at dinner, an immediate search would have been ordered, and Cedric would have entertained no reservations about invading the abbey to retrieve them. At this point, the impossibility of Ares' request began to weigh on her.

Upon entering Henry's quarters, Nicole saw Hillary laying out his nightclothes. "I will do this, Hillary. You may leave," Nicole said coolly.

The maid barely glanced at her. "Hmph. As if I took orders from you," she muttered.

"Get out, Hillary!" Henry demanded, and at that point she withdrew with a stiff curtsy.

Henry turned to Nicole in excitement. "Do you know what is being done for Ares tomorrow?"

Nicole knelt before him. "Henry . . . Ares thinks that the ceremony will not go well. He is afraid that someone may get hurt, and he asked me to take you and Renée to the abbey right away."

Henry studied her. "What is father planning to do?"

"I do not know for sure, Chatain. But Ares is worried, and wants us safely away."

Henry looked out of the window, over the moonlit fields. Nicole went to the door and opened it. When the sentry turned to her, she said, "Please tell the Chataine that her brother wishes her company for a moment." He nodded and moved off.

Nicole rejoined Henry at the window, where he was looking down at the broken eagle still on the portico roof. Then she looked down as well; it was only twenty feet to the roof. "If we only had rope," she mused, and Henry looked at her.

Renée appeared at the door, stately and beautiful in the ornate, beaded gown. Nicole sighed at the bulk of the skirts and the gemstones—she would not be escaping unnoticed in *that*. When the sentry had closed the door behind her, Nicole approached her quietly with a kiss on the cheek. "Darling, I spoke to Ares in prison. He asked me to get you and Henry to the abbey tonight."

"What?" Renée blinked. "Why?"

"He fears bloodshed, and—"

"I know." Renée turned away from her. "The Counselor is preparing a defense for him."

Nicole shook her head. "Darling, whatever he says will make no difference, for your father has already determined the outcome. I think Ares was afraid of . . . protest."

Now Renée looked at her coolly. "Rebellion, you mean? Has Ares been plotting rebellion?"

"Of course not!" Nicole said angrily. "How could you think that?"

"Then why is he so anxious to remove the heirs from the palace?" Renée asked.

"He fears for your lives!" Nicole replied.

"That is what I am asking: why should he fear?" Renée looked more regal than ever, almost defiant. Nicole stared back helplessly, unable to answer. So the Chataine made a little curtsy to her brother. "Goodnight, Chatain. Rest well." And she departed.

Nicole sank to the window seat beside Henry. Watching her, he said, "Ares is in prison?"

"Yes, Chatain," she whispered.

"And tomorrow Father will chop off his head," Henry said. Nicole was silent, hanging her head, and he shouted, "Tell me! Tell me the truth!"

"Yes! That is what he intends to do!" Nicole cried.

"I will not permit it," Henry said imperially.

"Henry, I don't know that you can prevent it. We must do what Ares said—we must get out of the palace," she urged.

"Then who will help Ares?" he asked pathetically.

Nicole clutched him, breathing, "Lord of heaven, we commend Ares to your hands, and ourselves to your hands, for we do not know what will happen tomorrow."

"Amen," Henry said, sounding just like Ares, and she squeezed him.

While she was holding him, trying to think what to do, there was a knock on the door and a sentry leaned his head in.

"Lady Nicole, the Chataine requests your presence in her chambers."

Nicole whispered, "Wait here, Chatain," and he nodded. She followed the sentry to Renée's chambers, entering after his warning knock.

Renée, alone in the room, rose from the sumptuous daybed to take Nicole's hands. "Darling, I've been . . . thinking about what you said, and if Ares wants us out of the palace, I believe he may have good reason for it. Tell me what to do," she whispered contritely.

Nicole inhaled in gratitude. "Very good. First, you must change. . . ." She opened the Chataine's wardrobe, searching through the many fabulous gowns for something inconspicuous. "Darling, do you have anything that does not glow like a thousand fireflies at night?"

Throwing up her hands, Renée opened a cedar chest to pull out the brown traveling suit she disliked so. "Yes. That will work. Turn around; let me help you," Nicole said.

She assisted Renée in changing, then peeked out the door to look for sentries. "Wait. I need to take some jewelry, at least," Renée whispered.

"Darling, if we are successful, your jewelry will be here waiting for you. If we are not, you will never need it again," Nicole uttered, and Renée nodded nervously. As the sentries were on guard in the corridor, Nicole threw a robe over Renée to obscure her traveling dress. Then, oh so casually, they sauntered down the corridor, giggling between themselves under the eyes of the sentries, and entered Henry's quarters.

He rushed forward with outstretched arms, and for the first time, Nicole saw Renée embrace her little brother. "Now how shall we do this?" Nicole murmured, peeking through the crack of the door at the guards. "Henry. . . . we must find out if your father is in his chambers. Can you go—ask to tell him goodnight?"

"Yes," he said, slipping out of his sister's arms. He

opened the heavy door of his chambers and looked up at the sentry as the door creaked to a close behind him.

Nicole and Renée waited, listening, until the door opened again a few minutes later. Henry entered and shut the door on the guard standing outside. "He is there with his lady friend. He would not come out of his bedchamber to tell me goodnight. He just said to go away," Henry reported.

Nicole closed her eyes. "We will not get out that way." She looked out of the window down at the portico roof, repeating, "If only we had rope."

Renée looked down as well, bemused. "Why go out the window when we can just go downstairs?"

"Why indeed?" Nicole murmured. "Here. We shall go down to Ares' quarters, and slip out from there." Henry began bobbing up and down in excitement. "Shh! Now, we just must convince anyone who sees us that we're going down for a lark, or—"

"To the kitchen!" Renée and Henry said in unison, turning to each other in laughter. Apparently, this was a time-honored, late-night, forbidden excursion.

"The kitchen is even better," Nicole agreed. "There is a door to the outside from the kitchen."

So, feigning a certain amount of lighthearted laughter, they openly departed Henry's chambers, carrying candles. They made their way down the staircase, Henry clutching Nicole's hand as he laughed nervously. Then they turned down the kitchen corridor, coming face to face with a sentry on duty. Nicole drew back with a startled gasp.

But Renée said, "Stand aside and let us pass."

He eyed her. "For what reason, Chataine?"

"We want something to eat out of the kitchen!" she exclaimed, as if that should have been obvious.

"The kitchen is closed for the evening, Chataine." He did not move, and there was no getting around him.

"No matter," Nicole said indifferently. "This beast shan't

spoil our fun." Tossing her head, she turned up the corridor toward Ares' quarters, and the royal children followed.

Gaining speed, they hurried into his chambers and Nicole bolted the door after them. While Renée held the candle up, Nicole opened the shuttered window. "Here, it's big enough," she whispered. "Henry, you first. Henry?" She turned to look around the darkened, shadowy room.

The louvered doors were standing open with the candle sitting at the edge of the closet. "I have to use the garderobe," Henry's voice said from within.

Renée exhaled in exasperation. "He can't ever come down here without using Ares' garderobe. It fascinates him."

"Henry, you must hurry," Nicole whispered urgently.

"I'm coming," the little voice said.

Nicole went to the door of the garderobe to help him out and pull up his pants. Gripping his hand, she whispered, "I am going to lift you out the window. Wait there under the portico for us to follow. We still have to find a way over the wall."

"I know where there's a secret opening," he whispered excitedly. "Ares showed it to me, in case I ever needed to get out!"

"We need to get out, Chatain," she said dryly.

Nicole held him under the arms to lift him as Renée opened the shuttered window again. Then she gasped. The moonlight was almost entirely blocked by the shadow of a soldier who stood pointedly with his back to the window.

20

Nicole lowered Henry and gestured silently for Renée to close the window shutters again. They stared at each other a moment, then Nicole crossed the room to unbolt the door and open it. Standing outside were not one, but two soldiers. Casually, Nicole made as if to leave the room, and she was not hindered. Renée followed her out without difficulty. But when Henry attempted to leave, the guards blocked his way. He looked up in surprise, and Renée snapped, "What are you doing? Stand aside."

"A thousand pardons, Chataine. We have our orders. For his own safety, the heir must not be all over the palace tonight," the guard said.

"Well, allow him to go to his quarters," Renée demanded.

"It is not safe, Chataine," he repeated.

"Whose orders are you following?" Renée asked.

"The same chain of command we have always followed, Chataine. We know nothing more."

The three of them withdrew to the room and shut the door. "What do you think?" Nicole whispered.

"Those are not Father's orders. He would never prohibit us from our own rooms," Renée said testily.

"What if Ares was afraid of assassins?" Nicole asked.

"Why should he be?" Renée exhaled. "Darling, no one wants to see him executed, but it's not something that would topple the throne."

Yet Renée did not know his lineage. After some thought, Nicole returned to the window and opened the shutters. Leaning out, she asked the soldier there, "Who are you loyal to?" He turned his face over his shoulder to her, but did not reply. "If you are loyal to your Commander, I ask you to help me carry out his command."

"To do what?" he asked.

"To get Henry and Renée to safety," she said.

"You and the Chataine may go where you wish. But the usurper's heir must stay," he replied. Her hands went clammy as she remembered her casual revelations. Was she responsible for the treachery at hand?

She closed the window. "What did he say?" Renée asked.

"We wait. That is our only hope," Nicole said.

So Henry and Renée lay down on the straw bed to rest. Henry thought it much preferable and more manly than his feather bed, and went to sleep directly. Renée tossed about like a ship on the raging seas, then sat up. "How can you sleep on this? It's horrid."

Nicole thought back to the Chataine's near escape from the slave markets of Corona, which would have been truly horrid, as bad as prison. That, in turn, gave her an idea. She would find out for certain to whom the sentries were loyal. Opening the door again, she said to the sentry, "The Chatain wishes to see his guardian, and the Commander would want to know that he is safe. Allow him to see his guardian."

"The Surchatain has forbidden the Commander visitors," the sentry replied.

"Ah. As you follow the commands of the Surchatain, then allow us to take Henry back to his chambers," Nicole said.

"He must be confined here," the sentry said.

"You are desperately confused, not to know whose orders you are following," Nicole said scathingly.

"That will be determined tomorrow, Lady," he said, reclosing the door on her. As he seemed not to care whether it made sense to her or not, Nicole realized there must be a third party grappling for power, and she thought of Thom. Or Carmine. She heard a scraping sound, and looked under the door to see chair legs resting on the floor directly against the door. The sentry sat with a grunt and stretched. It did not matter if he went to sleep, for they would never get out without waking him.

"You might as well lie down, darling. We have to wait until the sentry outside goes to sleep or goes away," Nicole whispered. Under those conditions, Renée took off the robe, as it was no longer useful. She lay down on the straw mattress in her travel suit, bunched the pillow irritably under her head, and went to sleep in the naive confidence that this irritating confusion of authority would be neatly settled in the morning.

Nicole rekindled the fire to help keep her awake and watchful, but the warmth and smoke made her sleepy. So she opened the shutters a crack to let in air and look out. If the sentry was sleeping, he was doing it on his feet. She gave him a long time to nod off, then experimentally widened the window opening and leaned out. He promptly turned his head, and she withdrew. *Probably someone Ares trained*, she thought ruefully.

She must get out. She must get Henry and Renée out; she had promised. How? She paced and prayed for a way out, looking under the door at the chair legs, looking out the window at the sentry's shadow. So she sat at the table and prayed, and the fire died down, and she got very sleepy waiting for the grappling hook to come through the window. Then she put her head down on her hands to pray.

The next thing she knew there was a loud scuffling, and she startled up. Soldiers were taking her arms. "You are summoned to trial, Lady," someone said, and she twisted around to see early sunlight streaming into the room from the cracks in the shutters. It was morning, and she had failed.

Henry and Renée were likewise roused from the straw bed, and the three of them taken together to the balcony, the seat of judgment, overlooking the grounds below. The stained, gouged block was already in place on the grounds, and soldiers lined up in rows behind it. Servants crowded the courtyard to watch, along with the townspeople who could finagle their way past the guards. Seeing it all, Henry began crying, and Renée's eyes filled with tears. Nicole was still stunned at her own failure.

The Counselor rushed up. "No, no—they're not to be here," he said to the soldier. "Take them down to the east wing to watch from there." The soldier complied. While they were being escorted away, Nicole looked at the Counselor as the next in the long line of traitors. He looked back at them all with an unmistakable expression of anxious love. But this she would not see.

The three of them were taken down to the portico across from Ares' chambers. Soon, the Surchatain appeared on the balcony, with the Counselor and amanuensis at his side. "Bring out the accused," Cedric waved, and the long, full sleeve of his fur-lined robe accented his command.

There was a rustling, and clanking, and tramping of feet, and Ares was led before the block, dirty, unshaven, with his wrists bound behind his back. The three of them were close enough to see him blink in the morning sun as he looked up to the balcony. Henry was weeping fitfully and Renée was taking shallow, shaky breaths. Nicole watched silently as her world began to crumble on its foundations.

Ares straightened, looking up to the balcony, and she could only think how beautiful he was. Cedric said, "Ares, you are charged with indecency with the Chataine Renée. How do you plead?"

"Indecency! Him?" Renée muttered indignantly, unheard. But she was not the only one who found the accusation ridiculous, for there was a general murmur. Apparently, Cedric had decided that one treason was as good as another, and this complaint was less risky to air than the other.

"Not guilty, Surchatain," Ares replied loudly.

"Have you lain with her?" the Surchatain demanded, according to form.

"No! As you well know," Ares said.

"Have you kissed her?" Cedric asked, continuing the form questions.

"A great deal. Because I was such a poor student, I could not get it right the first time," Ares said defiantly. Suddenly, Nicole realized that he believed them to be safe at the abbey. He felt free to reply boldly because, seeing that they were not on the balcony, he believed she had succeeded in getting them out of the palace.

"Enough insolence, soldier! The penalty for indecency is death," Cedric said.

"Surchatain, may I speak?" the Counselor bowed. Cedric did not look inclined to permit him, but being aware of the soldiers watching their Commander at trial, he waved him forward.

The Counselor bowed again, then addressed Cedric loudly enough for the soldiers to hear. "Surchatain, it is true that death is prescribed for extreme cases of indecency. But since you have been lenient in the past, and allowed lesser punishments for the crime, I ask you to take into account the Commander's many years of faithful service, and many accomplishments in your name. As his defense counsel, I ask that you allow him to live with the lesser penalty of castration."

There was a small stir among the soldiers, and Nicole heard one cry, "That's fitting!" Another objected, "Unjust!"

The Surchatain looked to be reluctantly considering it.

That would answer his main fear, but there was still the underlying question of loyalty. Could he count on Ares to be loyal the rest of his life, assuming he had no heir? To test him, Cedric called out, "Ares, who is your father? And how were you slashed?"

"My father was Erlend!" Ares shouted. "And I was slashed by your father Talus after he murdered my father and my grandfather Bobadil, the grandson of Roman!"

There was a commotion among the soldiers, and Cedric, livid, shouted, "Then you shall die!"

"No!" Henry cried. "No! I forbid it!"

At first, he went unheard except by one person. At the small cry of protest, Ares jerked his head around, searching. And when he spotted the three of them in the shadow of the east wing, his face went slack in dismay. "I sentence you to death for treason!" Cedric shouted, as Henry continued in his pathetic, childish voice to forbid it.

Thom looked where Ares was looking, then began pointing at Henry and shouting up to the Counselor to make himself heard above the soldiers, who were milling and muttering in a dangerous fashion.

Seeing him, the Counselor touched Cedric's sleeve and pointed down at Henry. Nicole watched Cedric look at his son and apprehend that he was defending the person who was the greatest threat to his life and his ascension to the throne.

Making himself blind and deaf to his own heir, Cedric held out his thumb down, ordering, "Executioner, to your duty!"

Thom, directly behind the block, spread his hands in frustrated anger as the masked executioner stepped up with a sharp, heavy sword. Ares was still looking toward Nicole, Renée, and Henry, and he was saying something, pleading, but she could not hear him.

Everything began moving slowly, too slowly, as she saw Ares pushed to his knees. Thom spoke hotly to the executioner, who paused with the massive sword in hand while Carmine argued with Cedric. The soldier who had forced Ares down was shoved in turn by the soldier next to Thom. Suddenly there was fighting in the ranks. Ares was thrust face first into the block and Thom drew his sword, then she could no longer see him.

"Death to the usurper! Death to murderers!" someone shouted. An arm arched from the crowd, and a knife shot upwards through the air to bury itself in Cedric's chest. The Counselor and the amanuensis jumped behind the pillars of the balcony for protection from the mob below.

Looking down in surprise, the Surchatain touched the exposed handle, raised his face in confusion, and then fell over the railing of the balcony to the roof of the portico below.

"Traitor!" another soldier shouted, attacking the assassin. Men were crashing together like angry waves, throwing fists, drawing swords, drawing blood. The servants and townspeople fled in terror, leaving the grounds to the army turned on itself. There was a horrendous uproar of shouting and running, blades flashing and plunging—Nicole, knocked off her feet, heard Renée screaming nearby.

Two men fell beside her, grappling in the dirt, and Nicole looked up in time to see a soldier grab Henry by the hair and lift his sword. Crying out, she fell forward, landing on top of Henry to shield him from the blow. Unwilling to stab her through, the man yanked her aside, only to be knocked backwards by a muddy boot.

Ares, rope dangling from his hands, was grasping the executioner's sword as he stood over Henry. The sight caused many of the soldiers to pause, and some began shouting, "Finish him, Commander! Regain your right!" Others began cursing him as traitor to his lord.

Panting, wild-eyed, Ares looked around to see who was shouting what and who was opposing whom. Almost at his feet beside Henry, Nicole looked up to see that he was bleeding from the scar. Renée was on her knees nearby, sobbing but unhurt.

Six or seven soldiers began to circle Ares as he stood over Henry, and he shifted constantly, watching them. In this defensive posture, with such a formidable weapon, the man who had been a soldier since childhood commanded everyone's attention, and the fighting slacked off.

The soldier who had tried to slash Henry said, "We know your oath, Commander. We know you can't break your oath and do harm to the boy. Just—stand aside, and we will see that it's done mercifully. You can't rule while the boy lives. Avenge your father's death!"

Ares glanced down at Henry trembling underneath his legs, but his attention did not waver from the confused mob. Some soldiers were calling for the usurper's death and others were shouting, "Traitor!" at the Commander himself. He seemed to be making sure he knew who was saying what before he committed himself to an action.

Then he said loudly, "You may kill the child. But you will have to make sure I am very, very dead first, and I can take out scores of you before that happens. Come, Roath, you are so bold—you be the first to die." Ares leveled the point of the sword toward him.

"Avenge your house, Commander!" Roath shouted in disgust, without advancing.

"My oath stands!" Ares shouted. "Anyone who touches the Chatain dies, and that I swear! Disarm yourselves!"

"Roath, look up here." It was the Counselor's voice. Roath and everyone looked up to where Counselor Carmine stood on the balcony with Thom and a battery of archers, bows drawn. "We are now informing you that anyone who does not comply with the Commander's order to disarm will be shot according to the law of military treason without a trial. Choose your sides, gentlemen."

The men became quiet, almost sheepish, and most of

them immediately thrust their swords point down into the ground as a sign of compliance. With reluctance, Roath and the others surrounding Ares did so, too.

Ares lowered the heavy blade. "Nicole, can you get this rope off me?" he murmured. She scrambled up to untie the knots on his wrists, biting at them if they would not come out. While she knelt before him, he raised his face to call, "Oswald! Rhode! Derrick! Alphonso!—" and ten other names —"Present yourselves!" Which command was almost unnecessary, as they had pushed their way toward him immediately upon being summoned.

"First—Denny—fetch the priest to say last rites over the High Lord's body, and prepare it for burial." They all looked up to where the lifeless hand with the signet ring hung over the edge of the portico roof. "You others, you will take these men [referring to the ones surrounding him]: Roath, Antony, Gammon, Witt, Dyer, Durrett, and Bruck, who threw the knife —you will take them to prison to be held on charges of treason."

The appointed guards took hold of the conspirators under the watchful eye of the archers while Ares shucked the last of the rope from his hands.

Standing, Nicole clung to him, trying to kiss him, but he held her in one arm as he reached down with the other to bring up Henry from between his feet. The boy clutched him around the neck in a death grip.

In Oswald's custody, Roath cried, "We saved your life, Commander! You would be dead right now if we hadn't killed the usurper! And this is the thanks we get!"

"You did not have to kill anyone to save my life," Ares responded. "All you had to do was listen to the Chatain." Henry stopped trembling and raised his face.

"He's a child! Who's going to listen to him?" Bruck shouted, struggling with Rhode and Derrick.

Carmine replied, "The Law hears him." He had descended

from the balcony in order to go to Renée, still sprawled near Ares, and lift her from the dirt. She collapsed on his arm.

"He's not of age!" Bruck argued.

"In certain circumstances, his age is irrelevant. The Law states that if the Surchatain has been in the habit of accepting the Chatain's judgment regarding certain persons or issues, then the Chatain's opinion must be respected on subsequent questions involving those same persons or issues. It has been well established that Surchatain Cedric gave his son great freedom in deciding minor questions involving his guardian. Therefore, his opposition to the Commander's execution must preclude it," Carmine explained.

"Thank you for mentioning that early on, Counselor," Ares said dryly.

"It was my next point, if he didn't buy the castration," Carmine said as an aside.

Ares had opened his mouth to address the Counselor's use of *that* argument when Roath protested, "The Surchatain heard him, and was going through with it anyway. We had no choice."

"Because you are stupid," Carmine snapped. "If you had been diligent in attending the required classes in Westfordian law and history, you would have known the proper course of action, as the Commander's Second knew: the execution was to be halted until the question was addressed. Surchatain Cedric's failure to follow the Law would have certainly meant his deposal. These laws were written by Surchatain Roman himself, whose house you thought to avenge, to prevent the very violence you perpetrated today."

When that had sunk in among the host of abashed soldiers, someone asked, "Then who rules now?"

"You will swear fealty to Henry," Ares said severely.

"Certainly, Commander, but—are we to be ruled by a child?" the same man asked.

Ares looked at Carmine uncertainly. "If you are content to

leave Henry in the position of ascension, Commander, then may I suggest a co-regency—you and I acting as advisors to Henry, until he attains maturity," Carmine said. "Which, of course, leaves you in the stronger position, as he is more favorably inclined to you."

"Except when you offer him bribes," Ares said scathingly. Henry issued a nervous giggle. "So," Ares said, bouncing him, "you defied my request to go to the abbey, eh, Chatain? You thought to take your stand here and deliver me instead?"

"Yes!" Henry shouted, and Nicole felt weak.

She buried her head in his soiled black shortcoat and her eye lit on Thom approaching, smiling. She raised her face to give him the hardest, coldest glare she had in her. He stopped dead upon seeing it and moaned, "I'm in trouble."

Ares looked over his shoulder as Thom fell on his knees and clasped her hand. "Forgive me, Lady Nicole, for refusing to hear your request. But the Commander had instructed that we were not to allow you to attempt his rescue, and I could not disobey his command, so the only way out was to not hear you, lest you break my heart with insisting."

She sniffed, "You're forgiven."

Renée broke away from Carmine to face Ares, and he raised his chin. Forcing herself to look him in the eye, she said with wringing hands and trembling voice, "All these years—I teased you and used you and ordered you around, when your ancestor was Roman and mine—a murderer."

"What has that to do with us? I am still your patsy," Ares said.

Renée clapped her hands to her mouth, but she could not hold him, as he had one arm full of Henry and the other full of Nicole. So the Chataine grabbed his face and kissed him full on the lips, and he did not protest.

"Lady, wait . . . Lady—glub—please, you will drown me," he said, spitting water as Nicole inadvertently forced his head under the flow of warm water, not for the first time.

"Hush," she said sternly, covering his face with her lips as she straddled him sitting in the tub. "As if you never got wet in your life. Show me what Renée taught you."

"I'll never hear the end of that," he groaned. Unheeding, she turned his head and pressed her lips to his. He opened his mouth for her, but a slight movement elsewhere caught his eye. He held back her wet hair to look over her shoulder at the door, minutely ajar. "Did you bolt the door?" he asked in mild alarm.

"Pay attention, my lord," she chastised, rising up to block his view.

"Oh, Nicole," he murmured in appreciation, and they heard a slight giggle.

Water surged out of the tub as she dropped down and he raised up, both looking past the bed and trunk of dresses. "Henry!"

(The story continues in *Ares of Westford.*)

Glossary

Agnes, Sister—the nun in charge of the abbey

amanuensis (a man you EN sis)—a secretary

Ares (AIR eez)—Commander of the Lystran army stationed at Westford

Calle (kail) **Valley**—province west of Lystra, famous for its wine and fairs

capon (CAY pon)—castrated rooster

capriole (CAP ree ole)—a vertical jump in which the horse kicks out its back legs to be completely airborne

Carmine (CAR men)—Counselor to Surchatain Cedric at Westford

Cedric (SED rik)—Surchatain of Lystra, son of Talus

Chataine (sha TANE)—daughter of the ruler of a province; the son of a ruler is a **Chatain** (sha TAN)

cog—a broadly built ship with a square mast and blunt bow

Corona (cor OH nah)—capital city of Seleca, notorious for its slave markets

Crescent Hollow—capital city of Calle Valley

dagging—trim on a coat or cloak

Danae (dan AY)—the Surchataine of Scylla; wife of Ossian and mother of Magnus and Tancred

Deirdre (DEE dra)—Thom's wife

Eleanor (EL en or)—Renée's maid

Elise (ah LEESE)—Surchataine of Lystra, Cedric's wife, mother of Henry and stepmother of Renée

Erlend (ER lend)—Ares' father, now dead

Eurus (YUR is)—the capital city of Scylla, the province east of Lystra

garderobe (GAR der obe)—a water closet; indoor commode

Genevieve (JEN e veeve)—the wife of the palace Steward, Giles

Georges (GEOR jes)—dinner master at Westford

Giles (hard *g,* long *i*)—the Steward of the palace at Westford

Gretchen—Ares' personal servant

hake—a fish related to the cod

Hathor (HATH or), **Lady**—the first of Cedric's guests after Surchataine Elise was deposed

hauberk—chain-mail armor

Henry—Chatain of Lystra, Cedric's son and half-brother to Renée

Hillary—Chatain Henry's maid

Hycliff (HI cliff)—former port city on the coast of Lystra, now unusable due to erosion

jerkin—a short, close-fitting, sleeveless coat

leek—a vegetable similar to the onion

Lieterstad (LEE ter stad), **Lord**—a rich nobleman of Calle Valley

linsey-woolsey— a fabric woven partly of linen and partly of wool

Lystra (LIS tra)—province once ruled by Roman the Great

Magnus (MAG nus)—the elder son of Surchatain Ossian of Scylla

Merle (murl)—head laundress at Westford

meurtrières (MUR tree air)—arrow loops; narrow window slits in a castle wall through which archers can fire on invaders

Nicole (ne COLE)—daughter of peasant tailor Robert of Prie Mer

Notham (NOTH am), **Lord**—nobleman of Westford

Ossian (AH shun)—Surchatain of the province of Scylla

parapet—the top portion of the palace wall, behind which runs a walkway

Passage—the river marking the boundary between Lystra and Scylla; the only navigable river emptying to the Sea from the southern coast of the Continent

Polontis (po LAWN tis)—mountainous province far northeast of Lystra, home of the hardy, courageous, but unsophisticated **Polonti** (po LAWN tee)

portcullis (port CULL iss)—an iron grating with pointed lower ends which can be raised and lowered as additional security at a castle's gates

portico (POR te coh)—a covered walkway, or the roof of such a walkway

Preus (proose)**, Lord**—the most sought-after dressmaker in Westford

Prie Mer (pree MARE)—small port town in the province of Calle Valley

Qarqar (KAR kar)—a mining-rich province to the northwest of Lystra

Renée (ren AY)—Chataine of Lystra, Cedric's daughter and half-sister to Henry

Reynard (ray NARD)—Talus' brother; Cedric's uncle

Rhea (ray)—daughter of a nobleman of Westford, Lord Notham

Roath (rothe)—a soldier who urges Ares to kill Henry

Robert—Nicole's father, a tailor of Prie Mer

royal—the basic monetary unit traded on the southern coast of the Continent; the value of one gold royal equals fifty silver pieces

Scylla (SILL ah)—a large, powerful province on Lystra's eastern border

Seleca—(SEL e kah)—a province to the northeast of Lystra, notorious for harboring slave markets

Surchatain (SUR cha tan)—ruler of a province; a woman ruler is a **Surchataine** (SUR cha tane)

Talus (TAL us)—Cedric's father, now dead

Tancred (TAN cred)—the younger son of Surchatain Ossian of Scylla

Tanny—senior diplomat and messenger of Westford

Tegge (teg), **Lady**—the last of Cedric's prospective replacements for Elise

Thom (tom)—Second in Command of the Lystran army under Ares

trencher—a board on which food is served

Verschoyle (ver SHOIL)—the Surchatain of Calle Valley

viele (vee EL)—an early form of the violin

Vola (VO la), **Lady**—a long-time, "respectable" prostitute of Westford

Westford—capital city of the province of Lystra

Wigzell (WIG zul)—the palace doctor at Westford

Yael (yale)—a woodworker of Westford

Books by Robin Hardy

The Streiker Saga
  Streiker's Bride
  Streiker: The Killdeer
  Streiker's Morning Sun

The Annals of Lystra
  Chataine's Guardian
  Stone of Help
  Liberation of Lystra
  (first published as *High Lord of Lystra*)

The Latter Annals of Lystra
  Nicole of Prie Mer
  Ares of Westford
  Prisoners of Hope
  Road of Vanishing
  Dead Man's Token
  Games of God and Men
  In Extremis
  All Mirrors and All Suns
  The Laughing Side of the World

The Sammy Series
  Sammy: Dallas Detective
  Sammy: Women Troubles
  Sammy: Working for a Living
  Sammy: On Vacation
  Sammy: Little Misunderstandings
  Sammy: Ghosts
  Sammy: Arenamania
  Sammy: In Principle
(continued on next page)

Sammy: Grave Agreement
Sammy: Love Shouldn't Hurt
Sammy: The Consolation of Bucephalus

The Idecis
Unknown Name, Unknown Number: A Wimsey Reade Mystery
Padre and its sequel *His Strange Ways*

Edited by Robin Hardy

Sifted But Saved: Classic Devotions by W.W. Melton